Praise for

ATLANTIS RISING

continued . . .

ATLANTIS AWAKENING

The Warriors of Poseidon

ALYSSA DAY

BERKLEY SENSATION, NEW YORK

THE BERKLEY PUBLISHING GROUP
Published by the Penguin Group
Penguin Group (USA) Inc.
375 Hudson Street, New York, New York 10014, USA
Penguin Group (Canada), 90 Eglinton Avenue East, Suite 700, Toronto, Ontario M4P 2Y3, Canada
(a division of Pearson Penguin Canada Inc.)
Penguin Books Ltd., 80 Strand, London WC2R 0RL, England
Penguin Group Ireland, 25 St. Stephen's Green, Dublin 2, Ireland (a division of Penguin Books Ltd.)
Penguin Group (Australia), 250 Camberwell Road, Camberwell, Victoria 3124, Australia
(a division of Pearson Australia Group Pty. Ltd.)
Penguin Books India Pvt. Ltd., 11 Community Centre, Panchsheel Park, New Delhi—110 017, India
Penguin Group (NZ), 67 Apollo Drive, Rosedale, North Shore 0632, New Zealand
(a division of Pearson New Zealand Ltd.)
Penguin Books (South Africa) (Pty.) Ltd., 24 Sturdee Avenue, Rosebank, Johannesburg 2196,
South Africa

Penguin Books Ltd., Registered Offices: 80 Strand, London WC2R 0RL, England

This is a work of fiction. Names, characters, places, and incidents either are the product of the author's imagination or are used fictitiously, and any resemblance to actual persons, living or dead, business establishments, events, or locales is entirely coincidental. The publisher does not have any control over and does not assume any responsibility for author or third-party websites or their content.

ATLANTIS AWAKENING

A Berkley Sensation Book / published by arrangement with the author

PRINTING HISTORY
Berkley Sensation mass-market edition / November 2007

Copyright © 2007 by Alesia Holliday.
Excerpt from *Atlantis Unleashed* copyright © 2007 by Alesia Holliday.
Cover illustration by Don Sipley.
Cover design by George Long.
Interior text design by Laura K. Corless.

ISBN: 978-0-425-21796-2

BERKLEY® SENSATION
Berkley Sensation Books are published by The Berkley Publishing Group,
a division of Penguin Group (USA) Inc.,
375 Hudson Street, New York, New York 10014.
BERKLEY and the "B" design are registered trademarks of Penguin Group (USA) Inc.

PRINTED IN THE UNITED STATES OF AMERICA

10 9 8 7 6 5 4 3 2 1

To my readers, who made the dream a reality.
To the booksellers, who spread the word.
To Judd, who had no doubts.
To Cindy Hwang, who always had faith.
And to Steve Axelrod, who said
it was never "if" but "when."
Thank you all from the bottom of my heart.

Acknowledgments

Thank you beyond words to the following amazing people:

This one was rough, in that "oh, wow, my brain is melting" sort of way. So I have to give huge chocolate-covered thanks to the best editor in the world, Cindy Hwang, who has the crappy job of herding creative-type authors to try to hit a point somewhere in the same universe as the deadline. Herding cats would be far easier. Hell, herding *tigers* would be easier. She gets the ulcers, and I get the lovely reader mail, which doesn't seem fair at all. So I tell her—a lot—how wonderful she is, and if you go to New York, you should tell her, too. She's the gorgeous one down on Hudson Street. Stop when you hear the sound of teeth grinding.

Leis Pederson, who is chief assistant tiger wrangler and is marvelous at it.

Steve Axelrod, who is so brilliant it's scary, in a world-domination sort of way; and Lori and Elsie, who make it all work.

Barbara Ferrer and Cindy Holby (see "brain is melting"); Michelle Cunnah (ditto, plus more last-minute critiquing); Eileen Rendahl and Lani Diane Rich (they know why).

My family, who helps me brainstorm. (Yes, I'm still thinking about that Were-Koala, sweetie.)

Dear Readers,

This is a shameless love letter to every one of you. There I was, working away at my writing career, hoping to never, ever be forced to go back to practicing law, and *you* happened. *Atlantis Rising* happened! You took a chance on a new series, and my book hit bestseller lists all over the place. And nobody could have been more shocked/happy/grateful/blissed out on champagne than me. So *thank you* for keeping courtrooms all across the country safe from me. *Thank you* for the letters and e-mails telling me you had fun with my warriors. And *thank you* for plunking down your hard-earned cash and coming back for more. You *rock*. (Oh, and for the official stuff they make me say, see below . . .)

Thank you for coming along with me on my journey to Atlantis. I hope you've enjoyed Conlan's story in *Atlantis Rising* and Bastien's story in "Wild Hearts in Atlantis," a novella in the anthology *Wild Thing*. Be sure to look for Justice's story in *Atlantis Unleashed*, and Ethan's story in the anthology *Shifter*, both coming in spring 2008. Please visit me at www.alyssaday.com for excerpts, bonus short stories, and downloadable screensavers for members only!

Hugs,
Alyssa

The Warrior's Creed

We will wait. And watch. And protect.
And serve as first warning on the eve of humanity's destruction.
Then, and only then, Atlantis will rise.
For we are the Warriors of Poseidon, and the
mark of the Trident we bear serves as witness
to our sacred duty to safeguard mankind.

Chapter 1

Seattle, Washington

"These are my kind of odds," Ven said, drawing his sword with his right hand and one of the seven daggers strapped to various parts of his body with his left. "Not even gonna bother with my Glock and its nifty new silver bullets for this mangy crew."

The vamp leading the gang—*flock? herd? What the hells did you call a group of vamps this big?*—of vamps that had cornered them in the alley hissed, making sure to show a mouthful of fang. "Prepare to die, human. You are vathhhtly outnumbered," it threatened, with that peculiar lisp so characteristic of the recently undead. They hadn't quite yet gotten the hang of talking with a mouthful of tooth.

The alley was everything an alley always was; gray stone and chipped brick, crumbled trash on the ground, and the smell of old urine and fresh despair combining to make Ven seriously twitchy.

Twitchy and amused. He laughed in the vamp's pasty face. "You've got a couple of things wrong, dead boy. First, we're not human. We're three of Poseidon's finest. Second, you're the one who's gonna die, so you can kitthh my atthh," he mocked.

The vamp's eyes glowed redder, but it sort of danced around a little instead of charging. Ven figured it wasn't quite prepared to take on six and a half feet of Atlantean warrior carrying a sword at least half that size. But the creature was working up its nerve, especially with his bloodsucker buddies egging him on.

"Silver bullets are not particularly helpful on vampires, as you know, Lord Vengeance," Brennan replied in his usual even, calm tone, as he pulled a handful of throwing stars, no doubt with some kind of magical spell crap all over them, out of the folds of his long leather coat. "I am unsure as to whether the newly turned, such as these, would be even slightly hindered by silver. It is an interesting question, although perhaps for another time, as to why we are encountering such increasingly high numbers of the newly turned here in the Pacific Northwest."

"Yeah, I'm thinking another time," Ven said, trying not to laugh. Trust Brennan to want to get philosophical when faced with imminent death-by-bloodsucker. The horde— yeah, horde was good—*horde* of vamps edged back a little bit.

They were hissing and screaming some truly vile threats, sure, but they moved back. After Ven, Alexios, and Brennan had spent an entire week in this rainy part of the world, the word had gotten out about how deadly Brennan was with his pretty little toys. Too bad he'd probably had to play footsies with some witch to get the weapons magicked up. Except for bloodsuckers and shape-shifters, there wasn't much that Ven hated more than witches and their kind. Especially witches who dabbled with the dark.

"Shut up, already. I'm counting," Alexios growled at them. "Seventeen, eighteen . . . oh, yeah, can't forget the big, bad, and seriously ugly one lurking behind the Dumpster. Nineteen to three odds, girls." He shook his head. "That doesn't split three ways. I call dibs on the leftover."

"Age before beauty, Goldilocks," Ven said, baring his teeth

in what might pass for a smile. Then he whirled around, sword arm already in motion, to catch the vamp who'd tried to sneak up on them by scaling his creepy ass down the side of the building behind them.

Ven yelled in triumph as the vamp's head smashed down on the ground. Its body followed a few seconds later. "Okay, we're all evened up. Six each, boys?"

"For Poseidon!" Alexios called out in response, grinning like a fool. The scarred half of his face pulled and twisted down the side of his mouth, so he probably looked like an insane apparition or a wickedly bad dream to the newbie vamps. Ven watched as three of them in the back of the mob did some kind of signaling thing to each other and turned to flee.

Quicker than a bolt of lightning riding the waves of a sea storm, Brennan's hand flashed out once, twice, three times, and the three went down, screaming, clouds of smoke rising from their backs. "I would never stab an honorable opponent in the back," Brennan said. "Luckily, these undead have no honor."

Brennan flashed a glance that Ven almost swore was smug—if Brennan could even do smug—at Alexios. "I believe that is fifty percent of my total?"

The vamps must have taken that as a sign, because they attacked in a swarm of hissing and shrieking, flashing their fangs and claws. Alexios shouted out a wild laugh and hurled himself into the thick of them, sword flashing and dagger plunging. Ven leapt into the air, shimmering into mist as he pushed off the ground and rematerialized behind the front row of his attackers. "Surprise, you sorry excuse for Dracula wannabes! Just call me *Ven* Helsing! Get it?"

Nobody laughed. Guess a sense of humor didn't travel well beyond the grave. With one stroke, Ven cut off the heads of three of the vamps, who'd very helpfully lined up, shoulder to shoulder, in order to attack him. "Personal best, Brennan! Three for one! Did you see that?"

"Lovely, Your Highness," Brennan replied, pulling his dagger out of the chest of one of the vamps with one hand and simultaneously hurling another shooting star with the other. "Your brother will be so proud."

Ven tore into two more, using his dagger and sword, then groaned as a vamp behind him got the drop on him long enough to dig its filthy, unhygienic claws into the side of his neck. "Damn you!" He finished off the ones in front of him and whipped his head to the side, but couldn't disengage the feral vamp, who now had a hand wrapped in Ven's hair and was trying to get close enough to bite him. "Get your nasty-ass fangs away from me! And where have your hands been? I'm going to have to disinfect myself after this."

The vamp reared its head back and struck, but Ven threw an elbow up to block its chest. Still, the undead thing was so close Ven could smell its rancid breath. Which was way, *way* too close. "Okay, but don't say I didn't warn you," he said, then reached up with the hand not holding off the vamp and sliced clear through its arm with his dagger. The vamp fell back and away from him, shrieking, but its hand still dangled from Ven's neck by its claws.

"I am so gonna need some freaking iodine," Ven snarled, ripping the now unattached hand out of his neck, pulling what felt like half his skin with it. He clapped a hand to his profusely bleeding neck and whirled around to gauge the remaining threat.

Only to see that the threat was entirely gone. Nineteen vamps lay all around him in various states of decomposing acidic slime. Alexios leaned up against the wall, boots carefully away from any of the crud, and Brennan crouched on the edge of the metal Dumpster, five feet off the ground.

"So. Good job, boys," Ven said, scanning the area for signs of any of the now permanently dead vamps' buddies.

"Yeah, nice of you to notice. I took out my six, by the way," Alexios said, grinning. "Your *Highness*."

"Call me that again, and I'll kick your ass for you, my friend," Ven said, leaning down to wipe his blades on a clean piece of cloth that had fluttered to the ground from somebody's shirt.

"My own tally was six as well, Lord Vengeance," Brennan said, leaping down off the Dumpster to a clear spot on the alley pavement. "You yourself accounted for the remaining seven, I believe."

"You must be slipping a little, Ven," Alexios said, shaking his head sadly. "You would have killed at least ten of them in the old days. Getting old, coming up on the big five-oh-oh."

Ven glared at him. "Yeah, yeah, laugh it up now, ladies. You didn't think *Ven* Helsing was funny, but you laugh at me now? Losers."

He glumly sheathed his sword, but then a cheerful thought occurred to him. "Ha! Just wait till the Council gets *you* in their sights for the maiden-in-stasis lotto. As high-ranking sons of your respective Houses, you know you're heading down the same path of doom that I am. But for now, we're free to find some women who meet my top two requirements: they have to be—"

A new voice cut him off. "Yeah, yeah, we know. Brainless and forgettable."

Ven had his sword up blocking his face before the second *yeah*, but now he lowered his weapon and laughed. "You got it, Christophe. Brainless and forgettable. Hanging back while we fought the vamps, were you?"

Alexios laughed and shoved his daggers back into their sheaths on his thighs. "His pedicure probably took longer than he planned."

Christophe floated down in the entrance to the alley, his body shimmering faintly with the essence of the elemental power he called. Ven knew that Alaric, Poseidon's high priest, had certain concerns about Christophe's untrained channeling of power.

Yeah. And Alaric isn't the only one with . . . concerns.

Ven watched the younger warrior until Christophe's boots rested solidly on the pavement. "I thought you were still in Atlantis? Is there news? Is it Riley—"

Christophe held up a hand. "No, no. As far as I know, Riley's fine. Or at least no worse off than she was before. It's about you, actually. Conlan wants you to go to a meeting with a rep from the main coven in this region. The Seattle Lights or something."

"The Seattle Circle of Light," Brennan said, a hint of censure in his voice. "Perhaps, Christophe, if you are honored with carrying messages from the high prince of Atlantis to his brother the Lord Vengeance, you might trouble to remember the correct phrasing."

Christophe's face darkened. The warrior had never been one to take criticism of any kind well. Ven studied him and made a mental note. Christophe might be in need of some serious ass kicking.

But that was a thought for a later time.

"What meeting? Where and when?" Ven asked, resigned. Conlan had been on an alliance-forming kick lately, especially since his new soon-to-be-wife's sister just happened to be one of the leaders of the human forces rebelling against vampire and shape-shifter control. "I need to get cleaned up, maybe pop a couple of stitches in my neck, and get a serious drunk on to wipe the taste of vamp breath out of my mouth." He shuddered. "Nasty."

"It's going to have to wait," Christophe said, with a shade less attitude. "The meeting is supposed to happen now."

Ven let loose with a string of words that called into question the parentage of every witch, wizard, and sorcerer in the Pacific Northwest, then hung his head, resigned. "Fine, bring it on. But, first, anybody got any iodine?"

Chapter 2

The Pink Pig Pub, Seattle

Ven wanted to smash something. Bad. Preferably the face of the jerk he was supposed to meet forty-five minutes ago. Bad enough he had to postpone his planned evening festivities to meet a wizard, but his neck was aching and he had the feeling that the bandage Brennan had slapped on it wasn't really doing the job.

His lip curled as he scanned the place, trying to avoid compulsively checking the time again. Dirt and bottle caps warred for space in every corner. Stale beer and the miasma of ancient cigarette smoke hung in the air in a foul cloud. Even all these years after the "no smoking in public places" laws went into effect, joints like this still reeked of the cancer sticks.

He scanned the losers slouching on the cracked red vinyl barstools of the dive where the coven rep had insisted they meet. Professional drinkers, all. Professional losers. Although who else hung out in a place like this at midnight on a Tuesday?

Well, losers, except for one highly pissed-off Atlantean warrior. He thought back to Alexios calling him "Your Highness" and scowled. He didn't like the title, even in jest. Prince

Ven, yeah, right. However much he didn't like the idea, he was stuck being second in line to the throne, at least until Conlan and Riley started popping out babies. Which had better be soon, because no way did Ven ever want *that* little obligation. King of the Seven Isles of Atlantis.

He shuddered, downed his beer at the thought. Nope. He was much better as head of the warrior training academy. The King's Vengeance, whose sworn duty it was to protect his brother the king. Taking names and kicking the ass of any vamp or shape-shifter who decided to snack on humans.

He glanced up at the cracked face of the Budweiser clock on the wall. Maybe he'd just kick some magical ass. Specifically, the asshole he was supposed to be meeting to discuss a Magickals-Atlantean alliance. The asshole who was now fifty-two minutes late.

The squeak of the hinges on the door alerted him, and he looked up into the mirror behind the bar, his gaze trained on the person walking in.

His eyes widened, and then narrowed in appreciation. If he had to waste time waiting for the jerk Quinn had sent, at least now he had something worth looking at. He whirled around on his stool so he was facing her. All curves and attitude in a small package, the blonde came striding into the place as if she owned it.

High-heeled leather boots worn under snug jeans, rounded hips he'd love to get his hands on, and a tight-fitting black leather jacket. Oh, yeah. She was exactly his type of woman.

And he must have been dreaming, because she walked right past the lowlife scum who were drooling at the sight of her and stopped in front of him.

Ven was used to the reactions of human women to him. Hell, after several centuries, he knew that they considered him attractive. Not a lot of six-foot, seven-inch muscled warrior types running around with *human* DNA these days.

This one flicked her icy-blue gaze down, then up him, and curled her lips back a little. He'd looked at steaming piles of peacock shit on the palace grounds with more enthusiasm.

"So," she drawled, disgust dripping from her voice. "*You're* the pride of Atlantis?"

She stalked around him and leaned back on the vacant barstool on his left, glancing his way again. Then she rolled her freaking eyes.

Ven had seen and heard way more than enough. He rose to his full height, which gave him more than a foot on her, and stared down his nose. "You're late."

Okay, *that* was lame. Sadly, it was all he could think of, considering his brain cells had gone south at the sight of the creamy cleavage nestled in the gap between the lapels of her jacket and some lacy thing she wore underneath it.

For some reason, he wanted to lick it.

And her.

"Oh, boy, you're just trouble with a capital—"

"Make that a capital W, warrior," she said. "And you can sit down now and leave your Intimidation 101 tactics for somebody who is impressed with them."

He sat down, feeling like a damn fool, gaping at her. "Capital *W*? How did you—"

She smiled slowly, sensual lips curving over a gorgeous set of teeth. God, even her *teeth* turned him on. Suddenly he was a horny fucking dentist.

He shifted on the stool, hoping she hadn't noticed the sudden tightness in his jeans.

"Capital W is for *witch*, warrior," she said. "Welcome to the revolution."

❧～～ऄ

Erin Connors cast a very minor look-away spell, and the drunks in the room found the contents of their glasses more interesting than the two people seated on the barstools. She drew in a long, slow breath, trying to fill her suddenly empty lungs. Quinn had never told her that Atlantean warriors looked like Greek gods come to life and had the capacity to suck the oxygen right out of a room. Except had Greek gods looked like predators who ate witches for lunch? This one sure did. He was pure alpha male warrior, and every feminine instinct in her body was begging her to flee—or to climb into his lap.

Alerted by the sudden heat encircling her fingers and the melodies whispering through her mind, she glanced down at the three rings of power she wore on each hand and saw them start to glow and pulse with heat and light.

Not now, not now, she thought and focused all her concentration on locking down the magic. She was in enough trouble with the coven without allowing the Wilding Magic to escape during her first meeting with the man. And she needed them both—the coven and the Atlanteans. She needed them *all*.

After the gemstones in her rings subsided back to inert lumps of mineral and their singing faded, she finally dared to meet his gaze, pulling the cloak of toughness back around herself like a shield.

She'd decided the only way to earn the respect of a warrior was to become a warrior herself. Tough to do when she was all alone, twenty-six years old, and the only Magickal in a three-state area who believed in her quest. She drew in a deep breath and prepared to channel somebody kickass. "So, do I call you Ven? Mr. Vengeance? Your Highness?"

He raised one eyebrow, wincing a little at the unexpected echo of his earlier thoughts. "Your Highness? Quinn's been messing with you. I'm just Ven. Or you can start calling me *sweetheart* now and save time later."

His teasing was double-edged, and she had a feeling the edge was honed steel. But the humor touched the Erin who'd once known how to laugh. All *this* Erin could summon was a nod. "Don't flatter yourself, Atlantean. Your charms aren't quite as impressive as you may have been led to believe. Or are the women in Atlantis fairly desperate? You have kind of an Alaska thing going on there? The odds are good, but the goods are odd?"

It was sheer bravado. There was nothing odd about this man; he was pure, potent male. The wavy, too-long black hair that framed sculpted cheekbones. Eyes as dark as the promise of revenge. A wall of muscled chest that strained the black T-shirt he wore under that leather coat. Not to mention the faded jeans covering huge muscled thighs. Her mouth suddenly got a little dry.

Yeah, nothing odd here.

He narrowed his eyes, but seemed more speculative than annoyed. "You think my goods are odd, witch? I'd be glad—"

"Not here!" She quickly scanned the room, but none of the drunks appeared to be paying them the slightest bit of attention. The dive bar was way too low class for the vampires or their spies, or so she hoped. People had died for making smaller mistakes. "That word still summons up genetic memories of burnings and stakes for far too many non-Magickals," she murmured.

He stood up off the barstool, a fluid motion that made her think of a caged panther and brought him way too close to her. The large opals gracing her two ring fingers began singing—a low, urgent call. Thank the Goddess that he couldn't hear them. "Let's get out of here, then," he said.

Ven held out a hand as if to assist her, then paused and tilted his head. "Do you hear that? What's that music?"

Erin felt the blood literally drain out of her face. Maybe she'd thanked the Goddess too soon.

~~~

Poseidon's Temple, Atlantis

Alaric, high priest to Poseidon, leaned against a slender marble column and folded his arms across his chest, studying the warrior who paced back and forth across the Temple rotunda before him. "What exactly is it that you're worried about, Conlan?"

The high prince of Atlantis shot Alaric an irritated glare. "I'm not worried, Alaric. Princes don't worry. Kings don't worry, either, and you keep reminding me we must go through with the Rite of Ascension and coronation within the next thirty days, or risk breaking some sacred tradition or other." Conlan snorted and resumed pacing.

"Then what is it that you are *not* worried about that has you pacing across Poseidon's Temple like a rat scurrying to escape a drowning ship, my prince who is almost king?" Alaric returned, voice mild. "And sacred traditions are sacred for a reason, but of course you know that."

Conlan halted again, turned to face Alaric, and shoved his hand through his hair. Alaric caught a fleeting glimpse of his boyhood friend in the gesture, and gathered his patience.

A troubled prince was of much concern to the high priest. A troubled friend was of much concern to the man.

"Tell me."

"It's Riley," Conlan said, his anguish clear in the deepened lines around his mouth and eyes. "The midwives say the pregnancy is not going well. She is so sick, every day, all day long. Instead of growing large and healthy with the child, she is wasting away before my eyes."

Alaric straightened. "And the human doctor?"

Conlan shook his head, face grim. "Nothing. They say the baby is fine, and that Riley will get over it. It's a 'phase.' Morning sickness, they call it, which is a damned stupid name—she's sick all day long. But Riley is *aknasha*—and as an emotional empath she can read the truth behind their placating words. The baby is in danger." He took a deep breath. "We need you, Alaric. You are the most powerful healer of any."

Alaric called for power, felt the elements instantly respond, and knew by the heat in his eyes that they were glowing bright green with the force of his channeling. Sent out a mental plea to Poseidon. Received the same response he'd gotten every other time he'd asked, even begged, for the power to help Riley.

Silence.

"Poseidon has never granted his priests the power of healing in any part of pregnancy or childbearing, Conlan. You know this. The midwives of the Nereid Temple are the only ones who may intercede in these matters."

"To the nine hells with that! They can do nothing. You're

more powerful than any high priest Atlantis has ever known—even the Council knows it. Break the rules, Alaric." Conlan stopped, as if realizing his voice had risen nearly to a shout, then continued, more quietly. Bleak. "Do it for me."

Alaric clenched his hands into fists, pulled power from the air around them, and hurled a ball of blue-green electricity across the room. It smashed into the wall, leaving a smoking, charred hole in the marble that was exactly the shape of the hole that anguish and frustration had burned into his gut. "Don't you think I would if I could, Conlan? For you—my friend? For your woman and unborn child? For the future king, queen, and heir to the throne? I don't give a good goddamn about the rules. I just don't have the power."

Conlan's entire body slumped, and his despair buffeted Alaric in almost palpable cyclone-force waves. "Then we have no options. There is nothing we can do."

Alaric pushed the words past lips gone suddenly numb. "Have you—did you contact . . ." He couldn't say her name. Berated himself for the coward he was.

Settled for the pronoun. "Her?"

Conlan nodded. "Yeah, we got a message out to Quinn, we think. At least we got word to that weretiger colleague of hers, Jack, that Riley needed her sister. Who knows when she'll get it, though. Last I heard, the rebel alliance was looking into a new vampire threat on the West Coast, and Quinn always has to be in the thick of any—"

The prince stopped midsentence, closed his eyes, and groaned. "I'm sorry, Alaric. I wasn't thinking. I'm sure she's fine. You know Quinn, she's a fighter."

Alaric cut him off, proud beyond reason that he'd controlled the trembling in his hands almost as soon as it had started. "No, my prince, I do not know Quinn. And I never will. Which is as it must be, decreed by Poseidon's laws and by reality." The harshness in his voice couldn't be helped. "We both know she deserves far better than me."

With that, he took two running steps and leapt into the air, dissolving into mist as he did, and escaped out of the high window of the Temple. Escaped from Conlan's pain and fear for his woman and child. Escaped from his own dark, soul-destroying hunger for a woman he could never have.

But even in the form of shimmering mist, he couldn't escape Conlan's final words, murmured though they were. "There is no such person, old friend."

~~~~~~

Seattle

Erin pulled into the driveway of the old Victorian home that served as headquarters of the Seattle Circle of Light coven and glanced into her rearview mirror. The sleek black Jaguar Ven drove purred its way into the drive behind her, blocking off any chance of escape. Her hands tightened on the steering wheel for an instant. *Trapped.*

"Not that I want to escape," she whispered to the empty car. "This is my chance to build an alliance with someone with the power to help me. Help *us*."

Her car door opened as she unbuckled her seat belt, and she blinked up at him, startled. "How did you—oh, right. Atlantean super powers, I presume."

"That's me. Super Ven, at your service." He stepped back almost far enough to give her room to climb out of the car. She took it as a challenge to her courage and stepped out, standing so close her face nearly touched his chest. She caught his scent, a compelling combination of salt water and spice and man. Forced herself to resist a sudden urge to bury her nose in his shirt and inhale deeply. To wrap herself in his warmth and defy the icy damp of a Seattle winter's night.

The opals on her fingers trilled a sudden, startling call that expanded through her senses. Lonely, haunting. Singing of want, hunger, and the darker sides of need. Erin's knees nearly buckled at the power of it, and the warrior's hands shot out to grasp her arms.

"Don't touch me," she gasped, but it was too late, too late, *far too late*. The song of the opals soared and crescendoed inside her mind, through her soul, and into the desiccated spaces inside her heart. And where the music smashed through boundaries in her control, the Wilding rushed to follow. It seared her nerve endings and sparked along her skin, electric bright.

Ven's eyes darkened, and he bit off a curse as he jerked away from her, releasing her arms. She fell to her knees before him, clutching her hands to her head, clamping down on the forbidden magic. Mumbling words of power under her breath. *"Restrictos, terminos, immediamentos!"*

Gasping for breath, she forced the magic to subside. Beat it down. Wondered how long it would be until she could no longer control the Wilding Magic's hunger to display its power through her. Over her.

She blinked her eyes open when a shadow crossed her closed eyelids and saw the Atlantean crouching down to look into her face. The traces of amusement were gone, and she instinctively recoiled from the hardness in his eyes. A very thin layer of sophistication lay over the primitive savagery of this warrior.

"What in the nine hells was *that*?" he rasped out, staring into her face as though he could read her secrets in the lines of her flesh.

"That was—" She stumbled over the lies she'd rehearsed so many times in her mind against this very possibility, trying desperately for reason. Another melody chimed in her mind. Sweeter, richer. Wordless lyrics of desire. The emeralds in her rings seared the skin of her index fingers.

Shock had her reeling back. The *emeralds*? But—oh. His eyes. His *eyes*.

"What is *that*?" she asked instead, staring into the bluish-emerald flame glowing in his eyes. Thoughts of Atlantean and Wilding magic crossing paths—water and electricity battling for supremacy—skittered through her mind.

Disaster. Electrocution. Pain. Death.

Before he could reply, she pulled herself up and leaned against the car, never taking her eyes off his. "What is that blue-green light flaring in your eyes? Do Atlanteans call the Wilding?"

He shot to his feet. "What are you talking about? What blue-green flame? What is the Wilding?" He lifted a hand as if to touch his face, then lowered it; clenched and unclenched his hands and inhaled sharply.

"If you'll excuse me, Erin," he said, biting off the words as he strode around her car to the passenger side and threw the door open. He slid onto the seat and looked in the mirror under the dimness of the car's overhead light.

As Erin took a shaky step away from the car, determined to hide the truth of just how badly his touch had shattered her defenses, she heard the passenger door slam behind her. The car shook so hard with the force she nearly fell again.

She whirled around to face him, and the sight that confronted her was entirely unexpected. The warrior, eyes closed and head bowed, pounded his fists on the top of her car once, twice, and then a third time, muttering in a liquid tongue that sounded like no language she knew. Then he seemed to catch himself and stared at her over the roof of her car, eyes flared wide with shock and something that looked a lot like desperation.

"Forgive me, please, but I have to leave. Now. I need to—Alaric—damnit. I just—oh, hells, I'm so outta here." With that, he turned and leapt into the air, shimmering into sparkling mist as he rose into the darkening twilight sky.

She caught her breath. It was beautiful. It was terrifying. It was exactly as she'd dreamed of Atlantis. Shaking her head to try to clear it of magic and fancies, she caught sight of his car, blocking hers in.

"Trapped. Oh, Goddess, what have you done to me?"

A rasping voice answered her murmured question. "Better you should ask what *we* are about to do to you, Erin Connors."

Before she could think or move or react, the amber on her fingers sang out a clear, sharp warning tone. A pulsing red light filled her field of vision and sliced through her powers and her personal shields, cutting off her access to the earth magic. For the first time since she'd turned sixteen, Erin was as powerless as a non-Magickal as she stood, alone, and faced the dark.

Chapter 3

Ven soared over the treetops, feeling a sick twisting in his gut. Naming himself something he'd have called anyone else to battle challenge for: a coward.

Running from a woman—running from an emotion—wasn't his style. Hells, *having* emotions for women wasn't his style. There was nothing, not one damn thing, that was in any way normal about his reaction to Erin Connors.

VEN! HELP ME!

The sharp call smashed through his skull, shattering his concentration so thoroughly he nearly fell out of the air. It was Erin, and somehow, magically, she'd managed to reach him telepathically.

And she was in trouble.

He changed direction midflight and sped back through the darkening sky, rage pounding through him. Trouble was something he could deal with.

Trouble was his *specialty*.

As he shimmered back over the tops of the trees bordering the headquarters building, he saw the sickly orange-red pulsing glow surrounding Erin and the two dark figures pointing sticks at her. Witches, then, or wizards. Vamps didn't use wands or like much to be around anything wooden or pointy.

He called to the elements, diffused the mist forming his body even further so as not to draw suspicion, and floated down behind them. The two figures—definitely human, one male and one female on closer look—never even twitched. Erin stood, apparently unharmed, but frozen, in the center of an orb of the weird light. She was moving her lips but either she'd lost her voice or else no sound could penetrate the bubble. But he could hear the bastards holding her prisoner just fine, and decided to listen for a minute or two before he killed them for touching her.

Gather information. Act like a freaking ambassador. Then he'd rip their lungs out through their rib cages.

The woman spoke, her voice low. "This was badly thought out. We should have waited. What if someone from the coven walks out here and sees us?"

The man replied. "Hey, I saw an opportunity and I took it. He will reward us well for this. We just gotta get her out of here, fast. The car's on its way."

"You expect me to keep this shield up all the way to the mountains? I'm already tired, you idiot. She's very power-ful," she hissed.

The man pulled something out of his pocket that glinted metallic in the pulsing red light. "No worry. She'll be out for hours after I stick her with this." He started walking toward Erin, and all ambassadorial thoughts vanished. A wave of primal fury roared through Ven, and he immediately trans-formed back into his body and leapt forward. He drew a dag-ger but changed his mind at the last second, turned it, handle first, and smashed it into the back of the woman's head. Not hard enough to kill her, but she'd have one hell of a headache.

The reddish light immediately flickered off and Erin col-lapsed to the ground, maybe unconscious, striking her head on the dirt, hard.

The man whirled around and saw Ven and gasped, raising what Ven now saw was a hypodermic needle into the air with one hand and holding a gun in the other. "Come closer and I'll kill her," the thug snarled, pointing the gun at Erin.

"You're not going to touch her," Ven said, striding toward him and unsheathing his sword on the way. "In fact, you're already a dead man for even thinking about hurting her."

Time slowed to the speed of a single grain of sand falling from an hourglass as the man's finger tightened on the gun and the image of Erin bleeding to death on the ground nearly blinded Ven with rage. Guns were fast. Bullets were fast.

Poseidon's magic was faster.

Before the man's finger could tighten sufficiently to pull the trigger, Ven had flashed between him and Erin and knocked his gun hand up so the pistol fired into the air. Then, wrenching the gun away, he smashed the bastard's face with his fist and smiled as the man hit the ground. He knelt to check Erin's pulse, which was strong and steady, and was relieved to see her eyelids were already flickering. The man groaned, and Ven grabbed him by the neck and yanked him up off the ground.

"Nice silencer. Now tell me who you are and why you're here."

The man flailed in Ven's hand, feet kicking the air and hands struggling to peel Ven's fingers away from his throat. He made choking noises as his face darkened.

"Oh, my bad. Guess you have to breathe to be able to talk," Ven said, loosening his grip a fraction. "Now spit it out before I kill you just for fun."

The man's eyes glared hatred at him. That and something else. Terror, maybe. "If I tell you anything, they'll kill me."

"Yeah, well, I hate to sound like a B movie, but if you don't talk, *I'll* kill you."

"You don't understand." The man practically spat the words at him. "There's killing and then there's killing. Do your worst."

And then he laughed in Ven's face, and almost before Ven heard the sharp report of the gunshot a hole blossomed in the middle of the man's forehead.

Ven dropped him and whirled around to face the new threat, only to see another dark figure by the trees flash a sword through the air and slice the head off of the kneeling figure who held a gun in a two-handed position. The shooter immediately began to dissolve into slime.

Remembering the witch, Ven shot a look at where she'd fallen, only to see she'd disappeared. He shot up into the air and scanned the area, but came up with nothing. Leaping back to the ground, he moved to place himself between Erin, who was still lying silent on the ground, and the new threat. The slime had almost entirely melted into the ground. "Vamp."

"Yes, he was. As am I," the one with the sword called. "But better the vampire you know, isn't that the old saying?"

Ven recognized the voice and felt marginally better. But only marginally. "Daniel. Or Drakos. Or whatever your name is. I think that's 'the *devil* you know.' And don't get me wrong, I'm glad to have the help, but what exactly are you doing here?"

Daniel stepped forward. He looked the same as he had the night he'd betrayed his former master Barrabas to the Atlanteans, for whatever twisted reason he might have had.

"Devils, vampires, is there really any difference, metaphorically speaking?" Daniel paused and inclined his head. "Lord Vengeance. It is . . . interesting . . . to see you here."

"I kinda thought Anubisa had killed you in D.C. for what you did."

Daniel's mouth twisted. "I removed myself from the battle when she appeared. Luckily her back was to me at the time, although who can tell what vision a goddess of the night may have? Perhaps I owe you a debt for her death on that day."

"Yeah, well, consider us even, then. Where did that bloodsucker—uh, no offense—come from? And did you see a female witch get by you?"

Daniel pointed to the driveway. "He drove a car and parked it just behind the tree line, then headed here to back up this one, I presume. I saw no female, nor sensed any beating hearts other than the three of yours—now two."

Ven glanced down at Erin, who was finally stirring, thank Poseidon. He desperately wanted to scoop her up off the ground but he wasn't about to trust a vamp—even one who'd maybe just saved his life—any farther than he could throw him. Maybe not even that far. "What's going on, Daniel? Why were they after Erin? Why are you here?"

The vampire's eyes narrowed, and he glanced down at Erin with a look that was way too interested for Ven's taste. A primitive protective instinct curled up from Ven's gut and washed through his body, his muscles tightening in its wake. "I think you'd better tell me now. I'm here to make an alliance with Erin and her coven, and I'm not about to stand for any interference with that."

He took a step closer to Daniel, staring him right in the eyes. "Just so you know."

"Just so you know," the vamp repeated, mocking him, clearly not the slightest damn bit intimidated, "I'm trying to protect Erin, too. He wants her, and he won't stop until he gets her."

Daniel's head whipped to the side, as if listening to a sound beyond Ven's range of hearing. "I have to go. The witches are coming home. I'll clean up your trash for you." He bent and scooped up the dead body lying at their feet. "Take care of her, do you understand? Don't let your guard down for an instant. He is too powerful."

With the preternatural speed so characteristic of the undead, Daniel shot across the ground toward the trees, lifting the dead body and rising into the air as he did so.

"Who in the nine hells are you talking about, damnit?" Ven yelled after him, sick to death of vampires and their half-truths and shadowed threats.

Daniel turned and stared back at Ven. "Oh, he may possibly be from some eleventh level of hell, Atlantean. I'm talking about Caligula."

As the vampire vanished, Erin sat up, blinking and holding

her head. Ven knelt to lift her off the ground, murmuring soothing noises against her silken hair, vowing with a fierce resolve to protect her. It was his job. It had nothing to do with the way his body tightened when he was near her.

Yeah. Right.

As he watched, a sleek limousine pulled up in the driveway and three women, all wearing long silk robes, piled out and pushed past the male driver to rush toward Ven. He tensed, but one of them, with long red hair, started chanting, and he felt the push of her magic, hard, against his skin before she'd uttered more than three words. Erin smiled at the newcomers, though, so he relaxed somewhat.

"Hey, friend here. Don't turn me into a toad. I'm Ven from Atlantis, and we need to talk."

Erin raised her head from his shoulder and drew in a shaky breath. "It's true, Gennae." She looked up at him with those enormous blue eyes. "He may have just saved my life."

The three women all began talking at once.

"What?"

"Who—"

"Did you—"

And the redhead cut them off. "Inside. We'll discuss this inside."

The witches started toward the door and Ven followed them. "Are you okay?" he asked Erin, his arms tightening around her. "Really okay? How about your head? What did that ugly light do to you?"

Her head fell back against his shoulder, as *if* it were too heavy for her neck to support. "I think I'm okay. Ven, it was black magic. My amber sang to me. And they cut me off from my own power, so that witch had to be more powerful than any I've met before outside of those three." She indicated the witches walking into the building in front of them.

"Yeah, well, we've got even bigger problems," he said, dropping his voice to a whisper so that only she could hear him. "Do you know the name Caligula?"

She gasped and her fingers convulsively clutched at his shoulders. Slowly, she turned her eyes up to study his face, and he'd never seen skin so pale on a living being. But all she spoke were two short words.

"Not again."

～～～

The sky over Puget Sound

Ven transformed back into his physical form seconds before his body arrowed, head first, into the icy water. A power far older than Atlantis had engineered the magic of the portal that would take him home to find Alaric. To find some answers.

Poseidon himself knew answers were in short supply. Erin had begged him to keep the name Caligula to himself until she could fill him in on something. From the look in her eyes at the time, he had a feeling that it was a seriously bad story. The head witches or whatever they were had sworn to him that the building was warded with more than a century's worth of magic and that Erin would be safe to rest there overnight. He'd very nearly demanded a demonstration before he agreed, but he'd gotten the distinct impression that Erin was about to drop where she stood. Either that, or that scary one, Berenice or something, was going to shoot some nasty-ass magic at him from the wand she was white-knuckling in the corner.

In the end, he'd been convinced that she was safe enough there, asked for and received a promise that she wouldn't set foot out of the door until they could talk, and left. Now he needed to get home and report in. Maybe find out what kind of complicated plot the vamps were up to this time. Gather the boys and kick some bloodsucker ass.

He dove farther, deeper, scowling at the inconvenience of having to enter the doorway to his homeland through a body of natural water, but nobody except Alaric could call the portal from dry land. He plummeted down into the darkness of the icy waters, wishing the waves crashing around him would help him escape the residual terror he'd felt when Erin had hit the ground. Couldn't be emotion. He didn't do emotion. The lovely little witch must have trapped him with some weird musical spell.

Yeah, that had to be it.

He dove down still farther, calling to the power with his mind and senses. Offering himself as a prince of Atlantis. Falling into the ritual of the ages, calling out to be accepted into the portal's will. Farther, deeper, he dove. Down past the memory of light, but still the melodies of her magic rang in his head. Resonated in the fibers of his being.

Deeper, yet. Still the portal failed to appear. Ven didn't worry. Princes never worry, or so Conlan had told him often enough. The image of Erin falling flashed into his head. Okay, *almost* never worry.

But the first tendril of concern snaked through his mind when oxygen deprivation banded its iron grip around his lungs.

Princes may not worry, but princes can drown.

The depth gauge hardwired into every Atlantean brain warned him that he was passing the safety zone. He'd been diving for nearly five minutes. Another minute or so and he'd pass the point where his lungs had enough oxygen to return to the surface. Superior Atlantean lung capacity.

The irony of an Atlantean prince dying in the sea should have amused him, but it was just pissing him off. With every ounce of power he possessed, he sent out another call, dropping into the formal speak of ritual he never bothered with except in times of high ceremony or extreme stress.

Portal! The King's Vengeance demands entry! I serve Atlantis and my brother the high prince—to fail me is to fail us all.

For another long moment, nothing. Stubbornness—or the memory of clear blue eyes—propelled him ever farther down, in search of the knowledge he needed so desperately. Deep, and ever deeper. Flickers of dark danced at the edge of his consciousness before—finally—the familiar iridescent silvery-blue sparkles appeared and formed an ovoid shape beneath him as he plummeted down through the frigid water. Falling into and through the shimmering magic of the portal, he had an instant to wonder why the only image that flashed through his mind was her face. And then his oxygen-starved brain gave up the fight, and the shimmers faded to black.

Chapter 4

A cavern deep below Mount Rainier,
Cascade Range, Washington

The weak light of torches and candles barely illuminated the room well enough to see the speaker, but his face was one better suited for the dark, in any event. "Think of it as a birthday celebration, if you will. It's simply that the birthday in question will mark two thousand years." The vampire's voice thrummed with an ancient power that boomed through the enormous empty space of the cavern, shuddered through the damp and mold that lined the black walls, and grated inside the listener's eardrums. It was a voice designed to assert its owner's pull over the weak, the servile, and the craven.

The listener was none of the three. But he was curious. "And you plan to use the occasion to do what? Regain the rule you lost all those long years ago?"

"I *lost* nothing. I was brutally murdered in the prime of my life." The vampire glared, his eyes glowing a fierce red that cut through the murky dark. But then his laughter rang out, hoarse and slightly rusty. The bones in his face stood out in stark relief, framing his prominent Roman nose. Straight-edged black hair was styled in an ancient military cut. "Besides, the

Roman Empire is long gone and was far smaller than what I plan to attain today."

He glided to the center of the cavern and floated onto a red velvet-covered platform. "The world shall know the name of Gaius Julius Caesar Augustus Germanicus again."

The listener kept his face expressionless, which was somewhat of a feat, under the circumstances. *Right. Perhaps Hollywood would be a better goal, considering your flair for drama.* "But did the world ever know that name? Or was it the name the soldiers gave you as a child that you wish to hear again? Blaring from countless television screens, ringing in the streets?"

He paused, jaws clenching in spite of his desire to remain impassive, before continuing. "Isn't *Caligula* the name you wish to make famous again?"

The most feared and despised emperor in Roman history smiled, his long fangs flashing. "And if it is? It is no less than my birthright." He turned his gaze to the listener, who still stood, shadowed, near the cavern wall. "You know, of course, that I do not trust you, Drakos."

Caligula's newest general finally met the gaze of his newfound . . . master. "As well you should not. My first words of advice to you would be this: never trust anyone."

～～～

High Prince Conlan's palace, Atlantis

"I don't like it," Justice said, pacing the marble floor of Conlan's war chamber. Ven watched as the warrior, his sword sheathed on his back as always, measured the length of the room with long strides. Justice had been pacing, nonstop, for the dozen or so minutes since they'd started assembling.

After meeting privately with Ven, Conlan had called his warriors for a council to discuss the threat from Caligula, the increasing vamp activity in the Seattle region, and whatever in the nine hells Erin Connors had done to Ven.

Ven blew out a breath. To say he was frustrated didn't begin to cover it. He didn't move, though, from his stance leaning against the wall across from the chamber's main door. Between any possible threat and his brother, as was his duty and right as the King's Vengeance. Not that Conlan couldn't take care of himself. Ven glanced at his older brother, heir to the throne. Conlan looked so much like him, if maybe an inch or so shorter. The prince sat in his usual seat at the large round wooden table, leaning back in his chair, watching the room but saying nothing.

Ven finally replied to Justice's rhetorical comment, just to shave some edge off the tension in the room. "You don't like anything, Justice. Care to elaborate?"

Justice stopped pacing and whirled to face Ven, that waist-length blue braid of his flying as he turned. "Do not mock my concerns, Lord Vengeance. You know full well my instincts have saved your royal ass on more than one occasion."

It was the simple truth, so Ven couldn't find it in him to be annoyed. "Your point? It's not like all the ass-saving over the centuries hasn't been reciprocated." He looked around the chamber at the others of Conlan's elite guard, the Seven, who'd shared more battles with him than he could count.

Brennan, emotionless as ever, unable to feel since the curse. He and Alexios had made it back to Atlantis just a short while before Ven. Alexios, grim, unsmiling. Something had died within the warrior when Anubisa had held him captive. These days he only ever smiled when he was killing something. Ven still didn't know how far Alexios had come from the feral state in which they'd found him; the vampire goddess had had a master's touch when it came to torture.

Damn, but it was great that she was dead.

Christophe, eyes gleaming with barely leashed power. The most unstable of them all, perhaps. Standing next to him, Denal, youngest in age, but a warrior who had died and come back to life due to Riley's mortal sacrifice. His two hundred and twenty–odd years weighed more heavily on the youngling than it ever had before.

And their missing colleague—Bastien—still in Florida forming an alliance with the shape-shifters. Forming his own alliance by way of the soul-meld with a werepanther he'd fallen in love with, if Denal's stories could be taken seriously. Ven was in "believe it when I see it mode" on that one.

Alexios spoke up, jolting Ven from his reverie. "Do we really want to waste our time comparing notches on our swords, Lord Justice?" He stood near the window, the scarred side of his face turned toward the wall and away from their view.

Conlan held up a hand, and Justice stopped before snapping out whatever reply had caused his muscles to tense up like that. The warrior was as bad as Christophe. Justice had a chip on his shoulder so big that somebody was bound to want to knock it off one of these days. Probably sooner rather than later. Ven hoped to be around to see it.

If he wasn't the one doing the knocking. Maybe he'd go two-for-one with Justice and Christophe, just to burn off a little tension.

"I don't like it either," Conlan said, voice even. "Ven is my brother and, for some strange reason, my future queen seems to have developed a certain sisterly fondness for him."

Denal laughed. "She's so sweet she likes everyone, my liege. She even likes Christophe."

Christophe mock-growled at the younger warrior and reached out to smack him on the back of the head, but Denal ducked, grinning.

Conlan's lips quirked in a semblance of a smile, but his face remained grim. "Regardless of the reasons, Riley would prefer that Ven remain in Atlantis to be near while she . . . faces these difficulties. However, she is a warrior at heart and realizes that we must continue our mission to protect humanity. We who are the Warriors of Poseidon can do no less."

An icy chill shivered through the room, and most of the warriors standing around the table involuntarily stepped back a pace. After nearly three centuries as high priest, Alaric's signature entrance was unmistakable to them all. He carried the power of Poseidon with him even when formless as air, invisible as a breath. Brennan, who had been leaning on the chair next to Conlan's at the table, bowed slightly and moved away from it toward his own seat.

Alaric shimmered into shape in the space between heartbeats—one moment a cool chill threatened a whisper of mortality down Ven's spine, the next Alaric stood before them, hands fisted on the emerald-inlaid hilts of his daggers. He was dressed all in black, as always, like some kind of Atlantean angel of death.

The high priest scanned the room, as if he weighed and measured the caliber of the men within it in mere seconds. His gaze rested last—and longest—on Ven. "Your witch is a gem singer," he pronounced, before gracefully dropping into his seat.

Of course, he was the symbol of Poseidon's magic made flesh, or so the tradition went, Ven thought with grim amusement.

If he wanted to rip my heart out of my chest while it was still beating, he'd probably do that gracefully, too.

The image of the Lord High Vampire Barrabas's death in that very manner at Anubisa's delicate hand surfaced in his memory for a cringe-inducing second, but he shoved it out of his mind.

Suddenly, Alaric's words sank in past Ven's reminiscing. "What? I thought gem singers were a myth. And whatever in the nine hells she is, she's not *my* witch."

"A myth? Like the *aknasha'an*?" Alaric asked, voice dry.

"Whoa, Temple Rat, did you just make a funny?" Ven's eyebrows raised. He hadn't heard even a hint of the priest's trademark dry-as-the-Dead-Sea humor since before Alaric had first met Riley's sister, Quinn.

"I find no humor in the fact that ancient myths are walking off the pages of our scrolls," Alaric returned, his eyes glowing emerald green and warning of his irritation. "First Riley and Quinn are discovered. Both *aknasha'an*. Emotional empaths straight out of legends lost in the waters of time. Now Ven describes a human witch who resonates with the lyrical power of a gem singer. Who knows what may be next?"

"My vote is for the Tooth Fairy," Ven drawled. "Maybe riding a unicorn."

"What's a tooth faery?" Denal asked, brows drawn together, looking much like the boy who'd so often driven Ven to distraction with his endless questions.

Ven snorted, but before he could explain—okay, *mock*—Brennan finally spoke. "If the woman—"

"Erin," Ven cut in, unaccountably annoyed. "Her name is Erin Connors. Not 'the woman,' not 'the witch,' but Erin. She's beautiful, and she's brave enough to volunteer to ally with us to go after Caligula, so she at least deserves the use of her name." He kicked at the floor with the toe of his boot. "Anyway, we don't know if she's a gem singer for sure. Hells, it was probably her iPod I heard."

Brennan continued as if he'd never been interrupted. "If Erin Connors is truly a gem singer, and her song strikes harmony in Ven, perhaps I should be the one to ally with the Seattle magical contingent. I am somewhat of a student of the ancient myths and prophecies. They state that the resonance of a gemstone sounds in the emotion of the singer." He looked around the room and then zeroed his focus in on Ven. "And apparently in the one with the ability to soul-meld with the gem singer."

"No!" Ven pushed away from the wall. "No," he continued, forcing himself to calm. "Conlan gave me this job, and I mean to see it through. Yeah, it's true that you have no surface emotions, Brennan. Ever since that damn curse, I mean. But remember that Quinn found something buried way deep down within you. If Erin really is a gem singer, and this resonance crap is even real, then it stands to reason that she'd crack right through that barrier of yours."

He turned to face Conlan and Alaric. "I'm doing it, Conlan. If anybody is forming any kind of alliance with Erin and her coven, it's damn well going to be me."

"It appears the King's Vengeance has made his decision," Conlan said, a trace of sarcasm underscoring the words. "In any event, I need Brennan to deal with a report of an emotional incubus who is murdering people in New York."

"More myths walking off pages," Alaric said.

"Possibly not even true," Conlan said. "But if it is, Brennan is in a unique position to battle such a creature."

"Fine, whatever. Can we get back to Erin and what in the hells a gem singer is? How do I deal with her?" Ven said, turning his back on Conlan and Alaric and staring down at his folded arms. Maybe Justice had a good idea with the pacing. He either had to burn off some stress or hit somebody. Not the greatest time for his sparring partner Bastien to be shacked up with a werepanther.

Alaric nodded. "A gem singer is one whose soul resonates with the spirit of the stones of the earth. Some records indicate it was primarily a talent of the elvenfolk among the Fae."

"Great. Now Erin is *related* to the Tooth Fairy," Ven growled, looking up.

"Let us discuss Caligula," Alaric said. "Perhaps he seeks to consolidate Barrabas's power to himself. We knew political movement would be made in the vampire hierarchy, however loosely structured it may be."

"Is there even a hierarchy anymore?" Christophe replied. "Now that their goddess is gone, does that make them all turn renegade? We may not have done anybody any favors by killing her. Did she at least keep them in line?"

Alexios stepped forward, clenching and unclenching his hands. "Do not doubt that Conlan and Riley did the world a *favor*, as you put it, by killing that evil obscenity Anubisa," he said, the strain to remain calm evident in his roughened voice. "At the very least, they did me a service that I can never repay."

Conlan stood and bowed to his warrior. "Alexios, if there were any debt, it was mine to you for putting your life in her hands in order to search for me. Never doubt that I remember this every day of my life."

Silence reverberated in the room, stretched tautly between

the two of them—both who had known torture beyond description at Anubisa's hands.

Finally, Brennan broke the silence. "I do not believe in coincidences. If Caligula is operating in that area, it is almost certain that he is behind the drastic increase in newly turned vampires."

"Why? Why would he do that? You can't control new vamps for the first year or two, so what does it serve him?" Justice asked. "Although that's assuming a vamp needs a reason to cause trouble, which is probably stupid to begin with."

Ven nodded. "I agree with all of that. No coincidence, vamps cause trouble for no reason, and Justice is stupid." He grinned at Justice as he said it.

Denal and Christophe laughed, breaking the tension, but Justice didn't seem to be amused. He glared at Ven. "Laugh it up, *Ven* Helsing. Sounds like your little gem singer got to you." He laughed. "Hey, if it's a problem, I'll be glad to take over for you. Sounds like she's quite a woman."

Ven had joked with Justice about women for more than two centuries, but suddenly, with that one sentence, something changed. Some*one* changed.

Ven changed.

"Don't even think about it," he growled, all traces of amusement gone from his voice. "Stay away from Erin."

Denal's sharp gasp sounded a warning, causing Ven to unsheathe his daggers in one smooth motion and whirl around to face the threat. But the chamber door remained firmly closed, and the only things remotely threatening in the room were the shocked expressions on the faces of Denal, Alexios, and Christophe. Ven took in their widened eyes as his own narrowed. "What? Why are you staring at me like that?"

As Conlan and Alaric shot up out of their chairs in unison, Denal strode around the table until he faced Ven again. "Your eyes. They're . . . they're glowing," he said, awe infusing his words. "There's a weird blue-green flame in the middle. It's like—"

"It's the flame of Poseidon," Brennan said. "Since one

can only suppose that you do not seek to achieve the soul-meld with one of us, it appears that the gem singer has affected you even more than you know."

Ven clenched his eyes shut to block their view. Douse the flame.

Hoped it would work. Somehow knew it wouldn't.

"Ven?" Conlan's voice rang out, still calm, but resonating with royal command. "Is there something else you meant to tell me about Erin Connors?"

Ven muttered a few of his favorite curses in ancient Atlantean, then decided to try to play it casual. "Well, now that you mention it . . ."

~~~~~~

Headquarters, the Seattle Circle of Light

Erin stood in the center of the circle, trying to control the trembling in her knees. She'd never been called to a special midnight gathering of the coven high priestesses before and didn't know what to expect. The candlelit room, lined with sturdy wooden bookcases and heavy midnight blue silk draperies, contained an air of solemnity underscored by the absolute cessation of her power from the moment she'd stepped through the doorway. The room must be shielded by the most powerful of wards; Erin couldn't hear even a glimmer of the song of the large geodes that rested on the bookcases. The gems on her fingers lay dark and still as well.

The rumors of Silencing she'd heard, growing up as a witch, swirled up through her memories to press against her mind. Unfortunately, the rumors had brought along their buddies: Terror and Despair. Twice in one evening she'd been blocked from her powers. She made a promise to herself: it wasn't going to happen again. She straightened her shoulders and took a step toward the massive table at one end of the midnight blue draped room. "I am here to report an incident, am I not?"

Gennae looked up from the papers she'd been arranging

at her place at the center of the table, her icy features, nearly as pale as the white robes they all three wore, were arranged in an expression of mild surprise. "Did we ask you to speak?"

"No, but I—"

"That will be quite enough, Erin," said Lillian, her fall of short gray hair swinging around her square jaw as she nodded for emphasis. "You will speak when asked to do so."

Berenice, the third and final witch at the table, pushed her dark hair away from her face and stared at Erin for a long moment. When she finally spoke, her silky voice held nothing but contempt. "Perhaps Erin feels she does not need to heed coven law, now that she is so adept at channeling the Wilding?"

Erin narrowed her eyes and tried not to glare at Berenice, in spite of the taunt. *That's what she wants me to do. Blow up and show them all that I'm unstable. Not going to happen.*

"We're going to talk about my use of the Wilding, instead of the attack?" She didn't bother to hide the disbelief in her voice.

They merely stared back at her, not speaking. So she did the only thing she could think to do. She answered the question. "I am well aware of coven law and follow it faithfully. As you all know, I have been working very hard to control the Wilding Magic. The force of it this evening took me entirely by surprise." Erin clenched her hands tightly together behind her back, but kept her face smooth.

"Not hard enough, clearly," Berenice sneered. "We felt it clear across town at our dinner meeting."

Gennae held up a hand. "I would hear no more of this. You especially, Berenice, know the Wilding chooses its wielders. If a witch could choose to channel such dark magic, only the ones with the most corrupted hearts would make that choice. And the dangers inherent in the Wilding are too great to be left in the hands of one with evil intent."

She turned to face Berenice. "Although done with the best of intentions, your own attempt to call the Wilding a decade ago nearly destroyed the entire city of Seattle."

Berenice's face flushed a deep red. "I will not defend or discuss that decision again, all these years later. When vampires and shape-shifters made their existence known, I felt I had the opportunity to destroy them before they could gain overt power."

Lillian murmured a sound of agreement. "And you were right to forecast the threat, Berenice. Now the vampires have their own house of Congress, and the Primus holds more power than the House and the Senate combined. With the shape-shifters controlling much of the mainstream media, the power structure of the world is forever tipped in their favor."

Gennae shook her head, her long red hair flying behind her. "No. And no, and no, and no. She was right in her premonition, but wrong in her methods. Had we not intervened when we did, the results could have been disastrous."

Erin couldn't keep quiet any longer. The rage had been building inside her until she thought her head might explode from the force of it. "What, exactly, would you consider *not* to be disastrous about the night the vampire Caligula murdered my entire family?" she asked, biting out the words.

All three of the witches at the table bowed their heads for a moment. When Gennae looked up at Erin again, her face had softened. "For that, I apologize. Losing your mother and your sisters was the greatest tragedy our coven has ever known and, on a personal note, Gwendolyn was my closest friend, more like a sister to me." Tears glistened in Gennae's violet eyes. "You must believe how profoundly we all understand and share your sorrow."

Erin held Gennae's gaze for a long, defiant moment, but then nodded. "I do believe that." She lowered her lashes and glanced at Berenice's angry face. *Mostly.*

"And, knowing your mother and her teaching, we would never believe you would risk the loss of your soul to the Wilding Magic," Lillian added.

"I have done everything possible to shield against it," Erin said, head held high. "I have spent countless hours researching my Gift of the singing stones, as well. But there's nothing in any of my reading to explain why a warrior from Atlantis brought out such a violent reaction in me . . . in my gems."

Gennae and Berenice exchanged a nearly imperceptible glance. "Actually, Erin, there is something you need to know," Gennae said. "About the reaction you say this Atlantean had to your Gift, and about what you will find if you continue to seek out Caligula."

Berenice's face paled even further, if that were possible. "You cannot tell her—"

"We must tell her. It's time. Especially if she's planning to involve the Atlanteans in this impossible plan for revenge," Lillian said. "Not to mention the attack tonight, which may be related."

Yeah, you're all pretty good at *not mentioning* the attack, Erin thought, wondering if sheer rage would overcome her exhaustion and keep her standing upright.

"She deserves to be punished for not controlling the Wilding," Berenice snapped.

"She deserves to know the truth," Gennae said.

"What truth? Just tell me," Erin demanded, the ice in her veins streaking through her body and congealing in her stomach in a frozen ball. She wished for her power and the comfort of her gems and their song; she wished to run— covering her ears—from the room.

Mostly she wished to be curled up, resting safely in Ven's arms, she admitted to herself even as she wondered at the strength of her longing for a man she'd only just met.

Gennae rose from her seat at the table and glided noiselessly around it until she stood in front of Erin, then put her hands on Erin's shoulders. "You have been like a daughter to me, Erin, and if you are so determined to follow this path of revenge, you must know the consequences."

"But it's not just about revenge and the past," Erin blurted out, searching the priestess's eyes for some glimmer of understanding. "It's about the future, too. It's about stopping Caligula from doing this again, to somebody else's family.

Maybe to the entire human population of Seattle, or the state of Washington. What about the entire West Coast? We've felt the darkness from the area around Mount Rainier. We've seen the mounting numbers rise on the tallies of those he's turned to vampire. Why can't you understand?"

Gennae's fingers tightened painfully on Erin's shoulders, and she leaned forward for a brief hug, whispering in Erin's ear, "Don't think we're not concerned about the attack tonight. There is a spy in the coven and we are investigating."

Erin focused on not changing her facial expression, since Berenice was staring at her with narrowed eyes.

Gennae released her grip and stepped back. "Oh, we understand all too well, Erin. Caligula is consolidating his power over as many of those called to the dark as he can." She paused and bowed her head, as though she couldn't bear to look Erin in the eye any longer. "That may in fact be who was behind the attack on you tonight. You said you felt dark magic . . ." Her words trailed off.

"You have to tell her, Gennae. Or I will." Lillian said. Her voice held so much sorrow that Erin blinked and glanced over at the older witch, then gasped at the tears streaming down Lillian's face.

"Gennae. What is it? Please tell me. You're frightening me," Erin said.

"And so you should be frightened," Berenice called out, standing up from her chair. "After what I saw—" She broke off, shaking her head.

Gennae finally raised her head to look into Erin's eyes. "Yes. It is time. First, we recently have acquired more detailed knowledge of the nature of your Gift. According to the representative of the Fae currently visiting the North American Magickals coven leadership conference, your Gift may be a rare inheritance from the elvenfolk."

Erin blinked. "You're telling me I'm part elf?"

Lillian barked out a laugh. "Don't ever let any of the Fae hear you say that. They're fed up with the popular culture misconceptions of the elvenfolk. I heard one of the Canadian

Fae sliced a vampire's head off merely for mentioning the North Pole."

It was too much to process. "So, I may be part elf . . . part elvenfolk. So what? We're all part something, I suppose. What else did this representative say?"

"He called you a gem singer, Erin, when I explained your Gift. He said it was a talent lost in the annals of myth even to his kind," Gennae explained, kindness and something that looked a lot like pity in her eyes.

Erin hated to be pitied. "Go ahead. Tell me the rest of it, already."

Gennae bit her lip, uncharacteristically hesitant. The shadow in the corner of Erin's field of perception was the only sign that Berenice had moved, but suddenly the witch stood next to Gennae. As Erin stared at the two of them, Lillian walked slowly up to flank Gennae on her other side.

"What is this? Strength in numbers?" Erin tried for a casual laugh, but it came out sounding strangled. "Just tell me already."

"The last recording of a gem singer in Fae history was before the Cataclysm that sank Atlantis," Lillian said, glancing at Gennae as if for the go-ahead. "You also may be part Atlantean."

Relief made Erin feel a little giddy. "That's it? I'm part elvenfolk and part Atlantean? That's not a big deal. In fact, it may make Ven and his men more willing to help me. We're long-lost cousins!" She thought of how he made her feel. "Very, very *distant* cousins."

Gennae sighed, a soul-weary sound that swept Erin's shaky attempt at humor away before it. "It's not that simple, Erin. There's something else you need to know." She drew a deep breath. "Your entire family was not murdered that night. Caligula captured your sister and later sent us proof that he had turned her."

Erin's knees buckled for the second time that night, and she nearly fell to the ground. "What? Who? My sister? Which sister? It's a lie! I would have known—I would have felt her—I, I—" She looked to Lillian in supplication, but the gray-haired witch simply stood there, nodding her head in agreement.

"No! No, you're all wrong. I would have known. Somehow I would have known—"

"It is truth, Erin," Gennae replied, cutting off her desperate attempts at denial. "Your sister Deirdre is vampire."

Chapter 5

Seattle

Erin stood in front of the enormous brick waterfront building, clutching the cardboard tray and the paper bag, and double-checked the address. Her complete lack of sleep the night before wasn't all that surprising, considering the attack and the impossible news about Deirdre. She swallowed around the lump in her throat. It couldn't be true. They had to be wrong, and she'd prove it. Deirdre would never choose to live as a vampire.

She fought back the tears and put the pain aside to deal with later. She'd had ten years of practice with that technique.

Ven's address looked more like a warehouse than a home. But he'd called and apologized for leaving so abruptly the night before, then invited her to his place to discuss their impending alliance. He'd made some cryptic comment about not worrying—her safety was guaranteed. She knew vampires did not walk in the daylight, and she was on guard now against any new witch attacks, so she hadn't been worried, anyway.

She glanced up at the four stories of the imposing structure again and shook her head. Maybe it was like those trendy downtown lofts? Only part of it was Ven's?

The massive steel door had only one buzzer next to it, so she pushed that and heard a faint gonging sound reverberate from inside the building. Seconds later the door swung open and Ven stood in front of her wearing only blue jeans, his damp hair brushing against his shoulders.

Erin snapped her mouth closed when she realized she was gaping at him. It wasn't every day a witch was confronted with a chest like that. Holy Goddess, the man was built. Ripped, even. And the unusual tattoo high up on the left side of his chest intrigued her, even though she wasn't much for tattoos. A circle and a triangle with some sort of symbol crossing them both.

She yanked her gaze up to his face, blushing a little, but quit worrying about what he thought of her ogling when she saw his face and the sleepy concern in his eyes. The opals on her fingers glowed and sang to her, but she closed her mind against their call. Not today. She had no time for this weird gem-singing stuff today.

"You look like I feel—total death warmed over, with a side of misery," she blurted out.

He blinked at her, but then he caught sight of what she held and seemed to wake up a little. "Gee, thanks. Hey, you brought coffee? You are an angel."

She smiled at the expression of pure longing on his face. "No, I'm a witch, but thanks for the compliment. Are you going to invite me inside, or are we going to have breakfast on your doorstep?"

He hastily backed up, holding the door for her. "Sorry. I'm kind of wiped. Only slept an hour. Is there food in that bag?"

He took the tray of four quad venti lattes from her, bent his head over the cups, and inhaled deeply as he kicked the door closed with one large, bare foot. "Bliss."

"I hope you like lattes. I didn't know if they'd be too girly for a big tough Atlantean warrior to drink, but if so, that's more for me," she said, nerves swirling in her empty stomach.

She should have eaten one of the pastries on the way over to help mitigate the gallon or six of stomach acid sloshing around in there.

"I brought an assortment of pastries, too," she said, looking around the huge entranceway. The skylights on the ceiling filtered the weak winter sunlight down to them. Farther ahead, the building was divided into floors in a bizarrely open architectural style. Industrial-style metal partitions, walls, and doorways lined the hall.

"I'm secure enough in my manhood to drink froufrou coffee drinks," he said, grinning at her. "Come on."

He led the way down the hallway and she focused really, really hard on not noticing what an amazingly muscled back he had. Or that the amazing back curved down into a truly fabulous backside.

She scowled, suddenly disgusted at herself for noticing how gorgeous and muscled Ven was when she had a job to do. More of a sacred quest, now, really.

She idly glanced into a couple of open doorways as they walked by. Through one of them she caught glimpses of intriguing metal statuaries. Through another she saw what looked to be an extensive luxury car collection, and an almost painful twist of warmth tightened in her chest. "Wait," she called out. "Was that—"

She backtracked to the open doorway and looked inside. A giant room, evidently used as a garage, held probably twenty classic cars and a few very modern, very sleek sports cars. She spotted the black Jaguar he'd driven the night before by the garage door, but then got distracted by a gorgeous cherry red roadster. Dropping the sack of pastries on the concrete floor, she wiped her hands on her jeans and walked over to the beauty. As she touched the hood with reverence, she glanced back at Ven, who stood in the doorway. "Ohhhhh. You own a Duesenberg?"

He followed her into the room, placing the tray of coffee on a small table near the door. "Yep. A 1929 Duesenberg J 350 Willoughby, manufactured here in the U.S. in the—"

"The Indiana plant, yeah, I know," she murmured, her hand

caressing the smooth curve of the hood. "My dad was born and raised in Indianapolis. He moved out here and met my mother and never moved back. He loved these old cars and took me to a lot of car shows when I was little."

"They still live around here?" Ven asked.

The iron fist squeezing her heart clenched down even further. "No. No, he died nearly nine years ago. After the . . . tragedy . . . he couldn't find the strength or will to keep living. I think he made up his mind to die, and he did." She tried to blink back the tears burning at the edges of her eyes, but a few escaped and slid down her cheeks.

Ven raised one finger and caught her tear as it fell, but never touched her skin. "You give honor to your father with your tears, Erin. I am so sorry for your loss. May Poseidon and the gods and goddesses of your ancestors watch over him on his journey into the light."

She wiped her eyes with her hand, trying desperately to silence the emeraldsong that had blazed out of her rings at his almost-touch. She had never once heard the emeralds sing to her since the day of her Choosing, and now they were a Broadway chorus. Nonstop music whenever Ven was around.

She looked up into his dark, dark eyes, afraid of what she might see. The fascinating blue-green light that had so disturbed him the night before was gone, and she was relieved. A tiny part of her whispered in her mind, *Or disappointed.*

She shut down the tiny voice and the emeralds through sheer force of will and concentrated on what Ven had said about her father. "That's beautiful, thank you. Is that a traditional Atlantean saying?"

He bowed to her, the gesture somehow not lessened by the fact that the man offering it was standing shirtless in blue jeans, clearly fresh out of the shower. Ven's natural gallantry was like something she'd seen in the old movies she loved so much. Something about him . . .

"Are you very old?" she blurted out.

Straightening, he grinned, then raised an eyebrow. "That depends. Do you like older men?"

She rolled her eyes. "Nice. Always with the lines, right? You must have women falling all over you."

He abruptly turned away from her, saying something under his breath that she didn't catch.

"What was that?"

"Coffee. I said coffee now, talking later."

Filing away his odd reaction to be considered at another time, Erin retrieved the bag of pastries and followed him out of the room, casting a last look at the Duesy on the way.

I'll get him for you, Dad. For all of us. And I'll save Deirdre, too.

∿∿

Ven gritted his teeth over the highly freaking inappropriate sensations sweeping through every inch of him. The second he'd reached out to touch the tear falling off her cheek, he'd known he should pull his finger back. But, somehow, he hadn't been able to do it. Now he battled the urge to touch that same slightly damp finger to his lips, but clenched his hand more tightly around the edge of the coffee tray instead.

Control. Command. Confidence. His watchwords for nearly half a millennium; suddenly in peril from the mere sight of one small human female sorrowing over her lost father.

How did she manage to look so damned sexy in blue jeans, boots, and a sweater, anyway? It was even a thick, bulky sweater that hid the curves he'd seen on display in that silky thing she'd worn the night before. But the pale blue of the wool and the sunlit-sky blue of her eyes—all that blond hair, even tied back in a ponytail—oh. Hells. He was in big trouble.

Just agreeing to let Alexios and Denal shadow her on her short trip here this morning, instead of going himself, had nearly caused him to growl like a wounded bear at the emotionless warrior and the youngling. They'd been right. He'd needed at least an hour of sleep. But logic didn't resonate with his fierce and growing need to protect Erin.

To protect her *personally.* Hells, maybe coffee would help.

He finally reached the restaurant-sized kitchen at the end of the hall and blew out a sigh of relief. Safety in numbers. Ignoring the curious looks from the three warriors who waited there to meet Erin, he strode over to the red formica-topped table in the center of the room and put the tray of coffee down with more force than necessary. The sloshing coffee splashed up through the drink spouts on the cups and splattered on the table, bringing dark metaphors to Ven's mind of his control splattering up against the charms of one gem singer of a witch.

Yeah, so I suck at metaphors.

"Ven?" Erin's voice came from the doorway, where she'd stopped and stood, frozen, staring at Denal, Justice, and Alexios.

"Come in, Erin, I need to introduce you to the Three Stooges here. Larry, Moe, and Curly," he said, grabbing his shirt from the back of a chair and shrugging into it. Then he took one of the cups out of the holder, wiped the side with a napkin, and took a healthy gulp.

"Who?" said Denal, looking confused. Hells, confused was Denal's default expression, especially when it came to pop culture. He really ought to give the kid a break.

"Three letters for you, Denal. D. V. D. It's never too late for an education in truly classic television." Ven walked back to where Erin still stood in the doorway, her eyes wide, and gently took the bag of pastries from her. "Erin, more officially, may I introduce three of my fellow warriors: Justice, with the fancy blue hair; Alexios, leaning against the wall; and Denal, the youngling of the bunch. All three serve Poseidon in the protection of humanity, as do I."

Erin turned those beautiful blue eyes toward Justice, nearest to her, and Ven fought the urge to step between them, as every muscle in his body tensed to battle-readiness. For some whacked-out reason, he didn't want Erin to look at Justice.

Whoa. Need to figure that one out.

Erin, clearly unaware that Ven was going batshit next to

her, nodded at each of the three warriors in turn. "My name is Erin Connors. I am very honored to meet you."

~~~❦~~~

Erin tried not to stand there gaping like a beached fish, but it was pretty darn hard. She'd never been in a room with so much testosterone in her life. The warriors all stood well over six feet tall, and wore enough weapons to stock an armory. Not to mention that they were all gorgeous, gorgeous men. She figured Atlantis must be some sort of heaven underwater for the women there. Except if the men looked like this, the women were probably all tall, slinky supermodel types. The thought made her shoulders slump a little, considering her own nonslinky, nontall, nonsupermodel self.

She smiled tentatively at Justice. "Blue" was such a lame, doesn't-come-close kind of word to describe the rich sea colors rippling through his long hair. Navy, midnight, cerulean, royal, and even a few strands of periwinkle gleamed under the bright lights of the kitchen. He'd been standing near the far wall braiding it when she walked in, and, as she watched, he tied off the end with a short length of leather cord, stepped toward her, and bowed. The decorated and engraved hilt of the sword sheathed on his back looked worn, as if well used, and the sight of it reminded her again of her mission. As if she could ever forget.

"I am at your service, Lady Erin, so long as our goals are in accord," he said so smoothly that it took her a moment to realize it hadn't exactly been unequivocal support.

"Thank you, I think," she said wryly. She caught a glimmer of surprise and then amusement in his eyes before he masked his expression back to impassivity. "Same goes. From what Quinn and Jack told us of the Warriors of Poseidon, your service is worth quite a great deal."

She held out a hand to shake his and nearly jumped out of her skin when the amber on her middle fingers sounded a discordant note in her mind. A note she'd never heard. The amber protected her from the threat of dark magic and called to her with a wild, jangling song when there were vampires or anybody else wielding black or death magic near her. This hadn't been that song; it was nothing like the warning from the night before—but it had been . . . something.

Something unnatural. She stepped back from Justice and sent out a slight whisper of power toward him to try to sense what he was. But something within him slashed out at her seeking tendril of magic and sliced it in two. His eyes flared with power and something else for a long moment. Something deadly.

"You *are* Atlantean, right, Justice?"

He raised one eyebrow and the corners of his lips quirked in a mocking smile. "As Atlantean as Poseidon himself. You are very intriguing, aren't you?"

"Quinn spoke truly, my lady," Denal said, drawing her attention away from Justice, but not before she resolved to keep a close eye on, and a safe distance from, the blue-haired warrior. "We are honored to help you battle the dark forces."

Denal also bowed to her, but added a flourish. He drew the two daggers from the sheaths on his massive thighs and crossed them before his chest as he bowed. As he resheathed the blades, he grinned at her, and she understood why Ven had called him the youngling. She had a mad urge to ruffle his hair.

"About that bag Ven's holding—it doesn't happen to have pastries in it, does it?" he said, looking an awful lot like a hopeful puppy.

She laughed and gestured toward the bag. "There is an assortment in there, but I'm sorry I only brought four lattes. I didn't realize Ven had company."

As he took the bag and rummaged around in it, Alexios stepped up and stood at an angle to her and gravely nodded his head. The swirling gold in his hair reminded her of some movie star whose name she couldn't remember. But then he raised his head and looked at her, and the edge of danger in his golden eyes reminded her of the fiercest of predators.

She glanced involuntarily at Ven. Well, maybe not *the* fiercest predator. *Tigers and lions and Atlanteans, oh my.*

"You bring us honor by your presence, gem singer," Alexios said, his voice a low rumble. "We will do our best to assist you in destroying the foul scourge Caligula."

She blinked at the formal language, but before she could respond, Justice laughed. "Don't mind Alexios and Denal, they always drop back into formal speak in the presence of great beauty."

"Or really great pastries," Denal chimed in, then shoved half a croissant in his mouth.

Alexios swung his head toward Justice, eyes narrowing, and Erin caught sight of the hideous scarring on the side of his face. "Oh, dear Goddess," she whispered. "What unholy creature could do that to a living being?"

Alexios whirled away from her and strode to a position against the wall farthest from her. "The unholiest of creatures, my lady," he said, ducking his head so his hair swung in front of his face. "Anubisa, the vampire goddess of chaos and the night."

Ven handed one of the cups of coffee to Alexios, then turned to Erin. "Anubisa and Caligula were great pals, before we destroyed her. We have powerful reasons to hate Caligula, Erin. We've run into him many times over the past two thousand years, but somehow he always sacrifices the minions of his blood pride to us and manages to escape."

As always, the mere sound of the vampire's name drove steel spikes into her temples. "Nobody wants him permanently dead more than I do, Ven. Especially after what I learned just last night."

"Yeah, I learned a few things, too. The most important is that Caligula is after you, personally, for some reason." Ven filled her in on what Daniel had told him. "Any idea why? Or any ideas on who those witches were?"

A chill shivered down her spine at the idea that Caligula wanted her. "Maybe he wants a matched set," she said bitterly.

Ven pulled a table chair out for her and handed her one of the cups of coffee. "You look like a strong sea breeze would blow you away, Erin. Sit down and drink some coffee and tell us about it. Also, you mentioned a tragedy?" The compassion in his voice nearly undid the strong defenses she'd built up against the sorrow. Against the pain.

She accepted the chair, she accepted the coffee, but she flatly rejected the sympathy. "Yes. The tragedy. If that word—or any—could come close to describing the night Caligula murdered my mother and sisters."

Alexios slammed a fist against the wall, and she flinched from the sound. "He has much to answer for; far too many mothers and sisters have died at his hand," he growled.

Ven said nothing, merely kneeled in front of her. "We will avenge your loss, Erin Connors. You may take that as my solemn vow. We will slice Caligula's head from his body and salt the ground where his bones dissolve into the slime that withers his soul."

She stared into Ven's eyes, wondering when she'd become a woman who wanted to stand up and cheer at the idea of bloody violence. Wondering how she would react when the specter of grim death stared back at her through her beloved sister's eyes.

She reached out to touch his face, and the emeralds on her fingers called out to her, a seductive siren's call. She yanked her hand back, not yet ready to test her theory that her reaction to him the night before had been a fluke. At least not in a room full of other warriors.

"There's something you all deserve to know," she said, wrapping both hands around her coffee cup. "There are . . . rumors . . . that Caligula turned my sister vampire. That may have something to do with whatever twisted reason he has for coming after me. I . . . I may have to face Deirdre when we find him, and I'm not sure I could bear to see her harmed."

"Maybe she's a good vampire?" Denal offered, doubt apparent in his voice in spite of his words.

Justice snorted. "There is no such thing. Hasn't the last decade proven anything to you? No longer content to haunt the shadows, now they stalk right out in the open. Aided every step of the way by you pitiful humans, who all but declared open season on your own fool selves."

The contempt in his voice pissed her off. "Don't judge us, Atlantean. Last I looked, vampires weren't the only ones hiding in the shadows. Not much in the news about a race of Atlantean super-warriors helping humanity, is there?"

Before he could respond, the crashing sound of something—or someone—smashing through glass sounded from the hall. In an instant, the four warriors were running for the door.

"Stay here," Ven barked out at her over his shoulder as he ran.

"Not likely," Erin said, and then she raised her hands in the air and began to chant.

Chapter 6

Justice was the first to make it to the doorway, unsheathing his sword as he ran, but Ven was right behind him. Crouching low, he burst into the hallway next to Justice, prepared for shape-shifters, human minions from Caligula's forces, damn near anything.

Anything except what he saw lying on the floor about twenty feet from him. He jerked to a stop so suddenly that Alexios crashed into his back.

"Brake lights next time," Alexios snarled. "What is it?"

"I don't know. I think it may be a bomb." Ven was almost surprised to hear how calm his voice was, all things considered. The wooden crate surrounding the . . . thing . . . had splintered at the force of impact. He looked up and verified that the sound of smashing glass had come from the skylight.

"There's no possible way that metal container is a bomb. A bomb would have gone off on impact," Justice pointed out.

"Yeah? Then *you* go check it out. Maybe they threw some kind of magic shield around it. I'd watch out for the flashing red numbers there on the side that seem to be counting down," Ven said, calculating the odds of survival as slim to no-fucking-way.

39, 38, 37, 36 . . .

"Those are seconds, not minutes, and we'd have no time to defuse a bomb even if Christophe were here," Ven said. "We've got to get out."

"What if we throw water at it?" Denal asked. "Really drown the thing?"

The flashing numbers mocked them. *28, 27, 26, 25 . . .*

"Who the hells knows? We'd probably just have a wet bomb," Ven said. "Out! Now!"

He was already turning to run back toward the kitchen and get Erin out of there when he heard her clear voice chanting in a language something like Latin, but not. As she walked down the hall toward them, he started yelling, "It's a bomb, we have to get out of here now." He raced toward her and smashed up against an unseen force that pushed him back against the wall.

"Not now, Ven, there's no time, we have to diminish the impact," she said, then continued chanting, her arms lifted in the air. For a heart-stoppingly brief moment, he saw a vision of another Erin superimposed over her body. The vision Erin stood, bathed in soft silver light, dressed in blue silk robes, standing in his favorite palace garden.

He blinked, hard, and sanity surfaced. "Look, Erin, unless you have a magic make-the-bomb-disappear spell, I'm getting you *out* of here," he yelled at her.

Then he turned to check out the timer on the bomb. The blinking red numbers flashed down, down—did seconds really go by that fast?

12, 11, 10, 9 . . .

The magical shield holding him back dissipated enough for him to break free of it. He tried, but still couldn't reach her through her shielding, so he yelled at Denal, Justice, and Alexios. For all the notice they took of him shouting at them to "Get out—*get out*—RUN," he might as well not have been there. Instead, the three of them fanned out to form an Atlantean shield between the bomb and Erin.

She waved a hand in the air, still chanting, and the three warriors flew back and away from the bomb and hit the walls. "Yes, run, get out, that's a splendid idea," she murmured, then returned to her chant.

It was too late, anyway, far too late, and even though he couldn't get to her, by Poseidon's balls there was no way that he would leave her, even if they had to die together. He called for his power and flowed into mist, hoping he could get past her shield in that form. It worked, and he shot over her head and then shimmered back into shape between Erin and the bomb, channeling water as he transformed. Knowing it was futile, he shoved the force of water at the bomb.

He barely noticed when Justice ran up beside him and added his own powerful channeling—all he could see were those damned red flashing numbers. Together they hurled a deluge of water at the bomb—drenching it, drowning it— and it had absolutely no effect.

7, 6 . . .

Erin's chanting grew louder and stronger, and a silvery glow formed around her raised hands, but it was too late. Too late.

5, 4 . . .

Justice dropped to the ground and covered his head in a futile effort to duck and cover. At the same second, Erin threw her hands out and a bolt of silvery light streamed from her hands toward the bomb—covered it entirely, sealed a cylinder around it—but it was too little, too late.

Justice mumbled something that sounded like, "Damnit, I wanted to tell Conlan and Ven a few things before I died—"

But the sound of Ven's heart pounding drowned out the rest of the words.

2, 1, 0.

The blinding flash of the explosion nearly fried Ven's retinas, and he could feel the floor shake and the walls rattle with the force of an earthquake. He rubbed his eyes and stared at the shield, which still glowed over and around the heat and light, and had somehow—impossibly—contained the explosion.

Ven watched, open-mouthed, as chunks of shrapnel slammed off the inside of Erin's magical barrier and clattered harmlessly to the floor. He tore his gaze away from the sight and stared at Erin, who stood shaking, her pale face drained and gray, her hands still out. As he reached for her, she let her hands fall to her sides.

"A little bit harder than I'd expected," she whispered, and then she collapsed into his arms. He scooped her up and stood there holding her, both of them trembling, while he swore viciously in Atlantean.

"What in the nine hells was that?" Alexios said, crouching down to stare at the wreckage of the bomb and the giant hole in Ven's floor.

"I didn't know witches could do that," Denal said, eyes wide.

"She's stronger than any witch I've ever seen," Justice mused. Then he looked up at Ven and Erin. "And Caligula turned her sister. So now we have a powerful witch-turned-bloodsucker on the side of the bad guys. I'm pretty sure we're fucked."

ᴓᴕ‿ᴕᴕ

Erin woke up belted into the passenger seat of a speeding vehicle. The rebound headache dug viciously at her brain; using magic always came with a price. Especially since she'd lost control for those final three seconds and called to the Wilding. She pushed the memory into a small, locked chamber in her mind and decided to worry about it later. She was still alive, Ven was still alive; the rest could come later.

The physical price had to be paid, though. Magic didn't take IOUs. No checks, no credit, cash on the barrelhead. Lay your brain synapses here, little lady. For her, the magic was a carnival barker from hell, always calling out his lures to the unsuspecting witch. *Play now, you can win, don't worry about the cost, the sky's the limit, lovely lady!*

But winners must be balanced with losers, and magic always came with a price. The universe of power was a zero-sum game. She had little doubt that a migraine was lurking at the base of her brain, waiting for her to move a fraction of an inch. She chanced it anyway, and turned her head slightly to see who was driving like a bat out of hell.

"Ven," she whispered. "We made it?"

A muscle clenched in his jaw. "Yeah, we made it. Although you risked your life in the fucking process."

The controlled ferocity in his voice startled her, and the spikes pounding in her skull started dancing a killer jig. "Profanity is the last recourse of the uneducated," she finally replied.

He barked out a laugh. "That's it? That's all you've got? You risked your life to throw a magical shield over a bomb—and you're jabbing at me for swearing?"

He had a point. She looked out her window at the interstate speeding by. Sunday morning was about the only time anybody could speed on I-5. "Why north?" she asked him.

"Somebody mad, bad, and deadly found us. We had to get out of there before they dropped a fu— a freaking nuke on us. I want to take you to Atlantis, but the portal can be . . . difficult. We're heading to another safe house so you can rest before we make the attempt."

That he'd try to curb his profanity at a time like this made her smile. That he'd done it for her made her cautious. "I'm sorry you were concerned for me, Ven. But I've always been the most adept in my entire coven at shielding; I once threw a temporary shield over a thousand people at an outdoor charity concert for nearly an hour when an unexpected rain shower struck. It really didn't seem like it would be that much different to throw a shield over the bomb."

There was silence for a long moment, but she noticed his large hands clenching the steering wheel so hard his knuckles turned white. When his voice finally came, it was rough and strained, probably from the effort it took not to yell at her. "Are. You. Kidding. Me? You didn't think holding in a *bomb* blast would be much different from holding out a few raindrops? Are you a complete idiot?"

Yes, she thought. *Yes, I must be. Because I looked at you, and I looked at that bomb, and I flatly refused to let you die.*

Pride kept her from saying the words. Anger kept her from remaining silent. "Listen to me, Atlantean. I have power. I'm not the strongest witch in the world, but I have power. The Wilding only chooses those who are strongest in the Craft. Do not underestimate me."

"I won't have the chance to underestimate you if you're dead, Erin. If you ever—" He paused and exhaled a long, deep breath. "If you ever try something like that again, I will lock you in a room and paddle your ass for you."

"How *dare* you—"

"Erin," he said, cutting her off. "I don't want to watch you die."

Startled by the emotion in his voice, she turned to study his face, but he wouldn't turn his gaze from the road. "Get some more rest, Erin. We have another hour to go."

"But—"

"Rest. You're exhausted. You can ask me all the questions you want when we get there. You're safe now. Rest."

He flicked on his stereo and something warm and classical filled the air. Another surprise; she'd expected headbanger music from the tough warrior. She relaxed, exhausted, back into the leather seat. As her eyelids began to drift closed, she heard him clear his throat.

"And Erin? Thank you. Your actions saved the lives of men I value as brothers, as well as my own. Though I would not have had you risk your life for ours, please know that I honor your aid more than I could ever repay."

Her throat tightened a little and tears stung the edges of her eyelids. "What is formal speak for 'you're welcome'?" she asked, smiling a little.

He finally looked directly at her, and the heat in his eyes seared clear through her, deep down to something she'd locked away ten years before. Trapped in his gaze, she couldn't speak, couldn't think, couldn't breathe. Finally, he wrenched his gaze from hers and looked back at the road. "Rest, Erin. You are still exhausted from calling such great amounts of power," he said, voice husky.

"Okay. But just until we get wherever we're going. Then I want to know everything that you know about Caligula."

Ven nodded, his narrowed eyes promising retribution. "Yeah, well, the first thing I want to know is how in the nine hells they knew where we were. If we've got a traitor in Atlantis, I'm going to unleash all the fury of Poseidon on his ass."

"I'll be standing right next to you, helping," she murmured as her eyes drifted closed.

She barely heard his next words, but they sounded a lot like "Over my dead body," and she smiled.

Your dead body is exactly what I wanted to avoid, she thought, and then she couldn't stay awake any longer and let the rhythm of the car's motion lull her into sleep.

Chapter 7

Caligula's cavern, below Mount Rainier

The pathetic human crouched in the corner, face turned away from the bodies of his dead colleagues. Blood dripped steadily from his open wounds, but Caligula forced himself to ignore the tempting aroma. Time enough to drain the fool after he'd gotten every bit of information from him.

"You swore to me that this device would be effective, Merkel," Caligula snarled. "Years of experience with explosives, you said. No possible way anybody could survive a blast of that magnitude, you promised."

He stalked closer to the quivering man, who covered his head with his hands and moaned. "Do you know what happens to people who fail me?"

He kicked Merkel's ribs, holding back at the last moment so his boot didn't go clear through the man's rib cage. Still, he may not have held back enough of his strength, because Merkel's limp body rose half a dozen feet into the air before smashing back to the ground. His moaning shrilled into a keening cry of anguish.

"I don't know what happened—I promise you, that bomb

should have gone off," Merkel blubbered. "I checked every single component three times."

Caligula's new general drifted down from his perch on the wall from where he'd been watching the interrogation. Drakos had offered to handle it for him, but Caligula preferred to think of himself as hands-on when it came to torture. As they said in this century, if you want someone killed right, kill him yourself.

"There is another explanation beyond this man's failure," Drakos offered. "We know the Atlanteans channel the elements, and we know they plan to ally with the witches. Two very different types of magic may combine to be powerful beyond our expectations."

Caligula leaned down and casually lifted Merkel by the back of his shirt until he hung in the air. He tilted the man's head to face his own and forced Merkel to look into his eyes. Between the pain and the fear, it was only a matter of an instant to enthrall him.

"Speak truth or die," he snarled. "Did your failure cause your device to malfunction?"

"No, Master," the human replied in a flat, dead voice. "I knew you would kill me if I failed you. The bomb was fully functional. The drop was perfect. The witch shielded it from exploding on impact, but detonation should have occurred when the timer ran down."

Caligula lifted his other hand, and almost gently caressed the side of the man's face. The sheep all worshipped him, as was his due; it was almost painful when he lost even one. Adulation was his birthright; slavish devotion from his subjects his coin of the realm.

"And the witch who shielded it?"

"I killed her, as you directed, Master."

"There, now," Caligula crooned. "You did a good job after all, didn't you?"

A glimmer of hope flickered for an instant in the man's eyes, and Caligula chuckled. Then he drove his fangs into the side of Merkel's neck and drained him dry. When he finished, he tossed the empty husk to the ground and carefully wiped his lips. "Their terror is so much richer when you give them a morsel of hope first, don't you find?"

Drakos stood there, impassive. "I was taught never to play with my food," he observed dryly.

Caligula narrowed his eyes and then burst out laughing. "Never to play with your food. Brilliant."

The voice that sliced through the air was jarring in its beauty. The lilting tones of a dark angel whispering words of bloody death. "Laughter? Tell me that I do not hear laughter from my admiral when his plans have gone so badly wrong."

Drakos shuddered and then moaned, the sound shockingly similar to the one the dead human had made, and hoarsely spoke a single word. A name.

A dark and twisted prayer for a redemption that could never be found.

"Anubisa."

Dropping to the ground, Drakos knelt and bowed his head until it touched the dirt. Caligula remained standing, defiant; testing himself and his strength in the face of the matchless power of the goddess of the night.

Anubisa floated down from a point far above them, descending from high in the blackness of the cavern. Her midnight black hair glowed as the unseen stars caressed her hip-length curls. The silken white folds of her gown, unaffected by gravity or the speed of her descent, draped demurely around her ankles. As she neared Caligula, pressure built behind his eyes until he thought they must explode from their sockets.

"Are you truly willing to sacrifice your eyes in service to this petty defiance?" Her voice sizzled across his skin like acid, and blisters rose up on his arms and face in its wake. The pressure behind his eyes grew unbearable, and he dropped to his knees beside his general.

Her laughter drove needles into his brain, and the pressure behind his eyes continued to build. "Giving up so soon, Caligula? I am disappointed. I expected so much more from the most depraved ruler of the Roman Empire. What was it you are claimed to have said? 'I wish the Roman people had but a single neck'?"

She took a step closer to where Caligula huddled next to Drakos on the dirt. "Singularly appropriate, or perhaps prophetic, don't you think?"

The pressure in his head increased, and he clenched his teeth together and drove his fingers, lengthening into claws, into the ground in a futile attempt to keep from crying out. But the pressure built and built and built—surely his eyes would pop out from the pain screaming, blazing inside his skull. Caligula had a sudden, sickening visual of his eyeballs rolling across the dirt, finally surrendered, and he screamed.

He sacrificed two millennia of pride and screamed long and loud.

He screamed, and she laughed.

And her laughter raised a swarm, black as an ancient plague, of squirming discolored maggots that boiled up from the earth beneath him to crawl up his body. The pressure behind his eyes subsided, but he was beyond caring about mere bits of orbital flesh. He rolled on the ground, pressing his palms against his face, protecting it from the bugs that feasted on the rotting dead.

He knew better than to try to flee.

Still she laughed.

"You disappoint me, but you amuse me. Since very little has amused me in these weeks since those cursed Atlanteans tricked me into killing my Barrabas, I will let you live," she said. The rush of relief that roared through his ears was so loud that he almost missed her next words.

"I want Conlan's baby brother," she whispered, trailing one long fingernail down her cheek. "I will take the King's Vengeance for my own."

Caligula sat up, forcing himself not to flail as a wave of maggots squirmed up his body. *It is illusion, it is illusion, it is illusion,* he told himself.

Then they crawled into his mouth.

She laughed again at the sound of his soul-rending shrieks, clapped her hands together, and the maggots vanished.

It took him a few moments longer to be able to stop shrieking.

"I had heard that maggots were your particular . . . weakness," she murmured.

He raised his eyes and dared to look at her face for the first time since she'd arrived, knowing he should not. Unable to resist. Immediately he sank, enthralled as any pitiful human, into the seductive flames in her red eyes, which glowed like unholy jewels set in her pale, pale face. Such spectacular beauty was obscene when imposed on the face of painful death.

Anubisa pushed him with one delicately shod foot and knocked him over. He fell on top of Drakos, who continued to moan quietly on the ground, finally catching the vampire goddess's attention.

"My Drakos, is that you? Where were you when Barrabas needed you?" she asked, her voice betraying the first hint of uncertainty Caligula had ever heard from her. But it vanished so quickly he was sure he must have been mistaken. He didn't dare to dwell on it for fear she would somehow know and make the maggots return.

"You are either unreliable, or you are a traitor, General Drakos," she hissed, lashing out at the cowering vampire with her foot. He soared a dozen feet through the air and crashed into the craggy rock of the cavern wall, then lay on the ground where he fell, still and silent.

Caligula watched as Anubisa hurled herself across the cavern toward Drakos. "Either way, today is your day to die. Be advised that it shall not go quickly for you," she called out, and her wild, insane laughter spiked shards of pain and madness into Caligula's eardrums.

As Anubisa landed in front of him, Drakos finally raised his head from the ground and almost—but not quite—looked up at the goddess. "I am no traitor, and I can prove it," he said, his voice rough and broken as his body soon would be. "I can give you the rebel leader, Quinn."

Chapter 8

The palace gardens, Atlantis

Erin stood, entranced, staring at the vibrantly colored masses of flowers, many of which were species she'd never seen before. She'd rounded a corner on the stone path from the castle and spotted lush, dark purple flowers that looked a lot like roses—except each blossom was the size of a dinner plate. The blooms covered the dark green-leafed bushes surrounding a small white gazebo. The visual contrast was stunning, and she wished with a fresh stab of pain that her sister Deirdre were there to share it with her.

She'd slipped out of the spacious room assigned to her in the palace and found a door to the outside; fresh air and the space she craved. Now she stood alone for the first time in the several hours since they'd arrived in Atlantis, surrounded by the wild and delicate fragrances of a cascade of flowering beauty.

"Atlantis," she whispered, tasting the syllables. *Atlantis.* A land born in myth, lost in legend. Yet, somehow, here she stood. It was impossible, but the impossible had become her reality.

The opals on her fingers sang out to her, warning her of

his presence mere seconds before iridescent mist shimmered down in front of her. The sunlight—*sunlight?*—fractured into a prism of sparkling diamonds, and suddenly he was there.

Ven.

"Somehow I knew I'd find you here," he said, bowing slightly. "Are you well?"

She stared up at him, not trusting the warmth she'd felt when he appeared. The feeling of safety. Of *home*. She did not know this man, regardless of what the rings on her fingers might be telling her. And it might be petty, but it didn't help that he looked so damn good in his white shirt and jeans, with his wavy hair hanging loose to his shoulders. Actually, it kind of ticked her off.

Her emeralds sang again, and the opals chimed in on harmony, and she gritted her teeth against hearing their song. *What do gemstones know, anyway? Useless hunks of rock.*

"I'm fine," she finally replied. "Other than the whole part where you dumped me into the frigid waters off Whidbey Island, expected me to believe some magical doorway was going to let me into the mythical lost continent of Atlantis, then brought me to the palace drenched and looking like a drowned rat."

She narrowed her eyes at him. "Perfectly fine, thanks for asking. And how is there sunlight down here however many miles under the sea?"

He blinked, then a slow and dangerous smile spread across his face, and her heart started dancing to a rapid beat. "I'm sorry about the freezing water and the drenched part. The portal almost always sends us through dry. But it does have a mind of its own and likes to play practical jokes sometimes."

She rolled her eyes. "Yes, I noticed that you came through perfectly dry, in spite of being right there in the water with me. I just figured it was a royalty thing." Not to mention that she'd been too busy fighting her gemstones and their reaction to him to shield in any way.

"No, trust me, the portal has no particular respect for my princely genes," he said, laughing. "It very nearly let me drown the last time through."

She gasped a little. "Really? Then why do you use it? It's pretty obvious you've got enough power or magic or something to be able to figure out another way in and out of here."

"You'd think so, wouldn't you? But when you have a source of magic that does a job for more than ten thousand years, sometimes you quit looking for alternatives." His voice was grim, and the shadow that crossed his face made her wonder if this was a conversation he'd had before. He held out his hand to her. "Shall we walk?"

She lifted her hand, and the emeralds in her rings trilled out a sharp, clarion call. She jerked her hand back and took a step away from him. His eyes widened, and he lowered his own outstretched hand to his side. "What is that song, Erin? What is that music I hear when I touch you or even come close to touching you?"

She took another step back, even as she realized flight was futile. She was standing on the lost continent of Atlantis, maybe miles below the sea's surface, and "nowhere to run" took on a whole new meaning.

"Tell me, Erin. Tell me what it means to be a gem singer."

◆～～◆

Ven's mind kept returning to the vision he'd had when the bomb had been close to detonating. Funny how the last thing the mind conjures up when the body is getting ready to be blown to hells and back kind of stays with a man. In his vision, Erin had stood in this exact place, near the gazebo that had been his hideaway as a child. Now she wore her jeans and sweater instead of the blue silk robes he'd . . .

His mind stuttered to a stop. *Complete and total, full-on, not going there, STOP.* But his brain—*heart?*—kept right on making the connection that he hadn't seen before.

Blue silk robes. The traditional wedding attire for Atlantean royal brides.

My lord Poseidon, if this is your idea of a joke, I'm not laughing.

When he opened his eyes and unclenched his jaw, he realized Erin was staring at him as if she saw something peculiar.

Well, she did. The Atlantean who'd sworn all his life never to be tied down to only one woman was suddenly having visions of a witch in an Atlantean bridal gown. Clearly he was having some kind of mental breakdown.

"Bad timing," he muttered, shaking his head.

"Excuse me? Bad timing? For what? Bad timing to be yanked out of my normal life? Okay, maybe it's not all that normal, but normal enough that nobody was dropping *bombs* on me." Her voice was getting louder and more high-pitched with each question, and Ven figured he wasn't the only one on the verge of that rubber room. They were all going to be swimming under the cuckoo's nest at this rate.

She stepped closer and jabbed her finger at him, almost but not quite poking him in the chest. "Bad timing to be whisked off to Atlantis? Bad timing to discover that my sister is not dead but may be a vampire slave to one of the most evil, depraved tyrants in history? And that the bastard wants me, too?"

He held up his hands in an "I surrender" gesture, but she wasn't done with him.

"Don't talk to me about bad timing, okay, Ven? Just don't." Her shoulders slumped, and her voice caught on the words. Suddenly, all the sane and practical reaons he had for keeping their relationship strictly professional flew out of his mind, and he wanted to hold her. Wanted to comfort her. Wanted to take away the pain in her eyes.

Couldn't think of one valid reason *not* to hold her. He took a step closer and pulled her into his arms and—for the space of a single, perfect moment—she relaxed into his embrace.

The scent and feel of her silken hair caused things low in his body to tighten. He pulled her against himself, fighting his own instincts in order to be gentle. The feel of her soft curves against the hardness of his own body licked flames through his skin wherever they touched. Even though they were both fully clothed, holding her in his arms shot a raging case of hunger and need through him that was more powerful than any he'd ever felt before. His body jerked a little from the rush of heat, and he tightened his arms, unable to deny his primitive desire to hold her, claim her. Never let her go.

She gasped a little, and then she mumbled something under her breath, and he flew up and away from her and landed on top of the gazebo, flat on his back, the breath smashed out of his lungs. He stared up at the magically created sunlight and clouds at the top of the dome, wheezing, while he tried to force his lungs to cooperate and inhale a little oxygen.

"Ven! Ven? Are you okay? I'm so sorry! I don't know what happened—I just cast a very minor move-away spell, and suddenly you were flying through the air. Ven? Ven!"

He tried to respond, but could only manage a rasping cough. Well, she could damn well wait for an answer. He rolled over and pushed himself up to a crouch, then jumped back down to the ground. He landed heavily and promptly fell on his ass. Before he could pull enough air back into his lungs to let loose with a flood of truly creative profanity, she rushed over to him.

"Oh, Ven, I'm so sorry!" she said, dropping to her knees beside him. "I didn't expect—I didn't know—something about the Atlantean magic must have combined with my own to give it some kind of turbo boost. I'm so sorry—are you okay?"

She put her hands on his face and stared down at him with those enormous blue eyes, huge with concern for him—for *him*. For so long he'd been considered the biggest, the baddest, the scariest warrior Poseidon had ever sworn to his service, and this little bit of a soft, curvy female was afraid that *she'd* hurt *him*.

His irritation vanished. In its place a powerful emotion he

couldn't quite classify welled up from his chest and soared through him. He wanted . . . he *wanted* . . . he needed.

Suddenly need was all that existed, spiraling in the air between them, curling through his veins. So he kissed her.

He put one arm around her waist and caught the back of her head with his other hand and pulled her off balance so that she landed across his lap, and he bent his head to capture her lips with his own. She gasped a little, and he caught her breath in his mouth and felt like he'd swallowed a wish or a prayer; captured a part of her soul in his own.

Music soared from her and into him, and the heat and welcome of her mouth was a symphony of desire conducted by a maestro. She made a moaning sound in the back of her throat, and he tried to swallow the sound, tried to swallow the music, tried to inhale her light and sound and magic into his heart, and still, still, he kissed her.

By the light and the water and O, Holy Poseidon, she was kissing him back.

In a flash the kiss changed from exploratory to possessive as every inch of him shouted out his need to lay her back in the flowers, tear the clothes from their bodies, and pound into her right there in the garden.

His zipper must have been damn near leaving a tattoo on his cock from the pressure, because just the taste of her was sending him up in flames. An inferno of hunger and wanting—and suddenly he realized she felt exactly like a dream come true in his arms.

A dream he could never deserve.

All the dreams he could never attain.

He wrenched his head away from hers, fighting a battle with himself to do it, and pulled great, shuddering breaths into his lungs. She stared up at him, her blue eyes darkened with passion and her lips swollen from his kisses, and a primal urge deep in his soul roared out his need to possess her.

A need he could never fulfill. He lifted her limp form up and away from him and prepared to try to convince himself— convince them *both*—that the kiss could never be repeated.

"Erin, we cannot—"

An icy wind sliced through the air between them and he pulled Erin behind him, knowing what it meant. Knowing *who* it meant.

"No, you cannot," Alaric said flatly as he shimmered into shape. "And you, gem singer, have broken the laws of Atlantis. Poseidon's penalty for the unlawful use of magic on our shores is death."

Chapter 9

Still dazed from Ven's kisses—from the power of the gem-song that had poured through her; through them both—Erin sat on the grass and stared up at the man who'd just pro-nounced her death sentence. He was huge, like Ven. Tall, broad-shouldered, and with muscles straining the shoulders and sleeves of the black silk shirt he wore so elegantly. He even had long black hair like Ven. But his features were so different. The sharp-cut planes of his face, his aristocratic nose, and his high cheekbones all shouted haughty arro-gance. Not to mention the whole death penalty thing wasn't making him look warm and fuzzy.

Ven flashed up off the ground to stand in front of her so fast she almost didn't see him move, and a horrible freight train of sound roared from his throat. Was he . . . *growling*?

"Touch her and die, Priest. Come near her, harm a single molecule of her being, and—Poseidon's chosen or no—you will die screaming," Ven said, his low voice far more menac-ing than another man's shouting would have been.

Erin jerked her head back and forth to snap out of the weird daze she'd been in since Ven had touched her. Then she scrambled to stand up next to Ven, and she glared at them both. "If we're going to talk about my death, perhaps I can be involved in the conversation?" she said, holding her hands out loosely at her side, in case she needed to call to her power quickly.

The man Ven had called "Priest" pointedly glanced down at her hands and bared his teeth at her. His eyes glowed a fierce emerald green that was shocking in its intensity. She'd never seen any creature but a vampire whose entire eye glowed like that, and that was usually right before it ate somebody.

"I am Alaric, high priest to Poseidon, gem singer, and this is my realm. Think you that your puny earth magic will work against one such as myself, the greatest power Atlantis has ever known?" For all the arrogance in his words, there was none in his voice; merely the calm assurance of somebody who knows his own worth.

She glanced up at Ven, who'd pushed his way between them and stood, feet planted, blocking her bodily from the priest. "You can back off, Ven. I am a ninth-level witch of the Seattle Circle of Light and can probably hold my own." She tried for a casual tone. "It's not like he's going to strike me dead right here, is he?"

Neither man so much as looked at her, and her nerve faltered a little. "Um, is he?"

A female voice from behind her answered. "No, he most certainly is not."

Erin whirled around to see a tall, pale woman with strawberry-blond hair walking toward them. The woman smiled at her, but the smile didn't quite reach her eyes. Then she looked at Alaric and sighed. "Alaric, please stop scaring our guests. Don't you have some super-secret Poseidon adventures to work on?"

Erin whirled to see how the scary "the penalty is death" guy was going to take being teased, or if he'd even realize that he was. Alaric's lips quirked up in a brief smile, and he bowed to the woman, who'd reached Erin's side.

"As you wish, my future queen," he said, and his hard

features softened for an instant before he turned back to Erin and Ven and did the glowy-eye thing again.

Which, frankly, is working for him, because he scares the crap out of me, Erin thought.

"Perhaps you will refrain from the use of your earth magic here in Atlantis, at least until such time as we might discuss how you can rein it in sufficiently. You may not care that you caused repercussions across the Seven Isles with your wild burst of magic—"

"No!" she said, too terrified of what she might have done to care that she was interrupting him. "The Wilding? I called the Wilding and didn't even realize it? I am so very sorry; I never thought . . . it never occurred to me—"

Alaric stopped her in midbabble, catching her chin in his fingers and staring into her eyes. Ven moved to stop him, making that weird growling noise again, but Erin held up her hand between them. "No, Ven. Let him look. Perhaps he can see that my intentions were never to hurt anybody. Especially not you."

Alaric's eyes glowed so fiercely that she was sure her skin must be burned from it, but after flinching for a moment, she stared right back at him, falling, plunging, spiraling down into the black whirlpools in the centers of his eyes.

This must be how it feels to be enthralled by a vampire, she thought, and then suddenly he released her and she staggered, nearly falling, until Ven caught her in his arms.

"She is innocent of any evil intent," Alaric said, raising his head to pin Ven with his piercing gaze. Then he looked back at Erin, but the glow in his eyes had faded until the green was almost human.

Almost.

"You will tell me more of this Wilding, I hope. Although I learned some of it from the fears you hold on the surface of your mind for Ven, I would learn more of how such a powerful magic can be channeled by one so young." He nodded his head to her and then bowed again to the other woman.

Finally he faced Ven. "Your role by birthright and by battle challenge is to act as the King's Vengeance, my friend. Consider well how your feelings for the gem singer will interfere with those responsibilities before you tread farther down this path."

Ven took a step toward the priest. "You are and have been my friend, Alaric. But be warned. If you threaten Erin again, I will come after you with everything I've got."

"Hey! Not so helpless here," Erin said, indignant, but the queen-to-be put a hand on her arm and shook her head.

Alaric and Ven never even spared her a glance, still caught up in some kind of intense, silent communication with each other. Finally Alaric nodded. "So that is the way of it. I had my concerns when I saw the Flame of Poseidon in your eyes. We need to discuss this in a war council before you go any further with helping the witches against Caligula. It may be that she will be your fatal weakness."

Erin was tired of being talked about as if she weren't there. She shook the woman's hand off her arm and moved forward to confront Alaric. "What is the Flame of Poseidon? And if you're going to discuss anything that has to do with Caligula and our alliance, you'd better be damned sure that I'm part of your war council."

A tiny noise had the three of them whirling around to see the queen bent over, clutching her stomach, clearly in pain. "Alaric, Ven, please . . . please help me," she cried out. "Something is wrong—I can feel it. Something is wrong with the baby."

Before she'd spoken the second *please*, Ven had swept her up in his arms. "Shh, Lady Riley," he murmured against her hair. "Shh, my dear one. All will be fine. The maidens of the Temple will help you and the baby."

He shot a glance at Erin and Alaric. "Please bring her to the Nereid Temple, Alaric." With that, he leapt up into the air in one powerful bound and shimmered into mist around Riley, so that it looked as though an iridescent, fast-moving cloud carried her rapidly away from them.

Erin gasped at the sight. "It's so beautiful when he—" She stopped midsentence and shook her head at the irrelevant thought, then looked up at the priest, whose narrowed eyes told her he was extremely anxious about Riley. "Will she be okay? And the baby?"

A horrifying thought seared into her mind, and she thought she might vomit up all that ocean water she'd swallowed a few hours earlier. "I didn't—I didn't cause this with my magic, did I?"

He shook his head, the grim look in his eyes softening for a brief moment. "No, you did not, though it goes far to reassure me as to your character that it would count among your concerns. Riley is having a difficult pregnancy and, for all my power, I am helpless to assist in her healing."

She had the feeling he hadn't really meant to share quite that much with her, because the lines in his face deepened as he clenched his jaw shut.

"Is there anything I can do to help?" she offered, knowing that if a powerful high priest of Poseidon couldn't fix it, there wasn't going to be much she could do.

At least he didn't laugh in her face. He just shook his head, closing his eyes as if to keep her from seeing too much of his pain. "No, there is nothing—"

His eyes snapped open. "Wait. There may be something. The history of the Nereid Temple . . . You are a gem singer—"

"What? First my coven leaders told me I was a gem singer, but they didn't know much more than that. I'm part elvenfolk and, well, maybe part Atlantean. But what does it mean? What *am* I?"

Ignoring her questions, he grabbed her arm and said, "Hold on." Then he swept her into his arms and leapt into the air just as Ven had done with Riley. Erin let out a huge *whoop* of surprise and grabbed on to his neck with all her strength. But instead of carrying her in a cloud of shining mist, Alaric went one better and did some kind of stomach-wrenching Atlantean transporter thing. Because not two seconds later, they were touching down in front of a white marble temple inlaid with jade and sapphires and amethyst, and Erin was trying yet again to keep from tossing her cookies on the pristine lawn.

A wave of sound emanating from the Temple reached out to her; tentatively, at first, and then with an all-encompassing full-body wave. "Oh!" she cried out as, with a rush of pure, diamond-sharp joy, she felt it. She *felt* it. The music from the gemstones soared into her and through her and she felt it, she lived it, she was one with the music, the rich, powerful symphony of the stones pouring into her soul.

She stood there as the music trumpeted through her bones and blood and sinews, and for the first time since she'd been a tiny girl in her mother's arms, Erin opened her mouth and she sang.

The high, clear notes of song soared into the open, airy receiving room of the Temple, and Ven turned toward the doorway—toward the source of the sound—and began to walk toward it, still carrying Riley in his arms. The First Maiden of the Nereids, Marie, dropped a ewer of water with a startling clatter and, leaving it there, rose from her kneeling position by the side of the cushions where Ven had been about to lay Riley's huddled form.

Marie followed him to the doorway, but Ven couldn't have said if any of the other maidens followed in their wake. His eyes were straining to see the notes of the music, which must have been written in golden script on the air of the Temple. No sound so unbearably lovely could exist only as an intangible; no gift of such unutterable grace could vanish with the breath of the singer.

Marie spoke from very near his right side, where Riley's head lay cradled on his arm, and her voice was hushed with awe. "The legend of the gem singer of the Nereids. She has returned to us."

Ven didn't respond—couldn't respond. He followed the music, a Pied Piper's melody of enchantment calling to him.

Calling him to peace and calm. Calling him to healing.

He bounded to the top of the three wide stairs. *Must reach the music; must touch the music; must . . .*

But the music was *her*. Erin stood, arms held up to the sky, head thrown back. A silvery light played around her body and soared upward from her hands as the notes she sang soared upward from her throat. She sang a wordless melody of love and loss and homecoming. She sang and somehow, deep inside Ven's soul, he knew she sang of healing.

Of *healing*.

Riley.

He glanced down at her pale, still face, resting on his arm in the same unconscious state into which she'd lapsed when they'd arrived at the Temple. He didn't think, didn't worry, didn't wonder.

He simply acted. In one leap he flew from the Temple doorway to the bottom of the outside steps. In another leap he stood in front of Erin and placed his precious bundle on the ground at her feet. Kneeling in front of her, he turned his face in supplication up to Erin, to the gem singer from legend who had somehow sung her way into his heart, and he spoke a single word.

"Please."

The song continued to pour from her lips, but she slowly bent her head to gaze at him. Wildness raged in the burning intensity of her blue eyes, and the planes of her face were cast in glowing marble. She was suddenly more goddess than witch: terrible and beautiful and pitiless. She looked down upon him, and she sang.

He tried again, tried to reach the softness—the humanity—buried below the hardness of the living gemstone she had become. He tried again because he loved Riley as a sister. Loved her and her child more than his own life.

He tried again because part of his soul demanded that he do so.

"Erin," he said, wondering how the simple voice of a warrior could be heard through a song fit to grace the stars in the night sky. "Erin, please. She's dying."

Slowly, ever so slowly, Erin knelt down until her face was a mere handspan from Riley's abdomen, and put her hands over the exact place where the tiny baby grew inside. The silvery light poured forth from Erin's mouth and from the aura surrounding her and over and around Riley. Somewhere, far distant, Ven thought he heard Alaric shouting, or maybe Conlan, but he didn't care, it didn't matter, all that mattered was the light burning in Erin's incandescent blue eyes.

She sang to Riley, and she sang to Riley's baby, and it lasted mere seconds. Or it lasted through the birth of a universe. But moments later—millennia later—she finally stopped singing. Ven was instantly bereft, as though his still-pulsing heart had been ripped from his body, and his throat ached at the loss of her song.

Erin lifted a hand to touch his face. "Oh, Ven," she began, and then her eyes rolled back in their sockets and she pitched forward. He caught her and lifted her up and away before she fell on Riley, and he touched his lips to Erin's forehead.

"Please," he said, but this time he said it for an entirely different reason, one that he didn't quite understand himself.

On the ground at his feet, Riley sat up, smiled, and stretched, eyes and cheeks glowing with health and vitality. "Wow, I feel better than I have in months. What happened?"

Alaric and Conlan rushed over to Riley, with Marie hard on their heels. Everyone shouted questions at Ven, but he ignored them all and headed back for the Temple and its inner sanctuary, which no man had ever been allowed to enter. The Temple maidens had always spoken of the Cave of Gems, and, somehow, he knew it was exactly what Erin needed.

He lifted her precious head as he walked and touched his lips to her pulse and felt it slowing . . .

Slowing . . .

Stopped.

Nearly blinded by the burning in his eyes, he almost missed the hidden doorway, but then Marie was standing in front of him, ripping a tapestry aside from a section of marble wall, and beckoning him to follow her. "It lies here, Lord Vengeance. Bring the gem singer home, and we will heal her for you."

As he followed her down the candlelit passageway, he prayed to Poseidon more fervently than he'd ever done.

She did it for Riley and for the heir to your throne. Please save her for them. Save her for me.

But the only response was the sound of his heels ringing as they struck the stone floor and the sound of the barricades inside of his soul crashing as they shattered against his stony heart.

Chapter 10

Caligula's cavern, below Mount Rainier

A sound unlike any Caligula had ever heard in the two thousand years of his existence tolled through the cavern, dolorous, mournful, and dirgelike. A funereal call heralding his own imminent demise.

Vibrations from the immense, booming noise reverberated through the stone of the walls and the dirt on the ground. The vampires in his blood pride, roosting to flee the dawn, shrieked and scattered from various craggy perches and tumbled to the floor, striking out at each other in panicked confusion.

"Enough!" he shouted, and put so much power behind the word that it rang through the cavern and cut through the babbling idiocy of his undead minions. But his power was insignificant compared to the depth and resonance of the sound that continued to toll like the bell at the gates of hell, calling to the damned.

He clapped his hands over his ears and shouted for the single being under his command who could be counted on to act with a modicum of dignity and sense. "Drakos!"

"Yes, my lord admiral?" The voice came from above and behind him, making Caligula whirl around and look up, sickeningly aware that, had Drakos been an enemy, he might have been in very serious danger. The thought clanged warning bells in his mind, though they were as nothing to the ringing still sounding in the cavern.

"What is that *noise*?" he shouted to Drakos, though the general was only a scant two feet from him.

Drakos did not show by the slightest flicker of his eyes that the hideous cacophony disturbed him in any way. That, to Caligula, was also disturbing.

"I have no idea," Drakos replied. "Shall I investigate—"

The sound cut off midchime, as though a giant hand had silenced it. Caligula didn't even like to think about what kind of being might own a hand sufficient to silence a noise like that. He'd let his imagination run away with him far too much since the humiliating incident with Anubisa and the illusionary insects.

Damn her. If a goddess of night and chaos can be damned. The idea is somewhat redundant.

His private joke at her expense calmed him somewhat, and he raised his head. "Yes, I want you to investigate. Also, I want a report on your progress. Where is Quinn? You claimed you could deliver her to me," he said, leaving Anubisa's name out of the conversation. It was said that to even speak her name attracted her notice, and he did not care to be the focus of her gaze anytime soon.

"I am working on it, my lord. She is . . . elusive," Drakos said.

"I don't want to hear excuses," Caligula snarled. "You will deliver her to me or face the consequences. What is the progress on another plan to capture the Atlantean? Now that we know that Anu—the goddess—does not want him dead, there can be no more of your ill-planned explosive techniques."

"We know that they have formed an alliance with the Seattle Circle of Light coven, my lord. We plan to use the coven sisters as bait to capture Conlan's brother for—*her*. And he seems to have formed an attachment to the woman you seek, which will work to our advantage."

Caligula smiled at the thought of the woman and was pleased that his general did not attempt to blame his own failures on anyone else. Though it was true that the bombing had been Caligula's own idea, a good general was supposed to plot out strategy on his own and not just blindly follow orders. "Bait? Will the Atlanteans care enough about a gaggle of witches to sacrifice the brother to the heir to the throne, no matter what noble stupidity he attempts on behalf of the woman?"

The voice that sliced through the dark carried a wealth of contempt. "That so-called gaggle of witches nearly destroyed you ten years ago, my *lord*. And I will be happy to help them slice your sorry head off your neck."

Drakos stepped back, as if to remove himself from a domestic quarrel. Wise vampire.

"Deirdre, my love," Caligula purred at the fair-haired vampire who floated to the ground between him and Drakos. "How lovely it is to hear the dulcet tones of your voice again. It is so rare that you rise from the ground these days."

She spat at his feet. "I would starve myself to the true death if only it were possible, and you know that. But you keep me guarded every second of every night."

She shot a glance at Drakos, and it was almost surprising that the scorn in her words and gaze didn't turn the general to ash where he stood. "I see you've found a new *minion* to follow your imperial commands."

"Although this has been lovely, Drakos has work to do, my dear. Perhaps you would care to take your rest with me this day?" Caligula held his hand out to her, knowing that she would not take it.

Knowing that, one day soon, he would break her. And he'd use her only surviving sister to do it. He'd been accused of obsession before, but all of that paled compared to his desire for Deirdre's surrender. She and her sister, who were virtually almost identical to the only two women who had ever escaped him—his two young cousins, who had drunk poison after he had used their supple bodies for the first and only time.

They would not escape him again. Not even by fleeing to death.

"I will see you dead and rotting in hell, Caligula, before I ever willingly take your hand," she hissed at him, leaping back a half dozen feet across the floor.

"Perhaps, my darling. Perhaps. But there are many ways of rotting in hell, and you may yet join me there."

He shot up and into the air of the cavern to a niche near the very top where he would take his rest and wait for the night. Very powerful wards protected him from disturbance while he slept; he'd tested them many times before he sucked the life out of the terrified witch who'd cast them. Glancing down at his general, who stood facing Caligula's reluctant bride, he called down one final direction before retiring to the darkness of sleeping death. "Progress, Drakos. Bring me progress, or I will find a general who will."

Chapter 11

The Cave of Gems,
below the Nereid Temple, Atlantis

Marie led Ven down ancient stone steps, worn smooth with the tread of maidens for thousands of years. Strange that part of his mind was thinking about the freaking steps, when he held Erin in his arms and she was either dying or dead.

Stranger that the rest of his mind was thundering in tortured agony that he could not survive the death of a woman he'd only known for a brief ripple in the waves of time. The anguish rose up from his gut, from his chest, and forced its way through his throat. He roared out his pain and rage as he followed the First Maiden ever farther down into the dark.

Several paces ahead of him, Marie stopped, clearly startled by the sound, but one look at his face and she simply nodded and continued to move, more quickly now, down the corridor.

Although they were descending into the heart of the Temple of the Nereids, Ven sent out a prayer to Poseidon:

She cannot die. I don't know why, I don't know how, but she has become more important to me than my own life. I owe you my service and my honor, Poseidon. Please spare this woman for me.

Marie made a sharp turn, and Ven had an instant to hope that Bastien's sister was as thoroughly competent as her brother. He followed her around the curve in the wall and stopped dead at the sight of an enormous glowing jewel. A jewel that Marie stepped inside.

"It is a natural geode and the center of the Nereid Temple. It is where the Nereid's Heart lay before the Cataclysm," Marie explained. "The ancient ones wrote that the Cave of Gems is a natural restorative and power source for gem singers."

She indicated a plain wooden table centered in the oval space. Six paces took him to the table; he immediately settled Erin's limp body on it. Marie pulled a green silken cushion from somewhere on the floor and slid it beneath Erin's head as he gently lowered her.

Ven scanned the room and noticed that there were gemstones everywhere—distributed in deliberate patterns throughout the room, fastened to the silken cushions that lay scattered about, and even embedded in the base of the wooden table. The walls of the geode itself were a multifaceted shimmer of sparkling violet stone. As he smoothed the hair away from Erin's face, he stared at Marie. "Do something," he demanded, despairing at the sight of Erin's still, pale face. Marie started to respond, confusion and distress plain on her own face.

That was when the music started.

A single clear, wild note soared out from the walls themselves. The single note was joined by a chorus of others flying at them from all sides. Soon the music was swelling from the floor and the ceiling and through every molecule of air in the room. The chorus became a symphony—an orchestra of music of compelling beauty. Ven stood, hands holding Erin's, and he prayed rusty prayers to compassionless gods.

The music became light, the light became music, until the two were indistinguishable. The silvery light Erin had poured over Riley and the baby magnified a thousandfold within the small space of the geode. With a corner of his mind, Ven realized that Marie had dropped to the floor and knelt at the side of the table.

The wild music swept through Ven until the song permeated the very cells of his body. He could *see* the music; he could *hear* the light; he could *feel* the rhythm thrumming through Erin's body. And under and over and around it all, he heard a delicate voice ringing simultaneously in his mind and in his ears, a dichotomy of fragile power.

You have only just returned to me, gem singer. I shall not let you go so easily.

With that, the music crescendoed into a wordless triumph of sound and light. Erin's body began to glow until it shone so brightly that Ven had to close his eyes against it. He called for faith—for the ability to find some ounce of faith inside his own damaged soul.

Finally—*finally*—he found some measure of belief.

I give her to you, Poseidon, and to you, Goddess of the Nereids. I give her to you. All I ask is that if you keep her, you take my worthless soul as well.

The glare pounding against his closed eyelids abruptly ceased, and the music cut off at the same time. He blinked his watering eyes open to see darkness lit only by the scattered sparkling of countless jewels. It took his eyesight a moment to make the transition, but before he could see Erin, he felt her hand squeeze his, and the prayer in his soul changed to one of gratitude.

"Thank you," he said, forcing the words out. "Thank you both for saving this courageous woman for me."

Erin looked up at him, and her eyes glowed more brightly than all the jewels inside the geode. "Did you hear it? Did you hear the music?" She drew in a deep breath, face rapturous as though she could still hear the gemsong spiraling through the room and through her emotions.

She tightened her hand on his. "I heard your song, Ven," she said, smiling, awe and wonder in her eyes. "I heard the song of your soul."

Before he could reply, she slipped into a normal sleep, her chest rising and falling. He pressed his lips against the pulse beating so strongly in the side of her neck and repeated the only words that seemed large enough to fit the gratitude in his heart. "Thank you. *Thank you*."

∼∽∿∾

Erin swam up from a dream of diamond necklaces, a giant, glowing ruby, and sword-fighting women wearing chain mail that looked a lot like fish scales. She struggled to escape what her conscious mind knew must be illusion. Opening her eyelids took almost more strength than she had, and her body felt like it had been run over by a truck. She had aches in places she hadn't even known were capable of aching.

She finally forced her eyes open. Ven's face filled her vision, and the blue-green flames in his black eyes were back and glowing more brightly than she remembered. But instead of startling her, it made her sigh in relief. "You're here," she whispered, trying to lift her arms to him.

"I will never be anywhere else," he said roughly, then he gently lifted her up and into his arms, hugging her so tightly her aching body protested.

"Ouch! Um, Ven, not so tight, okay?" she said, lifting a hand to touch the strands of his hair. The silky dark waves slipped through her fingers as her arm fell back to her side.

He loosened his grip on her and lifted her completely into his lap, compulsively running his hands down her arms and back. "You're alive," he said. "You came back to me."

She blinked at him. "Alive? Came back? Where did I go?"

"Beyond the doorway of death itself in order to heal my lady and our child," a new voice said.

Erin whipped her head around, suddenly realizing that she was sitting on Ven's lap and they were not alone. Her face flushed as she scanned the small crowd gathered in the bright, open room. Some women in jade green robes lined the walls, and a group of men who were clearly warriors formed a semicircle behind the couple who stood in front of Ven and Erin.

The man who had spoken knelt in front of her, while holding tightly to the red-haired woman's hand. "Riley," Erin said, remembering. "Are you okay? Is the baby . . ."

The kneeling man looked up at her. He wore a simple but elegant white shirt and dark pants, and he bore a striking resemblance to Ven. This must be Ven's brother, Conlan. But his eyes didn't have the blue glowy thing in the center. Instead, they held more pain than Erin could bear to see. Pain and something else.

Possibly gratitude.

"We're fine, Erin. We're both fine, because of you. I can never thank you enough," Riley said. It was true; her grayish, unhealthy pallor was gone and she actually glowed with health.

"Anything," the man Erin assumed to be Conlan said. "Anything you desire from us, you shall have, up to and including a share of the royal treasury or lands and a title here in Atlantis."

The warriors behind them—Erin recognized Alexios and Denal among them, but not the blue-haired one, Justice—all knelt as one and bowed their heads. "Our lives for you," Denal shouted out, and Erin started to really get alarmed.

"Okay, let me up, Ven. This is mortifying to be sitting in your lap," she whispered to him, struggling to sit up. Her strength was slowly returning, and she had the energy to stand, although she had to give Ven a serious glare to get him to release her.

She knelt in front of Conlan and Riley. "Okay, I don't know anything about royal etiquette, but it seems like I should be the one kneeling or bowing or curtsying, except I don't really know how to curtsy, so will you please stand up?" she pleaded. "This is awfully difficult for me, and I have no idea what happened or, really, what it was I did to help Riley, so I'm feeling seriously at a loss."

The man rose to stand and, taking her hand in his own, pulled her up to face him. "I am Conlan, high prince of Atlantis, soon to be king and ruler of the Seven Isles. I pledge my service to you in exchange for the gift of healing you have bestowed upon my family," he declared, and the utter sincerity in his voice killed the tiny urge to smile that the words had prompted in Erin. It wasn't every day a girl had a high prince pledging anything to her.

She suddenly remembered that he wasn't the only prince in the room and shot a glance at Ven, her cheeks heating up all over again. Well. *This* was going to be complicated.

She flashed a tentative smile at Riley, who had a hand protectively covering the tiny bulge in her abdomen. "I'm glad I helped. I'm not sure exactly what I did, but I'm glad I helped you and the baby."

Riley covered the space between them in two strides and pulled Erin into a fierce hug. "Thank you, Erin. I don't even have the words . . ."

As her voice trailed off, Riley pulled back from the hug, but didn't take her hands off of Erin's shoulders. Instead, she stared into Erin's eyes with her own dark blue gaze. Nothing swirly and glowy happened, like with Ven or Alaric, so Erin waited, cautious but unafraid. "Um, what?" she finally asked.

"So much pain," Riley whispered. "No one to hug you or offer you comfort in so many years. Your family—your mother—oh, I am so very sorry, Erin."

Erin jerked away from her, appalled that Riley was casually reading her most tortured memories like the front cover of some trashy tabloid magazine. "How dare you!" she snapped out. "You may be some kind of Atlantean royalty, but that doesn't give you the right to rummage around in my mind."

Ven put his arms around Erin, and the heat of his body at her back offered some measure of comfort, until Riley's words popped back into her memory. *No one to hug you.* She stiffened and pulled away from him.

Conlan started to speak, but Riley put a hand on his arm. "No, she's right. I'm truly sorry, Erin. I'm not Atlantean anything, yet, well, engaged to the prince, but . . . anyway, that's not important." She bit her lip. "I'm what the Atlanteans call *aknasha*, and it means emotional empath. When I touch someone and there are such strong emotions buried right under the surface, they sort of smash out at me. Plus, I didn't shield before I touched you. Anyway, I'm really, really sorry."

As had been true with Conlan, there was so much sincerity in her voice that it was hard for Erin to stay angry. Especially since she was so exhausted she was wondering how much longer she'd be able to stand upright.

"No, it's okay, I guess. I shouldn't have snapped at you, it's probably bad for the baby to hear loud voices," she said, offering a weak smile.

Ven laughed and tightened his arms around her, so she felt the rumble of his laughter against her back. "If that's true, we're going to need to get him some earplugs in order to put up with several more months of being around this crew," he said.

Denal had moved to stand near Riley, and he spoke up, grinning. "Not to mention those awful old movies you and Riley watch, Ven. If the baby comes out looking like Bela Lugosi or Vincent Price, we'll know who to blame."

Riley shuddered, but she was smiling. "My baby is definitely not going to look like the star of an old horror movie. *She* is going to look just like her daddy."

Conlan put an arm around Riley's waist, and the glance they exchanged was filled with so much love and hope that it caused a pang somewhere in Erin's chest. A longing that someone, sometime, would look at her like that.

The memory of Ven's face when she woke up flashed into her mind, but she quashed it. There was no time to think about longing or looks or anything else that began with L-O. Suddenly the weakness from her exhaustion viciously beat at her and the room swirled in a crazy kaleidoscope of light and color. She leaned back against Ven for support. He instantly caught her up in his arms and stood holding her as if she were a child.

Or someone he cared for.

Either way, she was too worn out to argue about it.

"Erin needs to rest. Tomorrow morning will be soon

enough to discuss what we need to do next," Ven said to his brother.

Conlan nodded. "Riley must rest, as well. To the palace, then, and we will convene in the morning."

Erin yawned a little, then smiled at Riley. "Are they always like this? Beating on their chests?"

Riley laughed as her husband swept her into his own arms. "No, trust me. Sometimes it's worse. Wait till we get to the tree swinging."

Erin laughed out loud as Ven made a little growling noise at her and strode out of the Temple. Behind her, she heard Denal's puzzled voice. "What did she mean, tree swinging?"

Erin grinned up at Ven, and a hint of a smile crossed his grim face. Then he did the shimmer thing and carried her off to the palace, and she put all thoughts of missions and vampires and gem singing out of her mind, just for those few precious minutes, and flew through the air like a faery princess from a child's story, loving every minute of it.

Chapter 12

The palace, Atlantis

Ven sat next to Erin's bed, in the chair he'd dragged across the room, and watched her sleep. The light of the Atlantean moon feathered brushstrokes of silver across her delicate features. He'd been there for hours, after nearly ripping Conlan's head off for suggesting he leave her long enough to get some rest.

His fingertips ached to reach out and stroke her hair, but he didn't want to take the chance of waking her. The metallic taste of anguish rose in his throat like bile at the memory of her collapse. All of his instincts were shouting at him to put his hands on every inch of her body, to prove she was still alive. Although, who was he kidding, he'd been wanting to put his hands on every inch of her body since the minute he met her.

He closed his eyes and leaned back in the chair, trying to relax, trying to remember any of the deep meditation techniques he'd learned in his long years of warrior training. Anything to keep him from tearing his clothes off and leaping on her would be good. Would be *great*, even.

The adrenaline rush from her collapse, combined with

the immense relief he'd felt when she revived and opened her eyes, had slammed him into an overload of crisis-fueled testosterone and full-on, balls-to-the-wall lust.

Just pulling off her shoes, sweater, and jeans had left him shaking with need. She was all rounded curves and soft, smooth skin in her plain white shirt and lacy underwear, and the glimpses he'd caught before he pulled the covers over her had made him wonder where the nearest ice-cold shower might be. Hells, he was a prince of Atlantis. He might just call an ice-cold downpour right there in the room.

He clenched his jaw, disgusted with himself. She'd barely survived with her life, and all he could think of was diving cock-first into her body. He was scum. He was lower than scum.

Talk about your highway to hell. Speaking of which, he'd love a little classic AC/DC right about now. Or maybe Elvis. Elvis was always good. The King was the standard bearer for "no ties, no commitments, all-play-all-the-time" bachelors.

Damn, but I miss Elvis.

She stirred in her sleep, maybe catching the strains of "A Little Less Conversation" running through his mind. She hadn't seemed to be a mind reader, but she had some freaky talents when it came to anything musical. Hells, with a woman like that around, he'd be afraid to sing in the shower.

He couldn't help it; he laughed out loud at the thought of Erin critiquing his croaking singing voice, then clapped a hand over his mouth to stifle the sound. But it was too late. She opened those incredible blue eyes of hers, and she smiled at him, and he was lost.

So long, Elvis.

"Have I been asleep long?" she whispered.

"A few hours. Go back to sleep, it's still dark," he said, finally giving in to the urge to stroke the pale strands of her hair away from her face. The long waves slipped through his fingers like the purest Atlantean silk, and the tactile sensation arrowed a bolt of heat straight through him. He shifted in the chair and hoped she didn't notice that he was so lame that he got turned on just by touching her hair. Okay, turned on even more than he'd already been.

Highway straight to hell.

She never took her gaze from his face, though. "It wasn't a dream, was it? I heard your music, Ven," she said, awe and wonder infusing her tone. "I heard the inside of your soul."

"Poor you. I bet that was pretty scary. What did it sound like? A little Wagnerian? Headbanger garage band music by sadly no-talent high school kids?"

She shook her head and smiled at his sorry attempt at a joke, then tried to sit up. He lifted her upright so she could rest on the pillows, then forced himself to let her go long enough to sit back in his chair and act nonchalant. Like touching her didn't affect him at all. Mr. Cool. Mr. Casual.

Mr. Full of Shit.

"What was that place? What happened to me? I heard a woman . . . She sang to me, Ven. It was so lovely I almost couldn't bear it. She said something about me returning to her. Did you hear it?"

"I heard her. I think that was the goddess of the Nereids, Erin. It had to be her. Marie heard her, too, and as First Maiden she's heard her before, but only three other times, she said." He reached for her hand, needing the contact.

She twined her fingers around his, then looked at their joined hands. "What is this between us, Ven? Why is the connection so strong, when we've only just met? How can you hear my gems singing?"

"I wish I knew." He gently tugged his fingers from hers and stood up to pace the room, using motion to counter the uncertainty. He briefly considered avoiding the question, but she deserved better.

Finally he stopped by the side of her bed, drawn back to her presence by a force stronger than his own will, and used the truth as a shield. "I don't know how to answer any of it, Erin. I serve as the King's Vengeance, and I am sworn to protect my brother with my life. It is my honor and my duty, and it is my privilege to extend that protection to Riley and their unborn child."

Something sparked, then dimmed in the crystal blue of her eyes. "Riley is pretty important to you, isn't she? Did you . . . are you in love with her?"

"Riley? No, I never met her until she and Conlan had already pledged themselves to each other, even though it took a while for them both to admit it. She's like the sister I never had." He sat on the edge of her bed and took her hand again. "It's interesting that you'd ask, though," he added, grinning.

She flushed, and even in the dim light from the window he could see her neck and face turn a dark red. "I'm not jealous or anything. That would be ridiculous."

"Yeah, well, I wanted to pound Justice into the ground when you smiled at him. Ridiculous doesn't seem to factor into this," he said.

Her lips parted, and he had to clench his jaw shut and brace his shoulders against the urge to bend down and kiss her until she begged him to climb into the bed with her. Begged him to take her, over and over, until he drove so far inside of her that she sang again. Sang for him alone.

His body was singing its own song at the thought, but it was more of a damn sailor's limerick. He had to shift in his chair to relieve the pressure of his tightening pants.

Again.

"What if we took a break from being reasonable and rational for a little while?" she whispered. "What would you say if I asked you to hold me—just hold me—until morning?"

Hunger flared inside him, demanding that he conquer, that she surrender. The warrior he'd been born and trained to be wanted to plunder. The man he wanted to be—for her, just for a little while—pushed the hunger aside and sought desperately for self-control. "Erin, if you need me to hold you, I would love nothing more. In fact, I've been thinking of nothing else since I first touched you, if you want to know the truth."

She gave him a shaky smile, threw the silken bed coverings aside, and held her arms up to him. "Then hold me, Ven. Make me feel safe again."

Carefully, so carefully, he climbed in the bed next to her and pulled her into his arms, realizing as he did so that he was the one surrendering. When she nestled her head against his chest, her music flared up between them, pulsing hot and insistent. He forced his breathing to slow down, tried to focus on something—anything—other than the urgency of desire clawing at him.

He caught one of her hands in his and considered the rings on her long fingers. "It's the opal, isn't it? The opals and the emeralds that sing when we're together?"

She trembled in his arms and turned her face to his chest. The scent of flowers and springtime from her hair tipped the lid off his sanity just a little bit more, and he couldn't help but inhale her scent. Rub his face in her hair.

Want to mark her, brand her, claim her.

"Yes," she answered, the words muffled by his shirt. "They are . . . yes, it's the emeralds and opals singing."

Her words distracted him a little from the flames searing through his nerve endings. "What does it mean, Erin? Why can I hear them, too? Can everybody hear them?"

She drew a deep breath and looked up at him. "No. In fact, in the ten years since I turned sixteen and my Gift manifested, no person other than you has ever heard my gems sing. And the emeralds—the emeralds have never sung before I met you. Not even to me, except on the day of my Choosing."

His arms tightened around her. They only sang for *him*. Like he wanted to make her sing. Something deep inside him raised its head and roared. His breath quickened and he rolled back a couple of inches from her, trying to maintain distance. Trying not to pounce on her like the predator he was.

The gems. We were talking about the gems. Focus.

"What do they sing to you?" he asked. "Do the songs have meanings? Why are they so quiet now? I mean, not to be crude, but this is skin-to-skin contact. I figured they'd be singing up a storm."

She scooted closer to him, and her own breathing quickened, roughened. "We could always experiment a little, with the skin-to-skin thing. Right now, though, I'm focusing on keeping them under control with everything I've got."

His arms tightened around her and he couldn't stop the words from rushing out. Couldn't fight it any longer. "Let it go, Erin. Let it go and see what happens."

～～～

Erin lay still in Ven's arms, frozen by what he'd said. Let it go? Let it go, when it felt like her entire body was near to catching fire from the contact with his hard, muscular body? The heat from the attraction between them would probably blow the dome clear off Atlantis if she let the magic out. Speaking of heat, the man was a furnace, and they were close enough that she could feel every movement when his muscles kept clenching.

Mr. Warrior was trying pretty darn hard to keep a lid on his self-control. A very wicked part of her wondered how hard it would be to smash the lid and his control.

Luckily, the cautious part of her was way stronger than the wicked part. "I can't let go. I'm afraid of what might happen," she whispered, trembling. "What if I accidentally channel the Wilding again? Atlantis seems to have some sort of magnifying effect on my magic. What if I let go and the shock waves set off an earthquake or something?"

"Shh," he soothed her, stroking her back and her arm, touching her hair. At least he tried to soothe her. Something about lying half dressed in the arms of a man built like her hottest sexual fantasies come to life was not what Erin would call soothing. He smelled like leather and spice and pure, potent male, and she wanted to rub herself all over him. Her nipples puckered to hard little buds at the thought of it.

Ven's breath caught. Oh, dear Goddess, he couldn't have felt that, could he? Heat washed through her at the thought, but then he rubbed the back of her neck and she shivered, giving in, her breasts pressed up against his chest, and the friction of the contact nearly made her moan.

She felt the liquid heat gathering in her core, felt her body opening and readying itself, felt the urgent need to have him hot and hard and deep inside her. Tried to push the wanting away. Tried to be calm. Realized Ven's mouth was moving and words were coming out, but all she could hear was the wild, keening sound of her emeralds fighting to break free of the lock she'd clamped down on them.

". . . and Alaric warded this room," he continued. "He was . . . concerned that you might experience some repercussions from the healing while you rested and, well, let's just say that Alaric is Alaric."

She forced a laugh. "Right. Mr. Death Penalty guy. I bet he wouldn't have any trouble flipping the switch, or hauling out the guillotine, or whatever you do down here, either."

Ven put a finger under her chin and tilted her head up so that only a breath separated them. "It's really flattening out my ego that you're thinking of another man when you're in bed with me," he said, those dangerous lips of his curved into a sexy smile, but his eyes had gone flat and wary.

"But—"

"Tell me later," he said, and then he caught her lips with his, and every attempt at rational thought flew out of her brain. It was a slow, patient kiss, as if he had all the time in the world to taste her lips. His tongue teased her until she opened to him, and he deepened the kiss, continuing his soft, gentle exploration of her mouth.

She lifted her arms to wrap around his neck, and a tiny moan of deep contentment escaped from her throat, a humming sort of sound that he caught in his mouth, and suddenly the kiss wasn't gentle or soft at all. He shifted so she was partially underneath his long, hard body, and the heat and weight of him pressed her back into the pillows. She clung to him, kissed him back, inhaled his warm, spicy scent into her lungs and wanted more.

He lifted his head, his breathing ragged, and stared into her eyes. "You asked me to hold you. You wanted to feel safe, and I'm taking advantage of that. Please forgive me, Erin. I don't know—"

She stopped him by pulling his head back down to hers and murmured her reply. "I think I'm the one taking advantage of you. Kiss me again, Ven. We only have this small window of time before reality comes back. Kiss me again, and let's see how good Alaric is at warding rooms."

His eyes flared with heat and surprise and he smiled—a fierce smile of triumph and almost feral possession that might have scared her if she weren't feeling the exact same way. Then he took her mouth again, and she was lost.

She released her tight control over her magic, over her gemstones, over the passion pounding through her body. Every inch of her was sensitized from his touch. Her nipples tightened painfully inside the lace of her bra, and she felt the heat and desire tearing through her body to throb between her legs. She shaped his rock-hard biceps with her hands, running her fingers up and down his arms and shoulders, marveling at the muscular shape of his chest and body.

The stones on her rings, released from the dampening she'd forced on them, sang out joyfully. Emeraldsong and opalsong harmonized to create a powerful symphony of joyous desire that played through her body, through his body, through the room. At the first notes of the music, Ven groaned and curled one hand into her hair to tighten on the back of her head. He shifted a little and suddenly the hard heat of him was centered between her thighs and she felt the liquid welcome of her body in reaction.

Still kissing her, he touched her neck, her shoulder, and then his hand softly caressed the side of her breast, and she gave up the fight, surrendered, game over, no more rational Erin. She bucked against him and rubbed every inch of her body against his, moaning in the back of her throat at the goodness, the rightness, the heat and the pure, pounding need.

The emeralds trilled sharply, then faded into background music as the sensations pouring through Erin took command of her senses. When he rubbed his thumb over her aching nipple, electricity seared through her body and she arched up against him, mindlessly repeating his name, moaning, pleading.

He stopped kissing her long enough to speak her name with such longing, such desperate desire that she shuddered beneath him. The opals sang to her, to him, to them both; sang a sonata of joy and home. But the emeralds pounded their thunderous pulse of desire and need over and around her and Ven until she thought the universe would surely explode if he didn't bury himself inside her right now, right now, right now *right now*.

He pushed her shirt up a little, eyes on her as if to ask permission, and she took a shaky breath and placed his hands on her breasts. He closed his eyes for a moment, gently caressing her through her bra, and then opened his eyes and flashed a very wicked smile at her.

"You shouldn't do that to a man, Erin. Because you are so fu— . . . *freaking* beautiful, and getting my hands on your breasts is like getting the world's best present."

She looked up at him, too swamped with longing and craving to attempt to return his joking in kind. "I don't know why, but I need you right now. My body is on fire and I need you to touch me, Ven. It has been so long since anyone touched me . . . I *need* you." Her voice caught, and she was surprised not to feel ashamed at the stark plea she heard in her own words. But she wasn't ashamed. She was flying, she was burning up, she was going to die if he didn't release the explosive pressure building inside her.

But . . . oh, Goddess. Protection. "Wait! I don't have any, I mean, we need protection!" Her face flushed hot red.

He instantly understood. "We're safe. Poseidon does not allow his warriors to father children until he has blessed the rite of fertility."

She bit her lip. "Um, what about . . . I mean, I'm clean, but—"

"Atlanteans are immune to human illnesses, as you are to ours, *mi amara*. There is nothing at all to fear."

A mischievous grin flashed across her face and she shot a pointed glance down between their bodies. "Sure, nothing to fear, easy for you to say. To use terms you warrior types might understand, I'm the one with the giant sword getting ready to try to fit in my sheath."

He burst into laughter, as did she, and the miracle of their laughter reignited their passion. Slowly, though, the smile faded from his face, replaced by something darker. More powerful. A predator stalked her from behind the blue-green flames glowing in his eyes, and she caught her breath for an instant. "I am honored beyond measure by your words and your wanting, *mi amara*," he said roughly, lifting his hands to frame her face. "Yet I must say this: I want to do the honorable thing and tell you I'll back off and just hold you, but my control is shredding. Never in my nearly five hundred years have I wanted anything or anyone the way I want you right now. So say no or say yes, but either way, be damned sure. Because I need to be inside you more than I need to take my next breath."

She stilled for a long moment, but her body and the song in her soul made the decision for her. She smiled at him. "Yes."

He paused, then nodded once, and stared at her with a single-minded focus that reminded her again of a predator stalking its prey. "Now," he rasped out. "Now."

Before she could catch her breath, he grabbed the top of her shirt in his hands and ripped it down the center. The sound of fabric tearing shocked her with its suddenness. His large hands were surprisingly nimble at unclasping the front of her bra, and he pushed it aside and stared down at her breasts with such fierce possession stamped into the lines of his face that she shuddered a little. No man had ever looked at her like that, like she was everything he wanted. Everything he needed. His desire became her aphrodisiac, swirling her further and deeper into mindless physical craving.

He pulled her up into his arms and kissed her again. Hot, demanding kisses, almost bruising in their intensity, alternated with long, slow, kisses that drove every rational thought out of her mind and had her clutching at his shoulders to pull herself closer to his body.

He stopped kissing her long enough to stand up and yank off his own clothes until he stood next to the bed, proudly nude, the erection jutting out in front of him as enormous as

the rest of him. The craving grew fiercer and her body coop-
erated, heat licking through her and liquid need preparing
her for his entrance. "Yes," she said. "Now. Please."

He pulled her underwear down her legs and tossed it over
his shoulder, pressing a kiss to her abdomen as he did so, his
hot breath making her stomach muscles clench in reaction.
His fierce look of triumph sent tingles of electricity through
her as he caught her shoulders and effortlessly lifted her up
into his arms and kissed her again, running his hands down
her back, cupping her butt, squeezing and kneading her until she couldn't stand it anymore. She needed to feel him
against her, and she leapt up, putting her legs around his
waist.

He shouted out a laugh, then said something to her, words
spilling out of him, fierce words in a beautiful language she
didn't know. He whirled around with her in his arms, then
walked, holding her, to the nearest wall and pushed her up
against it, so that she was sandwiched between the wall and
six and a half feet of hard-muscled, naked Atlantean warrior.
She rubbed her body against his, moaning, not caring that
she was going for shameless on the wanton witch scale, only
knowing that she wanted his hardness rubbing against her
most sensitive places. The contact of her nipples against his
chest as she moved drove her insane, and she moaned again,
wild with need.

"Ven, I need you. I know it's crazy, and I don't care, I
don't *care*, I just need you," she said, beyond embarrassment
or pretense. "I need you inside me now."

~~~~~

Ven heard the words and thought he must be dreaming some
fantasy of the mountain of the gods. The most intriguing
woman he'd ever known, the woman whose courage and
beauty and magic had captured his soul, wanted *him*.

Wanted him *inside* her.

Wanted him *now*.

Holy freaking balls of Poseidon.

He reached down between them to see if she was as ready

for him as he was for her, and the feel of her wet heat against his fingers shot a bolt of hot lust through his body straight to his cock. He thrust two fingers inside her, as deep as they would go, and growled a warning when she squirmed against his hand. The beast inside him that was more animal than man, that had battled and fought and killed for centuries, warning her not to try to escape him. But she said, "Yes, more, yes," panting as she said it, reassuring him that she wasn't trying to get away, and the beast calmed, gave way to the man. Ven almost had time to wonder what the fuck was happening to him before another wave of lust rode him, hard, and he groaned as his body clenched, his hips bucking involuntarily.

Praise Poseidon, she was riding his fingers and rubbing her breasts against him and he had to get inside her before he died. He bent his knees and lowered his head and caught a tight, perfect nipple in his mouth and sucked hard, fingers still moving inside her. He found her clit with his thumb, rubbing her in the same rhythm that his fingers were moving to, and she caught his hair in her hands and screamed out his name.

When she exploded around his fingers, shuddering in his grasp, he shouted out his triumph and his possession, and he turned and crossed the room in one leap with her still in his arms. Before she could change her mind, or come to her senses and realize a battle-hardened warrior would never be enough for her, he laid her down on the bed and yanked her legs apart. Put his hands on the bottoms of her thighs and held her open to him. Stared at her slick, swollen folds and murmured a promise that he would taste her soon. Would bury his face and lips and tongue in her honey and taste her until she screamed and came in his mouth.

She shuddered at his words, and he lost the power of speech.

He tried to tell her how beautiful she was—how special.

All that came out was "*Mine.*"

She stared up at him with a passion-drenched gaze, panting from her orgasm, desire still sparkling in the glorious blue of her eyes. "Ven?"

"Mine," he repeated, unable to form words, unable to understand them. Why could she still talk?

She moved, lifted a hand to push a strand of hair from her face, and the motion triggered the predator, the conqueror inside him who demanded that he stake a claim on this woman.

His woman.

"Mine. *Now,*" he growled, and then he centered himself over her and looked into her eyes once more, sanity trying to raise its head, honor giving her one last chance to change her mind.

But she smiled up at him and nodded and said the most beautiful word he'd ever heard.

"Yes."

At that moment, he shifted so that he was no longer blocking the window, and the moonlight shone across her body as it lay opened to him, transforming her back into the goddess she'd been outside the Nereid Temple.

He paused for a heartbeat, understanding on some primal level that he was about to make love to a goddess turned human. Not caring what price he might pay for it.

Mine.

In one powerful thrust, he drove his cock all the way inside her slick heat and he shouted again, shouted her name, shouted his claiming in ancient Atlantean, the only language his brain could remember.

She clenched around him and cried out, wrapping her legs around his waist and digging her heels into his ass, not pushing him away but pulling him closer, and he was only too eager to get with that particular program, oh, thank you Poseidon.

"Erin, if you do that again, I'm going to go off right now like some damn youngling," he said, panting, as he held still for a moment, then belatedly realized he'd said the words to her in his native tongue and repeated them in English.

"Well, then we'd just have to try again, wouldn't we?" she said, biting her lip to keep the smile from forming.

He leaned closer and captured her lips again, kissing her until he was inhaling her breath and her music and her soul.

"Say my name, Erin. Tell me you want me," he demanded, slowly pulling out of her body, then plunging back in, over and over, speeding up the rhythm in response to the little moans and gasps she made underneath him.

"I . . . yes. Ven," she breathed. "I want you, oh Goddess, Ven, I want you more than I have ever wanted anything in my life."

Some primitive instinct deep down in the primal waters of his genetic ancestry roared out its triumph. Every muscle in his body tightened at the sound of his name in her lilting voice. His cock swelled and hardened until the friction from her tight, wet sheath drove him insane with sensation.

Her music broke forth again; the emeraldsong and opalsong soared through the room and through the two of them as their limbs tangled together and their bodies joined. He thrust into her harder and deeper, driving farther into her with every stroke. Erin suddenly gasped, dragging her nails down his back, and tightened around him as she exploded, crying out his name as she came. The force of her orgasm drove him over the edge, and he thrust into her as far as he could go and kept still, holding her tightly in his arms, while he pulsed his release inside her. Then he collapsed beside her, pulling her with him so he remained in her body, careful not to crush her with his weight.

"Ven, I—" she began, but then she made a funny little gasping sound, and the music that had been soaring through the room exploded inside of his head. A rainbow of music, a sunrise of melodies, a concerto sung by angels and Nereids rang, floated, spiraled through the room and through both of them, and the force of it slammed Ven back against the pillows, still clasping Erin in his arms, satiation giving way to another wave of impossibly powerful, driving hunger.

But suddenly the splendor and power of the music blasted through his mental shields and maybe through hers, too, because he looked into her eyes and saw the depths of her soul.

Saw the murder of her family—she'd been there. She'd seen it all, tried to help, tried to stop it, been beaten and stabbed. Caligula and his minions had left her for dead.

The whole thing played out in his head like a violent movie, complete with a soundtrack from the lowest of the nine hells. Her mother and sisters sobbing and shrieking as they'd died.

Erin had dragged herself to the coven, wounded, nearly dead, and demanded that they train her, though she was only sixteen years old.

He saw her strength, her loneliness, her despair. Her driving need to avenge her family.

He saw himself, and her wonder at feeling such a tangible, powerful connection to a man she'd only just met.

He saw her soul, and he fell over the precipice into the abyss. Strong, fearless warrior that he was, Ven was suddenly more terrified than he had ever been in the half millennium of his existence, because he realized that if he'd seen into her soul, shining with her courage and light, it was highly likely that she'd seen into the black and twisted corners of *his*. He closed his eyes as a blade sharper than any dagger ever honed twisted in his gut.

Game over.

There was no freaking way that she'd want him now.

Erin stirred beside him, and he resisted the urge to open his eyes, afraid that she was climbing out of bed to run as far and as fast as she could. Straight away from him. Not that he could blame her if she did. If he didn't see her leave, maybe it wouldn't hurt as much.

"Ven. Ven, I know you're awake. Look at me."

He felt her touch on the side of his face, soft and gentle. His eyes snapped open, but he didn't speak. Couldn't speak.

Her eyes were huge, enormous, a drowning blue. He thought he could fall into the depths of them and never climb out. But he still couldn't talk.

"I saw inside you, Ven," she said, her voice breaking a little. "I saw the horrible things you've been forced to do. Awful things, for so very long. Dancing with death over and over to protect your family, to protect your fellow warriors. Most of all, to protect humanity."

The tears spilled past her lashes and rolled down her face. "Oh, Ven, your mother . . . your parents. I am so sorry."

He tried to push the words past the aching in his throat. Tried to come up with a defense that would make her see past the monster he'd had to be to the man he could become.

Tried to let her know he would never fail to protect her as he'd failed to protect his mother. As he'd failed to protect Conlan.

Tried to find the words that would make her want to stay.

But before he could find any words at all, she curled up against his chest, pulling the bedcovers up over them both. "I'm here now," she whispered. "Let go of some of the pain and let me hold you."

He tightened his arms around her in a wordless prayer of relief. She was nothing that he'd ever wanted—human, gem singer, and witch.

She was everything he'd ever needed.

For a very long time—long after she'd fallen asleep, exhausted from the day and from their lovemaking—he simply held her and watched her sleep.

Chapter 13

The palace, Atlantis

Ven opened his eyes, going from sound asleep to fully alert in the span of a split second, instinctively reaching for his weapons and finding his arms full of warm, soft woman instead.

"So, you're finally awake, sleepy head," Erin murmured. "Tell me about this symbol on your chest." She traced the symbol of his oath to Poseidon, high on the left side of his chest, with one finger. He caught her hand, brought it to his mouth, and gently kissed her palm. If she didn't want to talk about what had happened, he would give her time to process it. It's not like he'd been prepared to reach the soul-meld with a woman he'd only known for a matter of days.

Actually, he wasn't sure he was prepared to *ever* reach the soul-meld, he thought, faint strains of another Elvis song singing a fading farewell in his mind. The soul-meld was not a prison, however. Free will still ruled all choice. A brief thought of Erin choosing another man flashed through his mind and his gut wrenched with nausea and rage.

Free will sucked.

He drew in a deep breath and forced his mind away from

anything to do with the soul-meld. "Poseidon burns that symbol into each of his warriors when we swear our oath of service to him. How did you sleep, *mi amara?*" He twined his hand through the silken waves of her hair, amazed that it was real—that *she* was real and still with him in the bed.

She was still naked, too, which was always a plus.

Erin leaned forward and pressed a soft kiss on his lips, smiling but with a hint of shyness in her expression. "I slept fine. I was pretty much unconscious, to be honest. After the . . . um. Well. We can talk about that later."

He started to speak, not knowing what the hells he was going to say, but she held a finger to his lips. "Shh. Tell me about this symbol, for now."

She removed her finger from his lips and tapped it on his chest. "What does it mean?"

"The circle represents all the peoples of the world, and the triangle is the pyramid of knowledge handed down to your kind by our ancient ones," he explained. "Poseidon's Trident encompasses and protects them both—humanity and knowledge—to hold in trust for the future. As the sworn Warriors of Poseidon, we carry out this duty."

"So, is that what you're doing with me?" she asked, suddenly not meeting his eyes. "Your duty?"

He grinned and tumbled her onto her back and rolled on top of her. "Oh, no, trust me, duty has never been this much fun. But if you feel it's my duty to make love to you all day long, I can certainly—"

Loud pounding on the door cut him off midsentence and he jumped up and out of the bed, leaning down to snatch his daggers out of their sheaths from his discarded pants as he did so, and bit off a sharp command. "Identify yourself!"

He glanced back at Erin. She'd scooted backward up to the teak headboard of the bed and sat with the sheet tucked under her arms, covering her chest and body but keeping her arms free and her hands held out, palms up, clearly ready to call her magic. She didn't look the least bit frightened.

Which ticked him off.

"Maybe you ought to be a little more concerned for your safety," he said to her, then turned back to the door and shouted out a repeat of his earlier command. "I said, identify yourself!"

"Really? Am I in danger even in Atlantis?" Erin shot back at him. It was a reasonable question, and that ticked him off even more. But his instincts were shouting at him to protect and defend, and he was damn well going to do it.

Christophe's voice came through the door, and he sounded irritated. "Sorry, sorry. Alaric's warding knocked me on my ass for a minute. It's Christophe here. Conlan wants you to know that Alaric called a meeting. We're all supposed to gather at the Nereid Temple in about twenty minutes. Especially you and the witch."

Ven strode over to the door and pulled it open just far enough that he could see out, but Christophe could not see into the room. "Her name is Erin."

"Uh-huh," Christophe said, jerking his head up and staring at the ceiling over the door so that he was looking anywhere but at what Ven had forgotten was his entirely naked body. "Maybe you could get dressed before you head over. I know I speak for us all when I say you're ugly enough with your clothes *on*."

Ven slammed the door shut as Christophe stalked down the hall, laughing his damn fool ass off.

Erin looked like she couldn't decide whether to laugh or yell at him. Unfortunately for him, laughter lost out. She jumped out of the bed and started grabbing for her clothes. Ven spent about two seconds wondering what she was mad at him about and then lost his train of thought when she bent over and he got a perfect view of her extremely delectable ass.

"By the gods, you're beautiful," he said, his body hardening at the sight of her flawless skin.

She abruptly stood up, her chest, neck, and face flushing red, and held her clothes in front of her. "I wasn't . . . that wasn't for your benefit. Anyway, I thought you realized by now that I am not a helpless female who will hide behind you every time there might be trouble. I am what your friend named me: a witch. And a pretty powerful one, too."

His good mood disappeared, draining out of him in an instant. "Do not think to compare your ten years of dabbling in witchcraft with my nearly five centuries of battling vampires, shape-shifters, and the other creatures that stalk humans in the dark. You are in danger, and I will protect you. *That* is my *duty*, and I will carry it out with every ounce of skill and experience I possess."

He yanked on his jeans and shirt while he spoke. She opened and closed her mouth once, then again, the fury sparkling in her eyes promising that when she did speak, she was going to flay the skin off his hide.

"Well, so the arrogant Atlantean royal shows himself," she shot back at him. "Don't bother to waste the formal speak on me, bucko. I am *so* not impressed. Also, five *centuries*?"

A knock came at the door again, gentler than Christophe's pounding. He flung the door open. "What?"

The palace servant standing there with her arms full of clothing took a quick step back, bowing her head. "Your Highness, I apologize. I didn't know . . . Lady Riley asked . . . I can come back . . ."

Ven forced a smile. "No, I'm the one who should apologize, Neela. Thank you for your kindness. And please call me Ven."

He took the pile of clothing that she handed him and tried to think past the emotion clouding his brain to reassure the woman. "How is your son? He must be nearly ten now?"

She beamed, maternal pride overcoming her anxiety. "He is to be twelve this season, Your High— . . . Ven. He brings much joy to our home."

"And probably much exuberance, I'd guess, having once been a twelve-year-old boy, myself."

Neela sighed a little, still smiling. "It is ever so. If you or the lady need anything else, please call me."

"We will."

As he closed the door again, he took a deep breath, steeling himself to face Erin.

"So you're not all lord and master of the castle all the time, are you?" she asked. "Is this something special you just pulled out for me?"

"No, I'm pretty much a pain in the ass all the time," he said, turning around. "I don't really understand what I am with you."

She stood there for a long moment and finally sighed. "Well, that makes two of us, because I don't recognize myself, either."

Then she headed for the bathroom, leaving him to wonder what in the nine hells he'd gotten himself into.

～～～

The Nereid Temple was a faery tale of marble, jewels, and beauty. From the moment Erin walked through the doorway, her gems sang to her in a low, joyous tone that murmured of home and peace. Erin forced everything to do with missions and quests and stupid alpha male Atlantean warriors out of her mind and wandered around the open, airy main room, where Marie and her maidens had set up tables filled with a delicious breakfast. Fruits, juices, and pastries shared space with hot dishes in covered silver serving trays, and Erin's stomach growled at the delicious aromas.

But she was too fascinated with the history that was coming to life before her eyes to concentrate on food just yet. She sipped her coffee as she studied the statues gracing the room. Stopping before a particularly warlike figure bristling with spears and a trident, she felt a chill skate down her neck and knew who he must be.

She smelled a gentle mix of roses and something lighter

an instant before Marie stepped up beside her. "Yes, it's Poseidon. Even here, in our temple where the Goddess holds sway, we are reminded that Poseidon holds the power of life or death over us."

"Is it a reminder you need? I mean, not to tap dance on the obvious, but you are living in a bubble far down under tons of water with the force to crush you."

Marie laughed. "You humans are refreshingly direct, if you and Riley are a representative sample."

Erin turned to face her, stunned. "You've never met any humans before Riley and me?"

"No, I have not. Riley was the first human to enter Atlantis in more than ten thousand years." Marie's beautiful face was a study in calm elegance, her dark blue eyes peaceful. Her midnight black hair was pulled back from her face in a series of intricate braids. "Thus far, Alaric has transported her to the human doctors, rather than bring them here."

Erin nodded. "Ven told me that you're still deciding when to make the big 'Atlantis exists' announcement." She lifted a hand to her own unruly mass of wavy hair and sighed. "Not to be frivolous, but I wish my hair were more like yours."

Marie smiled. "Your hair is lovely, Erin. It suits you."

"Thanks, but I keep telling myself to get it all chopped off. Anyway, haven't you ever visited the surface? Come up to look around, catch a movie, go shopping?"

"Only the warriors are allowed to visit the landwalkers," Marie said. "But I am planning to ask the Council to make an exception. My brother, Bastien, has formed the soul-meld with a shape-shifter female, and I wish to visit them and meet her."

Erin tried to read the other woman's expression but couldn't. "What is the soul-meld? Sounds serious. Is it something like human marriage?"

Even before she saw the shocked glance Marie shot over her shoulder, Erin felt his approach. A low humming thrummed through her senses and her skin, and her emeralds trilled out a sweetly seductive call.

Marie's eyes widened. "Your gems sing for him, then? It is in the scrolls, but . . . we have never had a gem singer in our temple in living memory. Not since before the Cataclysm, in truth."

Ven spoke from just behind Erin, his voice washing warmth and desire over her. Apparently the fact that she was pissed off at him had no effect on her gemstones or her hormones. "We haven't had time to discuss all the circumstances involved in this situation, Marie." His voice held a clear note of warning.

Marie didn't appear to be intimidated. "The lady Erin was asking about the soul-meld. You must tell her, Lord Vengeance. It is her destiny."

Even without seeing him, Erin sensed Ven's utter stillness at the words. "Destiny is an overused word, First Maiden. Erin has free will, as do I."

Marie smiled, and there was something dark and knowing behind her eyes. "Do you?" Then she murmured some excuse and moved away, leaving Erin alone with Ven. She swung around to face him.

"So, spit it out, already. Soul-meld? What the heck is that?"

"This is not the time or place, Erin," he said, his expression closed and cold. "And don't believe everything you hear."

"I'm not stupid, Ven. We both felt something last night. Maybe you should explain exactly what it was? Was that the soul-meld? Or do Atlanteans always make love with all mental doors wide open like that?"

He was shaking his head before she finished the question, and he reached out to grasp her shoulders in his hands, then stared down into her eyes with his hot, penetrating gaze. "Never, *mi amara*. Never have I felt anything like that in all of my days. Do not think I take what occurred between us lightly."

Shaken, she considered responses, and finally just nodded slowly.

"Erin, I—"

"Ven." The voice that interrupted them was far too imperial to be anyone but the priest. "Your presence and that of your gem singer is required. Please take a seat."

Ven snarled a response over his shoulder in that language she assumed was Atlantean, and everyone in the room seemed to take a collective sharp breath. Silence hung in the air for a moment, then Alaric spoke again, dry amusement in his voice. "I cannot think of a way to perform your . . . request, since it is anatomically impossible. However, if you would care to challenge me, Lord Vengeance, it would be my pleasure."

Conlan stood up from where he'd been eating his breakfast next to Riley. "Enough, both of you," he said, the words holding affection as much as command. "Don't make me pull rank."

Marie glided across the Temple floor to the table and took a seat. "Perhaps all of you will remember that this is the home of the Goddess and you should behave accordingly," she said. Her voice was gentle but there was the unmistakable whip of admonition underlying her words.

Erin grinned. Speak softly and carry a big Goddess stick. *Way to go, Marie.* She edged carefully around Ven, not quite sure he wasn't going to simply toss her over his shoulder and pull a caveman. "Sounds good to me, Marie. Why don't we all sit down and enjoy this wonderful food."

She headed for the seat at the table farthest from Alaric and right between Alexios and Denal, figuring it would really tick Ven off. Something bitchy inside her chuckled at the idea. Served him right.

But before she could take a seat, he caught her from behind with one powerful arm around her waist and lifted her into another seat at the end of the table. He took the seat that blocked her from Alexios, lifted a platter of fruit and held it out to her. "Mango?"

"Don't think that what happened between us gives you any rights over me," she said, careful to keep her voice low. "I will sit wherever I choose and do whatever I want."

Deadly calm washed over his expression, belying the suddenly feral look in his eyes. "If you wish to force me to call battle challenge on my friends and brother warriors, feel free to push me in this matter. Be advised that battle challenge is almost always to the death, so choose carefully which of them you wish to see die."

Pure shock slammed into her. He wasn't kidding. She could feel the heat of the banked rage burning out from him. If she continued to taunt him, he would hurt or maybe kill one of his friends over it. "What kind of monster are you?" she whispered, suddenly terrified.

"I am worse than any monster you have ever known, Erin," he said bleakly. "The things I have done throughout the centuries would rot away at your mind if you knew of them. And apparently the soul-meld causes certain . . . possessive instincts . . . that I have never experienced before. I can't understand it or control it right now. Please don't challenge me until I can figure this out."

She leaned away from him, not understanding how she could simultaneously feel terrified and yet safe and protected in his presence, when he'd just admitted to being a monster. It was a conundrum she had no time to explore, though, because Alaric and Marie were standing up at the head of the table and raising their hands for silence.

Marie spoke first. "Let us give thanks to the Goddess for this bounty before us and for returning our gem singer to her home. Thanks be to the Goddess!"

"Thanks be to the Goddess," everyone replied, as Erin studied them. Conlan sat next to Riley, who was looking a little less rosy and well than she had the day before. Brennan and a warrior she did not recognize sat on the other side of Conlan. Alexios and Denal sat on her side of the table. Several women who must be maidens of the Temple fluttered around, serving drinks and carrying dishes, but none joined them at the table other than Marie.

Alaric spoke. "Thanks be to the Goddess, and praise Poseidon, who protects us all."

"Praise Poseidon," came the refrain, and then Alaric and

Marie took their seats and everyone continued to eat. Erin discovered that she was ravenously hungry, in spite of feeling the emotional equivalent of shell shock, and filled her plate, studiously ignoring Ven except to murmur thanks when he passed a platter.

For several minutes there was little conversation as everyone ate, and then Conlan pushed his plate aside. One of the maidens hurried to remove his dishes, and he smiled and thanked her, which surprised Erin a little. *Not a lot of royal snobbery going on here,* she thought, remembering Ven with the woman who'd brought the clothes. Thinking of that reminded her to thank Riley.

"Riley," she said, pitching her voice loudly enough to capture the woman's attention. "Thank you for sending the clothes. My stuff was getting a little ripe."

Riley grinned. "It's the least I could do. That blue looks wonderful on you, by the way."

Erin grinned, since she'd thought exactly the same thing herself. The sky-blue silk top mirrored her eyes, and she hadn't exactly hated the appreciative heat in Ven's eyes when he'd seen her in the top and jeans after she'd showered. Other than the lip gloss she'd had in her jacket pocket, her face was bare of makeup, but she never wore a lot, anyway.

Ven put a hand on her back, and the heat from his touch seared through the light fabric of her shirt. "Yeah, it does. Look wonderful, I mean," he said into her ear. The touch of his breath made her shiver as if he'd stroked other, more intimate places, and she caught the quick flash of passion in his gaze.

Trying not to be obvious about it, she pulled away from his hand and sent a serious look down the table toward Conlan. "Okay, what are we here to discuss? I'm hoping you're on board with the alliance to help us fight Caligula."

"Yes, we are definitely willing to work with your coven toward that end," Conlan said. "It can't be coincidence that Caligula's base in the Pacific Northwest is the center of the increase in newly turned vampires."

Alaric nodded. "He is clearly consolidating his power,

perhaps seeking to expand his territory to encompass that which Barrabas left."

The warrior that Erin didn't recognize lifted his head and she was surprised to see power glowing in his eyes. "Why in the hells do we need to work with the witches? They're not powerful enough to be a help or they would have done something about Caligula ten years ago when he attacked them the first time."

Erin's heart stuttered at the callous mention of her family's murder, and it seemed to attract his attention, because he swung his gaze to her. "Sure, maybe Ven found some pretty little witch to scratch his itch for a while, but that doesn't mean we have to include her in our plans."

Beside her, Ven leapt to his feet and roared out a challenge, then launched himself over the table in one mighty leap, knocking the warrior backward, chair and all, as they both crashed to the ground.

Erin shot out of her chair and rounded the table with some idea of intervening, but the sight of them stopped her cold. Ven had one large hand wrapped around the other man's throat and was crouched on top of him, snarling in a low, animalistic rage.

"If you ever mention her, look at her, or even think of her in a disrespectful way again, Christophe, I *will* kill you."

Christophe tried to speak, but could only manage choking noises.

Ven bared his teeth in a terrifying parody of a smile. "Give me a reason. Just one word. Give me a reason to call battle challenge right here."

Christophe's eyes glowed with fury, then the flames in them banked and he held up his hands in a gesture of surrender. Ven glared down at him for another long second, then shoved up and off of the fallen warrior. When he raised his head, he caught Erin in his gaze, and she inhaled sharply at the single-minded focus in his gaze.

Trapped again, she stood, frozen, as he stalked toward her. It never even occurred to her to try to resist him as he swept her into his arms and strode up the steps to the Temple doorway. Immediately outside the doorway, he turned right and put her down, backing her up against the marble wall, and slammed his hands against the wall on either side of her.

She tried to push words past the breath caught in her throat. "Ven? What—"

But he simply shook his head and caught her words with his mouth. Caught her lips in a demanding, passionate kiss. She couldn't help it, she twined her arms around his neck and kissed him back, unable to resist his claim of possession.

Not sure she wanted to try.

He kissed her with skill and hunger until her knees weakened, and she would have fallen if she hadn't been clinging to him, but he was careful never to touch her body. Finally, he wrenched his head away from hers and stood, panting, with his head hanging down. "I'm sorry, Erin. I know an apology isn't enough, but it's all I've got right now."

"What just happened?" she asked, her own voice shaky.

He lifted his head and stared into her eyes. "What just happened is that I very nearly fucked you right here up against the wall. All I've been able to think of every second of this day is pounding my cock into your body until you scream for me."

Heat and razor-sharp desire burned through her at his crude words, and she shivered. "Ven, this can't—we can't keep going like this. This is too distracting, when we need to go after Caligula."

He laughed, disbelief evident on his face. "Caligula? Are you insane? You're not going anywhere near Caligula. Fuck free will. You're never leaving Atlantis again."

Chapter 14

After that kiss that had rocked her foundation, Ven backed away from her and pointed to the doorway, unspeaking, his breath still coming in harsh, rasping noises. She hesitated, then ran for the door and escaped inside to the relative safety of the Temple and the people inside. Conlan stopped on his way out the door and stared down at her with that face so like his brother's, but with compassion in his eyes. "Don't be afraid of him, gem singer. He would give his life for you."

Alaric brushed by her on the other side. "Why am I the only one concerned by that fact?" he muttered, then continued to swoop out the door like some marauding grim reaper.

She put her hands on her hips, feigning a steadiness she was far from feeling. "He just told me I'm never leaving Atlantis. If he thinks he can keep me here against my will, then *he's* the one who should be afraid."

Conlan grinned and unexpectedly leaned forward to press a brief kiss on her forehead. "I could never have wished for a more worthy mate for my brother, little witch."

Her mouth fell open, but before she could form a single response, he was gone, following Alaric out the doorway.

Somebody immediately started shouting at somebody else, and she didn't want to hear it. She walked away from the noise and toward the table, head held high. The room was now empty except for Riley and Marie, so the warriors must have made their escape through a back entrance.

Riley didn't stand, but held out a hand to indicate the chair across from her. "Please join me while the boys beat on each other for a while," she said wearily, but with a smile.

Marie came up beside Erin with a silver carafe. "More coffee?" she offered, as if this were a normal ladies' brunch and Ven hadn't nearly killed Christophe on the floor near where she stood.

Erin shrugged. "When in Atlantis, I guess," she said. "Yes, I'd love more coffee, please. And maybe some chocolate-covered Valium?"

Marie smiled, poured the coffee, mentioned duties, and glided off in that serene, swanlike way she had. Erin watched her disappear down a corridor, then turned to face Riley. She could feel the heat of the flush burning her cheeks, but tried to ignore it. "So, you're going to marry Conlan. Is he much like his brother?"

Riley laughed. "I wondered when you'd get around to asking that. Two peas in a pod, except really sexy peas in an underwater pod, to stretch a metaphor."

"He pulls this 'I'm the warrior, you do as I say' stuff on you, too?"

Riley rolled her eyes. "Let's just say that he tries and leave it at that. In their defense, it's bred in their genes and then trained into them for years, Erin. For centuries after that, they live for nothing but to protect and defend humanity. Once you recognize you're dealing with a warrior you learn to make certain concessions."

Erin tried to wrap her mind around the idea. "So you're saying that you let Conlan get away with this?"

"Are you kidding? If I gave him an inch, he'd have me locked in my room 'for my own safety.'" Riley flashed a very wicked grin. "You have to stand up to him, Erin. No matter what your hormones might be telling you."

Erin's face heated up again. "Um, about that. This is kind of personal, but do you and Conlan—" She paused, unable to think of a delicate way to ask the question.

"Go at each other like bunnies?" Riley asked drily.

The burst of laughter escaped before Erin could stop it. "I was going to say have some sort of runaway flash fire raging between you, but the bunnies thing works."

"I figured a little laughter might relieve the tension," Riley said, reaching for her glass of juice. "Has he told you about the soul-meld?"

"No, but Marie mentioned it. What exactly does that mean? And don't tell me that Ven will explain it, or I may have to take your pastries hostage," she threatened, only half joking.

Riley put her hands up to cover the plate. "Touch my baklava and somebody gets hurt," she warned, grinning.

"Okay, okay. Your pastry's safe from me, since you're eating for two. But, seriously, I need to know what this soul-meld is about."

The smile faded from Riley's face, and she nodded. "You deserve the truth, especially considering the way Ven's acting about you." She glanced up at the doorway, but it remained empty, although they could still hear the faint sounds of the three men arguing outside.

"The soul-meld is an ancient legacy that apparently very rarely happened around here in the past few thousand years. As the legend goes, certain Atlanteans have the capacity to reach a higher, almost divine level of connection with the person they fall in love with. When this happens, the doors to their souls fall open and each can travel inside of the other." Riley paused and bit her lip, then continued. "It's a connection far more intense than anything else could ever be, and intimacy with someone you're soul-melded with will rock your socks off."

Erin stared at the other woman, her mind racing frantically. "But I'm not Atlantean. Well, maybe one-one-thousandth or something."

"Same here," returned Riley. "Apparently only one of the

pair needs to be pure Atlantean. In fact, Alaric has a few theories about some of us humans having DNA from the Atlantean ancients who left Atlantis just before the Cataclysm. It would make sense, in my case, because of my emotional empathy. My sister has the same talent."

Erin shook her head, relief sweeping through her. "No, that doesn't make sense. I don't have a drop of emotional empathy."

Riley leaned forward and touched her hand. "But you are a witch, Erin," she said patiently. "What do you think the proportion of witches is in the general population?"

"I don't know. Fewer than one percent?"

"Way fewer. Fewer than point zero one percent, to be exact. My sister is . . . well, she knows this kind of thing. From what we're learning from the Fae and from what Alaric has learned from the scrolls in Poseidon's Temple, it seems that the witches are descended from the ancient Atlanteans." Riley leaned back in her chair and sipped some more of her juice. "Throw in your gem singer Gift, and you're almost certainly descended from Atlantis."

Erin rubbed her temples, where a fierce headache was beginning to form. "Okay, let's assume for the moment that I am some kind of great great great to the nth power granddaughter of some old Atlantean couple. And let's assume the bunny thing, too," she said, ducking her head and staring into her coffee cup rather than look at Riley. "But Ven said free will. So just because we might have done the soul-meld thing once doesn't mean we're stuck together, does it?"

Silence. When she glanced up at Riley, the other woman's expression was troubled. "Nooo," she said, drawing out the word. "But I guess, considering the bond I have with Conlan, it's hard for me to understand why you'd ever want to leave Ven if you truly have reached the soul-meld with him."

"Because I'm not a possession. I don't mean to offend you, and I'm not saying that you are. But maybe Conlan is more of a modern thinker than his brother. Ven is a cross between some marauding Viking lord and . . . and a pirate! Or a big, hairy caveman. And I'm not about to be his captive or his wench or his, um, cavewoman . . ." She trailed off, running out of righteous indignation at about the same time the ridiculous nature of the whole thing hit her.

Riley was clearly having a hard time not laughing, from the way she was biting her lower lip.

"Oh, just laugh at me. I sound like an idiot," Erin admitted, smiling ruefully. "Cavewoman, for the Goddess's sake."

They both burst into giggles, and laughed so hard Erin actually felt tears rolling down her cheeks. A tingle of sensation warned her just before she felt Ven's hands on her shoulders. She looked up to see him staring down at her, unsmiling.

"Perhaps you would care to share the joke? I could use some humor right about now," he said.

Conlan did a sort of flashing thing across the table and lifted Riley up and into his arms, bending his head to kiss her in a "don't care that we're in public, can't wait to get you home and naked" kind of way that filled Erin with a powerful sense of longing.

Alaric rounded the table more slowly and took up a position at the end. "We need to talk."

Conlan gently helped Riley, who looked a little stunned, back into her seat. When Riley blinked up at her, Erin mouthed the word "bunnies" and it set them both off again, peals of laughter ringing out.

When Erin could catch her breath, Ven was seated beside her, one hand twined in her hair as if he needed the contact. She chanced a quick look at his face, but it was as forbidding as it had been before, so she decided to ignore the hair touching and turned toward Alaric. "Sorry about that. Private joke. Okay, what is the plan and when do we leave?"

Ven's voice was quiet, but filled with harsh command. "*We* don't leave. You're not going anywhere. Caligula is after you, for whatever reason, and you're not going anywhere near him until after we neutralize him and his entire blood pride."

She yanked her head away from his hand and stood up.

"Don't give me orders. Caligula has my sister, and I am most definitely going after him. For one thing, I am a pretty strong witch. I'll be able to help neutralize any witches he has working for him."

He raised his voice, but only said one word. "No."

She ignored him and went on. "The second reason is obvious. He wants me. Use me as bait."

Ven stood up and yanked her around to face him, fury raging in his eyes. "There is no fucking way you are putting yourself in danger, do you hear me? If I have to personally chain you to my bed, I'll do it to keep you away from that monster."

She tried to pull away, but his grip was too powerful, so she settled for kicking him in the shin. "Who is the monster? You told me you were! And just because you want to fuck me doesn't mean you have the right to keep me prisoner, chained to your bed or otherwise, you sick pervert!"

The tense silence that fell over the room reminded her that the two of them weren't alone, and she groaned, waves of mortification washing over her.

Conlan's voice sliced through the tension. "Put her down, Ven. Now. You have no right, as she says. Not this way, brother."

Ven actually snarled at his brother and prince, but he released his grip on Erin's shoulders and she staggered away from him. "How dare you talk to me of rights?" He shot the words at Conlan. "You know the power of the soul-meld. Think back to how you were with Riley when you first met and she was in danger."

Alaric raised his hands, palms up, identical glowing blue balls of power shimmering on them. "I will gladly blast you up against the wall if you need to be taught a lesson in free will," he said.

"Try it, priest," Ven growled. "You're pathetic. You had Quinn in your arms and you let her go, and now you suffer every day because of it. Don't think I'll make your foolish mistakes."

Alaric's eyes glowed a fierce emerald green, and he hurled

the balls of power at Ven, almost faster than Erin's eyes could track.

Almost.

She flung herself forward, between Ven and Alaric, and raised a shield more quickly than she'd ever done. The glowing spheres bounced off her shield and winked out of existence, and she lowered her hands and released her shield. "I don't need your help either, Alaric, so back off."

Ignoring Ven and the priest, she turned to Conlan and bowed. "Your Highness, you told me to ask for any favor. Well, I don't want the crown jewels or my own beachfront Atlantean cottage or even the new car behind door number three. All I ask is that you send some of your warriors to help me rescue my sister and destroy Caligula."

She drew a deep breath and tried to stop her knees and hands from shaking. "If you can't do that, then I ask only that you send me home and leave me alone. Because if you reward me for helping your wife and child by letting your brother keep me prisoner, well . . ." She paused, trying to think of an elegant way to put it, but came up empty. "Well, that's a pretty crappy way for a future king to act."

"Guess she told you, your princeliness," came a mocking voice from near the Temple doorway.

Erin whirled around to see Justice standing there, leaning against the wall, ever-present sword rising over his shoulder.

He leapt lightly down the stairs and strode toward them. "There's something else you might want to know before you go getting all kingly one way or another," he added, steering clear of Ven to head toward Conlan. Once there, he stopped and looked at each of them in turn, going for the dramatic pause, probably.

But Erin didn't have the energy to appreciate his showmanship, because something entirely unexpected was happening to her. The amber on her fingers had started shrieking out a shrill warning to her from the moment Justice began to walk toward them. Now it was so loud that it nearly drowned out his words, screaming at her of danger and threat and dark, powerful evil.

She pointed a finger at Justice and pronounced the sentence she'd trained for ten long years to carry out. Tried on a little formal speak of her own. "Death magic. You stink of death magic, Atlantean, and it's my sworn duty to kill you."

Chapter 15

Ven tried to put his arms around Erin, but she shot a look of fierce warning at him and, remembering the gazebo, he held up his hands and stood back, grinning. He never believed for a minute that she'd really kill Justice, but it wouldn't hurt old blue hair to get knocked on his ass.

It was Riley who broke the standoff. The only one with no power at all, except the gentle talent of emotional empathy, stood there and faced them all down.

Ven had never admired her more.

"That. Is. Enough," she shouted, loudly enough to cut through all the edgy magic shimmering in the room. "All of you, cut this crap out. It's not good for the baby."

Justice bowed to Riley, more deeply than Ven had ever seen him bow before, and then took two steps back and away from her. "I would not bring strife and discord to your presence, my lady," he said smoothly, flicking a glance at Erin.

"Right," Erin snapped. "You'd just bring death magic. Into Atlantis. Into a temple, even. Near a pregnant woman. You're just a peach, aren't you?"

Marie appeared from one of the corridors leading to the other rooms in the Temple. "Is there a problem?"

The situation went from amusing to deadly in a heartbeat when Erin and Alaric both called power, preparing to strike Justice down where he stood. Ven had never been particularly magically inclined beyond the simplest calling of the elements, but even he felt the whisper of the forces swirling around the witch and the priest.

Justice must have realized it, too, because he reached back as if to draw his sword, but Marie was suddenly there, next to him, and she shot out her own hand, lightning quick, and caught his wrist. Then she started chanting something in such a quiet voice that Ven couldn't catch the words.

Beside him, Erin gasped, then dropped her hands to her sides, as her head tilted upward as if pulled by the strings of an unseen puppeteer. He moved to hold her, fighting his way through a strange, liquid menace that curled around her like transparent mist. When he was able to put his hand on her skin, the mist vanished—or recognized a friend and dissipated—leaving him free to hold her tightly in his arms.

She opened her mouth and sang out several notes in the pure, wondrous tone she'd used to heal Riley, and the silvery shimmer rose to surround her body, and Ven with it, like it had before. At the same time, an identical gossamer mist of light rose around Marie and enveloped Justice where he stood, somehow trapped by her delicate hold on his wrist.

Abruptly, Erin closed her mouth. The final notes of her song trembled in the air and then floated, evanescent, down to earth. Ven felt the sense of loss again, as though part of his soul disappeared with the music. He shook off the feeling and shot a look at Justice, who now knelt on the floor next to Marie.

"It wasn't death magic at all, was it?" Erin asked, staring wide-eyed at Justice.

Marie knelt in front of Justice and framed his face with her hands. "How did I never know this about you before, Lord Justice? You have been in this Temple on many occasions."

He shook his head, the blue braid hanging down in front of

one shoulder until it nearly touched the floor as he crouched there. "There was no gem singer before, Marie. She must truly be a descendant in the direct line of the Nereids to recognize me."

Conlan bit off a command. "Will someone tell me what in the nine hells is going on? Right now?"

Marie slowly turned her head to look at Conlan. "Lord Justice has not been dabbling in death magic, Your Highness. He is half Nereid. The Temple Goddess just called him home."

∞∞∞∞

An hour later, they reassembled in Conlan's war chamber, on neutral ground. Ven had spent most of that hour trying to think of ways to wrap Erin up in a cocoon of safety and keep her hidden from anything dangerous for, oh, say, the rest of her life.

Maybe even the rest of *his*.

Although that would be a neat trick, considering the substantial difference between their relative life spans. Riley and Erin entered the room just then, and he tabled that miserable thought somewhere in the back of his mind. Erin took a seat near Riley, across the room from where Ven stood watching her, but he was reassured by the way her gaze sought him out.

Maybe he wasn't the only one caught up by powerful forces he didn't know how to handle. She smiled at him, and heat rushed through him, burning his skin and nerve endings with sizzling flames. All he could think of was how much he wanted to be inside her, and he put every bit of that longing into the slow smile he gave her, then felt a brief moment of fierce triumph when she blushed and clutched the arms of her chair. She wanted him, too, and that had to mean something.

It *must* mean something.

Justice sauntered in, trying for nonchalant, even though Ven could tell that he was shaken by what had happened at the Temple. Ven's first instinct was to block Erin with his body, but the warning in her eyes stopped him.

For the moment.

"Hey, the Scooby gang's all here," Ven said. "What do you say we figure this all out."

"We're not all here yet, Ven. Marie is coming," Conlan said, then nodded. "Here she is, right on time."

Marie walked through the door, looking around curiously. Ven figured it was the first time she had been in this part of the palace. None but Conlan, Alaric, and the warriors usually saw this room.

"Who wants to start first and explain the half-Nereid part to me?" Conlan looked from Justice to Marie and back again. "I knew your mother, Justice. She was a lovely woman, but she was no sea goddess and, as far as I know, she did not have forty-nine sisters."

Brennan spoke up from his position against the wall. "He speaks the truth. When we were children together, your grandparents used to feed us treats. I do not recall their names being Doris and Nereus."

Justice smiled, but it was an empty gesture that did not reach his eyes. "My adoptive parents. You met my adoptive parents, who were so thrilled to take in a child that they asked very few questions. Especially considering the circumstances."

"What circumstances are those?" Ven asked, leaning forward.

"I can't tell you."

"You mean you won't tell us," Alaric said.

"I mean I can't tell you," Justice repeated. "You know that old saying? I'd tell you, but then I'd have to kill you? Well, in my case, it's the literal truth."

Ven and Conlan rose to their feet. "Are you threatening us?" Ven asked the question first.

Justice waved a hand. "No, I'm stating a fact. It's a *geas* that was laid on me as a baby. I literally cannot speak the circumstances of my birth, no matter how much I might want to," he said bitterly. "If I do, I am forced by a powerful magical compulsion to kill anyone who might have heard me."

Alaric studied him, eyes narrowed. "Who could have laid a compulsion so powerful that it lasted for centuries?"

Justice looked him right in the eyes. "It was laid by the best, Priest. It was laid by a god."

Riley lifted her hand and touched Conlan's arm. "He's telling the truth."

Ven shook his head. "We can't know that. He's been lying to us for centuries."

"Hello? *Aknasha* here, remember? I can feel his emotions. He is absolutely telling the truth."

Erin finally spoke, for the first time since they'd gathered in the room. "Why did my amber tell me he was using death magic? I don't understand any of this. If he's half Nereid, why did the Temple Goddess freak out like that?"

Marie replied before Justice could answer. "I don't know the answer to that. He's the first blooded Nereid to enter the Temple in millennia, as far as I know. However, he has been there before, and there was never any issue. I think your gems called the warning to you when our Goddess recognized one of her own, and you processed it as a warning of death magic. It's not as if you had any other way to translate it, not having met a lot of Nereids in the past."

Erin nodded, although she didn't look fully convinced. "It does make sense, I guess. Now that we're out of the Temple, my amber isn't warning me, even though Justice is close enough to touch."

Something dark vibrated through Ven at the words, and he spoke before he could stop himself, moving to place himself between Justice and Erin. "It would be better if you did not touch him," he said. "Please accommodate me on this one issue."

She sighed and shrugged. "Fine. But we're going to need to talk about that, too."

Marie spoke up again. "There is something of vital importance I must share with you all. I believe it holds the key to healing Riley and the baby. Although Erin's song helped temporarily, the basic problem remains. Riley's body appears to be rejecting the pregnancy."

Everyone looked at Riley, who did seem paler than she had that morning and certainly less well than she had been after Erin had sung healing to her the day before. Riley only had eyes for Marie. "You can help my baby?"

Marie shook her head. "No, unfortunately, it is as I have said. I am unable to do anything more for you. It's Erin. Erin can heal the baby."

Erin lifted her head, blinking. "You know I'll do anything I can. But I don't really know how to do this gem singer thing yet. What I did yesterday may be all I had in me."

"No, you don't understand," Marie said. "You have the ability to find the Nereid's Heart, which is hidden in a diamond and emerald coffer also rumored to contain one of the lost gems from Poseidon's Trident."

Marie pulled something that looked like a scroll out of a pocket in her dress and handed it to Erin. "Study this well. With that ruby, you could cure Riley and the baby completely."

Erin watched, bemused, as preparations for the journey back to Seattle took place all around her. A floor-to-ceiling tapestry on one wall of the war chamber, depicting scenes from what she assumed to be the Cataclysm they'd spoken of, was pulled aside to reveal an arsenal. Weapons ranging from swords and crossbows to modern pistols and what looked like assault rifles were pulled from shelves and made ready.

She'd wanted a war, and it looked like she was going to get one. Ven's arguments against her placing herself in danger had faded when he realized she was the only one who could locate the Nereid's Heart. Now every inch of his hard, muscled body seemed to bristle with weapons. He'd only spoken to her once since the decision had been made, pulling her aside and ordering her to never get more than two feet away from him at any time on the mission.

She'd just turned away, not bothering to argue with him. She would do what she had to do to save her sister, whether Ven was there to help her or not.

Riley had taken a turn for the worse shortly after Marie's pronouncement, and Conlan and Marie had taken her off to rest. Conlan stepped back into the room now, face pale and drawn. "She's worse again," he said. "Much worse this time."

Erin jumped up from her chair. "I can—"

"No. You can't drain your strength before you leave," he said, his voice rough with strain. "Thank you for offering, but apparently the relief you can offer without the ruby is only temporary. Marie believes that the ruby will help you to cure her. Cure our child."

Ven put a hand on his brother's shoulder. "Know this, Conlan. I swear to you that I will do everything in my power to find this jewel, even at the cost of my own life."

Conlan nodded. "I know you will. I can't . . . I can't leave here. There's a chance that she won't . . . that—"

Erin felt the tears burning her eyelids at the utter despair in his voice. "We'll find it, Conlan. Tell her for us."

He nodded, then hugged her briefly. "Do your best, gem singer," he said, and then he was gone.

Erin turned to Ven, desperately needing the comfort of his arms, but he stood, arms folded, staring at her, his eyes gone glacial with pain. "I will risk my own life, but I will not risk yours, Erin. We must find a way to recover this jewel without harm coming to you. If I am forced to choose between your life and the lives of Riley and her baby, I will not survive it."

She had no response that made any sense, so she merely nodded and curled up on a corner of the couch as preparations continued, wondering what kind of callous bitch Fate really was to put so much at stake—all riding on the shoulders of one young, scared witch.

She glanced down at her rings but, for once, they were utterly silent.

Chapter 16

A warehouse, Seattle

If Ven's warehouse home (or what was left of it after that bomb blasted a hole in the middle of his floor) was old enough to be retro, then the place Quinn had directed them to was on the borderline between piece-of-shit-rattrap and condemned.

Ven was betting on condemned.

As he looked up at the stark front of the building, dark in the dim glow cast by the single working streetlight on the block, he noticed the holes, missing brick, and multiple broken windows, all of which could house enemies sighting down very expensive scopes at them as they stood there. He pulled Erin closer to his body so she made a smaller target, even though he trusted Quinn as much as he trusted any human, and Alexios, Justice, and Brennan had all melted into the shadows to circle the building and scout for trouble on the perimeter.

Christophe and Denal had gone hunting for lowlifes; scouting the bars and flophouses for anybody who might have information about Caligula and his activities. When a drug or drink habit rode a man hard, he could usually be persuaded to sell what he knew for a price.

Erin stiffened and started to back away from him, but then a rat bigger than most cats scurried around the corner in front of them and she let loose with a shrill yelp and tried to climb into his shirt with him. He couldn't help the grin that crossed his face. "My little warrior. Willing to take on bombs with nothing but her magic, but afraid of a little mouse."

She shoved him. "Little mouse, my foot! That was the biggest rat I've ever seen!"

He shrugged. "At least you can be relatively sure it's not carrying plague, which wasn't always the case."

"Plague? Oh, right. You're almost five hundred years old. I keep forgetting. You realize you're way too old for me," she said, trying to move around him to go into the building first. She'd been arguing with him about how she was better prepared to be first inside, considering her magic shielding, ever since they'd stepped through the portal that Alaric had created for them.

Ven's gaze flicked to the priest, whose face had gone so white he resembled one of the undead. Every step they took closer to Quinn was one that Alaric must feel spiking through his chest.

Before they reached the steel door, which hung drunkenly off its hinges, it swung open to reveal a small, slender woman standing in the doorway. To look at her, you'd never believe that Quinn Dawson was one of the coleaders of the human rebel forces. She was a few inches shorter than her sister and had short, dark hair that looked like she cut it with a lawn mower. In the oversized Bon Jovi T-shirt that she wore with faded jeans, she could easily have passed for a teenage boy. A teenage boy with enormous eyes and very delicate features.

From a short distance behind him, Ven heard a noise that sounded like the whooshing of air driven out of someone's lungs. Since the *someone* was Alaric, who could fry Ven's ass with those glowing eyeballs of his, Ven gave no indication that he'd heard a thing. As Erin tried to push past him again, he even felt a glimmer of sympathy with the priest's reaction to seeing Quinn again.

Without a breath of warning, Alaric suddenly shimmered into mist and soared up and over the top of the building. Ven watched him go, grimly amused. The most powerful high priest Poseidon had ever anointed was afraid of a girl. The thought cheered him up immensely, in spite of a certain lack of accuracy.

He solved the Erin problem by putting an arm around her shoulders and pulling her closer, not bothering to deny, even to himself, the sense of utter *rightness* he felt when she was in his arms. He knew he'd pay for his presumption later, but figured he'd worry about that when he got to it.

"Nice digs, Quinn," he said, offering his hand.

She smiled up at him, her quick gaze having already weighed and measured each one of them, and shook his hand with a firm grip. "It's good to see you," she said, sounding like she meant it. "We've got trouble."

"You and trouble in the same playground? Say it isn't so," he said, clutching his chest.

"Maybe we'd better get this off the street." She turned to disappear through the dark doorway. As Ven followed her, still holding tightly to Erin, his gem singer threw him an elbow. Hard.

He grunted, but didn't let go. "What was that for?"

"Oh, I don't know, let's see. Maybe an introduction would have been nice," she whispered. "Quinn, this is Erin. Erin, this is Quinn. See how easy it is?"

"She's right, you know," said a voice Ven remembered very well. The owner of the voice flowed around the corner, moving with a lethal grace that was uncharacteristic of such a big man. Unless the man were a shape-shifter who became a five-hundred-pound tiger when he was in a bad mood.

"Jungle boy!"

"That's jungle *man* to you, fish face," Jack said, holding out his hand to clasp Ven's. Then his eyes shifted to Erin, and he leaned toward her slightly and inhaled deeply.

"Who's the witch? Are you finally settling down, gonna raise some guppies?"

Ven tensed and shot out a hand, shoving the tiger back several inches. "Don't sniff my woman like she's your territory."

Jack blinked at him, then laughed. "Your woman? So that's the way of it, is it? Well, don't let it be said that the alpha of my streak doesn't recognize the rights of a mated pair."

Beside him, Erin murmured something under her breath and lifted her hands. The next thing he knew, he and Jack were both sitting on their asses in the hallway, staring up at her in shock.

She made an exaggerated show of wiping her hands together, and then held one out to Quinn. "I am Erin Connors, and I'm pleased to meet you."

Quinn shook her hand, grinning down at Ven and Jack. "Oh, honey. It is seriously my pleasure."

∽⌒⌒⌒⌒∾

Quinn introduced Erin to the dozen men and two women who stood around tables in the back of the warehouse, but she only used first names, and Erin had a strong feeling most if not all of those were aliases. Her magic sensed that at least eight of the group were shape-shifters. All of them, humans included, looked tough and somehow weary, and greeted her with cautious reserve. She had the feeling that only Jack and Quinn had met any of the Atlanteans before, and the rest were curious about them, from the way Quinn's group was scanning them.

Erin had never been around so many shape-shifters in her life, and her amber was singing a frantic song. The music was different from what it sang when vampires were around. This song was deeper, earthier. More sensual. As if the gems realized Erin wouldn't be all that averse to getting up close and personal with a handsome shape-shifter if the world were different. The big, gorgeous, scary guy, Jack, had slanted eyes that told her some kind of cat was the other half of his dual nature. From the deadly menace he projected, she was betting he wasn't your everyday, average housecat, either.

She glanced at Ven; somehow just thinking about getting up close and personal made her want to reach out to him. Memories of the way he'd touched her, held her, and slid his hard length inside her flashed through her mind, and her mouth went dry as her emeralds purred a sultry song. He caught her looking at him, and something must have given away her thoughts, because his eyes darkened and his gaze practically branded her as she stood.

She closed her eyes for a second and drew in a steadying breath, then purposely turned her body so he wasn't in her line of sight any longer. "Quinn, I understand Riley is your sister?"

Quinn smiled and the first real warmth she'd shown glowed on her face. "Yes, although you couldn't tell it to look at us, could you?"

Erin studied Quinn's face. "Actually, yes. You have the same delicate facial features, the same cheekbones, and the same terrific porcelain skin."

Jack started laughing. "Oh, that's not the way to make friends here, Erin. Call Quinn delicate, and she's liable to rip your arm off and stuff it down your throat."

Erin blinked, but Quinn only rolled her eyes. "Great, Jack. Scare the nice witch, why don't you?" She put her hand on Erin's arm. "Ignore the tiger. He gets grumpy if he doesn't eat a few natives every couple of weeks."

Erin glanced back and forth between the two of them, smiling uncertainly, because she had the uncomfortable feeling that there was more truth to the joking than she wanted to know about. Also, she'd never met any shifter whose other form was tiger, and the exotic nature of the beast under Jack's skin surprised her and sent a little chill of trepidation tingling through her senses. On the other hand, who needed allies who were wimpy?

Ven glowered at them all from the edge of a table, where he was staring down at what looked like a topographical map of Washington State. "What in the nine hells were you planning to do? And please tell me that you were at least going to wait for us to join the party."

Quinn strode over to him and pointed at an area circled in red. "We've been working our sources and tracking the frequency of attacks from the newly turned for several months. It all seems to spiral to the area around Mount Rainier."

Jack stabbed a finger down at the map. "We're guessing under here. There are a series of ice caverns and tunnels that are impassable to humans. Any entrance big enough to get through is magically warded so strongly that we've watched humans bounce right off of it and not even realize what they were doing."

"What about witches?" Erin asked.

Quinn shot a measuring look at her. "We don't know. The only witch on our team has been missing for more than a week. We don't know if she's been captured, killed, or . . . converted."

Ven spoke again. "We've got a problem with witches going bad around here, don't we? The woman who attacked at the Circle of Light HQ was strong enough to cut Erin off from her power. Does that sound like your witch?"

Jack and Quinn traded a long look, but finally Quinn shook her head. "I don't know how powerful you are, Erin, but she wasn't very strong. I doubt she could channel that kind of magic unless she'd been disguising her true strength from us."

"The witch who attacked me was channeling dark magic, which would automatically increase her powers from what she could call with the light," Erin said. "I didn't get a good look at her, though."

"Neither did I," Ven admitted. "I knocked her out, but then she disappeared when I was dealing with her colleague and a couple of vampires."

"Well, we won't know until we try, will we?" Erin walked over to study the maps. "I never would have guessed that there were caverns under Mount Rainier. I used to go hiking there with my family, before . . ." She stopped and shook her head. No need to go into that now. Sorrow might weaken her resolve.

Quinn raised an eyebrow but didn't ask her for an explanation. The dark, bruised look around her eyes gave Erin the idea that Quinn knew a lot about secrets and tragedies herself.

Ven cleared his throat. "Quinn, we need to talk privately. There's something I need to—"

"Is it Riley? The baby? What's wrong?" Quinn practically leapt at him. "Tell me right now, damnit."

The compassion in Ven's eyes touched a place deep inside Erin as she watched him. This fierce warrior talked a tough game, but he cared deeply for his family.

To add to her confusion, Erin had the idea he was starting to care deeply for her. She pushed the thought aside before she could examine it further. No time to think about caring for someone when she was on a mission that could very well end with one or both of them dead. Definitely no time to consider whether it was the kind of caring she would welcome and, perhaps, reciprocate.

"Riley is doing a little better, Quinn. Erin actually healed her, and Riley felt much better for a while."

Quinn's dark gaze turned to Erin. "You're a healer?"

"No. Well, yes. Maybe," Erin stumbled, trying for complete honesty. "The truth is I don't quite know exactly what I am, anymore. I know I'm a ninth-level witch of the Seattle Circle of Light, and I have an affinity with gemstones. The Atlanteans think I'm a gem singer, which means more to them than it does to me just yet. But something about the Nereid Temple and the proximity to its gemstones helped me to actually sing healing to your sister."

Quinn crossed to her, gave her a quick, fierce hug. "I owe you a debt for that. Riley is the most important person in the world to me. I'm planning to go to her as soon as we can get to the bottom of this problem. Far too many of my people have died trying."

As Quinn stepped back toward the table, she suddenly froze, her hands going to her pockets. In one smooth motion, she pulled a knife out of one pocket and a gun out of the other, and crouched low. "Trouble," she called out, and everyone in the place went into attack-and-defend mode.

Yet the trouble that floated down into the center of the room was no enemy, but rather an ally. Sort of. If you didn't count the whole death penalty threat thing.

Quinn's face went chalky white, and Erin noticed a faint trembling in her hands as she put the weapons away. "Alaric. You have a thing for dramatic entrances, don't you?" Quinn's voice was steady in spite of the obvious effect the priest's presence had made.

Alaric touched down on the floor mere inches away from Quinn and stared down at her. Erin was shocked by the expression on his face. The planes and angles had hardened until he appeared to be a marble statue rather than flesh and blood—a statue with oceans of pain in his eyes. He stared at Quinn as a dying man might look at his last chance for salvation.

Erin's gaze flew to Quinn, and she got another shock. Because Quinn was looking back at Alaric with the exact same expression on her face.

The priest finally spoke, his voice rusty. "Quinn. I hope you are well."

"I . . . I will be well when I know my sister is well," Quinn answered, her voice breaking on the words. "Why can't you heal her, Alaric? I know how powerful you are."

"I have done everything I can, but it's not enough." A muscle clenched in his jaw, and Erin felt an unexpected sympathy for the man. His failure to help Riley and the baby must have been eating away at his soul—there wasn't even a trace of his usual arrogance in his voice or expression.

"Actually, I may be able to help with that," Erin said, compelled to break the hideous tension between them. "There is a legend of a famous ruby that gem singers can apparently use to heal pregnant women and unborn babies. If we can find it, I can try to use it. Marie said she'd help me. The rumor is that it may be somewhere around Mount Rainier."

"That's quite a coincidence," Quinn said. "We just happen to be near Mount Rainier, and Caligula is probably underneath it. Now you're telling me this gem is there, too? I don't believe in coincidences."

"I don't either, but it's actually not a coincidence at all, more of a cause-and-effect relationship, from what Marie told us," Erin explained. "Evidently the presence of the gem in this area called to any child with the latent gem singer Gift, so it was more likely that a gem singer would develop her talent near the Nereid's Heart than anywhere else in the world."

"We've got reports of a tolling noise coming from the area around the mountain. Seismologists thought it was earthquake activity at first," Ven said. "But Marie said it very well could be the ruby coming to life, so to speak, after being hidden underground and inert for thousands of years."

Jack suddenly made a deep, growling noise and leapt to stand next to Quinn. "I smell vampire."

"That would be me," a voice called out from the area by the door, where two of Quinn's men were standing with pistols trained on Alexios and Brennan, who flanked a third man. The man in the center held up his hands. "Somebody needs to shoot me, quick, because you're going to be attacked in less than five minutes."

As they came closer, Erin realized he was a vampire, even though a golden patina disguised his pale skin. He'd had the darkened complexion to go with his black hair, once.

"Daniel, what the hell are you talking about?" Ven called out, as everybody in the room went into a blur of action and the sound of weapons being locked and loaded surrounded Erin. Alexios and Brennan strode forward, with the man who must have been Daniel keeping pace.

Erin's amber sang out with a deep, urgent song, but it was different from the discordant, crashing sound she usually heard in the presence of vampires. This had a haunting melody that sang of soul-deep loneliness and loss. "What are you?" she asked as he came nearer.

He flashed a dark look at her that measured and dismissed her. "I am nothing you have ever encountered, gem singer. Be warned to stay far away from me and my kind, because you have the scent of Fae in your blood, and magic and Fae combine to form a most potent aphrodisiac. It's part of the reason why he wanted your sister so badly."

"What? Deirdre? Who the hell are you? What—"

"No time." He cut her off and turned to Ven. "Less than four minutes now, Atlantean. Make it look good. But first, here's what you need to know. I was there when the tolling began, and it was nothing human-made. It may very well be that your ruby is awakening and calling for its singer."

He turned his head and pinned Quinn with his black gaze. "My hope is that your sister be made well, brave one. You need to know this: Caligula's plan is to take the country back to the time when your rules and laws did not apply; when we who ride the night created our own anarchy. Everything he does is to further that end. His blood pride goes out every night to turn more and more humans to his service, against all the laws of your Congress and against the wishes of the other, more conservative vampires of power."

Daniel looked up, as if listening to something none of them could hear, then nodded. "Time's up. Shoot me and make it good, Lord Vengeance. The stomach, perhaps."

"What? What's going on?" Erin thought she might be shouting, but she didn't care. "You want us to shoot you? Where is my sister?"

The vampire flashed over to the table and grabbed a pen, then stabbed it down on the map so hard it drove into the wood and stood there, quivering back and forth. "There. Now do it, Ven. If they catch me here, I am worthless to our cause. Oh, and one more thing." He paused, eyes focused on the gun that Ven drew from his leg holster.

"Anubisa still lives. She is plotting something that even Caligula does not know, and they have spies in all three of your groups." His gaze encompassed Quinn, Ven, and Erin when he said it. Then his eyes glowed red and he curled his hands into claws. "Now!" He sprang at Ven, and Ven shot him in the stomach. Daniel howled out a bone-chilling scream of agony, and before he hit the ground the few windows that still had glass exploded inward as a swarm of vampires came screaming into the building, the rage of blood fever in their glowing red eyes.

Chapter 17

They came in fast and furious, and there were a lot of them. Ven slammed his Glock back in its holster, dismissing it as useless against the horde of vamps. He shrugged out of his long coat and used one hand to unsheathe the sword strapped to his back, while he pulled a dagger with his other.

He headed straight for Erin, who stood frozen in the center of the room, and herded her backward until her back was against a wall. "Stay here, and stay shielded," he ordered.

When she started to argue, he cut her off. "I know you want to help, but we have more experience at this. Keep yourself safe."

Alerted by the screaming sound of displaced air, he whirled around to meet the vampire diving at him. Ven hurled his dagger with deadly accuracy and it smashed into the vamp's throat. Not enough to kill a bloodsucker, but enough to slow it down.

The vamp crashed into the floor, clawing at the dagger protruding from his throat, but Ven was there in a single leap. One swift downstroke with his sword, and the vampire's head rolled away from its body. He yanked his dagger out of what was left of the vampire's neck and turned to face three more coming at him.

Everywhere he looked, Atlanteans, humans, and shape-shifters engaged in fierce hand-to-hand combat with the vamps. The rebels fought almost as fiercely as Poseidon's warriors, but they were brutally overwhelmed in number. Ven heard shots ring out, but couldn't see who was doing the shooting over the shoulders of the vampires who were suddenly on him. Stabbing, slashing, and wishing for an armful of wooden stakes, he defended himself and blocked them from where Erin stood behind him.

There was no way he would let them get to her. He tried to console himself that her shield that could block the force of a bomb was good enough to keep her safe from vampires, but then his sword got stuck in the ribs of one of the vamps, and another came at him from above and sank its fangs into his shoulder.

He leapt sideways so that he slammed the vamp's head into the stone wall, which dislodged it from his flesh. The move gave him an opening to see Erin. She stood where he'd left her, arms out, a shimmering shield of translucent light surrounding her. Two vampires were trying to get through it, and they kept hurling themselves against the shield, which bounced them back over and over again. Either they weren't very bright, or they knew something he didn't about whether repeated force would weaken her shield or her strength.

The immense force of a massive energy burst thrummed against his skin, and he looked up to see Alaric standing in front of Quinn and calling power. Ven grinned in spite of the blood dripping from his shoulder.

"Oh, you're in trouble now, bloodsuckers! My man Alaric is going to fry some vampire ass." He laughed when he said it, and the four new vampires heading for him paused briefly, probably unused to prey who weren't quaking in their boots. "Come and get me, girls," he taunted them. "I don't bite. At least, not much."

The vampires screamed out their rage, their hellish eyes glowing bloody red, and they dive-bombed him. Ven did a rolling dive to the floor and got underneath them, then leapt to his feet and slashed out with his sword, killing two of them before the other two even managed to turn around.

A woman's high, piercing scream distracted him. He whipped his head to the side in time to see Erin fall to the ground. She still held her shield intact, but it had shrunk to cover her by mere inches. Four vampires now beat on the shield around her.

A killing rage washed through him in a red tide of fury. He flashed away from the two vamps attacking him and barreled into the ones surrounding Erin. Slashing and stabbing, he made short work of the first two, but then a searing pain pierced his back. He looked down to see the tip of a dagger protruding from the left side of his abdomen, and forced himself to leap sideways away from the vamps, pushing off on legs suddenly gone numb. He smashed into the ground on his side, hard, and smacked his head on the concrete. Before he could attempt to reach around and pull the dagger out, the vamps were on him again. The largest of the three yanked Ven's hair and pulled his head up off the floor, baring his throat to strike.

Another piercing female scream sliced through the battle noise, but this one came from the center of the room. A huge roaring noise—so fierce that the vamps attacking Ven cringed away from the sound—followed the scream. In the next moment, a familiar pressure swirled through the room, then rocketed up to an intensity that Ven had never felt before.

None but Alaric could channel the elements with a power level even approaching that. Ven attempted another laugh, and stabbed his knife upward through the bottom of the neck of the vampire trying to bite him. "It's all over now," he began, and then the air in the warehouse went supernova. A blinding blue-green light filled the room and seemed to sear right through the skin of the bloodsuckers who were pinning him to the floor. Their skulls lit up like Halloween decorations, and the unearthly blue light sizzled out from behind their eye sockets and their open mouths. The hideous stink of burning vampire wafted over him and he rolled out from underneath them, swearing when the handle of the dagger still protruding from his side pounded into the floor and stabbed deeper into his flesh.

He tried to push himself up, but was unable to fight his way through the pressure from the energy still crackling through the air. He shoved the smoking carcass of a dead vamp out of his way so he had a clear line of sight to Erin. She was crouching against the wall, somehow still holding her shield. The bodies of three or four vampires lay on the ground in front of her, flames licking over their clothes and skin.

Something inside Ven's ears popped with a sudden release of pressure, and he tried to stand up again. This time nothing stopped him, and he ran toward Erin, scanning the room. Humans, shape-shifters, and Atlanteans alike were all down. A quick glance told him that many were wounded and some might be dead. Smoking heaps of bloodsucker littered the room, and Alaric was the only one standing, completely unharmed, blue flames surrounding him and licking at his clothes and hair. Whatever in the nine hells the priest had managed to do, Ven wanted to learn it. Soon.

He reached Erin and crouched down, wincing at the pain from his side. He put a hand back and yanked the dagger out by its hilt, tossed it across the floor, and pulled her into his arms. "Are you all right? Did they hurt you? Are you wounded?"

She pulled back and put her hand on his side, where blood was streaming down. "I'm fine. I'm not hurt. What happened to you? You're bleeding. A lot."

He shook his head. "It's nothing. Don't worry about it. If they had harmed you—" He left the rest of the sentence unspoken, not sure how to say "my universe would have ended" without freaking her out.

He was freaking out his own damn self, with the intensity of the rage that swept through him at the thought of them hurting her. He covered the wound on his side with his hand, and they stood and faced the room.

"Right now we need to help everyone else," he said.

She nodded, although her face was white with exhaustion. They stepped around the disintegrating mess of dead vampire on the floor and made it two or three steps before she grabbed his hand and stopped. "The gems, Ven. I can try to use the gems to sing healing for you."

"No! You're too exhausted, and the healing would drain even more of your strength. I'm fine, this is just a scratch."

She glared at him. "I think we need to have that conversation about you telling me what to do sooner rather than later," she said. "But not right now."

With that, she placed one hand on the entry wound and one hand on the exit wound, opened her mouth, and began to sing. Before Ven could protest, the delicate notes of her song washed over and through him in a glaze of silver light. A burning heat centered within him in the path the dagger had taken, and he somehow knew the notes of her song were calling to the molecules of his skin to knit themselves together, to heal his torn flesh.

She stopped singing, sighing with weariness. As her song trailed off, the sensation of heat penetrating his skin did, too. He looked down at his side and was unsurprised to see the flesh sealed back together, the gaping wound gone, and nothing but a thin pink line remaining where the dagger had pierced him.

"Now I'll go help everybody else," she said. But before he could utter a word, her eyes rolled back in her head and she collapsed. He caught her before she could hit the ground and lifted her in his arms, then turned and started toward Alaric, who had dropped to the ground and was cradling Quinn on his lap.

Quinn's limp body looked lifeless, and the rage in Alaric's eyes promised a screaming death by torture to those who had engineered the attack. Ven's arms tightened around Erin, and he made a grim vow to the gods, speaking the words aloud to underscore his vow. "I swear on my own life and on my honor as a Warrior of Poseidon that Caligula will not survive to hurt any under my protection again."

~~~~~

Erin fought her way to consciousness, but lay still without opening her eyes, wondering why she ached so badly in every part of her body. Pain danced behind her eyelids, pirouetting through her brain, a macabre ballet of agony. The hangover of magic use was all too familiar. The level of intensity was not.

Intensity. The battle.

Her eyes flew open. "Ven," she croaked out. Her vocal cords burned as if she'd swallowed a fire-sword. She struggled to sit up, and in an instant Ven was kneeling beside her.

"I'm here, *mi amara*. How are you feeling?"

"I feel like a boulder smashed into me," she admitted. "But other than a massive magic hangover, I think I'm fine. And you?" Suddenly frantic, she pulled his shirt aside to see his wound. "Did I do it? Are you healed?"

He showed her the healing flesh that was the only sign of the vicious stabbing, and she collapsed back against the cushions in relief. He bent and pressed a quick, hard kiss to her lips. "Thank Poseidon you are well," he said, his voice rough. "And yes, as you see, your singing healed me, but we need to talk about this propensity you have to put yourself in danger. The healing drains too much of your energy."

She mustered up a weary smile. "Add it to the list of things we need to talk about, then."

Reassured that Ven was fine, Erin finally looked around the room and recognized the gathering room in the Circle of Light headquarters. She lay on the burgundy striped couch farthest from the windows, and several men and women she recognized as being part of Quinn's group were lying on pallets on the floor and on the other couches in the room.

Justice leaned up against one wall, streaks of dark red blood staining his blue hair. His shirt was unbuttoned, and bandaging encircled his chest. Alaric, Quinn, the tiger, and the rest of the Atlanteans were nowhere to be seen.

"Is Justice badly injured? And the others? Quinn? Are they—"

Ven shook his head and his eyes darkened. "Justice is the least injured. Quinn nearly died; she took a knife thrust in her lungs. Brennan and Alexios were badly injured, as well."

She struggled to stand up, forcing her bruised and battered body to cooperate. "Let me up! I can help them. I can sing—"

"Shh," he soothed, gently pushing her back against the cushions. "Alaric has healed them all, as much as he could before even his energy faltered. That trick he pulled off nearly killed him, I think, but he won't admit it. He saw Quinn fall and went ballistic. Your friend Gennae said that somehow he pulled magic from every witch in the city and channeled it along with his own in order to send that destructo-bolt of lightning through the warehouse. It was powerful enough to incinerate every vampire in a two-block radius on contact. We found piles of melting vampire slime all around the building. Clearly they were sending reinforcements."

"What about your friend? Daniel? Was he destroyed as well?"

Ven shook his head. "I'm not sure I'd call him a friend. Seems like a friend could have warned us earlier or warded off that attack completely. To answer your question, I don't know. The last I saw, he was hitting the ground with my bullet in his gut. It seems unlikely that he could have gotten away."

A flash of something grim crossed his expression, and Erin impulsively reached out for his hand. "It's not your fault. He asked you to shoot him. He must have known the danger he was in."

His dark eyes iced over, and he pulled his hand from hers and stood up. "I feel no guilt for the death of a vampire. It has been our sworn duty for more than eleven thousand years to destroy their kind. If you are sure you are well, I need to go find Jack and ask if he will help me search for Christophe and Denal. I need their assistance to transport our wounded to Atlantis."

She nodded and watched him walk away, thinking that

whether he admitted it or not, he almost certainly regretted causing the death of even a single ally when the world seemed filled with enemies.

A familiar tingle of magic flickered at the edge of her consciousness, and she turned to see Gennae crossing the room toward her, her arms full of blankets. A young novice witch followed her with a tray of cups and mugs. Gennae nodded at Erin, then distributed the blankets, taking time to be sure her patients were comfortable. She and the novice handed out cups and mugs to any who were awake, and then Gennae carried a steaming mug over to Erin.

"Drink this, child." She handed the fragrant tea to Erin and sat on the edge of the couch near Erin's feet. "Are you well? That warrior seems to have appointed himself your personal bodyguard and would scarcely let me get near you."

Indignation furrowed her brow. "As if I would hurt you. All he kept saying was, 'We have traitors, lady, and I don't know if you're one of them.' That Alaric person finally had to tell them that he'd scanned me, and I was no traitor. The nerve of them both!"

Erin swallowed a brief glimmer of amusement at the idea of Gennae facing up against Ven and Alaric. She'd never known a witch stronger than Gennae. But then again, Ven had said that Alaric pulled power from all the witches in Seattle . . .

"Did it affect you?" She knew the question was impertinent, but she suddenly needed to know. "When Alaric pulled power from the witches, did he pull yours as well?"

"No, I shielded. But I certainly felt it." Anger and then a trace of bewilderment flashed across Gennae's normally expressionless face. "I have only felt power like that once before, many years ago, from a wizard who was channeling death magic at the time. The power this Atlantean called was free of any taint of the dark, though. It was crystalline in its purity, and evocative of an ancient power that only the eldest of the Fae describe."

"That would make sense then, since the Atlantean race seems to be as old as that of the Fae."

Gennae nodded, then reached out to touch Erin's hand. "I am afraid I must tell you that we have had bad news upon bad news tonight, Erin. Attacks occurred in several parts of the city simultaneously with the attack upon you. Several witches are dead, and others captured. One entire squad of the new paranormal ops unit was murdered; all five members were left hanging, eviscerated, off the roof of the Seattle Police Department."

Erin shuddered at the image. "Caligula? It had to be him, Gennae, and you must see why we need to destroy that monster."

For once, the older witch did not disagree. "There's more. For me, personally, the worst news of all—" Her voice broke, and she bowed her head. Erin saw the tears fall onto Gennae's clenched hands.

"What is it?" She looked around again, suddenly realizing who was missing. "Berenice and Lillian! Where are they?"

Gennae's shoulders shook with the force of her suppressed sobs. "They are gone. Missing or possibly dead. What's worse—much, much worse—is that one of them may have betrayed us."

Chapter 18

Alaric watched Quinn sleep. Even while she was asleep, incapable of conscious thought, the force of her emotions swirled around him in an aura of deep blue, wine red, and misty gray. Some had named him the most powerful high priest ever anointed by Poseidon. Yet as he stood there and stared down at the fragile human female, he knew she had the power to destroy him.

He lingered, greedy for a few more stolen moments in her presence. Not knowing how she'd somehow climbed inside his soul. Not knowing why.

Not caring.

Only certain, with the knowledge born of dark and implacable hungers, that he wanted her—her touch, her mind, her soul—more than he'd ever wanted anything before.

Also certain that his duty and his destiny forbade it.

But duty surely wouldn't deny him a single taste of her lips. He bent down silently, but as he came near, her eyes opened.

"Alaric. We have to stop meeting like this," she said, her lush, soft, kissable lips curving in a smile. Somehow, he couldn't take his eyes off her mouth. Even a priest of Poseidon, sworn to celibacy, could fantasize about her mouth.

She licked her dry lips with the tip of her tongue, and a bolt of lust slammed through him. He staggered back a step on knees suddenly gone weak.

Quinn sat up on the narrow bed, and her gaze darted around the small room the witches had given him for her. "Are you all right? Your face is a shade of gray that can't be healthy. What happened? Where are my people?"

He held up a hand to stop the flow of questions and sank down into the single chair in the room. "A moment, please. It appears that my strength is not what I might wish it to be."

A shocked awareness dawned in her eyes. "The attack. That vampire—he stabbed me—I should be dead."

She swung her legs down off the side of the bed and braced herself with her hands. "The last thing I remember was feeling like I was drowning in my own lungs, and then either I passed out or the sky exploded. And why do I have a strong feeling that you had something to do with that?"

He stared at her and wondered how he ever could have mocked the poets. Clearly it *was* possible to drown in a woman's eyes. Or at least to wish to be trapped inside her for all eternity.

But thoughts of being inside Quinn led to dark and impossible longings to strip her bare and plunge inside her right there on the bed where he'd finished healing her. To drive so far into her that she would never let him go.

Never want to let him go.

Impossible longings.

"Alaric?" Her breath caught on his name, as if she had seen his fantasies, or read the hidden corners of his mind. She was *aknasha*, and perhaps he was not shielding enough.

As he stared at her, still unable to speak, the temptation flashed through him. Just to let go, to drop his shields. To let her fully inside his barren soul, only for a few moments. Only long enough to see if she could discover any trace of the humanity that centuries of serving as Poseidon's justice might not have burned out of him.

But duty was ingrained too deep. Destiny rode him too hard for him to imagine any other path. He locked down his shields and took a deep breath. "I am sorry, Quinn. I am . . . weary."

She pushed herself off the bed to stand, unsteady on her feet. "I understand. I have the idea that I may need to thank you for saving my life again." She crossed the narrow width of the room, knelt down in front of him, and put her hands on his knees. "So, thank you."

He sat, frozen in place, the heat from her hands searing through his pants to the skin below, to the nerve endings, to the very blood cells that rushed through his veins. Caught in a sparkling prism of sensation, he knew that her gratitude would be his destruction.

"You cannot—" He could barely force the words past the pain suffocating him. "You cannot touch me, Quinn. You cannot ever touch me."

She stared up at him, her enormous eyes gone as dark as despair and filled with an anguish beyond what could possibly be borne by such a fragile human. "I know, Alaric. I know I'm not worthy to touch you. I could never be worthy. But in this one moment, stolen from reality, please let me."

He shook his head. She didn't understand. It was he who could never be worthy of her, he who could not abandon his people and his duty and Atlantis, he who had performed such unredeemable actions that he could never erase the stains from his soul. "Quinn, no, you do not understand—"

But before he could finish the sentence he did not know how to form, she rose and touched her lips to his, and his world shattered. He leapt up in one powerful movement and yanked her into his arms and kissed her with all the passion and fury and urgent need that had been clawing at him since the first time he'd seen her face. She wrapped her arms around him and kissed him back, fervent longing in her taste, in her touch, in the glory of her warm and welcoming mouth.

He kissed her, his arms wrapped so tightly around her that a distant, sane part of his mind recognized that he might hurt her and he loosened his fierce hold, just a fraction. Not enough to let her go; he could never let her go.

She pulled back for a moment to draw a breath, and he pressed kisses to her face and neck and cherished her with a stream of words in Atlantean, words she could not understand, words she could not know spoke of longing and need and desperate, soul-deep hunger.

He lifted his face to claim her lips again, and saw the iridescent sparkle of her tears as they streamed down her face. "I knew it would be like this between us, Alaric," she whispered. "I knew, and I knew it would be so much worse for me if I ever touched you. If I ever had a single taste of what I can never find or have or hold."

Pain sliced through him, agony so fierce and grinding that his back arched from the strength of it and he jerked, startled, when his head bumped the ceiling of the room. He blinked and looked down, only to realize that he had floated, carrying her, several feet off the ground. He focused enough of his waning energy to gently lower them so that their feet touched the floor again, and then, his arms still tightly wrapped around her, he kissed the tears as they fell from her eyes.

"You honor me with your tears, *mi amara*," he whispered. "I cannot be what you need, but know this. There has never walked the earth or the waters of the oceans a more worthy woman than you. Your courage and spirit shine brightly enough to pierce the most evil darkness. If I could have nothing else in this lifetime or the next, I would wish for an eternity at your side."

She inhaled sharply, a harsh sound of pain that crushed the fragments of his heart that still remained in his chest. "Alaric, if you only knew . . . The things I've done. I can't—"

He could no more stop himself than he could cease his need for breath. He bent to kiss her again, to somehow claim a kiss that would suffice to warm the next several centuries of his barren, lonely existence, but then stopped, alerted by a noise in the corridor. He flashed to stand between Quinn and the door a mere second before it slammed open.

Denal stood there, misery etched in every line of his face. "Conlan sent a message to us with one of the warrior trainees. It's Riley. She's worse. If we don't get Erin and the Nereid's Heart back to Atlantis in the next seventy-two hours, Marie says Riley may die."

◦~~~◦

Ven drained the last of the coffee from his mug and refilled it, holding the pot up in a silent question to the rest of the room. The kitchen incongruously smelled like butter and cinnamon, homey scents that jarred with the grim mood of determination and despair that rode the room's inhabitants.

Only Quinn and Erin nodded yes, so he poured the remaining coffee from the carafe into their mugs, walking past Justice, who sat with his head propped up in his hands. The head wound must be causing him pain, not to mention the slice across his chest he'd taken from a vamp's sword, but the warrior had refused to allow any of the witches or Alaric to expend healing energy on him.

Alaric sat in a chair as far from Quinn as was physically possible in the spacious yellow and white kitchen, but the heat in the looks that the two of them kept shooting at each other was likely to set the place on fire. Ven didn't know when he'd ever seen such naked anguish on the priest's face, except maybe for when they'd learned that Anubisa had taken Conlan.

Gennae sat near Erin, speaking into her ear in a low tone, and Ven's hands itched to go lift his gem singer into his arms and get her far, far away from this damned town. Away from the entire fucking state. He'd kidnap her if he had to, if only so much more than their own lives weren't at stake.

He studied the weary droop to her head, the way she kept tucking her blond curls behind her ears in a nervous gesture, and amended that last thought. If her life were in danger, he might kidnap her anyway. Not that she'd ever forgive him if she believed Riley died through her own inaction.

Not that he'd ever forgive himself. The choice of risking Erin's life or risking the lives of Riley and the baby ate at him worse than any torture that Anubisa could ever have planned. Of course, the vampire goddess was alive, according to Daniel. So maybe she'd had one of her unholy hands in the making of this dilemma.

Denal stumbled into the room, grief and exhaustion harsh in the lines around his mouth and eyes. "Brennan—he almost died, didn't he? And Alexios, he's still in bad shape, too. If I'd been there, maybe I could have—"

"Maybe you could have been killed or nearly killed, too," Justice said, clenching his hands into fists and slamming one on the table. "We need to find out who the traitor is. They know every step we're making, and they're coming after us in numbers large enough to wipe us out."

Gennae nodded. "We are sadly afraid that one of our ruling three is possibly a traitor. I can hardly countenance it, but the evidence suggests that Berenice betrayed us to Caligula and his blood pride either captured or killed Lillian." Her voice contained only a hint of unsteadiness, and Ven got the idea that the women were very close to her but she'd be damned if she'd show any weakness.

Gotta admire that in a witch.

Erin's hands tightened on her mug until her knuckles went white. "Berenice," she said, all but spitting out the name. "I knew she was up to no good. Always poking and prodding at me with her jibes, trying to get me to give up my training and forget about my plan for revenge against that monster."

As if she remembered that he'd named himself a monster, Erin's gaze sought out Ven.

"They're after you," he said flatly. "They were after you in the attack here, and they were trying with everything they had to get through your shield tonight. Caligula wants you for some reason, and he's throwing everything he's got at us to try to get you."

The little color she'd had in her face drained out at the words, but she squared her shoulders and lifted her chin. "Well, he's not going to get me."

"Don't worry, little witch. He'll have to go through me to get to you, and that's not going to happen," Ven promised, amazed again at her courage. Amazed and—however reluctantly—impressed.

"It's not just about her, though, Ven," Denal said. "Christophe and I scoured the city. You wouldn't believe the destruction. The vamps tore through town in the space of an hour, from what we could learn. Anybody in their path is either dead or captured, probably to be turned. The P-Ops unit was caught completely off guard, and one entire squad is dead. Brutally murdered and left as a warning."

Christophe came through the doorway from the hall. "All clear outside," he said. "Whatever wards you've got on this place are apparently vamp-proof; we found more than a dozen smoking piles of decaying vamp slime around the perimeter. Two of your witches, one of our men, and Jack and a few of Quinn's shifters are patrolling outside."

"The wards of countless witches for more than a century protect this building," Gennae replied, a hint of pride in her tone. "They will not get inside."

"Wards are all well and good, but this ancient Roman emperor has entered the demolition age, don't forget," Ven said. "If he drops another bomb and Erin—or somebody who is awake and alert and can shield—isn't around, *kaboom!* So much for your wards."

Gennae shuddered but didn't disagree. Erin stood up. "Well, Erin isn't going to be around. I've changed my mind. He wants me, and he's going to get me. If that will stop this carnage, I will gladly go and slit his throat in person." The fact that her hands were shaking at her sides made the determination behind her words even more impressive, in spite of the fact that Ven wasn't going to let her get anywhere near Caligula.

"No. There is no way you are going to come within a mile of that bastard," he gritted out. "We will try to find the Nereid's Heart, but then we get out, and I take you and it back to Atlantis to help Riley. When Brennan, Alexios, and Alaric are back up to full strength, we will go after Caligula with everything we've got and take him out. But you are not going to be part of it. Do you understand me?"

She glared at him. "Don't talk to me as if I were a child, Ven. That monster has my sister, and I will do anything in my power to rescue her. Quinn's intel said that the resonance from the tolling sound emanated from the caverns under Mount Rainier. That's where we believe Caligula is based, too. So, hey, we've got a twofer."

"A what?" Denal asked, looking puzzled.

"A two for one," Quinn explained. "And neither of you need think you're going anywhere without me and my people. We owe Caligula a blood debt, and I plan to repay it in full. Not to mention that if you're going to seek something that will help my sister and my unborn niece or nephew, there's no way I won't be part of that mission."

A voice like thunder on waves came from the corner where Alaric sat. "You will not risk your life in this manner," he commanded, his eyes glowing such a fierce green that Ven was mildly surprised that they didn't burn holes in Quinn's face.

But Quinn only looked back at Alaric with such sadness that it was almost a tangible presence in the room. "Don't you understand by now? That's what I do. I risk my life, in order to perhaps one day redeem it."

Alaric started to rise out of his seat, but then closed his eyes and sank back down into his chair, silent. Quinn quietly stood up and started to leave the room, shoulders bowed under some immeasurable weight. At the doorway she paused, then glanced back at Ven. "Your guy Reisen serves with us in the same way, Ven. He calls himself a dishonored warrior, and takes every suicidal mission he can come up with to help the rebellion. He's hoping his death will redeem some wrong he says he's done you—some weird Atlantean stuff about 'restoring honor to the House of Mycenae.' If you ask me, he's one of the bravest men I've ever known."

Ven said nothing. There was nothing to say. He'd be damned if he'd ever forgive the warrior who'd stolen Poseidon's Trident for his own personal glory.

Quinn shook her head. "Right. Whatever. Just thought you should know. I've got to get some rest. Somebody call me when it's time to go." She cast one last, brief look at Alaric, then left the room.

Ven filled Christophe and Denal in on what Daniel had told them about Caligula's goals, and Christophe whistled. "If his goal is to convince the humans to turn the clock back to the days before the undead and shape-shifters had any rights under law, I'd say he is well on his way. We saw a mob gathering at the federal courthouse downtown, and they weren't talking about peace, love, and forgiveness, if you get my drift."

"This is going to affect our timetable for rejoining the world of the landwalkers," Ven said grimly. "Atlantis will be needed far sooner than we'd planned if this continues."

"They don't deserve our help," Christophe sneered. "Why protect the sheep who welcomed the wolves into their herd? Do you know there are clubs where humans go to voluntarily get bitten by a vamp? What kind of madness is that? If they want to die so badly, let them."

"And then what?" The force of Alaric's fury was a tangible thing. "Once they have turned more and more humans, even witches, to join the ranks of the undead? Then what? The entire surface of the earth will eventually belong only to those who can never face the sun."

Erin suddenly laughed, a shrill, sharp sound that held no humor. "Yeah, you do the math. If two vampires are on trains traveling in opposite directions, and each of them turn two humans, who then each turn two more humans, and so on and so forth, which train full of the walking dead will get to St. Louis first?"

Ven's eyebrows shot up. "What are you talking about? What trains?"

She laughed again, but despair stared blindly at him from behind her eyes. "Nothing. It's a child's math problem, it's . . . nothing. I think Quinn's not the only one who needs to rest."

Ven shoved his chair back and stood. "We all need to rest. Alaric, we will gather our wounded in one room so you can open a portal."

Alaric shook his head. "I am too drained from the events of this night and the healings. I tried earlier to open a portal and was unable to call it to me. I must rest for at least twelve hours, perhaps more, before I even try again. And Alexios and Brennan are far too badly wounded to be moved, let alone dropped into the ocean to attempt to make the water crossing. We must stay here this night and trust to the witches' warding."

Gennae bristled a little. "We will post guards, as well. Between the guards and the warding, we will be safe. Also, dawn will be here in less than an hour, and the sun means the vampires have to go back to their holes for the day."

Ven watched Erin droop in her chair, barely able to remain upright, and came to a swift decision. "You will all stay here and rest and heal until you can open a portal, Alaric. I'm taking Erin away to someplace safe. Someplace nobody but me knows about, so there's no chance of any traitor revealing its location."

"Far away from Caligula, I would hope," Gennae said.

Erin's head jerked up, and he saw the fire in her eyes as she prepared to argue the point.

"No," he said. "Quite the opposite. We'll go where they'd never expect. We're heading right for him."

Chapter 19

Point Success,
elevation 14,158 feet, Mount Rainier

Caligula crouched on the balls of his feet, knees bent, and surveyed the predawn landscape from one of the highest points on what he had come to think of as *his* mountain. "It amuses me to think that this spot is named Point Success," he told her, "when so much of my own success has been plotted here. Perhaps when the world has turned, I will re-name this entire mountain in my honor. Mount Caligula. I would enjoy that, I think."

Deirdre did not respond, not that he'd expected her to. After the first hour, her broken cries had become wearisome, and he'd caught her mind in his, allowing her to experience all of the pain and terror but not to vocalize any of it.

She trembled, naked and bruised, on the snow in front of him. But when he lifted her chin to drink in her surrender, it was not fear he saw in her eyes, but hate.

He smiled. "Fear, hate, it all means the same to me, my love," he said, tracing the edge of one bleeding cheek with his fingertip. "The darkness of violent emotions pleases me well, regardless of their source."

He cast a measuring glance at the sky. Perhaps twenty

minutes, no more, until the sun rose. He was ancient enough to countenance some of the day's light upon his skin, but she would burn and die, and he would never risk her. Twenty minutes, though, was long enough for the dessert he'd planned.

He caught her around her waist with one arm and pulled her to him until her delicious ass nestled against his groin, then slammed his cock into her with one hard thrust, feeling something inside of her tear at his brutal entry. She opened her mouth and screamed a long, utterly silent scream, and he threw back his head and laughed. "Yes, twenty minutes is surely long enough," he said out loud, making certain that she heard him over the wordless sound of her own agony. And then he fucked her until he came, howling out his own completion mere minutes before the dawn.

Chapter 20

The backcountry, Mount Rainier

Ven watched Erin trudge along next to him on the snow-covered path, her eyes on the ground in front of her feet, weariness clear in every stumbling step she took. She'd kept insisting she could carry her own backpack until he'd over-ruled her and simply taken the damn thing. Still, traveling the mile or so from where he'd stashed the nondescript sedan Gennae had loaned him had taken more energy than she had.

"I'd travel as mist and carry you, but Alaric warned me that even channeling that much Atlantean magic so close to Caligula's hideout might warn him that we were here. We can't afford to take the chance," he said for the third or fourth time.

She nodded, not bothering to respond. He probably sounded like an old woman, hovering around her. All he wanted to do was protect her, cherish her, make love to her for the next century or two, and here they were walking right into the belly of the beast, so to speak.

As they came to the top of another rise, Erin stumbled again, and he caught her before she fell, then lifted her into his arms. "I've had enough of this. Your exhaustion is beating at me."

She didn't argue with him, which scared him more than anything else had. Simply looked up at him with the skin around her eyes bruised dark and purple, then rested her head against his shoulder. "It sings to me, Ven. Can't you hear it? The Nereid's Heart sings so loudly, calling me. It needs me to rescue it from the dark."

He listened, focusing his Atlantean hearing on the sounds of the mountain dawn, but heard nothing out of the ordinary. "I'm sorry, Erin, I don't hear it. Is it unpleasant?"

"No, it's beautiful. Magical, even. If my gemsong is apprentice music, this is the sound of the master. So lovely . . ." Her voice trailed off, and he glanced down to see her eyelids fluttering as she tried to stay awake.

"Don't fight it, *mi amara*, just rest. We're here now." He stopped in front of a tiny wooden cabin that was so well camouflaged by the trees surrounding it that it was invisible from a distance of more than eight or ten feet. Setting her gently down, he untied a complicated series of knots in a rope pull that held the door closed, and then pushed the door open. Entering before her, he was greeted by a slightly musty scent, but no errant wildlife had made the cabin into a den, so it was as clean as it had been when he'd last used it, more than eighty years ago.

Erin walked into the one-room structure behind him and stopped, staring around. "What is this place? It doesn't seem like an official park structure."

"I'm not sure the park even recognizes its existence," he said. "It's been here for more than a century, I'd guess. Maybe it was a trapper's cabin. The tradition among serious hikers is to keep it clean and use what you have need of and leave what you can spare for others." He strode over to the crude wooden shelves built onto one wall and checked out the supply of tinned goods. "Most of this is fresh enough that it will be edible, and I can always catch some game."

"No," she said, shaking her head. "I know it's stupid, but I can't stand the thought of any more death right now, not even a rabbit or bird."

He didn't argue, simply nodded and dropped their bags

on a bench, then refastened the door from the inside. The two small windows were boarded shut against the winter, but there were cracks in the walls and the room was icy.

"We need to make a fire. There's chopped wood in the fireplace, but I don't see any matches." He searched the shelves, swearing under his breath at his failure to bring any with him.

"No matter," Erin said. She moved her fingers gently in the direction of the fireplace, and the kindling under the logs sparked and flamed until a steady fire crackled.

She raised one eyebrow. "It's a simple enough trick that even first-year novices can raise fire. Isn't it something you can do with Atlantean magic?"

"Fire is the forbidden element, the only one Atlanteans cannot channel. But I'm not completely useless." He grinned and pulled a clean-looking metal coffeepot and a deep copper pot off a shelf and put them on the table. Then he chanted the words Alaric had made him repeat, over and over, sensing the magical warding that surrounded the cabin as he called it.

"You've warded the cabin," she said, eyebrows raised. "Sealed it magically?"

"Alaric taught me that trick before we left. He believes that Caligula may be able to sense Atlantean magic, and certainly Anubisa can, if she's around."

She nodded and closed her eyes, mumbling something under her breath, and he sensed the power of his warding being reinforced. "That should help, too," she said, then unzipped and pulled off her heavy coat.

Ven stared at her, trapped in the tangled emotions rushing through him, damning himself as a randy fool for wanting nothing more than to strip the clothes from her and bury himself in her, to prove in some primitive way that she was alive and unharmed. To claim her as his, for now and always.

"Ven? The water?"

"Right," he said, almost dazed. He shook his head to break free of the lust- and longing-induced daze, raised his hands and called to the elements, called to the water that was as natural and necessary to his spirit as the air he breathed.

It came immediately, spiraling in through the chinks in the walls in shimmering sheets of droplets, then coalescing into waves and curls of shining water that heated in the air under his gaze and filled the pots until it boiled and bubbled inside them.

"Gennae gave me some coffee when we were packing our provisions," he said, then bent to rummage through his backpack. When he finally found the coffee, which had somehow ended up on the bottom of his pack, and turned back to Erin triumphantly, he promptly dropped the bag from suddenly nerveless fingers. Because she stood there, in the middle of the cabin, wearing nothing but her socks.

"My feet are cold," she said, biting her lip, as if unsure of his reaction.

"I'll warm them," he promised, silently thanking Poseidon yet again for the gift of this woman, this witch, as the heat seared through him, clawing into his gut and his balls and his heart. "I need you, Erin," he managed to get out in a voice gone rough and husky with hunger. Trying to be chivalrous. Trying to show restraint. "I need you so much that I can't promise to be gentle. Are you sure?"

"I don't want gentle. I just want you." She held out her arms, and restraint vanished under a maelstrom of fierce, desperate need. He used his last remaining moments of tightly leashed control to cast the magical Atlantean wards Alaric had made him practice, and then he leapt across the small room and pulled her into his arms, exultant, exhilarated.

Erin watched him come toward her with his eyes fixed on her in the fierce, focused gaze of a predator and felt a tiny shiver of unease mixed with excitement. She'd unleashed something by her words and her action, and now she stood, bare to him in more ways than one, ready to accept the consequences. She needed to know he was alive on a visceral level, needed to erase the image of the wound in his side, the pulsing blood, that continued to haunt her.

Staring at her, capturing her in his gaze, he ripped at his clothes and piled them, along with their coats, on the wooden bench that must serve as a bed. Then he yanked the thermal sleeping bag from the bottom of his pack and spread it out. The glow from the firelight caressed the muscles of his legs as he bent over the makeshift pallet.

A humming noise started deep in her throat as she watched him, and her emeraldsong rose to meet it. His shadow shimmered across the wall and it trembled slightly. Suddenly she realized the extent of the power she had over him and she almost took a step back. Somehow, impossibly, their desires had become entangled together, and they'd become more vitally important to each other than she could understand.

He stood from arranging the bed and turned to stare at her, naked emotion in his eyes. She calmed, finally realizing on a soul-deep level that mere time had nothing to do with the need she felt for this man. It transcended the mundane reality of minutes or hours or days. Her soul called to him, and his answered.

Caught in this stolen, carefully warded moment, she didn't need anything more.

Ven pulled her over to stand in front of the fireplace with him. The heat from the flames licked at their legs, but it was nothing compared to the heat clawing at him from inside. He bent his head to kiss her, and it was a fierce branding of possession, nothing gentle in it. He drove his tongue into the heat of her mouth the way he planned to drive his cock into her body. He wanted everything that she was, and he planned to take it. May the gods help them both if she would not surrender.

Erin clung to him, melting, helpless before the primal onslaught of his passion. Some distant part of her recognized that he was staking a claim to her, but she could only comply, accept, surrender. She shivered as his hands lifted her breasts and his thumbs flicked at her nipples, gasping her delight into the heat of his mouth. He pulled his head back and stared down at her, the blue-green flames flickering in the centers of his pupils, his lips curved into a triumphant smile. "You're mine," he said, voice husky. "I'm going to taste every inch of you."

She shuddered at the stark desire in his voice and then

moaned as he knelt in front of her and fastened his mouth on the side of her breast, sucking and almost biting at the skin until she was sure that he would leave a mark. She pulled back a little, suddenly afraid of the desperation in her own response to him, but he looked up at her and growled a warning before he caught her nipple in his mouth and sucked hard. The sheer electric pleasure of it buckled her knees, and she would have fallen if he hadn't caught her, steadying her thighs in his hands, pushing them apart and pulling her closer.

He released her breast and stared down at her body with such intensity that her skin sizzled in the wake of his gaze. Then he moved one hand to draw a finger through the damp curls between her thighs and she gasped again, remembering his promise to taste her.

"Ven, no, I want to please you," she began, but he laughed, cutting her off, and her words trailed off at the sound of his laughter.

"Oh, you will please me, my little witch, my gem singer, *mi amara*," he said. "You will please me well when I have the taste of you coming in my mouth."

The words shot a thrill of sensation through her body, centering between her legs, pooling in a rush of creamy liquid desire. Then he lowered his head and put his tongue on her and she went insane, helpless to do anything but stand there, bucking against his mouth, until he drove two fingers inside of her and caressed her with the long, hard strokes of his fingers.

She screamed, and she shattered.

When Erin screamed, Ven felt her orgasm sear through her, through him, through the room. The music from her gems soared into a crescendo, and the tension in his cock and balls tightened to a fever pitch until he thought they might explode with the force of his painful, frantic desire. He licked at her and sucked on the center of her heat, continuing to plunge his fingers in and out of her until he felt the tension build to an impossible level in her limp body. She clutched at his hair and moaned. "No, Ven, I can't take any more. Please—"

He lifted his mouth from the ecstasy of her wet heat and stared up at her, his fingers stilling inside her where her tight sheath clenched around them, clutching at them as she would soon clench around his cock. "Yes, you can. You will. I am going to make you come so hard and so often this night that you will never get the taste and feel and scent of me out of your mind or body. Just as I will never have the taste of your passion out of mine."

He bent his head to her again, licked around her swollen clit, then fastened on to it with his lips and sucked, hard, as he renewed stroking inside of her with his fingers. Erin's entire body went stiff under him for an instant, and then she screamed his name, shaking and shuddering out her release into his mouth, her creamy wetness dripping down his fingers.

His own body screamed at him for his release, and he stood on shaky knees and lifted her into his arms. He strode over to the pallet and lay her down, then yanked her thighs apart and stared down at her. "Tell me what you want, Erin," he rasped out.

"I want you," she whispered. "I need you, always you, only you, Ven. I need you inside me."

The words broke the final thread of his control, and he centered his cock over her slick, wet opening and plunged in so far his sac slammed against her as he thrust in to the hilt. He stood, holding entirely still for a long moment as his body quivered with the furious pressure for him to take and take and fuck her harder and faster and then harder still.

She quivered underneath him and lifted her arms to him. "Now, Ven. Come for me, this time."

"Mine," he growled, pulling back to plunge back into her, harder and faster and deeper. "Say my name again. Tell me that you know it's me who is fucking you, claiming you, taking you for my own."

"Yes," she said, arching her hips up to meet his furious thrusting. "Ven. Yes."

Her beautiful blue eyes, blue of the sky, of innocence, of the magic she'd wrapped around his heart and soul, stared up at him, and he felt a tingle of her magic wash over him.

Then the song of her gems burst forth from the control she must have been keeping them under and swept him away, swept her away, in a fierce tsunami of passion, of heat, of powerful hunger and need.

He came harder than he ever had, so hard he thought something in his balls must be rending, pumping his seed into her for what seemed like forever, and she came with him, clenching and spasming under him and around him, milking his cock with her feminine muscles, until finally, finally, he collapsed onto her and the world faded as her music sang exultation around them.

"If that's the soul-meld, how can we ever survive it?" she whispered, her voice trembling.

He smiled at her, reveling in the feel of her, in her music, in the light and color that was her soul. "Now that we have found it, *mi amara*, how could we survive without it?"

Chapter 21

Erin woke suddenly, a warm and unfamiliar heaviness across her stomach, and stared into a pair of very amused black eyes.

"You snore," he said, laughter lacing the words.

"I do not!" Indignation warred with embarrassment. She lay there nude, zipped into the sleeping bag with him, the warmth of his arm and one leg casually thrown across her body.

She had an instant to realize that she would be happy to wake like this every morning, and then the memories of the previous day crashed through her sleep-filled mind. "Oh, Goddess, Ven." She pushed at his arm and struggled to sit up. "How could we . . . when so many others—"

"No, Erin. Don't diminish what we shared with regrets. We needed to rest and regroup, and our bodies needed the reassurance of each other. Our souls—"

"No. Please. I can't talk about that right now. We may not survive this fight with Caligula, and I can't go into it if . . . just not now."

He pulled her into his arms and held her for a long moment, saying nothing. Then he spoke against her hair, his chest rumbling beneath hers. "As you wish, *mi amara*. But there is one thing I need to tell you, as much as I may not want to do so. The soul-meld does not negate free will. You are not bound to me, if you should choose—" His voice cut off, and he stilled before inhaling a huge breath. "If you should choose another path than mine."

She pulled away from him, and this time he let her go. "The soul-meld, that's what allowed me to see inside you? What allows you to hear my music?"

"Yes. It is a pathway between the souls of two who have the ability to find love on a much higher scale of intimacy than merely physical or emotional."

She laughed a little, shaken. "So, does using formal speak help you *negate* the fact that you're centuries old and I only have a human life span? Or that we might both die in the next day or so? How does that play into everything?"

A muscle in his jaw clenched at her words, but he answered her calmly. "If you were to die, I would end my existence as well. So it would be a good idea for us to get up and make that coffee and get to work practicing for what we plan to do, wouldn't it?"

She blinked, not even sure where to start in asking about the "end my existence" part of that statement. Not sure she wanted to know the answer.

∽⌁⌐∾

After they drank coffee and ate some of the food provisions they'd brought, Ven stood before the fire, staring into the flames. The wood he'd added crackled merrily, since he'd done some Atlantean thing to sweep it clear of every drop of water and snow that had clung to it. She glanced at her watch. "We slept most of the day away, but we still have about four hours of daylight. Dark comes early in Washington in the winter. And I may need the sunlight to try some of the spells in the scroll Marie gave me."

He turned to her, face impassive. "We have part of the day

tomorrow, as well, to plan and prepare, if we need it. You also have the book from Gennae? The one from the Fae?"

"Yes, although it really ticks me off that she took so long to give it to me. She's had it since I turned twenty-one—five long years—but Berenice convinced her not to give it to me. Said I wasn't ready," she said bitterly.

"No use crying over plucked peacock feathers," he said, shrugging.

"Spilled milk."

"What?"

"We say 'no use crying over spilled milk,'" she explained, smiling a little.

"Why would you cry over spilled milk? Does that injure the cow in some way?" His brow furrowed with confusion.

"Never mind. If we survive this, we'll have a crash course on stupid human sayings."

"*When* we survive this, *mi amara*," he said, voice coated with shards of ice that she knew weren't meant for her.

"That's another thing. What does *mi amara* mean?"

His expression softened for a moment. "That's another thing we'll talk about when we survive this."

"How much time do we have, Ven? Marie and Conlan told that messenger that they could only hold Riley in stasis for forty-eight hours without risk of harm to the baby. And that she was fading, fast."

"We must locate the Nereid's Heart within the next seventy-two hours if we're going to make a difference," he said. "There is something you must know, Erin. Her system is apparently rejecting the baby as a foreign body, which puts the future of any Atlantean-human mating at risk."

The room swirled around her as the implications of that crashed into her. "Mating? You mean . . . not that we know each other well enough to even . . . but we could never . . . I mean—"

He crossed the room in two strides, knelt in front of her, and took her icy hands in his own warmer ones. "Not now, Erin. Not now. Let us add this to the list of 'things to worry about later,' okay?"

She looked around the cabin, with its bare wooden floor and walls, the pile of Ven's weapons centered on the table, the scroll and book that might teach her some way to harness her gem singer Gift in front of her, and blew out a breath. "Sure. Why not? It's an awfully long list. That's going to be one humdinger of a conversation."

"Humdinger. Humdinger." He rolled the word around in his mouth, clearly enjoying the sound of it, then the amusement faded from his face in slow degrees, leaving the icy promise of death in its wake. "Yes, we'll have a humdinger when we have destroyed the monsters. For now, we train."

~~~~~

10,000 feet beneath the cabin on Mount Rainier

Caligula watched as the cringing, cowering fools from his blood pride shuffled into the main floor of the cavern, shivering as they assembled before him. The smell of dried blood covered them all, so some success must have been achieved, but there were far fewer than the nearly two hundred he'd sent out into the night to sow fear and dread into the humans.

Far more important than the missing vampires, however, was the other who was missing. He snarled at the leaders, who he'd turned many years earlier than these newest idiots. "Where is she? How is it possible that one weak human female managed to escape all of my best and brightest—all of my most powerful?"

They bowed until their foreheads touched the damp and icy dirt of the cavern floor. "She was protected, my lord. The Atlanteans and many shape-shifters were there in the building that you sent us to. And the witches had warded their home so strongly; there was no way for us to breach it."

He bared his fangs and hissed at them, too furious to form words. The leaders began to moan, knowing that he enjoyed nothing more than killing the bearer of bad news.

Well. Perhaps not *nothing* more. He glanced at the alcove

where Deirdre was imprisoned and licked his lips. Then he turned his attention back to the fools, suddenly realizing yet another who was missing. "Where is my general? Did Drakos not lead you to them?"

"He did, my Lord, but he was injured badly by the Atlantean prince. He shot Drakos in the belly. We might have retrieved him, but even as we tried to break through the witch's shield, the Atlantean priest called power beyond anything we'd ever seen. He blasted some kind of lightning strike through the building and destroyed every one of us within a mile."

The rage built inside Caligula's skull like a vat of boiling oil, until he was certain his very brains must be seared and bubbling from the intensity. "And yet you *managed to escape this catastrophe*?" He roared so loudly that sheets of ice and dirt and stone crashed down from the walls.

"I, uh, I retreated when the electricity began to build, my lord. I saw a vampire get electrocuted in a lightning storm once, and I was—"

"You were afraid," Caligula sneered. "You were more afraid of an Atlantean lightning strike than you are of me?" He dove down at the cowering vampire. "Truly you are a fool." With one slash of his extended claws, he ripped the man's head from his shoulders and then jumped up and down on the skull, shrieking, until nothing but a featureless lump of smoking slime hissed underneath his boots.

After a few minutes more, he leashed his rage and carefully wiped first one, then the other of his boots on the bent back of one of his blood pride who still cowered on the ground. Then he sought to center himself and find calm within. If he had lost Drakos, and all he had remaining to him were imbeciles the caliber of these, then he would need to retreat and regroup before he could press further. If he lost Erin Connors because of it, her sister would pay for it in agony beyond any he'd visited upon her thus far. He wanted them both—it had gone beyond obsession to him some time ago—and he would not be denied.

But at least he had begun the work of smashing the so-called civilizing advances the humans were forcing on the undead. He and his kind were born to rule the night, not to obey puny laws made by the sheep. His gaze raked over the worthless members of his blood pride.

Well, he amended, *some* of his kind were born to rule the night. Some were simply cannon fodder. But the most powerful generals and emperors learned to tell the difference early on, or they were assassinated by those they'd once trusted.

A slight disturbance in the air interrupted his bitter memories and heralded the approach of another vampire, one with a familiar cast to his thought patterns, although they were nearly unrecognizable under the throb of agony slicing through them. A black form plummeted to the ground before him and struck the ground hard, bouncing once and then lying still. The stench of blood and pierced intestines rose rankly through the air.

Caligula cautiously rolled the bundle of bloody clothing over with one foot and stared down into the burned and battered face of his only general.

Drakos slowly opened his eyes, his entire body wincing with the effort it must have cost him. "I am here, my lord, to report. And I know how we can capture the witch. She's on her way here to us, now." He broke off, coughing and groaning, very near to permanent death.

Caligula smiled and raised one wrist to his mouth, then tore it open with his fangs. As he bent to his general and held his wrist to Drakos's mouth, he smiled the smile that had once held all of the Roman Empire in terrified thrall. "Drink, Drakos. Drink and tell me everything."

As Drakos clamped on to his wrist and began to drink, the hideous tolling noise began to pound through the cavern again, and his blood pride squawked and scrambled away, covering their ears. Caligula bared his teeth and snarled out a challenge to the earth itself. "I recognize your noise as the herald of my own dominion, whatever you are!" he shouted into the darkness. "I am Caligula, and I will rule the world!"

The noise grew even louder, until he was forced to pull

his wrist away from Drakos and cover his ears against it. Somehow, however, even over the horrible noise of the unknown bell, and though his hands covered his ears, high above him he heard Deirdre begin to laugh.

Chapter 22

The Temple of the Nereids, Atlantis

Conlan looked down at Riley's pale, sleeping form and forced himself to believe in miracles. The flickering light of the candles reflected prisms of color from the jewels surrounding the low bed in one of the Temple's many healing rooms.

He forced the words out past a throat frozen with pain. "The stasis holds?"

"Yes, I can easily hold it for the full forty-eight hours," Marie said.

He shot a hard, measuring stare at the First Maiden, noting the gray pallor and the lines of strain in her face. "Are you sure? Marie, I know I have no right to ask you to risk your own life or health—"

She shook her head. "Do not finish that thought, Your Highness. As First Maiden, it is my right and my privilege to offer aid to the women and unborn babes of our realm. Can I do less for the future heir than I do for the least of us?"

"Why? Why is this happening?" His voice was a howl of anguish, more wounded animal than man. "Why does her body reject the child?"

"The energy of her pregnancy is . . . wrong. I've never

felt anything like it before. It's not a simple miscarriage, but something fundamentally off—discordant—in the energies between mother and baby."

He stared down at Riley, who had become more important to him than his own life. His beloved, his soul, his future queen. He finally asked the question that she had forbidden him to speak, or even to think, although it gouged bloody holes in his heart to form the words. "If you took the babe?"

Marie's face paled even further, and she swayed on her feet. "I cannot, Conlan. Riley spoke to me before she agreed to the stasis, and she made me swear on my oath as First Maiden that I would do nothing that would harm her child, if there were the slightest hope that the baby might survive. No matter who might ask."

He made himself ask. "Is there that hope?"

She touched Riley's forehead with one slender hand, then looked up at him, a quiet strength in her eyes in which he desperately wanted to believe. "As long as there is life, there is hope, my prince. Now we must pray to the Goddess and to Poseidon that your brother and the gem singer are successful."

~~~~~

The cabin

Ven finished reinforcing the magical warding that Alaric had taught him, then settled back to watch Erin. She'd spread the gemstones from the velvet bag Marie had given her across the table more than two hours before, and then spent the time since staring at them. She had not moved except to lift first one, then another, stare intently at them, then place them carefully back down on the wooden surface. He'd reined in his questions and his curiosity, but when she put her head down on her arms, the muffled sound of despair sliced through him like the sharpest dagger.

He pulled her up off the bench and into his arms. "Tell me," he murmured against her hair.

"I can't do this. I don't know enough. Marie expected me to somehow instinctively know how to use these gems; how to channel their power. I'm the gem singer, woo hoo," she said bitterly. "But even though I hear their song, I don't know how to use it. I don't know how to sing their songs." Her voice caught on a sob against his chest.

"I can hear the power of the stone in the mountain calling to me, Ven. It's so loud it's like thunder in my chest and bones. Every hour, on the hour, it rings and calls me."

"If you hear it, then we can find it, Erin. It's calling out to you to find it and we will."

"But will it matter? If I can't figure out how to sing these small healing gems, how will I be able to sing the healing of a jewel so powerful that it calls me through thousands of pounds of dirt and rock? I'm not enough, Ven. What if I try and fail and Riley's baby dies?"

His heart clenched in his chest, both at the thought and at the resonance of the pain in her voice. "We won't fail. I'll be there, and I'll be your strength."

He remembered her word. "Together, we'll be a humdinger."

A tiny laugh escaped from her lips, and she looked up at him and touched his face, her eyes bright with unshed tears. "Thank you. I needed to jump off the self-pity train and get back to work."

He nodded and pressed a brief kiss to her lips. "More coffee?"

"Yes. I hope you brought a lot."

As Ven gathered the pot and bag of coffee, he glanced back at her. She'd rolled up her sleeves and was choosing another gemstone. "Sing to me, damnit," she muttered, and a grin quirked at his lips.

If anybody could lay the magical smackdown on a hunk of rock, his money would be on Erin.

~~~~~

Hours later, Erin sat half covered by the sleeping bag, surrounded by Ven's unique spicy scent, and watched him pace the tiny cabin floor. "This isn't easy for you, is it? Being inactive?"

"No. I think I'd rather be stabbed than sit around waiting."

She curled her arms around her knees and sighed. "I'm sorry I'm holding us up, I really am. But I needed time to rest. My magic is drained. Plus, I have to study the scroll and the book of the Fae that Gennae gave me, to see if there's any way I can be prepared to find and then deal with a gemstone as powerful as the Nereid's Heart. I'm worried that it will knock me out or something, because I don't know what I'm doing, and then you'll be surrounded by attacking vamps with an unconscious witch on your hands."

He crossed over to her and touched her hair. "I wasn't criticizing you in any way, please know that. You are braver than any of us have any right to expect." He clenched his hands into fists at his side, and then forced his fingers open, but not before she saw the suppressed rage in the movement. "If there were any way I could retrieve the jewel without you—"

"You can't, so forget it. Marie said the Heart would destroy anybody who wasn't a gem singer who tried to touch it. You do hear it, though? I'm not going crazy?"

He nodded. "I do hear it, but very faintly. More like a quiet reverberation that I feel under my feet than a sound, really."

"I think it's the gem singer thing. I'm attuned to it, so it blasts through me every time it starts up. It's more frequent now, did you notice? More like every forty-five minutes."

"As if it recognized your presence and wanted to make sure you noticed it?"

She forced a smile. "Yeah, well no worries there. It would be hard to miss."

He began pacing again, and she tried to think of something that would distract him before he went nuts with the enforced idleness. The slight soreness between her thighs gave her an idea, but she wanted to actually talk to the man, not become some lust-driven bimbo. The thought made her laugh. If any witch in the history of the Craft had less likelihood of becoming a bimbo, lust-driven or otherwise, she'd like to meet the woman. They could form a club: only the grim and dedicated need apply.

"That's an interesting smile. You wanna share that joke?" Ven had stopped pacing and was leaning against the wall near the door, his arms folded across his chest.

"No, that was definitely an inside joke," she said, reminding herself to work on her poker face later. If she had a later. "Tell me about yourself. Tell me about Atlantis. What does it mean to be the King's Vengeance? Is Ven a nickname from that title, or your real name? Exactly how old are you?" The questions tumbled out as fast as she could think of them. Anything to keep the calculation of probabilities associated with *later* at bay.

"The King's Vengeance is my title from birth, as the second son to the prince and heir. But it is only an honorary title until I have earned it by battle challenge."

"What does that mean? You had to challenge the old King's Vengeance to some kind of duel?"

He smiled. "Not exactly, not like your movies with the swords or pistols at dawn. But there is a component of the position being passed down from uncle to nephew. My uncle served as King's Vengeance to my father, but after—" His smile faded so quickly that she knew his uncle hadn't merely stepped down from his job.

"Was it bad?" she asked hesitantly. "I saw some of your past when we . . . with the soul-meld. But I didn't want to pry into your privacy, especially when I know how those memories can burn."

"It was obscene," he said flatly, all warmth and humanity leached from the vast, icy darkness that looked out at her through his eyes. She shivered, and the movement seemed to bring him back from some faraway place, but the iciness in his expression remained. "My mother—Anubisa tortured my mother nearly to death while she made my father watch. She has some sick, twisted vendetta against my family— especially the males of our family—and she held my father captive for nearly a year before she killed him."

"Oh, Ven, I'm so sorry. Please, you don't need to tell me this now—"

"Yes. Yes, I do. You should know what you're getting

yourself into with me," he said, his voice gone flat and dead, as if he'd given up any hope that she would want him after he told his story.

He didn't know her very well yet if he thought that, she thought. Seeing his pain and hearing what he'd suffered only made her want him more; want to comfort him and heal him and sing solace to his soul.

"It wasn't the first time she'd captured my father. She held him briefly long ago, when Conlan and I were very young, and when he came back he was changed. Drained. Silent. As if she'd broken something inside him that couldn't be repaired. My mother helped him, but I never quite believed he came all the way back." He stared at the fire, and she had the feeling he was almost talking to himself, expressing thoughts he'd never before spoken out loud.

"That's how my father was after my mother and sisters were killed," she murmured. "It was almost as if they took his heart and soul with them, and all that was left for me was his body, hollowed out, going through the motions of life without the intent or the meaning."

Ven seemed to come back to himself at her words, and she saw warmth in his gaze again. "I am sorry you had to endure so much pain so young. I wish I could take some of the anguish from you."

"I feel the same way, but we all have to carry our own burdens, don't we?" She'd meant it as a rhetorical question, but somehow it came out differently. Almost as a plea.

"No, I don't believe we do. I would have said the same thing before I saw what Conlan and Riley are to each other. But somehow they share the weight of each other's burdens and, in so doing, lighten the load of both."

She thought back to the fiercely passionate looks the two had shared, whether or not anyone was watching them, and felt a moment of sharp envy . . . that vanished under concern. "What will happen to him if she . . . if she—"

"He will end his existence," he replied, and the ice formed over his features again. "If she and her babe die, he will die as well, and I will be left, alone, the last of my bloodline."

She pushed the sleeping bag aside and stood up, then swiftly crossed the room to him. "Then we will make sure that doesn't happen, won't we?"

He pulled her into a fierce hug, and she felt his heart thundering beneath her cheek. "I cannot believe Poseidon has gifted me with you, no matter how briefly you choose to stay."

She smacked his arm. "Hey! I'm tired of that kind of talk. It sounds like you're trying to get rid of me," she joked, trying to lighten the mood a little. He rewarded her with his quick grin. "Am I so annoying that you're already trying to dump me on some other man?"

The grin vanished, and the blue-green flames flared in his pupils again. "Simply because I bow to the dictates of free will does not mean that I would not want to kill any man you took to your bed, Erin. I am a predator and have been one for nearly half a millennium. I would ask that you do not tease me about this one subject."

Her breath caught in her throat, and desire flared at the stark need in his eyes. "You have an interesting way of going from caveman to polite gentleman in one sentence, Ven. I'm not sure I'm witch enough to deal with your contradictions."

His arms tightened around her, and pain flashed so briefly in his eyes she wasn't entirely sure she'd seen it. "You are all the witch—and all the woman—that I could ever ask for, my little gem singer. Do not ever doubt it."

She rose on her toes to kiss his nose, fighting the urge to rip his shirt off and kiss him senseless. She knew they were terrific together with their clothes off. Now she wanted to know how good they were with their clothes on. Just in case.

Just in case.

Pulling away, she took the two steps to put her in front of the fire. "So Ven is your real name?"

He took a long breath before answering, but she didn't look back at him, afraid that if she saw heat mirroring hers in his eyes she would be back to the naked thing in a heartbeat.

"Yes, it is. Ven, the King's Vengeance, of the House of Atlantis. There are seven isles that comprise Atlantis, each with its own House, and the main and largest of them is also named Atlantis, and houses the rulers of the Seven Isles."

"So it's a royalty thing, I got that, and it must be hereditary. What about the other Houses? Are the rulers there dukes or earls or something like that?"

He laughed. "No, we don't have such titles. The ruling families are simply Lady and Lord, but Atlanteans from nonruling families can also earn the title of Lord or Lady for acts of valor or distinction. Marie is the sister of my friend and brother warrior, Bastien, and she has earned the title of Lady many times over, for her great service healing the childbearing women and their babies."

Erin bit her lip. "Crap. I must have broken protocol a dozen times in the brief time I was there. I never called Marie 'Lady Marie' at all. Nobody mentioned—"

"She does not allow us to use the title, saying that she is content to be simply Marie, or First Maiden in service to the Nereid Goddess."

She heard the admiration in his voice. "You think a lot of her, don't you?"

"She was always following me around when she was little. The most curious and annoying little girl child I'd ever known," he said, fond amusement in his tone. "Who could have guessed that she would grow up to be such a serene beauty?"

She felt a tiny, petty twinge of jealousy at hearing him call the other woman a serene beauty. "Yeah, she's a lot different from me," she said glumly. "Tall and elegant and serene, not short and dumpy and frazzled."

Before she heard him move, he was standing behind her, pulling her back against his chest. "Dumpy? Are you having an attack of temporary insanity brought on by standing too close to the fire? You are beautiful, and your body is so perfect that I cannot look at it without imagining you naked."

Heat rushed through her that had nothing to do with the fire, but still, she was a woman who faced facts. "My butt is way too round," she said. "It's a family trait, so I can't really hate it, but facts are facts."

He tightened his arms around her so that she was pressed against the very hard, very unmistakable evidence of his desire. "Your *butt*, as you so inelegantly name this rounded temptation, is as perfectly curved as the rest of your body." He lifted his hands to cup her breasts, and made a growling sound into her hair. "Speaking of your body . . . perhaps we could spend some of the hours until dawn wearing fewer clothes?"

She turned her neck and lifted her head and he was simply there, fitting his mouth to hers, and any doubts she had about the rightness of them being together were swept away by the heat of his touch. He kissed her deeply and urgently, and she twisted in his arms and put her own around his neck, still kissing him.

She heard a low moaning sound but wasn't sure if it came from him or from her, because the sound was captured inside of their mouths, which were locked together, their tongues first dueling for supremacy, then surrendering in a tasting, exploring dance of passion. Ven lifted her up off her feet and she wrapped her legs around his waist, still kissing him, clutching his shoulders tightly, not letting go, never wanting to let go.

Suddenly he jerked his head back from hers and stared wildly around them. "Did you hear that?"

"Did I hear what?" she asked, still dazed from their kisses.

He whispered "*wolves*" in her ear, then lowered her to the floor, saying nothing else. As he lunged for his cache of weapons, eerie sounds resonated through the cabin. It was wolves, howling out something that must have been a warning or a threat. From the sound of it, there were a lot of them.

And they were surrounding the cabin.

Chapter 23

Headquarters, Circle of Light

Alaric startled awake out of the half-dozing trance he'd put himself in to speed his recovery. A noise—something unexpected. He looked up to see Justice standing in the open doorway to Gennae's small sitting room, sword in hand.

"You should get out here, Alaric. We're being attacked, and this time it's coordinated," Justice said grimly. The blood still stained his hair a macabre shade of maroon-streaked blue, and the dark shadows under the warrior's eyes spoke of more pain from his injuries than he'd admitted.

Of course, he'd admitted to none, following the ancient warrior code of "leave the healer to guess." Alaric snarled at the thought. "I cannot properly heal that which you do not describe to me, Lord Justice."

Justice, being Justice, snarled right back at him. "Don't bother wasting your time on me, priest. There are many far worse off, including Brennan and Alexios. But right now we need to figure out what's going on out here and make it stop, because there is no fucking way in the nine hells that I will put up with night after night of attacks from these bloodsuckers." With that, he whirled around and headed down the hall toward the door. As Alaric followed, he mentally tested his readiness to call the sort of power that would proclaim to the undead exactly what—and whom—they were facing.

As he walked out the door and looked up at the dozens of vamps darkening the night sky, a sudden certainty slammed into him that the one directing these attacks knew exactly who he was dealing with—and was coming after them because of it.

Gennae stood a small distance from the front door, holding a shield over the entire building. Even from a dozen paces away, he could sense the strain in her magic. He scanned the group of heavily armed shape-shifters who stood at the front corners of the building. "Quinn and her people are on all corners?" Alaric asked.

Justice hesitated. "Quinn's people are, and Christophe is with them around back."

Alaric pounced on the omission. "Quinn?"

"Don't aim those glowing eyeballs at me, priest," Justice growled. "She and the tiger took off several hours ago. I get the feeling they were headed to Mount Rainier to help Ven and Erin, but they dodged my questions."

Alaric wanted to roar out his rage and frustration, but fought his instincts and remained silent. He sent his senses out into the air to reach for her, but found nothing. She was nowhere near then.

"If Caligula harms her, he will never again know a single peaceful moment until the time that I flay the skin from his bloodsucking bones," he said, power thrumming through his voice.

"I'm an expert at flaying, so just tell me the time and place," Justice replied, examining the edge of his sword. "For now, we should prepare. That red-haired witch doesn't look as if she can hold that shield much longer."

Alaric nodded, began to stride toward the witch, then paused. "Where are the remaining of the Seven?"

"Denal went through the water to report back to Conlan some time ago. Alexios tried to drag his broken ass out of bed, and I knocked him in the side of the head hard enough to make sure he didn't go anywhere for a while. Brennan is still unconscious." Justice cast a sharp, measuring glance at him. "Are you sure you're up to this? You don't look all that great yourself."

"Keep your worries for your own well-being, warrior," Alaric said, raising his hands to call power. "I have some vampires to incinerate."

～～

The cabin

Ven peered through a crack in the boards covering one of the windows, while Erin did the same with another. "There are at least seven here," she whispered.

"Another half dozen on this side," he said. "Those can't be ordinary wolves."

She stood with her eyes half closed and her hands held out for a moment, then shook her head. "They're not. They're shifters. There's magic out there, too. Either one of them can call magic or they've got a witch hiding in the trees."

Just then a female voice called out to them from outside the cabin. "We know you're in there, Erin. You and your Atlantean need to come out now before we smoke you out."

Erin gasped and steadied herself with one hand on the wall. "That voice! It can't be her—"

"Who?" he demanded, tossing her coat to her.

"Lillian. My friend. She's the one we thought Berenice captured . . . that must be it. They must be forcing her to do this," she said, her voice gaining strength. A little color washed back into her pale cheeks as she shrugged into her heavy jacket. "She wouldn't betray us. I know she wouldn't."

He glanced outside again. "Regardless of her motive or whether it's voluntary, we'd better do what she says. Because she's standing there with a torch, and five of those wolves just shifted into their were-shapes. I'm game to take on a crowd of eight-foot-tall monsters on my own, but I'm not going to risk you, especially since there are more of them surrounding us."

She raised her chin. "We'll see what they want. Don't forget, I have power, too."

"I'm not forgetting anything, but are you as powerful as she is? Honestly?" He kept his voice gentle, but he needed to know the facts. "Exactly what chance do you have against her?"

"It depends. I'm stronger than I let any of them know, but if she's called the dark magic, I can't match that."

"Even with your gem singer powers?"

She shook her head. "I don't know. I don't know enough about what I'm doing, yet. I need—"

"Time's up, Erin," Lillian shouted. "Come out now or we're going to see how fast old wood burns."

"Let's do it," Ven said. "Stay behind me."

"Right. Because you have a chance against an eleventh-level witch? I don't think so. Maybe you should stay behind me," she replied, her voice hardly shaking at all. He pulled her to him and kissed her, hard, then threw the door open and stepped out.

"Why does this sound so familiar?" he drawled, scanning the growing crowd of Weres facing him and flanking the gray-haired witch who stood in the center. There must have been fifteen or more, all shifted to their were-shapes.

All acting like they were in a bad freaking mood. *Great.*

"Wait, I know. Wasn't there some story about the big, bad wolf who died horribly at the end?" he continued.

One of the Weres, a huge muddy-brown hulking monster, snarled at him, displaying dripping fangs. "That makes you the little pigs, human," he growled in the distorted voice distinctive to his Were form.

Ven drew his sword. "This little pig has teeth, dog breath. State your business and get out."

The witch spoke. "Very amusing bodyguard you've found, my dear. But then you and your sisters and your bitch of a mother always were good at attracting the handsomest men around, weren't you?"

Erin flinched as if she'd taken a physical blow. "Lillian? Are they controlling you somehow? How could you . . . why could you—"

Lillian laughed, and her laughter had an edge of madness to it. "Right. Poor, weak Lillian must have somebody else pulling her strings in order to step out from behind the shadow cast by Berenice and Gennae, right? Or, ten years ago, by Gwendolyn? She took your father away from me, did you know that? Pretended to be my friend and then stole him, bedded him, and married him all before I even knew what was happening."

Erin stood next to Ven, trembling. He watched her for signs of shock with the fraction of his attention he dared take away from the Weres, who kept edging closer.

"You must be insane! My father loved my mother, and both of them were never anything more than friends to you. But no matter what you think happened, does it justify this? Hurting people who love you? Are you . . . did you have anything to do with that attack on us?"

Lillian sneered at them. "Still a little slow, aren't you? Guess it's true what they say about blondes. I helped plan that attack, you idiot. Just as I helped plan most of the attacks for the past ten years. Caligula promised me a seat on his ruling council once we've taken over. Once we rule as we were born to do."

Ven whistled, a long, slow sound of disbelief. "Are you stupid? Or did you just skip history class a lot? If you think you can trust the word of a monster like Caligula, you should have maybe had a chat with Tiberius about who held the pillow that smothered him, back in March of thirty-seven."

Erin shot him a glance, eyebrows raised.

"Hey, I'm a history buff, what can I say," he said, shrugging. "Plus my great-grandfather used to drink wine with the man occasionally."

"Shut up, shut up, *shut up!*" Lillian screeched. "I am sick to death of being ignored! Gennae and Berenice spent the past decade ignoring and overruling me on coven decisions. Your parents ignored me when they fucked their way to wedded bliss. But no one will ignore me any longer!! I'm taking over the Circle of Light tonight!" Lillian raised her arms and glowing balls of fire formed in her palms.

Erin mirrored her action, calling her own fire, and Ven interrupted them. "Wait! How are you taking over the coven if you're here? Not to douse your enthusiasm, but the Circle of Light HQ is a couple hours north of here, depending on traffic. Of course, I guess you could ride your broom," he said.

Lillian's face turned a vivid shade of purple, and she hurled one of the balls of witch fire at him. Erin threw a quick shield up, blocking it, and it bounced into a tree, which immediately exploded.

"You idiot! I'm here taking care of you while Caligula and Drakos are in Seattle! I don't know why you're his obsession, but I'm not going to stand by and watch him drool over you and your sister the way I had to watch your father drool over your mother. If you're dead, Caligula and I can focus on more important matters, like *our* plans."

The Were next to her roared what was probably supposed to be a spine-tingling, terror-inducing roar. "I give it a six point five," Ven said. "Maybe throw in an extra point for pure ugly."

The Were snarled at him and crouched, clearly preparing to attack.

"No sense of humor in the pack these days, hmm, boys?" Ven said, drawing a dagger from its sheath with his left hand and holding up his sword with his right, then he glanced at Erin, who stood frozen beside him. "Why do they always have to blather on and on about their quest for world domination, the glory of evil, blah blah blah? If you knew how many times I've had to listen to this self-serving whale shit over the centuries, you might understand how much fun I'm going to have skewering these furballs."

Erin finally seemed to snap out of the fog of pain and shock and betrayal that had paralyzed her, and she looked up at him, then back at Lillian. "One question, you traitorous bitch. What did you do with Berenice?"

Lillian's lips curved in a smile of such concentrated malice that even Ven felt the chill of it snake down his spine. Then she held up her hands again, and the balls of witch fire raised a few inches from her palms, illuminating the dark red stains coating her hands and arms. "Even you should know that I needed a blood sacrifice to call the dark. Let's just say that it didn't have to be a willing sacrifice."

Erin threw back her head and howled, a cry of such pure anger and grief that it rivaled the wolves' howls. "Then this is revenge, Lillian," she snarled out.

"Try your best, Erin," Lillian replied. "But know before you die that at least one of your sisters fell to my hand."

With that final thrust, Lillian said, "Go!" and the Weres attacked. Ven had time to see Erin throw an arrow of glowing witch fire at Lillian before the first ugly hulk of a Were was on him. He channeled water and smashed their front line with a six-foot-high tidal wave of everything he could pull to throw at them, but it only knocked them off their feet for a few moments and then they were back on the attack.

He had time to think that he'd always been better with his blades than with calling the elements, and then all he could do was defend and attack—slash and stab and slash again, ducking and rolling and leaping as he did so, cutting down first one, then another. Flashes of lightning-bright explosions of witch light illuminated the sky over them, telling the tale of Erin's battle with the traitor.

He fought furiously, slicing through hamstrings, through hearts, through necks, taking blows to his kidneys, his back, his head, claws and fangs and feet kicking and tearing at him until his skull rang from the pain and both he and his blades dripped with blood. He heard a distant roaring and realized it was him, calling Erin, calling Poseidon, shouting out his oath to protect her.

He grinned—a fierce, feral baring of teeth—and the Were coming at him hesitated for a moment, staring into his face with its beast eyes, which gave Ven time to gut it on his sword.

A loud, thunderous noise began to shake the ground around and under them, and Erin screamed. "Yes, sing to me, sing with me," she screamed, and he realized it must be the Nereid's Heart somehow responding to the gem singer. Then she started to sing, and the remaining Weres around him flinched back as if from something even scarier than Ven's blades. They clapped their paws over their ears and fell to the ground, letting loose a discordant, terrified howl, rolling and cringing on the ground. Ven started to slice heads from bodies, but the warrior that he was could not in honor take the lives of helpless, cowering victims, so he turned to face Lillian and determine the threat she posed.

Erin's song reached a high pitch far above soprano, a song that surely humpback whales would have recognized, and she threw her hands straight out in front of her and a bolt of pure silver light shot forth, straight toward Lillian. As he watched, keeping an eye on the fallen Weres and gasping for breath, Lillian's body lifted off the ground and somehow expanded, as though the light filled her and was pushing out at her flesh, trying to force its way through. Then, in an instant, the light vanished and she fell, hard, to the ground. Erin dropped her hands, bent her head, and stood, panting, apparently exhausted but unharmed.

The Weres began howling even more loudly, still cowering and rolling on the ground, so Ven ran toward the fallen witch, sword raised, prepared to take the final killing stroke and spare Erin that pain.

But when he reached her, her neck lay at an impossible angle to her head and her eyes gazed blankly at the sky.

"She's dead, Erin," he said. "She can't hurt anyone else anymore."

"I know," she said, and—for a brief moment—the pitiless goddess he'd seen in her in Atlantis shone forth from her eyes. Then the moment passed and she put a hand over her mouth and ran to the side of the cabin where she vomited, violently, into the snow.

He wanted to go to her, but there was the matter of the eight remaining Weres to deal with, and he swore viciously under his breath as he stared at them.

"Need some help with your animal control problem?" A

female voice came from behind him, startling him, and he whirled around to face a small woman sitting astride an enormous tiger. As he gaped at her, Quinn hopped off her snarling mount and walked up to him. "Jack and I are here to help."

Erin stood up, scrubbed fresh snow over her face, then walked toward them. "Quinn. It's good to see you. We have news to share."

Quinn nodded grimly while Jack stalked around the group of cowering Weres, viciously snarling at any who dared to raise their heads. "We have news, too, and it's not good."

Chapter 24

The treetops near the
Circle of Light Headquarters

Daniel stared down at the vampires circling the magical shield through his new and improved vision, which now bizarrely kaleidoscoped into a prism of infrared gone multicolored. If he'd known he'd gain this kind of power from drinking the blood of an ancient vampire, he would have drained the bastard the first time he'd met him. His wounds were entirely healed, and he felt the life force of more energy than he'd had since becoming undead pumping through his body.

Although he'd come closer to the permanent death than he ever had before in the doing of it, dragging his bloody carcass back to the mountain had sealed Caligula's trust in him. Now he would finally have the opportunity to destroy the monster, and the world would be a much better place.

At least until the next would-be conqueror popped up. He'd thought Barrabas's death would have thrown off course—even a little—the evil vampire's insidious encroachment of power over the human political infrastructure. But even after permanent death, Barrabas's influence continued to spread. The perfect example of what a good strategist with absolutely no boundaries could accomplish.

Daniel watched the members of Caligula's blood pride scurrying along the edges of the shield below and admitted the grim truth to himself. Four days out of five, he was discouraged enough to consider facing the true death. If he hadn't met the Atlanteans and Quinn and finally had partners in his covert efforts, he certainly would have done it sooner. Life—even undead life—needs hope, and Daniel was all out of that.

"Drakos!" Caligula thundered at him. "Get over here and help me determine how to break through that witch's shield!"

Daniel nodded and floated through the treetops toward his so-called master. *Soon. The very first chance I get, Caligula, your ass is mine.*

～～～

The cabin

Ven entered the cabin and his gaze immediately went to Erin, who sat curled up into a ball on their sleeping bags. She'd probably drained all her power again, but somehow she'd overpowered a witch who sat two levels ahead of her on the power grid, or whatever the magical folk called it. Unless he was reading her wrong, she'd also killed her first person, which was never an easy thing to get past.

It never should *be an easy thing to get past,* he thought grimly, *no matter whether it was your first kill or your hundredth kill.* Even if, like him, you'd killed so many you couldn't even keep track anymore. Killing was killing, and the gods more than likely kept some kind of giant scorecard until the end of your days. If they did, surely they'd note Erin's courage, which had shone more brightly than her witch fire. He walked over to her and pulled her onto his lap, then simply sat in silence, arms encircling her, and breathed in the scent of her hair.

The door banged open and Jack, in human form now,

although he didn't take up all that much less space on two legs, strode in with Quinn right behind him. "They didn't know anything about Caligula's plans," Jack said, brushing wet snow off his hair. "They were way down on the food chain, so to speak."

Ven raised an eyebrow. "They *were* way down on the food chain?"

Jack's eyes looked more big cat than human when he replied. "Yeah. They were."

Quinn's face was nearly as pale as Erin's, and her eyes had gone flat and dead. Either she was a stone-cold killer or she retreated from the world when she was forced to do horrible things in the name of her cause. *Their* cause, he silently amended. Knowing Riley, Ven was pretty sure that Quinn was no cold-blooded murderer. So it must be an extremely tough road that she walked. Even as Ven admired Quinn's dedication and her courage, he promised himself that Erin would never need to face that bleak path.

"There's coffee," Erin said, her voice nearly inaudible. "And some canned food on the shelves and nonperishable stuff we brought with us."

Quinn aimed her intense focus at Erin. "You don't need to play hostess, gem singer. We can—" She broke off midsentence and swiftly crossed the room to crouch down in front of Erin. "Oh, no, Erin. You can't feel like that over her. She was a traitor."

"What?" Erin lifted her head, then dropped it back on her knees. "Oh, the emotional empath thing. Riley's sister, so you, too, I guess. Well, stay out of my head." There was no heat behind her words, just a dull apathy that scared Ven more than an emotional outburst would have.

"Ven, Jack. Get out," Quinn said, standing. "Now."

Ven's arms tightened around Erin. "I don't know what you—"

"Get. Out. Now," she repeated, but she didn't take her gaze from Erin, and the sympathy and understanding in Quinn's eyes decided him.

"Okay with you, *mi amara?*" he murmured to Erin.

She shrugged, but then moved off of his lap, so he took that as assent and stood up to leave. "I'll be right outside if you need me."

Quinn quirked an amused grin at him. "I'm not as scary as I look, big brother."

"Big . . ." He clapped a hand to his forehead. "Oh, by the gods, I never considered that. When Riley and Conlan wed, we'll be family. How am I going to survive that?" he groaned.

Quinn reached up and ruffled his hair, as if he were a tiny youngling. "It's okay, Bro. I promise to take it easy on you at the family reunions."

Still groaning, he followed Jack out of the cabin, sneaking a final glance at Erin as he went through the door. He was relieved to see a shadow of a smile on her face. Maybe Quinn could impart some measure of peace where he could not. All he could think to do was love her senseless until she slept, and that wasn't really practical at the moment.

"Come on, fish boy," Jack said. "I'll teach you how to hunt for dinner that doesn't come out of a can."

Ven waited until the golden shimmer of transformation ended and the tiger stood where the man had been before he answered. "That's fish man to you, fur face."

The tiger growled and bounded off into the woods, and Ven followed, shaking his head at the realization that his circle of friends suddenly included witches, rebels, and tigers.

~~~~

Headquarters, Circle of Light

Justice stalked the perimeter of the shield and thought for the third or fourth time in twenty minutes that he was glad to be on Alaric's side. The priest had added his strength to Gennae's, and the shield was entirely impermeable to the maddened vamps who repeatedly hurled their bodies against it, fangs gnashing and red eyes glowing with murderous intent.

He swore under his breath as one of them dove straight at him out of the overhanging trees and smacked off the shield inches from his head. Scanning the treetops, he caught a glimpse of somebody who looked a lot like Daniel, at least from a distance, which would mean the vampire had survived Alaric's blast at the warehouse.

Justice didn't know whether to call that a plus or minus. Daniel in Drakos guise would have a plan to get at Caligula from the inside. Or so the theory went.

Personally, the idea that Daniel/Drakos was playing them all as some sort of undead double agent had crossed Justice's mind more than once. The vamp looked like a man with secrets, and Justice was definitely in a position to recognize secrets. Like calling to like.

Not that Justice could ever tell his. At least to anyone he didn't want to kill.

"Justice," Alaric called out to him. "I think we need a plan. That is Caligula with Drakos, and he is commanding this attack. But if I release the shields to retaliate, these vampires will overtake the field."

"They cannot enter the building without being invited, isn't that true?"

"It should be true, with the warding, especially. But the arcane rules of vampire abilities as pertains to public buildings may hold sway here," Alaric replied, his eyes glowing a fierce emerald green.

Gennae lowered her arms. "Thank you for humoring me, but it's clear you're holding this shield without me, Alaric. Perhaps if you release it to me, you could step through in the moment we transfer? And we have had vampires attempt to gain entrance to the headquarters below, with very bad results for them."

Justice narrowed his eyes. "I'm not sure what you mean by 'very bad results,' but a couple of things spring to mind. One, they could have been faking in order to get you to let your guard down. Two, what may affect a baby vamp is not going to be the same thing that affects a master vamp as old as Caligula."

"If they were faking, spontaneously catching fire as they forced themselves past our wards is a pretty convincing way to do it," she snapped. "And I am well aware of the power of ancient vampires. But you Atlanteans have fought them for centuries, haven't you?"

Alaric inclined his head. "We have, lady. But never until recently have we had to combat coordinated attacks. The undead are not the community type, nor have they ever been, and defeating isolated attackers is an entirely different proposition."

Christophe came running around the edge of the building. "I don't know how deep that shield runs, but the vamps behind the building just started digging underneath it."

Alaric swore viciously in Atlantean, then his eyes glowed even more brightly and Justice's skin sizzled with the zing of sheer, raw power being channeled by the most powerful high priest in the history of Atlantis. Several seconds passed, and then he nodded. "The shield now runs twelve feet deep into the ground, and I can extend it into a seamless sphere around this place if need be."

"Did I mention I'm glad I'm on your side?" Justice muttered before beginning to pace back and forth in front of the shield's edge again. "Why not just let them in? If they can't get in the building—although, granted, that's a big *if*—we're only outnumbered eight or nine to one."

"Which would be reasonable for Atlantean warriors, perhaps, but we have tired and wounded shape-shifters fighting with us, and we are not at full strength, either," Alaric said, glancing down at the bandages wrapped around Justice's chest that gleamed white in the darkness under his open shirt.

"It's a scratch," he protested. He scanned their group, grudgingly recognizing the weary, stumbling gait of exhaustion in most of the shape-shifters, many of whom were recovering from their own *scratches*.

"Okay, you may have a point," Justice admitted. "Then what's the plan?"

"Gennae's plan has merit. I will go out and . . . discuss . . . the situation with Caligula, while she holds the shield," Alaric said, baring his teeth.

"If *discuss* is Atlantean for 'wipe the murdering monster off the face of the planet,' then I would be completely in agreement with that plan," Gennae said.

"You're not going anywhere without me," Justice snarled, daring the priest to disagree.

"Same goes," Christophe stated, drawing his daggers.

Alaric raised one black eyebrow. "I would not have expected otherwise."

Chapter 25

The cabin

Erin warily raised her head to see what Quinn was doing. The woman had been silent for several minutes; she hadn't spoken a word since she'd ordered the men out of the cabin. Quinn sat on the floor, cross-legged, in front of the fire, staring into the flames.

"Did you want to talk to me or something? Girls-only pep talk? Maybe a bunch of 'it's all right to kill in the name of Life, Liberty, and the American Way'?" The words came out with more weariness and less sarcasm than she'd intended. Maybe she just didn't have any fight left in her.

Quinn pinned her with a dark look. "Is that what you need to hear? Will that make it better? If so, rah rah, go, you."

Confusion broke through the numbness. "What did you want to talk to me about, then?"

Quinn sighed. "Mostly, I just wanted to listen. Do you think that it gets easier to kill just because you've done it more than once? It doesn't. If anything, it gets harder."

"Then how do you do it? How do you do what you do, day after day, month after month?" Erin clenched her hands together so tightly her knuckles turned white. "Even staking vampires isn't a black and white proposition—many of them are neighbors, friends, contributing members of society who just happen to drink blood. How can you look at faces that are exactly like ours and kill them?"

"Some of your best friends are vamps, is that it?" Quinn said bitterly. "Look, you're not telling me anything I don't know. Like I said, it gets harder and harder. Every life taken, even an undead life, is another black mark on my record. Another stain on my soul." She laughed. "Listen to me: 'stain on my soul.' Suddenly I'm a drama queen."

"What if it is? What if my soul is irreparably stained because I killed Lillian tonight? She wasn't a shape-shifter or a vampire. She was human."

"She was a monster," Quinn said flatly. "Ven told us that she boasted about killing both your sister and your fellow witch and helping to plan the murder of your family. Do you really think she deserved to live?"

Erin stared at Quinn. The light from the fire played over her face like an eerie foreshadowing of the flames of hell. Erin shook off the fanciful sense of dread and considered the question for a while. Finally, she shook her head. "I did what I had to do, and I'd do it again. It was self-defense, and I was defending Ven, because even if he'd killed every one of those Weres, she would have murdered him, too. But don't ask me to decide who deserves to live. That is a question for the Goddess."

Quinn turned back to face the fire. "Maybe. Or maybe your Goddess and my God gave us the power to defeat them as an answer to the question. Either way, I refuse to let this go on any longer. I can't stand by and pretend not to notice that the vampires are taking over our political leadership, enacting law after law in favor of the undead over humans. I can't stand by and let groups of rogue shape-shifters kill humans who get caught up in their territorial struggles."

A wave of hopeless despair washed over Erin. "Can we make a difference, Quinn? Do you really believe that your efforts amount to anything? I feel like we're all playing a carnival game for giants. Do you know that game where you whack the plastic gophers with a mallet as they pop up out of the holes? No matter how many you hit, more keep coming and coming?"

A ghost of a smile crossed Quinn's face. "Yes, I've played that game. Back when I had time for things like street fairs and carnivals. Seems like ages ago."

"Well, the vampires with plans to take over the human race and treat us as sheep, the rogue Weres, more and more of the witches who are turning to the dark—they're the gophers. They're everywhere, and it feels more and more like a never-ending game where the odds are stacked against us," Erin said.

"What you did tonight was not useless or futile. It wasn't wrong, either, no matter what the law might say. The legislation hasn't caught up with what we need to do to put down this threat. Until we remove the vampire conspiracy, it never will. Because they're the ones writing the laws, and anybody who disagrees conveniently disappears." Quinn pushed another log into the fire. "We have to keep the faith, Erin."

"I don't know. I—"

Quinn smacked her fist into her palm. "Stop! You don't have time for self-pity. I need you to be strong to find this ruby and save my sister. She's the only goodness left in my life, and if she and the baby . . ." She shook her head, tears streaming down her face.

Anger and resolve, in equal measures, swept through Erin and sent steel through her backbone. "I'm not feeling sorry for myself, Quinn, believe me. I don't know if you even will understand what this means, but I channeled the Wilding tonight without any backlash. The gem singing seems to have enhanced my powers enormously. Suddenly, I'm not so worried about coven law telling me not to call the Wilding, either. So why don't we figure out exactly how we're going to go about finding the Nereid's Heart in the morning."

Quinn stared at her for a long moment, then smiled and

stood up. "I knew back when you knocked the boys on their asses that I was going to like you."

"Same goes."

~~~

Headquarters, Circle of Light

Justice stood, sword held high, at the edge of the shield, next to Alaric. Christophe stood on the priest's other side, and the strongest of the shape-shifters spread out on either side of them. Gennae stood well back, protected by several men as she held the shield.

"Now!" Alaric snapped out the command, and the shield vanished. He, Justice, and Christophe stepped forward and the shield shimmered into existence almost immediately behind them. A couple of the vampires who'd been in the process of hurling themselves against the shield had broken through, but Justice was grimly pleased to see the shifters ripping them to shreds behind the shield.

"Shall we talk, then, Emperor?" Alaric called out.

Justice couldn't believe he'd accord the fiend the respect of the title, but it was probably a strategy move. Vamps were notoriously vain, and Alaric and Conlan nearly matched Justice's father for bold and intelligent strategy. He spat on the ground at the thought of his father, then shoved the bitter memories out of his mind and focused on the present.

Caligula floated down from the trees, with Daniel at his side. *Drakos.* Must remember to call him Drakos, or the jig was up.

"You dare much, Atlantean," Caligula hissed. He'd put power and his thrall voice behind the words; they reverberated across the dark lawn. "Yet clearly you know who I am."

"I know you, Germanicus. I know your cruelty, your excesses, and your insanity," Alaric proclaimed in a voice like thunder over tempest waves. "I am the high priest of Poseidon, and your reign is nearly over."

Caligula sneered. "I once named my horse after a priest. Incitatus at least had a jeweled necklace and a house with a golden manger. All you have is a ragtag bunch of warriors who belong in the last century."

Alaric raised one eyebrow. "At Poseidon's grace, I wield power you cannot imagine. A horse, one would imagine, gave a self-proclaimed god such as yourself exactly what you deserved. Steaming piles of it, in fact."

Daniel leapt at Alaric, snarling. "You dare to insult him! I will enjoy ripping your head from your neck and drinking the blood that the sea god so cherishes."

Justice drove forward with his sword to block Daniel, but Alaric waved a hand almost casually and the vampire flew backward more than fifty feet until he crashed into a tree and fell to the ground.

"I don't have time for foolish displays of bravado by your underlings. What do you want here?" Alaric asked.

"I want the blood of humanity running freely underneath the soles of my boots," Caligula said, baring his fangs. "I want to crush your underwater continent so that you never even think of coming back to the surface to challenge me again. I want to build floating palaces that far exceed my vessels that the humans found in Lake Nemi." He laughed. "Do you want a detailed list? How about just one final desire? I want all of humanity to tremble at the sound of my name."

Justice rolled his eyes. " 'Let them hate me, so long as they fear me,' right? Can't you come up with new material after nearly two thousand years?"

Caligula turned his glowing eyes toward Justice. Before Justice could look away, he was falling into the red flames, falling into the thrall of a master vampire. He heard a vast roaring noise, and suddenly Daniel was rushing up toward him and leaping on top of him, knocking Justice's sword out of his hand.

Daniel bared his fangs and turned Justice's head to the side before the fog of thrall had fully lifted. Then the vampire stuck, driving his fangs into the side of Justice's neck. Justice clenched his jaw so tightly his teeth ground together, to keep from howling at the pain of it. Daniel almost instantly withdrew his fangs, but did not lift his head.

"There's a warded opening at the top of Point Success," Daniel whispered in his ear. "Find it and help me save your friends. Now yell, loud."

Justice yelled, putting his lungs into it. It wasn't that difficult to do. That damn bite had *hurt*. Daniel shoved at Justice's leg to push himself up, making a show of wiping blood off his mouth.

"Something about these Atlanteans tastes better than ordinary human, don't you think?" Daniel said.

Caligula and Alaric stood in a silent face-off, both of them calling power, in different ways. Both of them unwilling to back down. Justice dragged himself up, making sure to act like he'd been drained of more blood than he could afford to lose, especially in his wounded state. He staggered a step, scanning the area for Christophe.

"He's over by the shield, Justice," Alaric said, only a hint of strain in his voice. "I think his leg may be broken. Perhaps you would check on him."

Justice limped off slowly, careful to stay in hearing range.

Caligula was the first to step back. "This is futile. We are equally matched, priest. Give me the witch and I'll call off the siege."

"Which witch? As you might guess, the coven headquarters is currently housing more than a few," Alaric replied calmly.

"Erin Connors. Give her to me and I will give you my word to leave the rest of them alone."

"Your word means nothing, vampire. It meant nothing when you yet lived," Alaric said. "We will give you no one."

Christophe, who lay on the ground by the shield half propped on his elbows, started laughing. "You stupid vampire!! You spent all this time and effort to get a witch who isn't even here! She's halfway to Canada by now!"

Alaric slashed a hand toward the ground and flicked a glare at Christophe. "Silence! Tell them nothing."

But it was too late. Caligula leapt into the air and floated over the top of the shield, staring down at it. When he was centered over the highest point of the glowing magical barrier, he floated down until he was touching it with his hands and face, then stayed there for several seconds.

Suddenly he shrieked, a sound like a demon from hell rising through the dark, and spiraled up into the air so fast Justice could barely see him move.

"To me, Drakos! She's gone, and I know exactly where she must have gone," Caligula shouted down at them. "Point Success truly will earn its name very soon."

Daniel cast one last glance at Justice, who nodded. Then he shot into the air to follow the insane emperor, and all of the rest of the bloodsuckers scrambled to follow.

Alaric strode over to Christophe and crouched down to put his hands over the fallen warrior's leg, which was pretty obviously broken in two different pieces. As the blue-green light flared between his hands and Christophe's legs, he said nothing. But when he was done, and Christophe stretched his now-healed leg, Alaric met Justice's gaze.

"What did he say to you?" Alaric said.

"There's a warded opening at the top of Point Success," Justice said.

"Anything else?"

"No." Justice started to shake his head, and then remembered that strange push against his pants. He put his hand in his pocket and drew out a crumpled piece of paper. "Directions and a crudely drawn map," he said, holding it out for Alaric and Christophe to see.

Alaric tilted his head toward the sky again. "I was pleased with your attempted misdirection of Canada, but I would have preferred that you not give away the fact that the gem singer had gone, Christophe."

Christophe inclined his head. "I am sorry for that. I'd hoped to send him off on a false lead."

Alaric still stared at the sky, in the direction where the vampires had vanished. "Did you notice the direction they took?"

"South," Justice said. "They went south."

Gennae shouted at them, waving her arms to catch their attention. The shield shimmered and vanished. "I don't think we need this anymore, do you? But your warrior needs you, Alaric. Brennan is worse."

Alaric nodded at the witch. "I will attend him momentarily," he called out, then turned to the warriors. "It would appear that Erin and Ven are in more concentrated danger than we had hoped, and I am drained beyond use for much except basic healing."

"I'm going after them," Justice said, sheathing his sword. "Their idea of a stealth mission just got blown to the nine hells, in any event."

"I will go, as well," Christophe said, but he stumbled when he took his first step.

"You will stay here and continue healing," Alaric commanded. "You are weak enough to be only a hindrance to Justice, but I have need of your skills here to help protect the coven."

Anger flared in Christophe's eyes, but he whirled and headed for the building.

"Go now, Justice. May Poseidon be with you, that you may save Erin and Riley and the baby," Alaric said. "Help Ven to assist the gem singer in singing the Nereid's Heart out of the stone, or the future of all Atlantis is in jeopardy."

Before Justice could move, Alaric caught his shoulder in a firm grip and heat seared through his body. The priest's eyes flared brightly, then dimmed back to their normal green, and Justice felt a renewed surge of energy pour through him and a lessening of the pain from his head and the dagger slice across his chest. He clasped Alaric's arm in a gesture of thanks and farewell, and then he shimmered into mist and shot into the sky, following the trail left by the vamps.

The future of all Atlantis is resting on my shoulders, after all these centuries of anonymity, he thought, as he soared over the treetops.

We're all doomed.

Chapter 26

The cabin

Ven waited until Jack and Quinn headed outside to patrol the perimeter, and then he took the untouched plate of food out of Erin's hands. "We'll pack this out with us in one of those sturdy plastic bags on the shelf," he said. "Definitely no littering in a national park."

"Are you really worrying about litter?" Erin asked tiredly. "We may not even survive this. Who'll carry the plastic bag out then?"

"What we need to focus on right now is rest. You must have drained your energy going up against Lillian."

She shook her head, and the firelight kissed golden highlights in her blond curls, making him want to touch her hair. Touch every part of her.

"No. I didn't," she denied. "I channeled the Wilding, and for the first time, ever, I didn't have any backlash from it. I'm not sure whether to be glad or afraid."

He sat down next to her and took her hand, needing some form of contact. Needing to touch her skin, even in such a small way. "Tell me. Tell me about the Wilding, and why it's forbidden. I don't understand why you're not making use of every means of magic at your disposal to defend yourself."

She was silent for so long that he assumed she wasn't planning to answer him.

"Is this some sort of witch secret? Your super magic handshake that you're not allowed to share with outsiders?" He grinned. "Cross my heart, I promise I can keep a secret."

A ghost of a smile crossed her face, but quickly faded. "It's not that. It's no secret. It's just that I'm beginning to believe that the traditional thinking on this subject is wrong. The rationale for never using the Wilding is that it's a dark magic. That using it could open the door to dark forces intent on usurping a witch's power."

He leaned over and tucked a loose curl behind her ear while he considered her words. "You don't believe that anymore?" he finally asked.

"I don't know what to believe. I know that my intentions are good. I know that I would fight against the dark magic with everything in me. But I also know that—right or wrong—I just killed a human being. A woman who was like family to me."

"That was self-defense. She would have killed you. She *told* you she was going to kill you. She killed your sister. She also killed Berenice—sacrificed her for the death magic. There's nothing of the dark inside you, Erin." He struggled for persuasive arguments, but didn't know how to convince her of what he knew to be true. The most basic law of nature—kill or be killed—had struck home with her in a brutal way, and her emotions were blocking out reality to protect her.

It was rational, but not particularly helpful, considering their circumstances.

She pulled her hand away from him and jumped up, then started pacing the small space. "How do you know that? How do I know it? How can I *ever* know it? Isn't that like insanity? The truly insane people never guess that they've lost touch with rationality, do they? So, maybe you never realize the dark has taken you over until you're entirely submerged."

"Or maybe it's the other way around. Maybe questioning whether you're going crazy or surrendering to the dark side of magic is a tangible sign that you're not," he countered.

She stopped and turned to face him. "I don't know, Ven. All I know is that I'm drowning and can't seem to find my way back to the surface. All I have ever wanted is to destroy Caligula and get revenge for what he did to my family. Now I'm finally about to face him, and so much more is at stake. He has my sister. He may have the Nereid's Heart, which I need to help Riley and the baby. And suddenly I'm easily channeling a type of magic I've been forbidden from using my entire life. I'm playing a game of chess against a master strategist and all the rules have changed."

"Maybe. Maybe everything you say is true. But now you have me. I'll be the knight to your queen. And we have Jack and Quinn for pawns. Or bishops. I doubt Jack would agree to be a mere pawn," he said, imagining the look on jungle boy's face if he heard himself being called a pawn. "You need to rest, Erin. We'll go after him in the morning—in the daylight. And we will succeed."

He crossed the room and pulled her into an embrace. "We'll succeed, because we have no other choice. Now we need to rest until it's my turn to stand watch. I'd like nothing more than to hold you while you sleep. Will you grant me that gift?"

She tilted her head up and flashed him a mischievous smile. "Really? You'd like *nothing* more than that?"

He groaned and dropped his hands to her hips and pressed her even closer to him, demonstrating the hardening evidence of the effect she had on him. "I think you know better than that. But you need to sleep, and there's also the problem that a certain rebel leader and weretiger could walk through the door at any minute. Once we've saved your sister, retrieved the ruby, and healed Riley, I'll have you safely back in Atlantis. Then I'll show you *exactly* what I'd like to do more than anything else. In fact, I think I'll show you for several days and nights in a row."

The sound of her low laughter tugged at something in his

chest, something he shoved out of his mind. Erin needed a warrior. He was one of the best.

Simple.

Everything that *wasn't* simple could wait until he'd had the singular pleasure of slicing Caligula's head from his body. Ven bent his face to her hair, so she wouldn't see the bloodthirsty expression on his face. He might be a monster, but it took a monster to defeat another. He would find soft words, gentle expressions, and everything she might want when his mission was complete and his woman was safe.

He lifted her into his arms and walked back to the pallet. As she curled up next to him under the blankets, he realized an undeniable truth: no matter who he had to kill to protect her, no matter what he had to do to keep her, he was never going to let her go.

∿〜∾

Quinn shivered with a bone-deep chill that wracked her body. "Look, Jack, I don't have a fur coat and this goose-down jacket isn't doing it. I think we gave them enough time to play footsie, talk about what happened, or whatever they needed to do. Let's get the Atlantean to patrol for a while. Maybe he can at least use his super-magic water powers to melt the snow and make a hot tub or something."

The tiger nudged her with its large head, then paced forward and shimmered back to human shape. The sight still awed her. Natural magic would never become ordinary to her through repeated viewing.

"You whine a lot for a kickass rebel leader, woman," Jack growled at her, the timbre of his voice still carrying a hint of his animal form. In either shape, he was pure predator.

"Yeah, whatever. And I still want to know where the extra pounds go. You're five hundred pounds, give or take, in tiger form, and, what?" She cast a measuring gaze from his head to his toes, probably four or five inches over six feet. "Maybe two fifty in human?"

"Two sixty, the last I checked," he drawled, one eyebrow raised. "Your point?"

She scrambled to catch up with him as he headed for the cabin. "That *is* my point. Where does that extra two hundred and forty pounds go? If we could figure out how you do that and bottle it, we could make a fortune."

He slowed down until she matched his stride, although she had to take two steps to his one. "Quinn, I have no idea what you're talking about. Bottle what? Make a fortune how?"

"Weight loss secrets!! Somebody uses our patented 'Tiger Super-Magic Pounds Off' formula and magically transforms her body so that she weighs fifty pounds less," she explained, biting the inside of her cheek to keep from laughing out loud.

He exploded, right on cue. "Are you nuts? First off, they'd have to be a shape-shifter. Second—"

The laugh escaped; she couldn't help it. He just looked so damn irate. He whipped his head to the side and glared down at her. "Great. *Great.* We're patrolling for vamps, after we just put down half a dozen Weres, and we've got what has all the makings of a suicide mission to face in a few hours, and you're making jokes," he grumbled.

Pain swept through her, washing out any trace of the laughter. "Don't you think I know what we're facing, Jack? Don't you think I'm doing everything I can think of to keep from falling apart? That's my sister and my niece or nephew whose lives depend on our success. Don't think I've forgotten that for even a second." To her utter humiliation, her voice broke on the words. "Sometimes a little stupid black humor is the only thing that keeps me sane."

Jack put an arm around her and awkwardly hugged her. "I'm sorry, Quinn. Sometimes I forget that our fearless leader is also a girl." The kindness in his voice threatened to break through the shield she'd put around her emotions, and she was terrified that if she started to cry, she might not stop for a long, long time. So she resorted to her usual defense— toughness.

Stepping away from him, she started walking faster. "Yeah, well, try to keep up, little kitty. And if I ever hear you call me a girl again, I'm going to break your furry balls for it."

"Thanks for the warning," he said drily. "I'm rather fond of my balls, furry or otherwise."

They tramped toward the cabin in silence, continuously scanning the ground, skies, and trees for any threat. After several minutes, Jack cleared his throat. "So. Alaric. Do I need to take him out for you?"

She stumbled, taken completely off guard by his obviously sincere offer. "No, I don't need you to try to kill the *Atlantean high priest* for me, Jack. I think they might take that rather badly. Create some kind of international incident, probably."

He shrugged. "Like I care about politics."

"Very funny. Cut it out, Jack. I'm not a girl, and I can take care of myself," she grumbled at him.

He stopped, caught her arm, and yanked her to a stop. She looked up at him, startled, and was shocked by the feral rage in his suddenly slanted tiger eyes. "You're my partner, Quinn, and no, you're not a girl. You're very much a woman. You already know I'd kill for you—or for our cause. Maybe you ought to know that I'd also die for you. If this priest is giving you a hard time, you say the word, and I'll do my best to make sure he never does it again."

Before she could think of a response, he dropped her arm and started forward again, muttering something she was sure she didn't want to hear under his breath. It took her a minute to process. Jack hadn't been talking to her as his partner. He'd been talking to her as a woman.

She felt the shockwaves of an emotional earthquake rock her mental landscape as she watched him walk away from her. Somehow in all the time they'd worked and planned and fought together, she'd forgotten one thing about Jack.

He wasn't only her partner. He was a man.

Still bemused by the sudden turn in conversational topic, she was caught off guard when a dramatic drop in the already frigid air temperature was her only warning before Justice shimmered into shape between her and Jack. Jack's tiger senses must have alerted him to the Atlantean's presence, because he whirled around, crouching low and going for one of the knives he always carried before he realized who it was and stilled his hand.

Quinn rushed forward. "Justice, what is it? News from Riley? Is she worse?"

He bent slightly in a brief bow, the moonlight through the trees dappling his hair into silvered midnight blue and black. "No, and I am sorry that my appearance should give you cause to fear on her behalf. She is unchanged, to the best of my knowledge. However, there is other news."

He filled them in on the attack and what Caligula and Daniel had said. "Unfortunately, the undead emperor now appears to realize that Erin is on her way here."

"Erin is already here," Jack said. "She and Ven are resting at the cabin. They had some excitement of their own."

Justice raised one eyebrow, and Jack told him about Lillian and the shape-shifters. "It does not appear that Caligula knew anything of Lillian's plans," Justice said. "He would not have come to Seattle after Erin if he had. Nor did Drakos mention it."

"Speaking of finding Erin, how did you find us?" Quinn asked.

"We of Atlantis can communicate on a shared path, and even when we silence the link, as now, for fear of who or what may be listening, we have the ability to sense one another to a certain extent."

"Let's move this conversation indoors," Jack said. "Quinn's freezing her ass off."

Justice flicked a not unappreciative glance down and back up Quinn's body, and she had a momentary glimpse of exactly how irresistibly sexy the warrior would be to any normal woman, before she focused her gaze on the path again.

There was that word again. *Normal*. Something she could never be. She heaved a sigh and started trudging toward the cabin. "Yeah, let's get indoors. Why did you come out here anyway, instead of heading straight for Ven, if you could track him?"

"I sensed movement in the area and wanted to scout whether you were friend or foe," Justice said.

Quinn suddenly froze midstep, and eased her hands down over the handles of her guns. "Speaking of foes," she whispered. Justice immediately drew his sword and dropped into battle stance, and Jack shimmered into the transformation in seconds. But, almost before he'd fully achieved his tiger shape, a hailstorm of darts came soaring through the air and struck him hard, piercing his thick coat. The tiger roared out his rage and fury, twisting in midair in a futile attempt to avoid the tiny missiles.

Quinn nearly staggered as she watched Jack paw at the air, snarling at the stinging darts. If they contained poison, he could die. The man who'd fought at her side, saved her life too many times to count, and offered to battle a powerful Atlantean high priest just because Alaric might be giving her a *hard time* might die in front of her.

A terrible ache started in her heart and spread outward. If he died, they would pay. All of them.

"Justice!" Quinn pitched the command in a low but urgent voice. "Do the misty thing and get out of here and warn Erin."

"I will not leave you undefended, Quinn," he snarled, whipping around in a circle to try to see their hidden attackers.

"Damn you, I don't need your help, but Erin's mission is vital." She had her guns up and pointed, her back to Justice's position, scanning the area. Jack's snarling shrieks slowly faded, and then he collapsed heavily to the ground. Ice coated Quinn's heart when she couldn't detect any sign that he was still breathing.

"Then we will both warn her," Justice said. "Prepare to defend our position and your tiger."

A new voice that held the gravel of the grave skittered across the clearing. "Oh, it's far too late for that, Atlantean. We're going to take the tiger with us for Caligula's amusement."

The vampire who stepped into the open from behind the cover of the trees wasn't one Quinn had seen before, but it wasn't like they posted their pictures on some bloodsuckers' website. He had long, ragged brown hair that fell over skeletally thin shoulders, and the same glowing red eyes that she was so damn sick of seeing. "You'll have to go through me to get to him," she said flatly. "And these guns are loaded with silver. I know it won't kill you but it will certainly slow you down."

The vamp flinched at the word *silver*, but then bared his fangs in a grotesque parody of a smile. "The silver is inconvenient, I admit, but there are only two of you."

Justice raised his sword. "Come out and play. I will fight you with one hand tied behind my back to even things up, if you like," he said icily. One glance at Justice and the concentrated focus apparent in the hard lines of his body reassured Quinn that Justice was every inch the predator that Jack was. She was suddenly fiercely glad to have him at her side, though her stomach ached at the thought of Erin and Ven, possibly asleep and defenseless, back at the cabin.

"Oh, things are as even as I care for them to be, Atlantean," rasped the vamp. He waved his hand almost casually and dozens of dark forms spilled out into the clearing from behind the trees. Some were clearly vamps, the moon reflecting a glow off their pasty-white skin. Others moved like shape-shifters, maybe kin to the wolves from earlier.

Worse—far, far worse—at least two of them were witches. Quinn opened up her emotional shields enough to discover their intent, but it was too late. Even as she aimed her guns directly at the lead vamp's face, a large rope net fell heavily down from the trees to land on top of Jack, and five or six of the attackers, hissing, snarling, and carrying another of the nets held high between them, headed toward her and Justice.

"Shoot and your tiger friend dies," the vamp shouted at her. Relief washed over Quinn. Jack must still be alive.

Quinn shot a glance to the side and saw that they'd surrounded Jack, who lay, unmoving, on the snow. She lowered her guns.

"Now! Do the mist thing and get out of here, now," she yelled at Justice, past caring that the vamps could hear her. But before he could move, a swishing sound heralded the approach of two more darts, both of which struck him in the back. Enraged, he tried to rip them out of his skin. She leapt to help him, but an arm like a block of concrete smacked into her chest and knocked her back and away from him. She stumbled and nearly fell, but the vamp caught her, and she could only watch, helpless, as Justice flailed around, his arms jerking and waving in the air in a bizarre fashion.

But it was too late. Justice's arms dropped to his sides and the sword fell out of his fingers. As she screamed and tried to get past the vampire, Justice's eyes rolled back in his head and he fell, facefirst, onto the snow.

Two of the larger men, surely shape-shifters, caught her arms and lifted her off of her feet. Another took her guns and three of her knives. She had time to hope they didn't do a more thorough search, and then the leader was strolling forward toward them.

"I'd wondered about that," he said, glowing red eyes trained on Justice, who lay silent on the ground. "If keta-mine, which works so wonderfully on the animals, would have an effect on the Atlanteans. Appears that it does."

"You didn't know? You could have killed him," she shouted at him.

He laughed. "You say that like I should be concerned about the possibility. The dose in each of those darts is enough to bring down a werewolf during the full moon, so maybe it will kill him. I guess we'll drag him along and see."

He turned his back and gestured to the others, who hefted Jack and Justice and followed. Quinn was grimly pleased that it took half a dozen of them to lift Jack's limp form.

Quinn noticed the angry looks exchanged between the two shifters holding her, and she forced a mocking smile. "Interesting the choice of dosages the vampires use, isn't it? Wonder which of you so-called allies they'll use those darts on next?"

One of them cuffed her in the face with his huge hand, splitting her lip against her teeth. As the blood ran down her chin, she savored the bitter satisfaction of seeing the doubt on their faces.

Discord and discontent among the ranks, maybe? We'll just see how we can use it to our advantage.

Quinn fought for the calm she needed to come up with options. She'd been in worse situations, but her terror over what they might do to Justice and—especially—Jack was threatening to overwhelm her reason. She tried to slow her breathing, but the head vamp trained his red gaze on her.

"I don't like the sound of this one's mouth," the leader said, coming closer. He raised one hand, and the last thing Quinn saw was his fist coming at her face.

Chapter 27

The cabin

Erin shot straight out of sleep, fighting her way through dreams slashed with fangs and claws and red, glowing eyes. She screamed and fought against the weight suffocating and trapping her.

"Hey, it's me, *mi amara*. It's Ven. Calm down."

She forced her eyes open and stared into his face. His forehead was furrowed with concern. "Ven?" She glanced down and realized the weight pinning her down was simply his arm, which had been resting across her abdomen as they slept.

"Yes, you had a bad dream. It's okay—" His soothing words abruptly cut off. "No, it's not okay. That's sunlight streaming in through the chinks in the west wall. Quinn and Jack should have woken us long before this."

He vaulted out of the bed and reached for the weapons that he always kept near, and Erin sat up hastily and pulled on her boots.

"Maybe they slept somewhere else?" She realized as she said it that it didn't make sense, a feeling he confirmed with a quick, decisive shake of his head.

"No way. They're professionals and they would have known we'd expect them to check in as they said they'd do or we'd assume the worst." He finished stowing his various daggers and his sword in their sheaths on his body and then pulled on his long leather coat to cover it all.

"So we expect the worst," she said grimly. "But it doesn't change anything. We still have to go after the Nereid's Heart now, while the sun is up and the vamps will be at their weakest."

He strode to a window and peered out through the cracks between the boards covering it, then repeated the action everywhere there was a chink or crack large enough to see through. "I don't see anybody, but that doesn't mean anything. Any shifter worth his fur will be hiding in the trees, not sitting out in the open."

He stopped, back to the door, and looked at her for a long moment, then he growled out a vicious-sounding stream of words. She might not have known the language, but it was easy enough to guess the meaning.

"Ven, quit cussing like a wounded bear and tell me what is going on in that five-hundred-year-old head of yours," she said, trying for a smile.

"I'm not five hundred yet and I'm not likely to get there at this rate," he muttered. "Look, Erin, I'm not sure I can do this."

"Do what?"

"Allow you to risk your life. Why don't you tell me how I can find this ruby and you head your pretty little ass back to Seattle and your people?"

Her mouth had fallen open back at "allow you." "I'm sorry?"

He blinked. "Why are you sorry? You have nothing to apologize for."

"I *know* I have nothing to apologize for, you . . . you . . . overbearing Atlantean dunderhead! *I'm sorry* is another way to say *excuse me*. Or—better—what the *hell* do you think you're talking about?"

"I get that you're angry at me, but—"

She finished lacing her boots and stood up. "Two words. 'Allow you.' Figure it out."

As she yanked her coat on, he crossed the room and caught her waist and lifted her up off the floor until she was equal in height to him. "My choice is this, gem singer," he said, biting off the words. "I can lead you into what is almost certainly a suicide attempt to discover a priceless, magical ruby that, from all accounts, is hidden somewhere in the middle of Caligula's home base."

"Put. Me. Down. Now."

"Fine." He glared at her but put her back on her feet on the floor, then crowded her until her back hit the wall.

"Second choice," he continued, eyes narrowed and a muscle clenching in his jaw. "I can get you out of here and safe and try to recover the ruby without you."

"Which is crazy, Ven. Marie told me that a gem singer would need to find the Nereid's Heart. Do you think it's just lying around on the ground with signs saying 'This way to the priceless ruby of Atlantis'?" She put her palms on his chest and shoved, but it was like shoving a wall.

"Right. So my other choice is to protect you and forget the ruby, and Riley and the baby will probably die."

The bleak words hung in the air between them for several seconds. Then she put her hands on the sides of his face. "It's a choice no man should have to make, Ven. Especially a warrior who lives to protect others. But you must listen to me. This isn't your choice. It's my decision to make, and I've already made it. I hope Jack and Quinn are somehow fine, but we can't worry about them right now. We have to find the ruby, and if we can destroy Caligula as we do it, so much the better. If not, we can return later for him."

She tilted her head up and pressed a gentle kiss to his lips. "It's my choice, Ven. All I can ask you to do is respect it and help me."

He wrapped one hand around the nape of her neck and bent his head to kiss her so fiercely that she was unable to do anything but hang on to his shoulders and kiss him back.

When she was completely out of breath and trembling, he finally stopped and rested his forehead against hers, groaning a little.

"Brainless and forgettable," he muttered. "What a fool."

"Hey! Those words had better not be aimed at me," she threatened him.

He stepped back and swept into a full bow. "Oh, no, my lady. Trust me, no one could ever mistake you for either brainless or forgettable. In fact, you are the most courageous, most beautiful, and most unforgettable woman I have ever known."

She had to wait a moment for her heart to stop stuttering before she could respond. "Thank you. I . . . thank you. I feel the same way about you. Well, without the woman part."

He grinned. "I like your woman parts."

She studied him, suddenly realizing exactly what he was doing. "It's not working, Ven. You can't distract me from this. We have to go, and we have to go now."

All humor vanished from his face, and the hardness in his eyes would have terrified her if she hadn't known him. Hadn't seen inside his soul. Hadn't seen the darkness that he believed defined him—and the courage that truly did.

She watched as he finalized the few preparations they needed to make and carefully doused the remaining embers of the fire with water that he casually channeled from thin air. Anticipation and anxiety warred inside her until her stomach roiled with nausea.

"Tell me we're going to succeed, Ven. Even if you don't believe it, tell me that we're going to succeed."

He stopped what he was doing and met her gaze, his own fiercely determined and utterly sincere. "We will succeed, Erin. Count on it."

He headed for the door, and she fell into place behind him, the knots in her stomach loosening somewhat. It didn't make sense—it wasn't logical in any way—but she was somehow reassured. "Well, since you have five hundred years' worth of experience, I'm guessing I should take your word for it," she said, trying for humor. "You know, I think I've said this before, but you realize you're too old for me, right? We should probably talk about the whole May-December romance thing at some point."

He smiled briefly, then his face returned to its grim lines. "Add it to the list."

As they walked out of the cabin and into the cold and sunny morning, Ven with his weapons drawn and at the ready, Erin cast one last glance at the room. "Please, Goddess, may we have time to write that list," she whispered, not knowing even as she spoke the words if she uttered a hopeless wish or a prayer.

~~~~~

Justice felt the first stirring of consciousness and realized he was being carried by his arms and legs, face down, over uneven ground on a descending path. His captors made no sound except for the harsh rasping of their breath and the ringing of boot heels on stone.

Resisting the urge to open his eyes, he gave no sign that he was waking up from whatever drug the darts had pumped into his system. The poison was strong, but his immune system was proof against all but the most virulent poisons and had undoubtedly been attacking the molecules of the foreign substance until his bloodstream was recovering from its effects. But the properties of Atlantean health and recuperative powers were not widely known, and he was counting on the attackers to believe he'd be unconscious for quite a while.

He slowly lifted one eyelid a hairsbreadth of space and saw nothing but darkness. He mentally counted off a full thirty seconds before opening his eye a little more, and still saw nothing but darkness. Vamps and shape-shifters had night vision that was superior to his, so they undoubtedly didn't need light.

As they continued their descent, he considered his options. He wasn't entirely sure the poison's effects were diluted enough for him to be able to manage the transformation to mist, at least before they could stab him with another dart.

Awake and feigning unconsciousness, he held a temporary edge. He decided to stay as he was until he could determine what had happened to Quinn and Jack. Careful not to give any hint that he'd woken up, he began counting footsteps. It was always a good survival tactic to know the direction and duration of any exit routes.

Exactly three hundred and thirty-seven steps later, the quality of light on his closed eyelids changed. Instead of the constant black, a reddish glow came through. Again, Justice cautiously raised one eyelid just enough to see that they were not walking in total darkness any longer. From his facedown position, he could see a flickering reddish-yellow glow reflected off the small pools of water on the ground. Wherever they were headed, there was either fire or torches. Either way, he'd finally be able to see what he'd gotten himself into. He couldn't look up high enough to see if any of the men following his captors held Quinn, but he did see the legs of several of them who were walking in a closely gathered group. When one of them stumbled, a long orange and black striped tail swung free and smacked the man right in the groin, prompting a howl of outrage.

Way to go, Jack.

"Keep it together, you lot," snarled the man on Justice's left, clearly a shape-shifter. "I don't want to be anything but model wolves until we find out what exactly that bastard plans to do with those vials of Special K."

The one who'd gotten his nuts smacked growled, but subsided, and then the shifter carrying Justice's right arm and leg spoke up in a low tone. "I didn't like the sound of that. The mouthy little human had a point. What *are* our supposed allies doing packing ketamine? That Calgoolie fellow has a rep for offing his help."

"It's Caligula, you illiterate asshole. Used to be a Roman emperor, right? Anyway, he says he had the Special K for the tiger, although why anybody'd want to play with a live tiger, ancient vamp or not, is beyond me. I've heard of this Jack, too. He's one of the meanest shifters around. Vamps killed his whole pride."

"That's lions. Tigers call 'em something different, I think. Streaks?"

"I don't give a square shit what they call them! Whatever the name, the result is the same. Killed his entire pack or streak or whatever, and he's been dusting vamps ever since."

"Can't say as I blame him for that. If somebody came after our pack . . ." His voice trailed off into guttural growls, and the fierce need to get his hands on a sword gripped Justice so hard he had to fight a mental battle with himself to remain limp in their grasp.

"I hear you. But that ain't our concern. We do this, we get paid, we move on. First we got to survive meeting the big man himself, and we're almost there."

They made a jerky, awkward turn to the right, bashing Justice's already wounded head against the stone wall, and then stopped. The orangey light flared brighter in this space than it had in the tunnel. Justice snapped his eyes closed, in case the room boasted guards who were a little more alert than the two carrying him.

Justice fixed the information in his memory. At least three hundred sixty steps, then a right turn.

"Get out of the way, you two. We need to dump this damn tiger before our arms fall out of our sockets." The group carrying Jack must have crowded past them, because the jungle-sharp smell of tiger strengthened and then waned as they passed.

He carefully opened his eyes again, in time to see the shape-shifters dump Jack on the ground, hard. The large tiger lay still, his chest barely rising and falling with shallow breaths. Justice still couldn't see Quinn. When one of the ones who'd been carrying Jack turned to face his captors he hurriedly shut his eyes again.

"Why are you still carrying that piece of shit? Throw him over on top of the tiger. With any luck, the cat will wake up in a rage from the drugs and eat him."

The "Calgoolie" idiot laughed. "Good idea. At least that would be a little entertainment for a change around here. I'm not much for icy, damp places."

They took a couple of steps and tossed Justice. He maintained the appearance of limp unconsciousness, even when his face smashed into what had to be Jack's unyielding rib cage and his knees smacked the stone floor hard enough that he could only hope nothing had shattered.

Though he was relieved to find that Jack's chest was still rising and falling with the tiger's breaths and a steady heartbeat thudded under his head, he made another, far more unpleasant, discovery.

Jack smelled like wet cat.

Before he could figure out a way to turn his head to the side, undetected, so that he could scan the area, he heard the tramping of more footsteps. These came from the opposite direction of the way he'd been carried.

"It's about time you got here." The voice hissed with menace, and Justice instantly recognized the leader from the very short-lived battle above.

"Yeah, well, you weren't carrying several hundred pounds of smelly tiger. Damn thing was pure dead weight," one of the shifters said. "I'd like five minutes alone with the idiot who decided we had to bring him, instead of just killing him on the spot."

With his face still mashed into Jack's side, Justice had to agree with the smelly tiger part. Also with the killing part, except the killing he had planned involved a certain group of shifters and vamps.

By his oath to Poseidon, there was going to be much, *much* killing. And he was going to enjoy every bloody moment of slicing heads from bodies, just as soon as he could figure out where he was and how to get Jack and Quinn to safety.

"Drakos took the woman to Caligula, so why don't you come along with me and you can voice your complaints directly to the emperor?" The vamp's voice was sly with amusement. "I'm sure he'll be glad to find some way to . . . accommodate you."

The shifters growled and stamped their feet a bit, then the one who'd been talking about "smelly tiger" finally spoke up. "Naw, just blowing off a little steam. We'll stay here and guard these two. You go ahead and do your vamp stuff."

The vamp laughed. "No, our 'vamp stuff,' as you so eloquently phrased it, is something that Caligula wants to share this time, so two of you stay here to stand guard until they start to stir. The rest come with me. The woman is important to the human rebellion in some way, and he wants to make an example of her. It should be quite a show." He laughed again, and a chill whispering of torture and death skated down Justice's spine.

Almost simultaneously, the tiger's muscles clenched. The movement was so slight none of their captors would have noticed it, but it gave Justice very specific information and concerns:

First, Jack was waking up.

Second, depending on the reaction Jack had to the drugs in his system, Justice might be defending himself from a five-hundred-pound tiger any minute.

Without his sword.

The day kept getting better and better.

Chapter 28

Ven watched Erin as she walked—almost staggering—forward through the woods beyond the cabin, holding her hands out in front of her, palms facing down. "What is it?"

"There were vampires here very recently. At least one of them called death magic," she said. "We need to—"

"What is it?" He raised his sword and pushed past her, scanning the area for danger.

"A battle," she said, her eyes going dark. "I don't know how, but I'm sensing the emanations of what happened here, not long ago. The Wilding is coursing through me, calling to me, but not . . . I don't know how to describe it."

She pointed to a cluster of trees. "Through there. Death, but not death. Perverse joy . . . evil. Evil."

Ven ran forward, sword held high, searching ground, trees, sky for possible attack. He slammed to a stop at the sight of an eight- or ten-foot-square spot of trampled snow. Vivid red spatters of blood showed up starkly against the bleak white. "Something happened here, all right. Looks like we found out what happened to Jack and Quinn."

Erin's face paled to the color of the snow surrounding

her. "But maybe they're still alive. If they'd killed them, wouldn't the bodies be here?"

"Maybe. Unless they didn't want to leave any evidence. Another snowfall would cover up the signs of the fight," Ven said. "Wait! What . . ."

The breeze had ruffled the low branches of the lacy pines, and sunlight had flickered off a flash of blue. He swiftly crossed the trampled snow to a spot on its edge, under an overhanging branch, and knelt down. The sight of the familiar blue strands, ripped from their source, tore the breath from Ven's lungs.

It was Justice's hair.

Erin ran up beside him and dropped to her knees in the snow next to him. "What is it? What—oh, no. Is that your friend's hair? Is that blood?"

She put her hand on his arm. "What is happening? Why was he here? If they captured him, too, what can we do—"

"Stop. Stop it, Erin. There's nothing we can do but go forward," he said. "If Justice had the opportunity to protect Quinn and Jack and kick a little vampire ass, he would have gone for it. We can only hope that our quest for the Nereid's Heart brings us to all three of them."

"Damnit, when will this end? Every step we take seems to bring us further and further into Caligula's trap." She slammed her hands down on the ground, then curled her fingers into claws in the snow. "I don't know how much more . . . Wait! What's that?"

She lifted something white and shook snow off of it, then handed it to him. "It's paper, probably trash, but it's a big coincidence that Justice's hair was right here, and I don't believe much in coincidence. You open it."

He carefully unrolled the ball of paper and read the words written in dark, slashing handwriting, then looked up at Erin and gave a shout of triumph. "Finally! Chalk one up for the good guys! It's a note from Justice with directions and a map. It says *warded opening Point Success*. Does that mean anything to you?"

She took the paper from him and examined it. "Yes, it means we have to get to fourteen thousand feet and figure out a way to pass through another witch's warding."

Turning her vivid blue eyes up to meet his gaze, she bared her teeth in a feral smile that would have made any warrior proud. It certainly made Ven proud, even as fear for her ripped at him. "Then we can join Justice in the vampire ass-kicking party."

～～～

Quinn lay still in the darkness, slowly working her way back to consciousness, and wondered if anybody had gotten the license plate of the truck that had run her over. The image of the vampire's fist coming at her face flashed into her mind, and she sat up fast.

Big mistake. *Huge.*

The concussion she'd probably sustained swirled nausea through her body, and she leaned over and threw up the remainder of her previous night's dinner onto the stone floor. When her aching stomach had pushed out everything it had, she scrubbed her mouth with a shaky hand and wished for water. Actually, she wished for a toothbrush and some mouthwash, too. Why not go all the way and wish big?

The thought forced a rusty laugh past her parched lips, and, as if in response to the sound, a viciously bright light seared into her eyes.

"If you hadn't turned your head at the last second, my fist surely would have driven your nose into your skull," said an unpleasantly familiar voice from behind the headache-inducing light.

"Well, nobody wants that, do they? How would I even blow my nose without my brains coming out?" She was pleased to hear that her voice sounded faintly mocking, instead of faintly terrified. Which, to be honest, was a more honest description of how she felt, considering they'd stripped her of her weapons, may have killed her partner, and she was acting with diminished capacity.

Guess Jack was right. Sometimes the rebel leader *was* a girl.

The light lowered so it wasn't shining directly in her eyes, and she breathed a sigh of relief. Dry heaving had been imminent, and that was definitely *not* on her top ten list of fun ways to spend her free time.

But now she could see the vamp's face, and that wasn't much better. He looked a tad bit angry.

"If Caligula didn't want you for his little demonstration, I'd take care of you myself," he hissed. "But don't worry, bitch. I may still get my hands on you when he's done. And I'll make sure you scream for a very long time."

At the mention of Caligula's name, Quinn ran strategies through her mind, considering and just as rapidly discarding most of them. There wasn't much she could do until she found an opening. For now she'd have to wait and watch. But if they gave her the slightest chance, she was going to dance on the salted grave of one very old ex–Roman emperor.

"Bring it on, fang face," she said, forcing herself to her feet. "Let's go meet the big bad."

"Bold words, considering they may serve as your epitaph," he snarled.

She shrugged, then winced. Right. No shrugging until large bottle of extra-strength acetaminophen found and consumed. "It's better than 'Here lies Fred. He's dead.'" She laughed again, faking a humor she didn't feel in the slightest. "Or how about 'Here's old John. He's gone.'"

He snarled a truly obscene curse and smacked her between the shoulder blades to shove her along. Her headache picked up drumsticks and started pounding out something with a heavy beat right between her eyes. Aerosmith, maybe.

"Sheesh. None of you dead guys ever has a sense of humor," she managed, and then she stumbled in the direction he indicated, chin up and shoulders squared, praying that Erin somehow found a way to save Riley and the baby. If Quinn could help her by playing cat and mouse with a two-thousand-year-old vampire, that's exactly what she was going to do, even if the thought of it sent ice searing through her veins.

She glanced over at Mr. Undead and Unfriendly. "Hey, ugly. Do you think Caligula has any Tylenol?"

~~~~⁕~~~~

Point Success

After Ven had transported them up the mountain at a dizzying rate of speed, he'd shimmered back to his form and now stood silently, watching her. Erin found the warded area easily enough, but deciphering the magic was far more challenging. She paced back and forth before the area of ground that would be indistinguishable from the rest to any non-Magickal. Aside from the magic, only a slight decrease in the ambient air temperature marked it as different. Her amber sang out a warning whenever she stepped too closely to the warded area, and heat seared her skin when she reached out with her magic.

Ven tried brute force, in spite of her warning, and bounced off the edge of the transparent magical shield. "Isn't that a little odd? I mean, doesn't your average hiker kinda notice when he gets knocked on his ass by an invisible wall?"

She sighed and held out a hand to help him up. He shook his head and pushed himself up off the ground, grumbling something about *warrior, swords, and freaking witches*. She figured she was better off not asking him to repeat it.

"It doesn't work that way, Ven. A non-Magickal would simply be directed subconsciously slightly away from this area. It's probably no more than three square feet, so it wouldn't be noticeable. Especially since the spell is reinforced with a look-away spell, so they literally would not see this spot or even know that they'd been guided away from it."

"Right. No offense, but I don't care how the spell works," he said, stabbing the shield with his sword and cursing when it zapped a bolt of electricity up the sword to his arm. "All I want to know is, can you break it?"

She focused all her concentration on the ward's intricate patterns and sent her own magic out to meet it and unravel tangled skeins of power. For every step forward she made in the process, it seemed that the ward's magic knocked her a half step back. Finally she pulled back and looked at Ven.

"I'm going to have to call the Wilding. I can't get past this warding any other way."

"So do it. You've already proven that you can control it," he said. "I'll be right here with you."

"It's not that, Ven. It's that vampires and anybody who is part of the dark seem to be able to sense the Wilding. By calling it, I'll be giving our position away."

He turned those dark, warrior eyes on her. "I think we're past worrying about that. Breaking the ward may set off some kind of magical car alarm, for all we know. And if there's only one way in, it's bound to be guarded. I'd already given up any hope for stealth a while ago."

He bent to place his sword on the ground, then scooped her up and kissed her fiercely. "No matter what occurs, remember that your soul has melded with mine, Erin Connors. I do not plan to let you escape me so easily."

"Same goes, Lord Vengeance," she whispered. "Same goes."

Then she gently pulled away from him and opened her mind and soul and the power of her gems to the Wilding, and reveled in its power as it immediately came to her call and spiraled through her body. It was a matter of seconds to undo the ward, which now seemed almost pathetically simple to her. As the last strand of its magic snapped, destroying the warding entirely, the ground shook beneath her feet. The powerful sound of a tolling bell—or possibly a ruby calling to its singer—rang through the ground and up into the air through a dark opening that slowly appeared in the snow.

This time, even Ven heard it, if the startled glance he sent her way was any indication. "That's the Nereid's Heart?"

"I think it must be," Erin said, finding it hard to speak over the gemsong, rubysong, and heartsong flooding through her senses. "It's lovelier than I ever could have imagined."

He retrieved his sword and raised it, then peered down into the darkness of the hold. "There are steps carved into the rock, like a stone ladder, and what looks like a tunnel branching off from it," he reported.

Erin simply smiled at him, feeling drunk with the wonder of the pure, undistilled power that poured through her, circled around her, and wrapped her in its heat.

His eyes narrowed as he watched her, but he said nothing, just held out a hand. She placed her own in his, and he squeezed it briefly and then started down into the hole. The ruby continued to toll its clarion call to her, to her, only to her.

The power. The power. Oh, the *power*. She could lose herself in it. She *wanted* to lose herself in it. To hide away from the pain and desolation of the past ten years.

"Erin." The voice was faint and barely penetrated the music, but it kept nagging at her. "Erin! Snap out of it! I need you with me if we're going to do this."

Ven. It was Ven, he'd climbed back out of the hole, and he was saying something. With difficulty, she focused her gaze on him. "Do you hear the ruby, Ven? It's singing to me and tempting me with so much power. A seduction of power," she said, lifting her arms and twirling around, her voice lilting with the cadence of the rubysong.

"Erin! I need you to concentrate." He grabbed her shoulders, stared down into her eyes, and spoke a single word. "Caligula."

The name was a slap of cold water against the fog permeating her brain. Clear, sober thought instantly returned as she clamped all of her control down, hard, on the Wilding.

"I'm sorry. I'm so sorry. It just caught me for a minute." She shuddered against him. "It's so seductive, Ven. It wants me to call it and own it, and it would be so easy to fall into the whirlpool of its power and never return."

"You have to fight it. You must control it, or we'll never succeed." The blue-green flames were back in his eyes, and for a momentary flash of time, she could see into his soul to the deep concern he had for her safety.

She twined her hands in his silky black hair and closed her eyes, not speaking, not thinking, just letting the pure tactile sensation of his thick hair sliding through her fingers occupy her entire present.

She stood that way for at least a minute, and then she released him and nodded. "I'm back. I've got it under control. It's okay."

"Are you sure? I will not take you into the darkness if there is no hope of return, my lady," he said quietly, dropping back into the formal speak that underscored the intensity of his words.

"I am sure. Into the belly of the beast, Ven," she said, trying to smile. "Well, I don't mean that literally, of course."

"I'm the only beast whose belly you're going to get near," he growled, flashing a grin that belied his mock ferocity.

"Then lead on, beast. The sooner we go, the sooner we get through this," she said. And then she followed him down the stone ladder into the dark.

Chapter 29

Caligula's cavern lair

Quinn sauntered forward into the enormous cavern, hands in her pants pockets as if facing a criminally insane master vampire was just another day in the life.

Sadly, since she'd started working for the rebel cause, it kind of *was* just another day in the life. Another step toward the redemption she could never earn. She didn't even fear death anymore as much as she feared the idea of never seeing Riley again.

She tried to ignore the rapid pounding of her heart and studied the space, which was lit by torches placed strategically on the stone walls. Dozens of vamps lurked and skittered against the walls, hiding in shadows, making hideous hissing sounds that she figured translated into "yummy, fresh blood walking."

But the centerpiece of the room—*and, hey, want to bet that he'd planned it that way?*—was the vamp floating about fifteen feet above the floor, slowly twirling in a circle, black silk cape flowing behind him. He had a Caesar-type hairdo, which she supposed made sense, but he looked like he should be wearing a toga, not a cape.

Well, "no guts, no glory." Or something like that. Maybe, "mouth off and he'll eat your guts."

Either way, she knew it was something about guts. And that was something she had plenty of, notwithstanding the acid curling and roiling around in them. A sense of enormous power, barely leashed, washed over her, and her emotional empathy shut down completely in the face of the pure evil in his intentions.

She took a deep breath and looked straight at him. "Seriously, dude, a *cape*? Are you kidding me? Too many Bela Lugosi flicks? Or are you more a Frank Langella or Gary Oldman fan?"

Before he could reply, a huge tolling sound, like some kind of King Kong of a Liberty Bell ringing to alert the soldiers or something, started booming through the cave. This meant that it also started booming through her skull, which was definitely not a happy development in the world of Quinn.

As she clutched her aching head and moaned, she noticed that she wasn't the only one suffering. The vamps and shifters were all clutching their heads, too, and moaning, snarling, and hissing out hideously tormented sounds. Clearly the bell was affecting them on a far more visceral level than it was affecting her, which meant white magic was involved somehow.

Which might mean Erin. Way to go, Erin. It boomed through the cave for several minutes, and then stopped with one extra-loud, final gong. She hesitantly lifted her hands away from her ears, wondering if a person's skull could actually explode from a headache, and getting the feeling she might be close to finding out.

Caligula raised his hands from his ears and snarled, then he lowered his levitating form down closer to the floor and to her. As he approached from above, he almost caught her eyes, but she was careful to quickly lower her gaze. She might have a talent or two in the area of rebel strategy, but there was no way she could pit her emotional empathy against a master vamp's mind-thrall powers and come out a winner.

Or even come out alive.

"What was that noise? Not a happy noise for vamps, I'm guessing," she said, unreasonably proud of the near-steadiness of her voice.

A flicker of uncertainty crossed his face, as if he didn't know what the noise was, either.

"That noise is none of your concern, Quinn Dawson. I have heard much of you. The infamous rebel leader who drives even master vampires out of their home territories. And yet here you are, and you're nothing but a little girl," he sneered.

Quinn clenched her fist around the hilt of the wooden stake that was strapped to her leg underneath her pants. Cutting holes in all of her pockets was second nature these days.

"I'm getting really tired of being called a girl," she observed. "Plus, if you're trying to piss me off, Emperor Fang Face, you can do better than that, surely. Bet your former enemies back in the old days would laugh so hard to see you skulking around in a damp, dark cave like this."

She deliberately turned her head from left to right as she scanned the room. "Not even a good interior decorator could help this dump."

She tensed, waiting for him to strike, but he merely laughed. Somehow his laughter was far more chilling than his snarling had been. "I see through your pathetic ploy, Ms. Dawson. You want to enrage me to the point where I kill you quickly."

"Right, because so many of my more successful plots involved me getting bloodsuckers to kill me," she said, rolling her eyes. "Not a lot of the brain power survived the past two thousand years, did it?" She tried not to flinch as a dark wave of hatred washed over her, nearly crushing her.

"You know as well as I do that a quick death would be a boon to one whose eventual death will be neither painless nor quick," he said. He floated down the last few feet until his boots touched the floor. Then he smiled at her, and her spinal fluid turned to ice water. His smile held the promise of unspeakable atrocities of pain and torture beyond anything she could imagine.

Not that she wanted to imagine it.

She was literally scared speechless, but tried to remember that he had the power to feed her fear and increase its intensity. She tried to fight through the terror that was paralyzing her and whispering urgently to her of her own defeat and death.

A crushing pressure smashed into her, forcing her to her knees, paralyzing her limbs. He could walk right up to her and bite her neck at his leisure now, because she couldn't move a single muscle to stop him. All she had left were the tarnished prayers of a woman who wasn't sure she even believed.

I'm going to die right here in this crappy cave. Please, God, if you even exist, tell Riley that I love her.

"I'm going to make an example of you, little rebel," Caligula crooned. "I'm going to turn you vampire, and then make you one of my generals. Any who look into your lovely dark eyes gone red and glowing will know my power."

A powerful voice thundered through the cavern. "I ask a boon, my lord. I ask that you give this woman to me, that I may turn her to vampire for your use. It is beneath you to do the task yourself and spend the slightest effort on this pitiful human."

Caligula turned to face the newcomer, and the pressure holding Quinn in place lessened, allowing her to raise her head and see who wanted to play "drain the rebel" this time.

Except it was Daniel. And the sight of him gave her that most dangerous of weapons—hope.

∽∼∾

The tunnel

Thanking Poseidon that the ruby had let up on the tolling, Ven led the way, banging into the wall occasionally and wishing for the night vision that the shifters had. Not that he'd want to get furry just to be able to see better in dark places, but not smacking his damn head into the damn walls every damn minute would be nice.

"Ven?" Erin's whisper floated through the darkness to him. "Would you like some light?"

He gave himself a mental smack for not thinking of it earlier. "Yeah, that would be nice. A little witch light to illuminate the path. Can you conjure up just a flashlight-sized ball?"

She sighed. "We're going to have to discuss all of these misconceptions you seem to have about witches at some point, you realize that, right?"

"Add it to the list," he muttered. A light flared behind him, and then a fist-sized ball of light bounced over his shoulder through the air until it floated about five paces in front of him. "Thanks, Erin. That helps a lot. My head couldn't take much more self-inflicted pounding."

"How far have we walked?" she asked.

"One hundred and sixty-four steps," he answered automatically.

"You're counting the steps?"

"It's good to know the direction and length of any escape routes."

Silence for several more steps.

"Okay, that's a good point. Maybe when I give you lessons in 'witch,' you can give me lessons in 'warrior.'"

He nodded, grimly amused. "Sure. Add—"

"It to the list," she finished for him. "That's getting to be quite a list."

"Works for me, since I'm planning—" The faint scratching sound alerted him before his eyes could find its source. "Erin, shield!"

Ven bent his knees into a fighting stance and raised his sword. The scratching turned into the scrambling of claws on rock, and it was coming from overhead. "We've got company, and I'm guessing vamp," he called out. "Watch out from the roof."

A hissing sound and foul smell like noxious air escaping a tire was his only warning before two vamps attacked him from above. He twisted and plunged his sword into the neck of one of them as the other smashed a fist into the side of his head, bouncing his poor abused skull off yet another wall.

He swore a blue streak in Atlantean as he wrenched his sword sideways and down, crudely but effectively slicing the head of vamp number one from its body. Vamp number two hissed at the sight, then leapt at Ven. He pulled his sword up into the ready position, but before the vamp ever made it to him, a bolt of sizzling energy zapped it right in the middle of its forehead. The silvery-blue energy shot through all the vamp's limbs and into its skull, illuminating it from inside like a bizarre, anatomically correct piece of modern art. Bloodsuckers by Damien Hirst.

Then it exploded into a pile of smoking slime, and he barely jumped back out of the way in time to avoid getting splattered with decomposing vamp.

"Hey! If you're going to use the Wilding to explode vamps, I'm entirely in agreement with that plan. But give a man a chance to get out of the line of fire, so to speak," he said, turning to face Erin.

She stood, mouth hanging open, with her hands still raised. As he watched her, she slowly blinked once, then finally lowered her hands. "What? That was . . . oh, wow. Wow. What just happened? Did I really do that? I had no idea . . ."

As her voice trailed off, he shot a glance farther down the descending tunnel, to see if more vamps or maybe a few shifters were hot on their buddies' trail. Her witch light, amazingly, still hung in the air. "We need to get going. I have a feeling that those vamps may have been reacting to you busting through their warding, which means more will be on the way when they don't come back and report."

He carefully studied her for signs of shock, but other than the slightly stunned expression in her eyes, she seemed fine. More than fine, considering the fierce look of joy that slowly lit up her face. "I exploded a vampire, Ven. I called the Wilding and *exploded a vampire.* Do you know what that means?"

"I should be careful never to get on your bad side?"

She ignored his feeble attempt at humor and raised her arms until a silvery-blue translucent glow covered her entire body. "I can destroy them, Ven. I can destroy them all."

He grabbed her arms, noticing and filing away the slight zap of electrical shock that sizzled up his hands to his shoulders from touching her. "You're not invulnerable, Erin, and a master vamp has defenses and powers these baby vamps never dreamed of. Also, if you throw some kind of shock wave, you run the risk of harming your sister. So, yeah, it's great that you're Super Wilding Witch now. But be careful."

She stared at him, remote and unyielding, reminding him again of the Goddess she'd become at the Nereid Temple. "Lead on, Lord Vengeance," she said in a voice that was subtly deeper and vaster than her own. "Your concerns are noted."

Not knowing what else to do, sure that an army of shifters and vamps was swarming up the tunnel toward them at that very moment, Ven did as she asked and led on. His concerns might be *noted*, he thought. But they damn sure weren't *relieved*. He could finally admit that he'd fallen in love with a witch. But he wasn't at all prepared to be in love with a goddess.

Chapter 30

Erin followed Ven down farther and farther into the dark heart of the mountain, feeling oddly as though she were no longer alone in her own skin. She was more—was other. She sensed the presence of the Nereid Goddess, who would serve as midwife to the birth of Erin's true gem singer Gift.

She wasn't sure how she knew this to be true, but didn't question the knowledge. She followed Ven, who would defend her to the ninth level of hell, and walked with the Goddess, who would help her to become, fully, who she was meant to be.

She floated on the rubysong that now sang only to her, and not to the others, and gazed at stone walls turned red by the shining brilliance of the Nereid's Heart. Suddenly she heard its song with lyrics—words that spoke directly to her:

Come to me, gem singer. Sing me free of this rock prison. Sing me to my home.

The part of her mind that was pure Erin was amused at the idea. What was the protocol for talking to an inanimate hunk of rock?

The part of her filled with the Goddess serenely responded. "We come, blessed ruby. Lead the way." Somehow the size and shape of the Goddess had filled her so that there was no room left for fear or uncertainty.

Ahead of her, Ven glanced back at her, hesitating, as if he wanted to ask her a question. Or shake some sense into her, knowing Ven. But she narrowed her eyes in warning and shook her head, so he began grumbling under his breath again and kept walking.

Trapped between an Atlantean who cared for her and a Goddess who wanted to use her, Erin focused on the only things that mattered: she had to find the Nereid's Heart, she had to rescue her sister, and she had to save Riley and the baby—somehow getting through who knew how many vampires and shape-shifters to do it.

She called to the Wilding and gloried in its instant response. Oh, yes, she was going to have no problems at all.

~~~~~~

Headquarters, Circle of Light

Alaric paced circles around the pallets of still-healing shifters in the great room of the building. Justice or Ven should have communicated with him in some way by now. Something had gone wrong.

Quinn might be in danger.

Quinn might be in *danger.*

Coming to a decision, he strode rapidly through the rooms until he found Christophe, drinking coffee in the kitchen and talking to one of the witches.

"Christophe, a word."

The warrior excused himself and immediately followed Alaric into the corridor.

"I must leave now. You will be in charge of guarding those in this building until I return."

Christophe inclined his head. "As you wish, Alaric. Are you returning to Atlantis?"

Alaric could tell from the warrior's wary expression that

his eyes were radiating the power he channeled. "No. I go to Mount Rainier."

❦

Ven smelled the wolves before he ever saw them. The dark passage had been steadily brightening for several paces, and the smell of wolf crossed with something stronger thickened in the air. He stopped and held out a hand to Erin, not sure if she'd even accept the reassurance. He was relieved when she placed her small hand in his, but her fingers were icy cold. He glanced at her and saw that even more of her warmth had drained away, leaving her eyes an icy silver-blue, almost the exact color of the power she'd channeled to heal Riley.

"Are you still in there, Erin?"

She slowly turned her gaze up to meet his, but he couldn't see anything of Erin in her eyes. "We are well, Ven. The ruby calls me, so strongly. We're almost there, now." Her voice was still different—wrong. But there was at least something of *his* Erin left in her voice.

Ven had seen Alaric go dark and scary many, many times over the centuries, and the priest always came back from it. He had to trust that Erin would do the same.

"We're here," he said quietly. "It's going to be game on from here on in. Are you ready?"

Her lips curved in a sultry smile that was so sexy it would have made him go up in flames if the circumstances were different, but merely fed his concerns as things stood.

"A better question, Lord Vengeance, would be if they are ready for us."

❦

The tiger coughed, a deep, barking sound that nearly scared the two shifters guarding them clear out of their fur. Justice would have laughed at the sight of them if he hadn't still been pretending to be unconscious. He'd needed a distraction to take out the two of them, since he didn't have his sword or any of his weapons on him except a dagger inserted into the heel and sole of his right boot. Tough to get to it in his current position, facedown on the side of a drugged tiger who was about to wake up any minute.

The sight of the tiger chewing Justice's legs off would probably be a great distraction, but not exactly helpful to Justice's cause.

"I think the tiger's waking up," one of the guards said. The stupid one. Justice recognized the voice. "Wonder if he'll eat the guy. Bet he chokes on all that hair. What kind of color is blue for a man's hair? Bet he's some kind of gay guy."

The other one snorted. "You're an idiot. Plus, you're always seeing gay guys around every corner. A person could begin to think you're homophobic for a reason."

Stupid got belligerent. "What does that mean? I ain't no gay guy! I got a mate. A female mate."

This was getting interesting. Justice hoped they started beating each other's brains out before Jack woke up and turned him into Atlantean catnip.

"Oh, I was just kidding. Relax, you moron. I'm bored. I want to go see what they're up to out there, not hang out here with these two. There's no way the dose of Special K they took will wear off anytime soon. Wanna go sneak a peek?"

Justice tried to use his nonexistent psychic mind control powers. *Yes, yes, go watch the vampire show. Leave the unconscious man and the unconscious kitty.*

"No way, man. Calgoolie would have our balls for earrings, and I'm kinda partial to my balls," said Stupid.

"There you go, talking about balls again. I'm telling you . . . nah. It's too easy," said the one with moderately more intelligence. "Look, we can hide behind that rock outcropping right next to the entrance. We'll be close enough to check back in here every few seconds but still see the action."

"Well . . ."

Yes, do it, do it, do it.

"All right. But only for a few minutes, or till they show any signs of waking up. I don't think there's anywhere far enough to hide from that vamp when he's in a bad mood."

They started moving away, apparently trying to be stealthy.

For shifters, they were as stealthy as water buffalo, which at least gave Justice a big advantage. He'd know when they started to come back.

"Vampires are always in bad moods. I wish we'd never . . ." As their voices faded away down the tunnel, Justice whipped his head to the side, figuring that even if there were some silent guard who'd remained entirely still in order to fool him into moving, he'd rather face that than one second more of his face mashed into the side of a wet tiger.

He leapt to his feet, wincing as his bruised knees complained, then scrubbed tiger hair out of his nose and mouth. "Damn, Vengeance better appreciate this," he growled.

A very familiar chuckle sounded quietly from the opening to the tunnel behind him, and he whirled around to see Ven standing there, sword at the ready. "I'm sure I'm going to appreciate it. A lot. I'm already appreciating the hell out of it. Especially the part where you're covered with cat hair and lying around on a tiger pillow. Care to explain?"

Before Justice could respond, the booming sound of the unseen bell rang through the cave again and he clapped his hands over his ears. From behind Ven, he saw a woman enter the cave, her arms and face lifted rapturously up toward the ceiling. She looked familiar. Almost like Ven's gem singer.

At that moment, the tolling of the bell ceased and the woman dropped her arms and stared at him, an eerie bluish silvery light glowing fiercely from her eyes. It was Erin. Erin and something else—or some*one* else—sharing her consciousness.

Justice froze, nearly paralyzed, suddenly overcome with a fierce wave of longing for her, for them, for the essence of the Nereid who was the female to the male of his Nereid half. Insanity and battle lust ripped through him with a slicing pain. He dropped into a crouch and snarled at Ven. "I will take her from you, Vengeance. I am done with watching you rule over territory that should be mine."

Ven blinked, confusion clear on his face. "What did they do to you? What in the nine hells are you talking about?" He raised his sword, but it was a halfhearted gesture. The King's Vengeance didn't have the stomach to kill a fellow warrior.

A red haze of fury washed over Justice's vision until Ven's face appeared to be already covered with blood. Ven might not have the stomach for murder. Too bad for him that Justice did.

Erin spoke, but it was not entirely Erin's voice that issued from her mouth. "You will stop this now, Nereid. The drugs in your system are influencing your judgment and bringing you perilously close to telling tales you cannot share." She raised her arms again and spheres of pure power glowed in the palms of her hands.

Before Justice could launch himself, bare-handed, across the ground in a killing leap, she hurled one of the balls at him and it smacked him in the gut. The punch of it knocked him back, smashing him to the ground. Even as his head slammed into the stone floor, the healing silvery-blue light of her energy ball surrounded him and sank into him. Into his skin, into his blood.

Into the dark and empty space in his soul that had briefly seen in her a vision of home. The light washed color and song through and around him, and he gained a too-brief *knowing* of what it was to be a gem singer.

Then it was gone.

Blinking, Justice sat up and realized that he felt about a hundred times better. His headache was gone, the constant aching across his ribs where the vamp had slashed him was gone. Both wounds now felt as if they had never existed. He didn't check underneath his bandages. He felt no need.

"You healed me," he said to her. To them; the gem singer and the Goddess.

"We did," she replied, still in that immense, musical voice. "And now we must find the Nereid's Heart before its rubysong consumes me."

He jumped to his feet and bowed to Ven, who stood there still looking confused. "My apologies, Lord Vengeance. I was . . . overcome."

Ven just stared at him, then finally shrugged. "I don't pretend to know what just happened, but we don't have time for this now. We need to—"

But Justice never heard what Ven believed they needed to do. Because the two reluctant guards rounded the corner back to their post and stopped dead at the exact moment that Justice heard an angry roar. Five hundred pounds of tiger hit him in the back like a freight train, and he went down.

Chapter 31

Ven saw the expression on Justice's face signal the approach of what smelled like wolf. He'd been standing a little to the right of the opening, out of the line of sight of anybody coming back into the cave. He leapt even farther out of the way, holding up a warning hand to Erin to stay back. The thunderous tolling sound started up again and she got that dazed look on her face, but at least she stumbled back against the wall.

He turned to face the approaching shifters, so he had less than a split second of warning before Jack—all fangs and claws and pure, enraged muscle—attacked Justice. He couldn't hear the snarling over the sound of the Nereid's Heart, or whatever was making that enormous noise, but he could tell from the tiger's wide-open jaws that there was definitely snarling going on.

He'd known they must have drugged or poisoned Jack to knock him out. What he hadn't known was what effect the drugs might have on a ferocious weretiger.

Figured it wouldn't be good.

He raised his sword and plunged it into the chest of the

first shifter to hit the room. The Were had been moving fast enough that the impact drove Ven back a few paces. Before he could yank his sword out, Erin moved away from the relative safety of the shadows against the wall and headed for the fierce battle going on between Atlantean and tiger.

"Damnit, Erin, get back!" he shouted at her, not that she could hear anything but that damned ruby. This plan was fucked clear to the nine hells and back.

He had time to see Erin throw a shield around herself, and then the second shifter was on him. He abandoned his sword and went hand to hand, dropping to the ground and using one leg to sweep the Were's legs out from under him. The man dropped hard to the ground, then snarled at Ven out of a rapidly lengthening muzzle. He was about to have a fully transformed werewolf to deal with, and he just wasn't in the mood. Before the sparkling shimmers of transformation had fully dissipated, Ven balanced the silver and orichalcum dagger by its tip and then hurled it the short distance to his target.

Silver in a Were's heart stopped them like nothing else. Ven didn't have time to enjoy his victory, however. He whirled around and leapt into the ball of fur and blue hair snarling and growling on the ground. He managed to get an arm around the tiger's huge neck and pull it back a couple of inches so its fangs weren't quite so close to Justice's throat. Then Justice, his vision blocked by a tiger's head, slammed out blindly with a fist that smashed directly into the side of Ven's already throbbing head.

"Damnit, I'm trying to help you here," he yelled, hoping to be heard over the feral snarls of the cat and the gonging of the ruby. "Quit punching me!"

"Perhaps we could help?" A lilting voice that sounded less and less like Erin smoothly asked the question that was clearly rhetorical. Somehow her soft voice pierced the resounding noise of the ruby that continued to gong out its call.

Before he could answer, she'd already twined her magic into separate bubblelike shields that individually captured the three of them. After gently floating Ven and Justice to the floor a short distance away from the tiger, she released them.

Then she crossed to the final bubble that encircled the enraged jungle cat.

She placed her palms on the bubble and leaned her cheek against it, and then she started to sing. It was a quiet and gentle song, holding nothing of the immense power Ven had heard her sing before. It was a delicate song of healing and peace; a tapestry woven by a master weaver with silken thread. The pulsing noise of the ruby faded away as if in response to her song.

As she softly sang, a silver mist filled the bubble until Ven could only see flashes of orange, white, and black inside. Her song lasted less than a minute, and then she stood back from the bubble and the mist cleared. Sitting inside the bubble, entirely nude, Jack had returned to his human shape. As Ven watched, Jack raised his head and stared into Erin's eyes, then slowly nodded. She made a slight circular motion with one hand and the bubble vanished.

Jack stood up and bowed to her. "I'm in your debt, Erin Connors. The drugs had trapped me in the basest urges of my animal nature. I wouldn't have wanted to do something I might later regret."

Justice rubbed his head. "Sure. Apologize to *her*. *I'm* the one you damn near killed."

The edges of Jack's lips quirked up in a grin. "*You* probably had it coming."

"Enough," Ven commanded. "In case you two have forgotten, we're in the middle of enemy territory. Justice, check out that entrance and see if anybody else is coming. I can't believe they didn't hear the commotion in here, but that damn ruby probably drowned us out. So that's one good thing."

He frowned as Jack stood up, way too casual about having his bare ass hanging out. "Put on some clothes, Jack," he ordered, pointing at the fallen shifter. "Maybe this guy's pants will fit you."

Jack grinned again. "Right. You're as bad as the humans with your prudishness over a little nudity."

"No need," Erin said. She chanted something under her breath and a silver shimmer spiraled around Jack. Seconds later, he stood there, fully dressed in dark pants and shirt, frowning at her.

"Thank you. But it occurs to me that your powers are magnifying exponentially, witch," Jack said. "Is someone or something giving you more power than you can handle?"

"Do not concern yourself with my power, shape-shifter," she snapped, and again Ven heard the Goddess.

Jack tilted his head looking wary. "Oh, I concern myself with all sorts of things."

Ven stepped between him and Erin, tightening his hand on the hilt of his sword. "Not her. Not now, not ever," he said flatly.

For a moment he almost thought the tiger would challenge him, but instead Jack leaned forward and spoke so quietly Ven nearly didn't catch the words. "She's not alone in there, Ven. I am dual-natured by heredity and by experience, and I can recognize this. Be cautious and aware."

Seeing nothing but sincerity in Jack's eyes, Ven nodded once and stepped back, then crossed to Erin and put an arm around her waist. "Are you ready?"

She looked up at him, and for an instant it was only Erin staring at him through her eyes. "Kiss me, Ven. Please kiss me, in case—"

He cut off her words with his mouth and kissed her with all the desperation in his soul, breaking it off far sooner than he would have liked. Her kiss tasted of light and goodness and home, and he almost forgot where they were. Almost. Enemy territory, he reminded the primitive force inside him demanding that he take her lips again.

"We're going to have to talk about this bossy nature of yours," he said instead. "When—not if, but *when* we get out of here."

She smiled a little. "Add it to the list. I love you, Ven. I need for you to know that."

His heart expanded at the words. "I love you, too, Erin Connors. Do not even think of leaving me."

She smiled again, and then the life and warmth drained from her expression, and his gem singer went cold and still in his arms and pushed away from him. "Now, Warrior of Poseidon. We retrieve the Nereid's Heart now."

With the icy sound of her dual-natured voice ringing in his ears, he stepped in front of her, and they headed toward the glow of the lights.

∾⌒⌒∾

Quinn knew that the booming bell sound signified something important, but she wasn't sure what. Hopefully it involved the gem that Erin and Ven were searching for and the noise meant they'd found it.

No matter what it meant, she had the feeling that her luck had run out with the final, fading peals of the bell. Daniel and Caligula were both bearing down on her with fangs bared, and she wasn't entirely sure that this Daniel was still the Daniel that she'd known. This vampire had red, intensely glowing eyes, and all she could see was the threat of Drakos in the feral way he stared at her.

So much for hope.

"Are you going to fight over me, boys?" she crooned. "There's not really enough of me to go around. Kind of skinny, probably low on the O negative. Or, actually, A positive, I think. Seems like something a person should know these days, doesn't it?"

She smiled at Daniel, studying him for any hint that this was another guise in his covert mission. All she saw in his eyes was her own death. Or worse. Her own future as one of the mindless undead Caligula so enjoyed keeping in his blood pride.

"Over my dead body," she snapped.

"That's rather the point," Daniel said, smiling widely so she was sure to notice that his fangs had fully descended, which they only did when a vamp was preparing to strike.

She'd learned that one in a very personal way.

"If I only had a stake, you'd get my point, bloodsucker," she said, hunching her neck down into her collar in an attempt to look weak and helpless.

Caligula finally spoke, glancing back and forth between

the two of them. "If you truly would serve me, Drakos, I would be most pleased. I have had certain . . . concerns about your loyalty. It would go far to alleviate those concerns if you should take care of this little problem for me."

Daniel bowed. "It would be my utmost pleasure, my lord. I will remove her worthless carcass from your presence."

As he grabbed her arm, she screamed and fought to get away, not convinced that this was all a show for Caligula's benefit. She'd seen bloodlust before, and she was seeing it now in his eyes. Daniel really might be irrevocably Drakos. If so, she was truly screwed.

Caligula's voice sliced through the air. "Oh, no, my general. That would not please me at all. I prefer that this human serve as an example to her pathetic rebel forces and an entertainment to our loyal soldiers."

The vamps and shifters lining the walls cheered and stamped their feet at the word "entertainment," which reminded Quinn of the whole emperor thing. Throwing Christians to the lions or something. Murdering slaves in the coliseum. Russell Crowe dying in the dirt.

She was tough, but she was no Russell Crowe.

"I want her turned, and I want you to start the process now, my Drakos. Tie her to you with the blood bond and prove to me that you are truly mine to command."

"No fucking way!" she screamed. "Never. I'll kill you myself, you bloodsucking bastard!"

She shifted into primal attack mode, screaming and clawing and punching and gouging at Daniel with a ferocity that must have startled him, because he grabbed her and threw her across the room toward the opening to the tunnel. She crashed into the wall and slid into a limp heap of aches and possible broken limbs onto the floor. In an instant, he flashed across the cavern and bent over her, baring his fangs. Just before he struck, he caught her gaze in his own. "It will hurt less if you let me enthrall you," he whispered. "I promise I will find a way to fix this."

Then, even as she began to sink into the glowing red whirlpool in his eyes, he struck. She screamed as she felt him draining her blood and energy from her body. As she sank into the darkness, she looked up and over Daniel's shoulder and right into Ven's furious face and nearly laughed at the sheer unexpectedness of seeing him there.

Please, God, please save Riley and the baby, she thought, and then the world faded into shades of scarlet and bloodred, finally tunneling down to black.

Chapter 32

Ven heard the screaming and fought to keep from rushing out into the cavern, sword drawn. The correct battle strategy was always to scout out the opposition. He peered around the corner and saw Daniel driving his fangs into Quinn, who fought like she had werecat in her DNA.

Screw battle strategy. He raised his sword and charged, roaring an ancient Atlantean battle cry that surfaced from the depths of his being. He caught a glimpse in his peripheral vision of an enormous space filled with more vamps and shifters, and then he was on Daniel. "You soul-sucking bastard. Prepare to die the true death, vampire," he snarled, trying to find a place on Daniel's body he could skewer without injuring Quinn.

Daniel released Quinn and stared up at Ven. "All is not as it seems, Atlantean." He flashed twenty feet across the room, carrying Quinn, so there were now about fifty vamps and shifters Ven had to slice his way through to get to them.

From behind him, the first notes of a dark song began. Then a glowing sphere of power shot through the room and struck one of the vamps in the front row. It exploded in splatters of decomposing slime, and the vamps surrounding it shrieked and backed up. The shifters milled around, not quite retreating, but not attacking anymore, either.

On either side of Ven, Justice, Jack, and Erin stepped up so that they formed a solid line of attack. Jack and Justice were armed with the fallen shifters' weapons and Erin held two more of the glowing spheres in her hands.

"Can't shift back to tiger form for a while, but I'm a fair hand with a knife," Jack said.

"Less talk, more killing," Justice said.

"Now they die," Erin and what Ven had come to think of as Not Erin said.

Ven nodded. "Now they die."

With that, they started forward toward the enemy, hopelessly outnumbered if you didn't count the fact that they seemed to have a seriously pissed-off Goddess on their side.

"*Stop!*" The voice roaring through the room was icily inhuman, and it came from directly above them. The vampire floating down toward them was one of the oldest Ven had ever seen, if the whiteness of his skin were any indication.

"Ex-Emperor Caligula, I presume?" he drawled.

"Once an emperor, always an emperor, Atlantean," Caligula sneered, then he turned his laser-like focus on Erin. "Finally, Erin Connors. You are even more lovely than your sister."

The master vampire laughed, and the sound skated chills across the room. "Of course, she has had a rather difficult decade, so she's rather the worse for wear, as you humans might say."

Ven raised his sword and stepped in front of Erin. "I will happily show you a little difficulty of your own, Atlantean style, you monster."

"Ven. No. He has Deirdre," Erin said, choking on the words. There was no trace of the Goddess remaining in her voice, and he wondered where she'd gone.

"Yes, I have Deirdre," Caligula said, baring fully descended fangs. "Would you like to see your sister? She might be a bit angry at you for abandoning her to me all those years ago, but I'm sure you can work it out."

"I never knew," Erin screamed. "I thought she was dead. All these years, I thought they were all dead. I thought . . ." She broke off, sobbing.

From high above them, a new voice—eerily similar to Erin's—called out. "You truly didn't know? All these years he told me . . . I believed—"

"Yes, you believed me," Caligula said, doing an obscenely gleeful dance right there, still standing on air. "Not at first, not even for the first few years. But finally you believed that your own family had abandoned you to me in exchange for their own worthless lives. The joy of your surrender to my lies was truly sweet."

A female vampire soared down from a place high above them. As she came closer, Ven saw that she had Erin's hair and a certain similarity in facial features. There was no doubt that she was Erin's sister, even with the red glow in her eyes. She wore a bulky black gown, loosely belted with a length of rope, and the naked emotion on her face must have been driving a stake through Erin's heart.

"Deirdre, he lied to you," Erin said, tears streaming down her face. "He killed them all and left me for dead, too. I managed to make it back to the coven, but by the time I recovered from my injuries, everyone told me you were dead."

Deirdre started to float down past Caligula, but he snaked out an arm and caught her by the hair, twisting it cruelly. "Very touching, but I'm not about to let them get their hands on my trump card, now am I?"

He drew a dagger and pressed the edge of the blade against Deirdre's throat until a thin red line appeared against her pale white skin and blood trickled down from beneath the blade. "I propose a bargain, Atlantean. You give me Erin Connors, and I kill the three of you in excruciatingly painful ways."

"That's not exactly a bargain, bloodsucker," Jack growled. "Or are you better in Latin than English, even after all these years?"

"Ah, yes, the kitty speaks," Caligula said. "If you prefer Latin, then so be it. Let me set the stage for you: I hold the witch's sister, and if you attack my blood pride or my shapeshifters, I will kill Deirdre. Your witch won't care for that at all, will you, Erin?" He flashed a nasty smile at Erin.

"Furthermore, I hold the rebel leader, and my general is now going to take the second step toward forming the blood bond with her," he said, waving a hand toward Daniel and Quinn, who still appeared to be unconscious. "Therefore, you can do nothing, and I will enjoy seeing you die. Slowly. *Res ipsa loquitur.*"

"What the hell does that mean?" Jack snarled.

"The thing speaks for itself," Ven replied.

Deirdre, still caught by her hair in Caligula's fist, laughed a high, piercing laugh. "Sometimes the thing *sings* for itself," she said. Then she ripped the top of her gown in two, baring her breasts and a cloth-wrapped bundle, which she tossed down toward Erin. "Take this, baby sister, and join me in a duet."

Ven snatched the bundle out of the air as it plummeted toward them, but was unprepared for its heavy weight and nearly dropped it. Together, he and Erin tore the cloth covering away, and the fierce red glow of the sunset on the waves shone up at them. The ruby was in the shape of an enormous solid heart, as big as Ven's head.

"What is that?" Caligula screamed. "What did you give her?" He backhanded Deirdre across the mouth so hard that blood spurted from her lip, but she only laughed at him.

"You vain fool!" She spat blood out of her mouth and laughed again. "Did you really think that you could wear me down?"

Erin clutched the gem close to her breasts and closed her eyes. When she opened them, the Goddess was back. She raised her head and locked gazes with her sister. "Now we sing."

As one, the two sisters began to sing, and the ruby joined in, singing bass to their clear soprano. The symphony of pure power and light soared through the cavern, illuminating the darkest corners and shining a spotlight on the vamps and shifters cowering in the corners.

Caligula shrieked and released Deirdre to clap his hands over his ears, as the rubysong danced and played over and around him, casting him in a red glow that was somehow pure and innocent—a stark contrast to his putrid evil.

The rubysong trapped the ancient vampire in a glowing, crystalline prison made entirely of light and song, but Caligula's ineffective beating against the shimmering walls made it clear that he could not escape. The music dimmed the sound of his shrieks, but his open mouth and the cords straining in his throat told the tale of his capture. A surge of fierce joy swept through Ven at the sight.

Deirdre dropped to the ground directly in front of Erin, and the two embraced. Drawing back a little, Erin effortlessly raised a shield over the two of them and turned to Ven. "I am safe, my warrior. You may leave my side with confidence."

"You stay safe!" he said fiercely. "Stay behind that shield, no matter what happens."

She nodded and then hugged her sister again, and the two turned as one to focus on Caligula, who remained trapped. Reassured, Ven raised his sword and looked to his brother warriors. "Now!"

He, Jack, and Justice sprang forward into the throngs of moaning and howling vamps and shifters. They weren't too incapacitated to fight back, however, and the battle was on. Slashing and slicing anything that moved to fight him, Ven fought his way through to where Daniel leaned over Quinn.

But he was too late. Even as he plunged his silver-enhanced dagger into the heart of a wolf in full, snarling Were shape, he saw Daniel raise his wrist and slice into it with his fangs, then press it against Quinn's half-open mouth.

"No!" Ven sprang toward them, but again he was too late. Quinn had raised her head and was clutching Daniel's wrist with both hands as she drank from his vein.

The traitorous bastard had completed the blood bond and would forever after have a connection with Quinn and power over her. Ven raised his sword, remembering a crucial fact. The blood bond was severed at the death of the vamp who'd created it.

"I'm going to enjoy separating your head from your body," he snarled.

Daniel raised his head, unspeakable weariness in his eyes. "She was dying, Ven. She had been weakened by the earlier battle and healing, and I must have taken too much blood. She was going to die if she didn't get a transfusion, and there's not exactly a hospital nearby."

Ven saw the truth in Daniel's eyes, and slowly lowered his sword. Quinn finally released Daniel's wrist and stared up at Ven, tiny dots of blood on her lips. "Are we dead yet?"

"No," he said. "But we may be in hell."

Daniel fixed a bleak stare on Ven. "I am Spartan, warrior. We invented hell."

Daniel stood and scooped Quinn up in his arms. "I am taking her to the surface, or at least as far as I can go before the sunlight stops me. Good luck with your quest, Atlantean."

"If she dies, or if you hurt her in any way, I will track you down and stake you out for the sun," Ven said, grim promise in his tone.

"She's going to despise me when she becomes fully aware," Daniel said bleakly. "Do you think facing the sun could possibly be any worse? Behind you on the left!"

With that, Daniel shot up through the air and toward the ceiling, toward what Ven figured was a vamps-only exit. He turned to face the threat coming at him from the left, and plunged his sword into the vamp's mouth, nearly taking off the top of its skull. As it slammed into the ground, he jerked his sword out of its mouth and then sliced it down to finish the job.

Stepping back from the puddle of decomposing vamp, he immediately confirmed that Erin's shield was holding, then headed back into the fray. One down, a couple hundred to go.

Chapter 33

Erin held her sister's cold, cold hand and sang. She sang of the past ten years' loss and pain and loneliness. She sang a battle song to rouse the fury of the Nereid's Heart and defeat the enemy.

She sang of love—her love for her sister and the consuming love she finally admitted she felt for Ven. The ruby warmed against her body until she felt as though she held a living flame. It added its voice to hers and to Deirdre's—an ancient counterpoint to their living song. The immense power rose through her until she felt she could expand to fill the entire cavern with her body and her song.

The reality of Ven fighting all of Caligula's minions, even with Jack and Justice, finally penetrated her rubysong-induced haze. She had to do something, and she had to do it now.

She turned to her sister. "I seem to have acquired a talent for exploding vampires, but I am afraid to use it with you here. I don't know if I have the control to direct it at specific individuals."

Deirdre clutched her hand. "If I must face permanent

death to save you, I'm ready to do it. The things he put me through . . ." She shuddered. "I cannot face our father ever again, Erin."

The look on Erin's face must have given it away. "Daddy, too?" Deirdre asked, her face crumpling. "No, not Daddy, too."

"I'm sorry, Deirdre. He thought you were dead, too. We thought they'd killed all of you. He couldn't . . . he couldn't face life without you."

A sudden bright flash of light exploded in the air of the cavern, and a female form appeared in the center of it. "I do so love family reunions." The voice was like nothing Erin had ever heard; the sound of an ancient, formless evil that rolled wetly in the dark.

Erin's shield collapsed, and she and Deirdre both stopped singing, their vocal cords frozen in their throats. As she clutched her neck, Erin saw the Weres drop to the floor, cowering and whining, and the vamps fall flat on their faces, hissing. She caught sight of Jack, lying still and bloody on the ground, and Justice leaning against one wall, hands on his knees, gasping. She couldn't see Ven.

The rubysong prism around Caligula vanished, and he made an odd, grunting noise, then dropped his hands from his ears and bowed deeply to the newcomer. He levitated down to the stone floor of the cavern and fell to his knees. "My lady, you are come. You grace us with your presence."

The vampire—for she must be that, with the white skin of the grave and glowing red eyes—spiraled down toward them, her silken white dress floating delicately around her. She had hip-length black hair and was so beautiful that it nearly made Erin's eyes hurt to look at her. Deirdre dropped to her knees and then lowered her face to the ground, moaning. "It's the vampire Goddess of Death, Erin. It's Anubisa."

"Ah, the witch turned vampire knows her betters," Anubisa said, smiling. Her tiny fangs were barely longer than the rest of her teeth. That and her beauty combined to give her a deceptively harmless appearance.

Then she turned her eyes toward Erin and any façade of

harmlessness vanished. Before Erin could lower her gaze, Anubisa captured her, sweeping her into thrall. Her mind could only scream helplessly as her body was paralyzed.

The vampire Goddess swept down and toward her and plucked the ruby from Erin's arms, then held it up toward the light of one of the torches. "What a pretty thing. It must hold some power, or you wouldn't have wanted it so badly, and even now, with the two of you silenced, it hums with suppressed power."

She shrugged and tossed it casually to the ground, where it landed on the folds of Deirdre's gown. "A bauble to play with later."

She turned to Caligula and pointed one long finger at him. "Where is he?"

"Where is who, my lady?" His voice wasn't nearly as smug as it had been, and Erin took a fierce joy at his cowardice in the presence of his Goddess.

"Where is my Vengeance? I smell the blood kin to my pet, Conlan," she said, twirling around to scan the room. "I have a certain promise to fulfill, and I fully intend to enjoy years of service from him. Willingly or not."

Erin stared around but couldn't see Ven anywhere. Good. Maybe he'd escaped.

Anubisa clearly thought otherwise. "I smell you lurking around, Atlantean. Are you such a coward that you will let these women die on your behalf?"

Ven stepped out from behind an outcropping of rock about fifteen feet above the ground. "Oh, I'm here, you unholy bitch." He raised his sword. "I was trying to get into position to give you a *pointed* reply."

"You warriors and your toys," Anubisa purred, gliding over to Erin and Deirdre. "Do you need a demonstration?"

She bent to Deirdre and grabbed her by the hair, yanking her head up.

"No!" Ven shouted, and he leapt down to the ground. "I will go with you. Let the women go."

Anubisa paused, glancing slyly up at Erin, who was still frozen in place and unable to access her magic. "It's this one you care for, isn't it? Not the undead plaything of my Caligula. No matter."

She swept out an arm and a wave of energy crashed across the room, smashing Ven across the cavern and into a stone wall. Then she struck hard with her fangs and drained Deirdre while Erin watched, utterly helpless, screaming a silent promise of revenge.

Anubisa delicately wiped her mouth with a fold of Deirdre's torn dress, then dropped her head on the ground. The hollow thunking sound when her sister's head struck the stone seared Erin down to her soul. "I enjoy these little demonstrations, gem singer," Anubisa said, touching Erin's face with an icy finger. "So you think to fight with your Gift when you do not know even a fraction of its power? The one who first wielded that ruby had enough power to destroy even me."

She stepped back and her hand lashed out to slap Erin in the face, rocking her head to the side. "You have nothing. You *are* nothing. Your sister will soon be dead, and I will now take your lover from you."

She turned her back on Erin and started to laugh. "I may kill you, but for now it's so deliciously fun to watch you realize that you have lost everything, little witch."

Ven had pulled himself upright, and he headed back toward them, limping slightly. Erin could no longer see Justice and hoped he was somehow getting in position to slice Anubisa's head off her shoulders, so she could spit on the vampire's decomposing remains. Rage burned through her, trying in vain to break through the bonds Anubisa had trapped her with. She mentally called out to the Presence that had shared her body with her and then vanished.

All right, Nereid. You took my body over easily enough when you wanted something. Where are you now? I could use a little divine intervention.

"How much does the witch mean to you, Lord Vengeance? Will you willingly serve me in any capacity I demand, if I let her live?"

"Yes," he said, his voice ringing strongly throughout the

cavern. "You let her go free and swear an oath that this monster will never again go near her."

Noooooo, Erin screamed in her mind.

"Done," Anubisa said.

"No," Caligula cried out. "My lady, you took my pet from me. The least you can do, in your benevolence, is leave me with her sister."

Anubisa tilted her head, as if in thought, then leaned down to retrieve the Nereid's Heart. "Mustn't forget my new jewel," she said to Erin. Then she turned back toward Caligula. "Oh, you have a point, I suppose. Very well, you may have her."

Ven roared out his defiance, hurling himself forward toward Caligula, murderously slashing and stabbing the shifters and vamps who dared to try to block him. "You will not have her!"

Anubisa held her dagger to Erin's throat. "Ven!" she thundered in her ancient voice. "Stop now, or she dies this moment."

Ven stumbled to a stop, his face twisted with despair. He stared directly into Erin's eyes, and she faintly heard the ringing of the ruby through Anubisa's thrall. Then she somehow heard Ven's voice in her mind.

I love you, Erin. I will love you for all eternity. No matter what you must endure, remember that and wait for me.

Anubisa's mocking voice sliced through the room. "You have no leverage, Atlantean. I have your beloved's life in my hands."

Ven raised his sword and everyone near him fell back, but he turned the point until it pressed into his own heart. "As I have my own life in mine. If you truly wish for my voluntary service, release her now and swear the oath for her safety. Or I will run this sword through my heart and you will be cheated of your goal."

Anubisa laughed, but the sound was tentative. "You would not do this, knowing that your gem singer would die a thousand deaths at my hand if you did."

He shrugged, and only Erin knew what the movement

cost him. She felt his pain sear her own heart. "If I do not, you will give her to Caligula. It will make no difference, ultimately."

The Goddess hissed, but she dropped the hand holding the dagger from Erin's neck. Several long moments passed, and then she nodded. "Very well. What is she to me, anyway? Caligula, you are bound never again to approach this woman."

Caligula began to howl, and she kicked him in the face, rocking the vampire's head back. "Never, ever defy me, or you will wish you walked the face of the sun for a respite from my punishment," she snarled.

Ven dropped his sword, and it clattered to the ground. His daggers and two guns followed. "Never use the damn guns," he said, forcing a smile as he watched Erin the whole time. "Don't know why I bother, even with the silver bullets."

She knew he was sending her a message about getting the guns after he'd gone with Anubisa, but she was too heartsick to care. When he left the cavern with the vampire, everyone she'd ever loved would be gone.

Joining them in death no longer held any fear for her.

Anubisa flashed over to Ven's side and stared up at him with greedy lust. "Do you voluntarily accept my service, Lord Vengeance, blood kin to Conlan?"

Justice's sarcastic voice interrupted before Ven could respond. "Of course he doesn't, you evil bitch. You're holding his girlfriend as collateral. He has no choice."

Anubisa whirled around as Justice lightly leapt down from the same rocky outcropping from which Ven had prepared to attack. She took a step closer to him and tilted her head, then inhaled deeply. "You smell like—"

"I smell like the blood kin of Conlan and Vengeance," Justice said, flashing a grim smile. "I'm their brother, and I offer myself in his stead."

Chapter 34

Ven stared at Justice after he made his ridiculous claim. "Don't do this, you idiot! I expect you to save Erin for me."

Justice laughed. "You think I'm lying, don't you? Precious pampered royal princes, never imagining that dear Daddy may have done the nasty with someone who wasn't their mother. Someone who wasn't even their *species*."

Anubisa studied Justice, awareness dawning in her eyes. "The mating I forced on Conlan's father bore fruit? Oh, that is entirely too delicious!"

"Yeah, well, this delicious fruit is going to start killing everyone in this room, thanks to the *geas* laid on my ass, if you don't get me out of here," Justice said bitterly. "You wanted voluntary? Well, trust me, after centuries of having to take orders from my brothers, with their overblown sense of entitlement that came with being the royal heirs, I'm more than ready to try out the other side."

Ven shook his head, trying not to believe what every one of his senses told him must be the truth. "Why? Why didn't you talk to Alaric about some way to lift the *geas*?"

"Don't you think I tried? There was no way to achieve it

without telling him the truth of my birth, and that would lead to me killing him. Or at least dying in the attempt."

Justice sheathed his sword and crossed to Anubisa. "Me for him. Willing service." He flashed a dark smile at her and, so quickly Ven didn't see him move, bent his head and kissed her. It was no gentle kiss, from what he could see. It was more of a punishing, claiming kind of kiss, brutal and possessive, and it lasted a long time.

When Justice finally raised his head, Anubisa's eyes had faded from glowing red to black and she looked dazed. She stared up at Justice, her lips swollen from his kiss, and then finally spoke.

"No man has willingly kissed me for more than five thousand years," she said, so softly Ven almost didn't catch the words. "I accept your offer, Lord Justice, blood kin to Conlan and to Vengeance."

"No!" Ven bent to retrieve his sword and leapt toward them, but she shot up toward the ceiling, with Justice firmly in her grasp. As they rose, Justice kissed her again and managed to knock the ruby out of her arms. She clutched at his shoulders and didn't even seem to notice. Justice lifted his head and stared down at Ven, and his lips formed a single word.

"Brother."

Then he bent his head to the vampire goddess again, and the two of them vanished.

Ven caught the ruby before it could shatter on the stone floor, and he ran toward Erin. Finally released from Anubisa's thrall, Erin sank to her knees over the body of her sister, who appeared to have suffered the true death. She was sobbing so hard her entire body shook with the force of it, and as he watched her she screamed and shot an energy bolt at Caligula that smashed him into a stone pillar.

When Ven reached her, Erin raised her head and stared through him, her face drenched with her tears, and the ancient power of the gems again in her eyes. "Now we kill them all," she said, rising.

He held the ruby out to her and agreed. "Now we kill them all."

As she began to sing, vampires began to explode in waves. The shifters were unaffected by her song, so Ven waded into them with a killing fury, slicing out with his silver daggers, whirling around to destroy them, two and three at a time, shouting out a fierce battle cry. "For Atlantis!" he cried. "For Lord Justice! For my brother!"

And all around him, vampires exploded and shifters died, until he was covered with blood and gore and surrounded by dead and dying bodies. Still he raged and stabbed and roared out his anguish, until the sound of the silence permeated his berserker fury.

He whirled around in a full circle and realized he was standing in the center of the cavern, surrounded by few who still lived.

Erin stood tall, shining so brightly with silver-blue light that he had to squint to see her. Deirdre still lay at her feet, and Caligula himself knelt in front of her.

Ven ran across the room with some thought of protecting her from the master vamp, but she stopped him with one up-raised hand. "This is mine to do," the dual voice that was Erin and yet not Erin proclaimed.

He slowed to a stop and drew a dagger, recognizing her need for revenge, but not wanting her to suffer another death on her soul.

"I sentence you to the true death, Caligula of Rome. For the thousands of innocents you have murdered. For your heinous atrocities. For the evil pleasure you took in destroying lives."

She raised her hands, and basketball-sized spheres of pure light formed on each one, as Caligula cowered before her.

"Your sister is dead," Caligula sneered, a final act of defiance. "You can live with the knowledge that I raped her a thousand times, in a thousand different ways, after I turned her to the undead."

"You can die with the knowledge that Deirdre yet lives," Erin replied. Then she slashed her arms down, and the spheres of power rocketed across the space between them, smashing into Caligula's chest, at the same time that Ven let his dagger fly, straight and true, into the vampire's black heart.

Caligula shrieked the shriek of the damned, which he surely was, and as Ven watched, he incinerated from the inside out, blue flames shooting out from his mouth and eyes and nose before he finally exploded.

Ven put an arm around Erin's waist and yanked her back and away from the disintegrating vampire, but she threw up a shield and none of the acidic slime touched either them or the body of her sister.

"Is she really alive?" Ven asked.

Erin suddenly collapsed, all of her strength and any remaining vestige of the Goddess vanishing. He caught her and the ruby before she hit the ground.

"She is not truly dead, but so close it hardly matters," Erin said, weeping. "I want to stay with her until the end, Ven."

A weary voice interrupted before Ven could reply. "That may not be necessary."

Ven jerked his head up to see Daniel slowly approaching them. "I can help her, Erin. From what I hear, you need to get that ruby back to Atlantis."

Ven raised his sword. "As if I'd trust you ever again, you traitorous—"

Erin touched his leg with her hand. "He's telling the truth, Ven. The ruby would warn me of any dark purpose."

He hesitated, unwilling to trust Daniel again but urgently aware of the need for haste in returning to Atlantis. Finally he nodded. "Fine. But we'll be back to check on her. If she's—"

"I know, warrior," Daniel said, dropping to the ground to raise Deirdre's head into his lap. "I know. Now go."

Erin pressed one final kiss to her sister's forehead, then stood, clutching the Nereid's Heart. "Now, Ven. Something tells me we have to go now."

An icy wind swept through the cavern at her words, and Ven smiled. "Picked a fine time to show up, Alaric. Didn't want to get your hands dirty?"

The priest shimmered into form and raised one eyebrow. His face was pale and drawn, and he looked as though he'd aged centuries in the space of a few days. "I do what I can, Lord Vengeance. May I interest you in a portal to Atlantis?"

"Best idea you've had in a long time," Ven said. "But first we have a tiger to heal."

He took Alaric over to where Jack lay, seriously wounded but still breathing, in spite of the numerous claw and teeth marks streaming blood from his body. Alaric knelt down and held his hands over Jack's body, and the shifter's eyes suddenly snapped open as the healing blue-green light shimmered over his body, leaving whole skin where wounds had been.

Jack sat up, holding his head. "Why do I feel like I missed something?"

Ven held out a hand to help him to his feet. "You missed a lot. Daniel will fill you in. Find out what he did with Quinn."

Jack bared his teeth. "He did something to Quinn?"

"It's a long story, and we have to go."

Ven returned to Erin and lifted her and her ruby into his arms, then shot one last look at Daniel. Alaric called his magic and the portal appeared, and they stepped into the glowing oval that would take them home.

"Home, Erin," he murmured to her as her eyes drifted shut. "Let's go home."

Chapter 35

The Temple of the Nereids, Atlantis

Erin and Ven stood, hands linked, and watched Riley sleep. Healthy color had returned to her cheeks as soon as Erin had added her song to the rubysong from the Nereid's Heart and sung healing to Riley and the baby. For the past several days, Riley had spent most of her time resting, eating nutritious food, and resting some more, only grumbling a little at the constant coddling from the maidens of the Temple.

Marie smiled at Erin. "As you see, she and the baby continue to thrive. I can find no hint of any problem remaining with either of them, and the human doctor Conlan and Alaric brought to us agreed. You truly performed a miracle."

Erin shook her head. "The rubysong was the miracle. Your Goddess performed the miracle. Knowing her sister was safe finished the job. I simply used my Gift to aid the process."

She and Ven had chosen, at Quinn's urgent request, not to tell Riley about the blood bond Daniel had forced on Quinn.

The last thing Riley needed was more stress during her pregnancy.

Ven squeezed her hand. "Putting your life in jeopardy, facing down a master vampire, and sharing your skull with a Goddess along the way. I'd say you have nothing to be humble about."

"I would agree," Marie said. "And now I will leave you so that I may continue my preparations to visit my brother on the surface in this place called Florida."

"I'm glad they let you go, Marie," Erin said. "I hope to meet your brother someday."

"So you shall, gem singer. As I am sure you shall lead the Temple wisely in my absence. Thank you for choosing to stay and study your Gift with us." Marie smiled again and left them alone with Riley.

"This is the first time your brother has been away from her side since the healing," Erin observed.

Ven flinched at the word "brother" but simply nodded. "She and the baby are his life."

She put a hand on his arm. "Let's leave her to sleep, Ven."

They left the room and the Temple and wandered through the gardens with no particular destination in mind. Finally he spoke. "I am sorry that Daniel and your sister have disappeared. He left that cryptic message with Jack about 'going deep,' and I'm sure it means he took her somewhere safe until she can recover. He did retrieve the jeweled coffer that held the Nereid's Heart and send it to us. Alaric was well pleased to recover the ruby that had been taken from the Trident."

The sadness that hovered constantly at the edges of Erin's mind washed through her. "That's great about your jewel. And I'm trying to continue to trust Daniel, Ven. But in the end, he is a vampire, and they all seem to have hidden agendas."

"The new drive among the vampires and the rogue shifters to form coalitions is of great concern to us, Erin. Together, they will be a more powerful foe than any we have ever faced.

Yet at the same time, the ancient legends of Atlantis are awakening. *Aknasha'an* and gem singers walk the waters at our side. How can we fail?"

The question didn't need a response, so Erin tightened her fingers in his and they walked for a while longer. She was content to enjoy the peace and stillness in the midst of the mingling scents of masses of flowers. Then they turned a corner on the path and a tiny gazebo, much like the one she'd accidentally lifted Ven onto during her last visit to Atlantis, came into view. She grinned up at him. "I promise not to put you on the roof if you tell me what you're thinking about."

A trace of a smile crossed his expression, but quickly faded. "I'm thinking about Justice and his sacrifice for me."

"For us," she said. "He did it for us, so that we could have each other. Don't doubt him for a second. He put on that show to convince her to let us go."

"I know. But that makes it harder to bear. I won't rest until I find him and rescue him, Erin, even if it takes the rest of my life."

She gazed up at the strong, proud face she'd come to love so well. "I know that. I'd expect no less."

"I love you more than I have ever loved a living being, but I cannot ask you to wed with this task hanging over my head, Erin. It would be unfair." He rasped out the words, as if they'd been wrenched from the deepest corners of his soul. As if everything in him fought against saying them.

Just like everything in her fought against hearing them.

She considered and rejected responses for several minutes, while he stood next to her, his hands clenched at his sides. Finally she found the perfect answer and flashed him her most brilliant smile.

"So you're unfair. Add it to the list. You're not getting out of marrying me that easily."

His face lit up with savage joy. "That's getting to be a very long list, my beloved gem singer witch. It's going to take us a lifetime to work our way through it."

"I love you, and Atlantis is beginning to feel like home. So a lifetime sounds just about right," she mused, and then his lips stopped hers from saying anything else for a very long time. When he finally lifted his head, she smiled and realized she was right. She'd finally come home. The future might hold darkness, but Ven would be her light.

Atlantis had awakened, and she was reborn.

Turn the page for a special preview
of the next book in the
Warriors of Poseidon series

ATLANTIS UNLEASHED

by Alyssa Day

Coming in May 2008 from Berkley Sensation!

Justice floated in a dark dimension composed entirely of pain. Viscous like a thick, murky liquid, the pain surrounded him, taunted him, buffeted him, and cradled him until he no longer existed other than as a supplicant, a slave, an unwilling participant in a twisted and torturous game.

His consciousness had dwindled down to the barest pinprick of flickering light. He knew his name, knew he was Justice in a vastness of injustice, knew that his sacrifice had saved Others whose names had long been torn from his mind. But nobility was nothing against the pain; the pain ate nobility, consumed strength, devoured pride. Ate the Body until what was left of the Body burned in acid rebellion against the Mind. The Mind screamed and howled, silent shrieks of protest against an unyielding evil that licked his blood, feasted on his terror, and laughed a dark, breathless humor of longing.

He was Justice, and he had been buried in the pain for years or centuries or millennia or merely minutes, but the pain existed outside the reality of time, and only the insanity of stretched and tortured perception remained.

But the flickering point of light that was all that remained of his Being waited and watched and plotted. Because he was Justice and—no matter the eons of time that passed before his time finally came—Justice would be served.

As if to reward the courage flying in the face of utter futility, the hope crouching in the shadow of utter hopelessness, a window opened into the darkness, and he saw through the shadows to a face. The face was Other, not his face, not his Mind, not Justice. The face was Female, and as he watched it, watched *her*, entranced by the shimmer of light in his eternal darkness, he realized one undeniable truth.

She was *his*.

GLOSSARY OF TERMS

Aknasha—empath; one who can feel the emotions of others and, usually, send her own emotions into the minds and hearts of others, as well. There have been no *aknasha'an* in the recorded history of Atlantis for more than ten thousand years.

Atlanteans—a race separate from humans, descended directly from a mating between Poseidon and one of the Nereids, whose name is lost in time. Atlanteans inherited some of the gifts of their ancestors: the ability to control all elements except fire—especially water; the ability to transform to mist and travel in that manner; and superhuman strength and agility. Ancient scrolls hint at other powers, as well, but these are either lost to the passage of time or dormant in present-day Atlanteans.

Atlantis—the Seven Isles of Atlantis were driven beneath the sea during a mighty cataclysm of earthquakes and volcanic activity that shifted the tectonic plates of the Earth more than eleven thousand years ago. The ruling prince of the largest isle, also called Atlantis, ascends to serve as high king to all seven isles, though each are ruled by the lords of the individual isle's ruling house.

Blood pride—a master vampire's created vampires.

Landwalkers—Atlantean term for humans.

The Seven—the elite guard of the high prince or king of Atlantis. Many of the rulers of the other six isles have formed their own guard of seven in imitation of this tradition.

Shape-shifters—a species who started off as humans, but were cursed to transform into animals each full moon. Many shape-shifters can control the change during other times of the month, but newly initiated shape-shifters cannot. Shape-shifters have superhuman strength and speed and can live for more than three hundred years, if not injured or killed. They have a long-standing blood feud against the vampires, but old alliances and enemies are shifting.

Thought-mining—the Atlantean ability, long lost, to sift through another's mind and memories to gather information.

Vampires—an ancient race descended from the incestuous mating of the god Chaos and his daughter, Anubisa, goddess of the night. They are voracious for political intrigue and the amassing of power and are extremely long-lived. Vampires have the ability to dematerialize and teleport themselves long distances, but not over large bodies of water.

Warriors of Poseidon—warriors sworn to the service of Poseidon and the protection of humanity. They all bear Poseidon's mark on their bodies.